# INTO THE LIGHT



UNIVERSITY OF ISLES 2

## VEE TAYLOR

TO THOSE WHO UNDERSTAND HOW
CONSUMING GRIEF CAN BE. MAY YOU
CONTINUE TO FIND YOUR LIGHT.

& TO MY OWN SLEEPING ANGELS ABOVE.
I HOPE I AM MAKING YOU PROUD.

# AUTHOR'S NOTE

This book, while strictly a work of fiction, is not a horse-and-carriage romance. While I do not condone these situations or actions between characters, it is simply a work of fiction. There are no characters in this book based on anyone, it is just part of my imagination.

This book is not a stand-alone. Before you open this, please read the first book in the series, Into the Darkness.

This book has heavy mentions of suicide, Mafia and Cartel settings, possessiveness/ownership of partners, groomed and institutionalized machismo/toxic masculinity, primal play, miscarriage/stillbirth.

Please see my website for additional content notes before continuing. They do contain spoilers, but your mental health matters.

These are also organizations that don't exist in today's world, so because this is a work of fiction, we can safely assume these are stretched to fit our imagination.

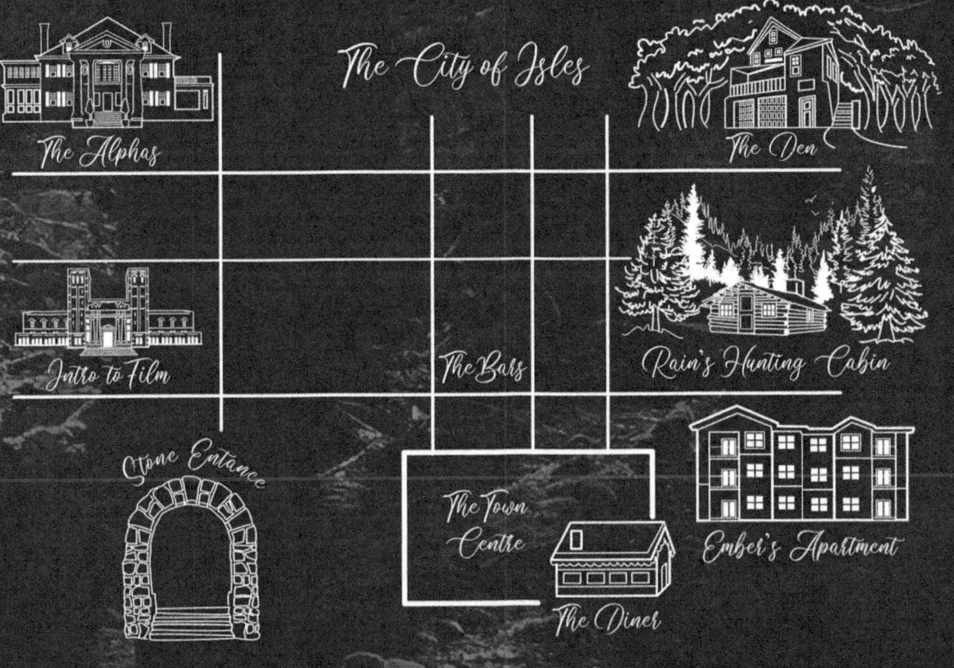

The Alphas
The City of Isles
The Den
Intro to Film
The Bars
Rain's Hunting Cabin
Stone Entrance
The Town Centre
The Diner
Ember's Apartment

# EMBER

## PROLOGUE

*The Next Day*

"I'm going to fucking murder her." The words played on a loop in my head as I forced my eyes open. The dim room was illuminated by the soft daylight, signaling a new day. A sudden movement in front of me caught my attention as I sat up on the couch.

"Step back, now." The voice was urgent and commanding, prompting me to snap, fully awake. Throwing off the blanket, I took in the scene before me. The memories of last night rushed back, flooding my mind with a mix of emotions.

My chest wanted to fold in on itself at the memory of getting that call, then Maddy's cold words hit me along with Rain telling me what had happened. I felt as though I was suffocating, trying to get air, but nothing was there to fill my lungs.

"What's going on?" I asked, piecing together the situation and the ache in my heart. It was as if reality was a cruel dream that wouldn't let me escape. Rain had positioned himself in front of me as a barrier from four angry men shouting at me. His black hair was tousled, his bright-blue eyes filled with worry and anticipation. His hand lifted, almost like he wanted to touch me but pulled away quickly when he realized what he was doing.

"Ember, please, just quiet down." Rain's words cut through the chaos, his tone a mixture of concern and frustration.

"It's her fucking fault," one guy screamed in my direction as another one reached for my arm. I'd seen him around before, but this time he had a gun tucked into his waistband, so as his towering body came closer, I moved away to keep him from grabbing me.

I moved as far back onto the couch as I could, then realized there was an angry mob coming for. . . me? They piled in from the back door.

What. The. Fuck?

"What is happening?" I bellowed a little louder while dodging someone's hand. I leaned to the side, so the hand grazed over my forehead, then I blinked a few more times, willing myself to get my bearings straight. Someone pushed Rain away from me, but he rushed over to my side of the couch, and most of the mob were waving around weapons.

"Your fucking brother killed him." M-my brother? There was no way Walsh was involved. He promised.

As I let my guard down, a hand grabbed my arm. Their expressions were full of anger, most of them with Glocks in my face.

Bile rose in my throat as someone dragged me off the couch. I yelled bloody murder for someone to save me, for Rain to save me, but he never came.

"He didn't. I swear," I cried out. "Please. Stop."

Walsh promised me, and my brother was anything but a liar. He was a cold and calculating asshole, but never a liar. This was not what I expected to happen the day after my boyfriend . . . I couldn't finish that sentence. This was not what I wanted to deal with, as every bone in my body felt brittle, my heart felt tattered, and my brain was complete mush.

This was not happening. Why couldn't life be gentle? Why couldn't things go to plan like I had expected them to? Fuck. Why was there so much fucking death in a life that I, too, didn't want to live anymore.

"Stop. Immediately." I glanced back at Rain, and the hand released me as I shuffled away on the floor.

Rain's eyes, red-rimmed and swollen, told me he hadn't slept last night. He looked as broken as I felt. The cracks inside his heart were as earth-shattering as the ones scarring mine.

"Rain . . ." I looked at him with pleading eyes.

"Get up, Ember," he demanded while looking around the room.

"They're coming back from the rock." Quite a few more people trickled in from the back door, all angry based on their tones, and whispered conversations about Ash's scene.

I shook my head and unsteadily got to my feet, rushing to hide behind Rain, but he moved to the side, so I was exposed to everyone in the room. I was still in my clothes from yesterday, my hair wavy from the rain.

"My brother promised—"

"Not now, Ember," Rain said, and I crossed my arms over my chest. It was a demand to shut up, either for my protection because we were still around everyone, or because he didn't want to hear it. He looked at everyone and told them to fucking leave.

"If we fucking kill her now, they will never know. We can say it happened with Ash," one guy said, and my heart dropped.

Killing me? The thought never crossed my mind.

"We need her to leverage the answer to what happened to Ash. She stays alive!" Rain boomed, quieting the hushed voices.

"Ash would want her here," he whispered, turning toward me. That sentence was meant for me, yet my stomach kept churning, the contents threatening to spill over.

I turned toward him, reaching out to see if he'd take my hand. My need for comfort was so intense and he was the only person around, but a shift happened between us. I could feel him retreating. Everyone in the room left, leaving us alone.

"Leave," he demanded, and as the events over the last few hours came rushing back, tears welled in the rims of my eyes. The comfort

Rain had shown me last night gave me the impression we could get through this together, but the person in front of me was different.

"But . . . Rain . . ." I couldn't find the words I needed to string a sentence together.

"There is no 'but Rain,' Ember. I need to figure out what happened with Ash." No longer was he the guy who held me last night while I cried in his arms. He'd somehow been replaced by the bitter anger I'd been well-acquainted with since knowing him.

There were two sides to Rain. The person who brought me a phone when Ale took mine, then the Rain who ignored me as if I was repulsive. Right now, he was the latter.

"You told me what happened . . . I thought h-he—"

"I have to figure it all fucking out, Ember. Leave this fucking house now." His tone was frigid. I'd always known Rain to be cold and impenetrable, but this was different.

I turned toward the door to walk out, and the hole in my heart grew and the thoughts in my head swirled around. What if Walsh didn't keep his promise or my dad double-crossed me? What if I was always supposed to be a pawn, like my mother had been?

As the thoughts spiraled out of control and I moved toward the front door, my knees buckled, and I fell to the floor.

Ash was happy, aside from our having broken up . . . er, at least that was what I thought. I never once thought he battled with any inner demons. He never mentioned feeling sad or depressed, aside from growing up without his mom. This had to be more than Ash jumping off a cliff. There had to be more to the story, and I needed to figure it out.

"I'll come with you," I cried up at him.

"You can't." He reached down, and I stared at his empty hand as if he was holding the world full of lost promises between the spaces of his fingers. I shook my head before pushing myself up, refusing to let him help me.

"Please." Rain's face fell even further, and he ran his hands through his dark hair.

"Ember"—he closed the distance between us, his voice low—"you need to leave right fucking now because when Ash's dad gets here, you don't want to be here." I understood why he was pushing me out.

I feared Ash's dad. He wanted revenge, and this would fuel his anger even more. The air was suffocating. I needed to call Walsh or go home.

But fuck. Where was home? Without Ash, I didn't know if I'd ever be able to feel at home again.

"Will you call me with updates?" Rain looked up at the sky as rain fell on the otherwise sleepy town.

"Go back to the city, Ember. Go to Dansport. Take Walsh."

That wasn't what I asked.

"Please, Rain." I needed to know what the plan was and needed to figure out what happened to Ash.

"Go." Rain's hand landed on my lower back, and there was something warm, comforting about the gesture.

"I don't want to go with my brother. If he had anything to do with this . . ." I looked around to make sure no one could hear us.

"Shit," Rain muttered, his frustration palpable. Taking my hand in his, he led me out of the house, skillfully maneuvering us to the back. He handed me the keys to a Jeep that bore a striking resemblance to Ash's, with subtle differences: distinctive chrome hubcaps, a unique license plate, and an almost pristine condition that stood out among the other cars in the driveway.

"Take my car. Do not go to your apartment. Go straight to Dansport, and don't stop until you get to this address." Rain handed me a small folded-up paper. I opened it to an address, with a scribbled door code underneath.

"What is this?" Rain gripped the back of his neck and looked around.

"An apartment Ash got for y'all. It's all secured and in your name, so untraceable to us otherwise." An apartment? But if he was planning on . . . I couldn't say it. Why would he get a place for us to live?

While Rain explained, the salty tears rolled down my cheeks, over my lips, and seeped into my mouth. I swallowed . . . hard. "Ember, fucking listen to me. Do not stop for anyone."

I nodded.

"My stuff . . . Ash's . . ." The words weren't coming out in any sensible way. My entire life was being left behind. My entire potential, my future, my past. It was all just . . . gone.

"I will get it delivered." I heard an engine approaching. "Please, Ember."

I wasn't sure he realized he was crying, at least not until I lifted my fingers and wiped away the lone tear falling down his cheek. We were both so fucking broken by losing someone we loved so deeply.

"Okay," I whispered, sliding into the driver's seat of the Jeep, and left Isles behind. The road ahead seemed endless, winding past the town's stone archway. As I drove, the shock that had shielded me receded, leaving behind a torrent of emotions. The pain hit me with a force I couldn't evade, overwhelming me.

The weight of Rain's plea echoed in my ears. I wiped away tears and focused on steering as I navigated the descent down the mountain toward the city and the apartment.

"In and out," I muttered to myself, my mind haunted by Ash's final moments. Questions crowded my thoughts, each more painful than the last. As I drove, the city lights twinkled in the distance, so I knew I was close to Dansport.

I followed the road indicated by my GPS, leading me to a street that seemed like the outskirts of Isles even though we were in the city. It appeared isolated, with only imposing black gates signaling the presence of residences. However, these were not ordinary apartments; instead, they were expansive properties with grand houses adorning them.

"It must be at the edge of this area," I said aloud to the darkness.

The GPS turned off, telling me I'd arrived at my destination. Welcome home, I guess?

How had I arrived so quickly? I typed in the gate code, driving toward the building at the end of the driveway. It was tucked close toward the edge of the mountain. I drove past the gate toward . . . a giant ass house.

If you could even call this a house. It was a giant cabin, with wooden beams on the outside like the real life-version of Lincoln logs. I stopped at the end of the driveway and got out as the oxygen left my lungs. In a city full of high-rises and mega mansions, of course Ash would find the one house that reminded us of Isles.

I looked up at the sky and imagined Ash was here with me. The way he would say, "*Mi sol, this is for you.*"

I'd look back at him and be entranced by the way the corners of his lips would twist into a smile. He would wrap me in his arms, and we would sit here staring at the oasis he'd built for us in the city.

"Why?" I cried, dropping to my knees to the earth beneath me. This pain was nothing I'd ever wish upon my greatest enemy. My phone rang incessantly in the car, but nothing in that moment mattered.

Because all I needed was Ash, and he wasn't coming back.

# EMBER



*Eight Months Later*

My dad had come by as I was packing the last of my house up, like he had every single day since the moment I moved out here. All his secrets were now out in the open. My father was the capo of one of the most prominent Mafia families, not by birth but through marriage. He hated it, but he was damn good at it, too.

It made me sad for him. I was proud that he did a good job, but sad he wasn't able to live out the life he wanted to. He wanted to be a poet and an author, and love blinded him from all of that. My mother walking out on his marriage also fucked him up. But every day since I spiraled into my deep, dark place and Santiago called him, pleading with my father to assist me, he had shown up to offer some form of assistance. Sometimes, he would simply deliver food, while other times, like today, he attempted to stay and engage in conversation.

"Ember?" he rasped from the porch as I carried a few boxes out of the house and to the trunk of the car. He sounded tired, and I was close to caving and telling him I forgave him, but I didn't believe him yet. I just . . . couldn't.

"Dad." I lifted my chin as I passed by him toward my car. Well, I guess it still wasn't my car, but at this point, eight months later, I considered it mine. No one came to collect it. No one, aside from Walsh, my dad, and Marissa came at all. "I'm a little busy."

My dad followed as I turned back toward the house where a few more cardboard boxes sat on the front steps, and he picked up a box and helped load it into the Jeep. I didn't complain because I needed to get out of Dansport and back to Isles. School was starting soon, and I wanted to live a normal life again—as normal as I could get.

"Where's Santiago?" my dad asked, looking around for my bodyguard. His brown hair was tousled, and his brown eyes were almost golden today, but there was worry etched into the lines on his face.

"He's in the guesthouse. I told him I'd be okay since I was staying on the property." It was one of the many mysteries I'd discovered since Ash's death. I woke up the morning after I arrived in Dansport, and Santiago was on my doorstep in full tactical gear. After I insisted he change into regular clothing, we had spent everyday together since.

He told me Ash had hired him and paid him enough for "a lifetime." I guess Rain had called to tell him when I was arriving, so he showed up ready for work. It was his responsibility to care for me and stay on the property in a guesthouse out back. I didn't complain, because I was all alone here, refusing to see my brother, dad, or anyone else from the family.

Plus, a part of me knew this was another string that connected my life to Ash's, and I realized over the last few months, I was desperate to hold onto every single string possible. Over time, Santiago and I had become close, and I looked up to him like a protective older brother. He dragged me out of some really dark times.

It thoroughly pissed my dad off that I accepted a bodyguard from the Cartel and not *la famiglia* but over the last few months, he gave up expressing that grievance and instead focused on me refusing to talk to him.

"You don't have to go back to Isles. You can continue your online studies through them."

I shook my head.

Following what had happened with Ash, my professors had all agreed to let me complete the last month of my freshman year and my first semester of sophomore year online. They had also extended the offer for me to continue remote learning, but I was determined to go back. I believed I'd grown strong enough to confront my fears, and I couldn't shake thoughts of what Ash would have wished for.

I knew now that he would have wanted to see me grow, get my degree, and have the college experience I should have had. Rotting away in Dansport and not leaving, sometimes for months on end, wasn't healthy. Finding a path to reclaim my life, even with the bone-shattering grief that was still woven tightly into me, was necessary.

"I can't wrap my head around you buying this house," my dad said, eyeing the grand log-cabin mansion behind us. I'd kept this one under wraps from him as well. Once we were on speaking terms, which basically meant I answered his questions when he showed up on my front steps when I'd let him in past the gate, he stumbled upon the house deed with my name on it. Truth be told, I didn't buy it. It was a gift, but he was in the dark about that part. Knowing about Santiago was more than enough for him to chew on.

"Yup." I popped the p and pivoted back to fetch the last couple of boxes. Just as I was about to grab them, my dad's hand gently landed on my elbow.

"I'm sorry," he whispered. I didn't turn, didn't budge. I just sucked in a deep breath, held it for a slow count of three, then let it out. A trick I picked up in therapy to handle those waves of crushing grief and sadness that sometimes hit me.

Swallowing, I replied, "I get it, Dad, but I can't bring myself to trust Walsh. There are way too many gaps in the whole story around Ash's death for me to just brush it aside."

There was no note, and I knew Ash. He wouldn't just leave me without a reason or explanation as to what he was doing. My brother was missing that night. My dad confirmed there were several people who saw Walsh leave and head in the direction toward the rock outside of town. Walsh refused to tell me if he saw him and what happened.

Walsh was a calculated man. Growing up, he was always the one with a meticulous plan and structure for the day. The fact he refuses to tell me where or what happened that night felt very suspicious. My dad had asked him many times over the months where he was, and even my dad had no clue.

I knew my dad was being honest when he said he had no hand in Ash's death. I saw the sincerity in his eyes when he begged me. He'd shared that when Mr. Ortiz found out about Ash's passing, the scheduled sit-down between our families got scrapped, and that was that. They were at each other's throats, still acting like grown-ups throwing kindergarten-level tantrums with way more dangerous toys.

"You know your brother wants to tell the truth . . ." My dad's comment earned an eye roll from me. I crossed over the lawn that had gone a bit overgrown in the last month. Ash had thought of it all, hiring both a housekeeper and groundskeeper. Last month, I gave them a long, paid vacation because I wanted to make sure going back to Isles was the right decision, and I needed some peace to figure that out.

"I'm done hearing about him, Dad." Walsh danced around the topic of Ash's death. He wouldn't talk to Dad about it. He refused to confirm or deny his role. "I'm not the same person I was a few months back. If Walsh doesn't want to open up, then I've got nothing to share with him."

When I asked Walsh eight long months ago if he had any role in Ash's death, he skirted around the topic, telling me he kept the promise he'd made, but that was all he could tell me.

I'd tried to call Rain to tell him . . . but . . . well, that whole situation didn't turn out how I'd expected either. Through therapy, I learned I couldn't change people or their actions, I could only control my reactions toward them. So I didn't give Walsh the time of day, and stopped giving a fuck about Rain and what he was doing.

It felt like another betrayal, with Walsh and Rain both leaving me when I needed someone the most, the pain cutting deep each time. I was emotionally exhausted by it. I was tired . . . really fucking tired.

"Where are you living while you're up there?" my dad asked, snapping me out of my thoughts.

"My friend Marissa helped me get a small apartment. It's near where I was last year."

Marissa was the one person who always called. Although she still lived with Pico in Isles, she was always there for me, checking up on me and making sure I'd eaten. It took a while for me to come around to letting her in, but once I started my healing journey, I invited her into my world.

Pico wasn't allowed to be around me, for whatever reason, so it meant a lot that Marissa didn't follow suit and still cared.

"You're living with Maddy again?" my dad asked, which only prompted a laugh from me.

"God no," I responded, and his eyes narrowed at me.

When Ash died, half the town accused my brother of murdering Ash while the other half thought it was what was in the police report—suicide. Both sides agreed it was my fault . . .and although I'd been working on removing that narrative from my mind, I still blamed myself because it felt like the only logical reason.

Maddy was on team *Ember was such a bitch to Ash, which led to his passing.*

"After Maddy called me multiple times a day for weeks berating me about how it had been my fault for Ash's . . . er . . . passing," I mumbled. It was still hard for me to say death aloud. "I told her off for being a shit friend and roommate last year, so we haven't been on speaking terms. I have no idea who or what she's doing this year."

It made me sad to think about Maddy. I honestly pitied her because it looked like she was going through a lot herself. I'd been there, I was there, but I also was trying to be a good friend, too. I would have never cast her aside like she had done to me.

"You should have told me, Ember," my dad said, patting my shoulder, but I just shrugged away from his touch, avoiding his gaze.

"I've done a lot of things alone these last eight months. I've learned a lot about myself and the way our family works, and I am determined to end this shit bonfire tradition in Isles." I shoved the box in the back of the car.

"I still have your other car, you know?"

"Sell it. I like this one better. It's bigger." It was a lie. Another string attached to Ash. I mean, technically, it was Rain's, but it felt like it was part of my old life.

"Are you going to be okay?" he asked.

"I am going to be living next door to Marissa. The one person who actually stuck around through all of this shit, so I'll be fine."

"And this Marissa . . . is she . . . part of the other world?"

I threw my hands in the air. "Come on, Dad, you can say their name, but yes, her boyfriend is part of the Cartel." My dad swallowed, then offered me a quick nod.

"I gotta go, Dad. I'm just going to lock up, then head out." I gestured toward his car, hoping he would take the hint and get outta here.

"Oh, okay, Em." My jaw ticked at the familiar childhood nickname.

"Can I give you a hug?" he asked.

I walked over and gave him a quick hug before heading into the house. Turning around, I watched him from the bottom of the steps drive down the driveway and through the gate, then walked into the house.

Entering the log cabin was like stepping into a world carefully curated by *his* touch. The massive space, adorned with oversized cozy furnishings, seemed to beckon with a warm embrace.

Ascending two stories, the cabin's size was both impressive and inviting. The kitchen, a perfect blend of modern convenience and rustic allure, held the essence of Ash's thoughtful choices. It was as if he had picked out each piece of furniture and décor with a purpose, infusing the space with his essence. Walking through the rooms, the surroundings exuded the same warmth he had, making it feel like his love was an invisible thread woven into every corner.

"I'll be back for spring break, house . . ." I said aloud before exhaling slightly, my palms sweaty. I locked the door, metaphorically closing this chapter of my life as I readied for Isles.

Santiago met me in the driveway, and I inclined my head in his direction. He had beautiful tanned skin and was wearing his typical outfit: a black leather jacket, black jeans, and a black T-shirt. He had long brown hair that curled at the bottom and deep-green eyes.

"I'm serious, I don't need you at Isles. It's all neutral territory," I grumbled, a fight we had been having since I told him I was considering going back.

"I've got no family, friends, or life here, Em. I'm coming with you." I rolled my eyes but had agreed to our terms, so alas, it was go-time.

"Did you talk to the apartment owner about getting your keys?" I asked. Santiago would be staying in the apartment next to mine. We would share a wall, which made him feel better about coming and still allowed me the privacy I needed. Marissa would be next to us, and we were the only three people on the floor, which also alleviated Santiago's security concerns.

I appreciated that I had a support team I could rely on, especially since I would be in the place that carried so many memories of him. I was grateful that Santiago and Marissa were willing to be in the same building as me, even though I hated feeling like I needed other people to lean on.

"Got them." He dangled the keys in front of me. I jumped into the car and waved him off as he followed me out of the driveway and onto the road to Isles.

Eight long months had passed since I last drove down this familiar road leading to the mountain town. The memory of how swiftly the three-hour drive had felt during my previous visit came to mind. But this time, everything was different. The change wasn't just in the landscape; it was within me. I was no longer the naive and sorrowful Ember Solis who first arrived in Isles. Nor was I the shattered and defeated Ember who had left those mountains behind.

I was a different Ember. One who hungered for answers, who demanded them with a newfound strength. No longer weakened, I stood tall, mentally and physically fortified. I was fucking underground royalty, unyielding and fierce, ready to confront whatever challenges lay ahead without faltering.

As I continued driving, the memories of that fateful night flooded my mind. The rain, the darkness, and the pain . . . they were all etched into my memory. The trauma and pain I experienced afterward was indescribable, but I was determined to uncover the truth, to understand what had happened to Ash and why he had left me in this world with questions and uncertainty. With every mile I covered, I was one step closer to unlocking the secrets that had torn us apart, and with every beat of my heart, I vowed to fight for the truth, no matter where it led me.

# RAIN

"Shut the fuck up." I yelled as I dropped the fucker's head back down into the bucket of water until his screams muffled and his body went slack.

The smell of the hunting cabin was usually warm and welcoming beneath the pines, but now it was filled with the stench of a filthy human. Mr. Ortiz suspected him of having information about where Walsh Solis was the night Ash was found dead. I was tasked to torture him, so I brought him out to the woods to do so.

"I think that's enough, Boss." I snapped my head toward Pico, my eyes bored into his before he laughed and threw up his hands.

Pico had been with me throughout the last few years. He was a born leader, so I'd been leaning on him when Mr. Ortiz tasked me with fucking people up. He was better at it. We looked like we could be blood related, both of us dressed in all black with our long black hair gelled back. Pico was bigger than me though, which was the only defining marker.

I pulled his head out of the water before questioning him. "What the fuck did Walsh do?" Grabbing his throat, I stared into the poor sap's eyes.

"I swear to God . . . I don't know anything," the guy cried out. "Is-isn't this against territory laws?"

I hesitated, looking at Pico. He gave me a silent nod to continue, ignoring his comment. As long as I wasn't killing anyone, it wasn't breaking the rules.

Leaning over, I pulled him by his shirt until our faces were mere inches apart. "Does it look like I give a flying fuck?"

He shook his head.

"I-I swear…" Tears now slid down his cheeks. Fuck that. Crying was for weak men.

"We aren't in Isles. It's free game." After the words slipped from my mouth, shock laced Walsh's right-hand man. We had grabbed him in Isles and dragged him out here. When my brother/best friend was potentially murdered, I didn't give two fucks about the rules and regulations, but I knew better than to do this in the open fucking public, so we came to the cabin, only accessible by ATV. The one cabin that …

Ash was supposed to hide out here. He was supposed to be safe.

"Fuck," I mumbled, turning toward Pico.

"He doesn't know anything." I concluded, and Pico tilted his head.

I didn't want to torture this guy. I knew in my soul that Ash wasn't murdered. Mr. Ortiz just couldn't comprehend that his son, the one he groomed for leadership, would want anything other than that life.

"Is it my turn to say I told you so?" Pico's eyes narrowed on me, and I punched him in the shoulder.

I opened the door, letting the cold winter air into the small cabin before telling the guys they needed to take him back to town.

"You're letting me go?" the guy asked.

"Yeah. Go back to the Alphas and cry about this shit, though, and you're dead."

"O-okay. I-I swear." He was useless. The moment he shed a tear, I knew he was too fucking scared to say anything.

Two of my guys came in after they parked their ATV and grabbed, blindfolded, and loaded him onto the back of the vehicle.

"Vamos," they said before peeling out, weaving through snow banks between the tall pines.

"You coming?" Pico asked as he grabbed his black leather jacket.

"In a second," I responded. "I'm going to clean this up."

"You good, Rain?" Pico's voice lowered, and I hated this tone. It was something I'd heard many times over the last eight months. Sympathy . . . or fuck, empathy, whatever you wanted to call it, but I fucking hated it.

"I'm fine," I grumbled. Over the last few months, Pico was the only fucking person who actually gave a shit about me. With Mr. Ortiz constantly breathing down my neck, pressuring me to unravel Ash's fate, I juggled roles. I went from being the Vice President to the President of the Den, a title I had no intention of seeking.

All I ever wanted was to finish my damn studies, slip under the radar of the Cartel, and let my stepbrother take the reins. But no, life threw me into this position, and I damn well knew that after graduation, I'd be taking on the full leadership role, a prospect I vehemently resisted. My dreams involved lying back, escaping into books, and crafting worlds that offered respite from real life. Because reality often sucked, and reading was an escape.

Yet, these past eight months carved fury into me, molding me into this hardened exterior. That's why I reluctantly agreed to this plan—to appease Mr. Ortiz and maybe uncover buried truths at the Alpha house and untangle the enigma surrounding Ash's gut-wrenching demise. Alas, our efforts resulted in only dead ends, which was the common conclusion and theme throughout these last few months.

I'd have to go back to Mr. Ortiz and let him know we still had nothing and maybe we should consider that Ash did actually . . . kill himself. While I understood that to be a possibility, Mr. Ortiz refused to believe it. My mother, his wife, sided with him, too.

"You taking classes again?" Pico asked, snapping me out of my thoughts.

"Yeah, gotta repeat last year's spring semester." I shook my hair off my shoulders. I really needed a fucking haircut. It was just one way I had stopped giving a shit.

"I cannot believe your professors failed you," Pico said, shoving his hands into his jacket pockets.

"*Me*, either." I failed one semester of classes, but my adviser assured me that if I took summer classes, I could graduate with the rest of my class. Mr. Ortiz was upset that I wasn't taking business as a major, but it was too late to change majors since I was already a senior.

"Are you taking any electives?" he asked. A conversation that would have been so normal for two college students to have, but after waterboarding a kid mere moments ago, it felt a little ridiculous.

"Yeah. I gotta go see my counselor about what I need to do." I shrugged.

"Sounds . . . dope?" We laughed, knowing electives were just filler classes to complete my schedule.

"See you back at the house." Pico opened the door, and that cool winter wind blew through the small hunting cabin again.

"Hey, Pico?" I asked right as he was about to step out.

Pico's gaze locked onto mine, and I saw that familiar sympathy in his eyes. He knew what I was about to ask—it was a question that had become almost routine between us. His girlfriend, Marissa, was connected to *her*, and I couldn't help but wonder about her. I hadn't spoken her name in eight long months, and I had no intention of breaking that streak.

Reality had hit me hard, forcing me to take on the responsibility of protecting her as Ash would have wanted, but as time passed and the influence of those around me took hold, resentment built. I couldn't help but blame her for what had happened. A part of me harbored anger because her brother stayed in Isles all summer, hiding out on neutral ground, while she enjoyed her life in her house, free from the aftermath of that night.

Anger had consumed me to exhaustion. I thought about Ember every single day, wondering how she was doing, and would get

updates from the housekeeper I'd hired for her. She had sent them on vacation this last month, so it'd gone silent.

"How is she?" The words finally escaped my lips. Pico's lips pulled into a tight straight line before he said the same thing he always did.

*"She's good," he'd mumble, and then be off on his merry way.*

His hesitation made me step closer to him. The way his eyes darted to my feet, then back up, made me think there was something else.

"What?" I shot out. "Tell me."

"She's . . ." He scuffed his boot against the wood floors of the cabin.

"Fucking spit it out," I demanded, my tone getting more intense and anxious with each passing second.

"She's back in Isles for the semester," he said, his voice barely above a whisper, so I had to lean in to make sure I understood what he said.

"B-back in Isles?" *Why didn't I know this?*

I was so caught up in my own issues I didn't check with Santiago about her plan for the new semester.

I gripped his jacket, pulling him closer. Pico was larger than me in most ways—taller, broader, and generally more built, however, my relentless training at the gym since the bonfire incident had leveled the playing field between us.

"Why the fuck didn't you tell me?" I growled.

"Chill, man. You asked me not to talk with her, and I told you I wouldn't. Marissa just told me." He shook me off like I was nothing.

"Why is she coming back?" I rubbed my temples. This wasn't part of the plan.

This wasn't part of the damn plan . . . not even close. I slammed my fist against the wooden wall next to the door, my frustration boiling over. Ash would've known how to handle this shit, how to turn it around. But no, fate thought it would be funny to make me the leader, me—a guy who never asked for this, who never wanted to be in charge, who was stumbling through the mess like a raging idiot. Just a pissed-off college kid forced into a role I never signed up for.

"I don't know. I didn't ask." Pico stood on the threshold, shuffling from foot to foot.

"What's wrong?" I asked.

"She's staying on campus."

"I mean, if she's coming back to Isles, there really isn't anywhere else to stay." I was exasperated at how long it was taking him to get to the point.

"What I meant to say is that she's staying in the same apartment building as Marissa." I closed my eyes momentarily, imagining the look on her face when I told her to leave Isles and the way she broke in front of me as I told her the news of what happened.

"Okay." This wasn't a big deal, and honestly, I was glad she was staying with people she actually knew and not strangers that could ostracize her. I swallowed, walking away from the door, letting Pico leave.

"You know you can talk about it. He's not around, it's okay if you li—"

I growled. "Shut the fuck up."

I didn't want to talk about it. My feelings confused me enough. She was Ash's, and even though he wasn't here anymore, she still was.

"Okay, okay." He let out an exasperated sigh before saying goodbye and leaving one ATV and a radio with me in case I needed anything.

I closed the door and turned back to the small cabin. It was just one simple room with a small outhouse in the back. It had been built for the Den for the spring bonfire, and in the ten years it had been standing, no one from the Alpha house had found it.

I dropped to the edge of the small full-sized bed and looked toward where I was torturing the fucker from the Alpha house.

"Fuck you, Ash," I whispered.

My existence was meant to be veiled in shadows, a phantom lurking in the background. This transformation into someone else, someone unexpected, was forced upon me, and I would give anything to revert to the simplicity of before. I wished everyone could grasp the unfiltered truth I carried, the truth of what truly unfolded. Ash's internal battles were known only to me, even more intimately than Ember could fathom. I knew Ash had killed himself, so searching for a murderer was pointless. I needed to arrange the puzzle pieces to see the larger picture.

I guarded the knowledge of his struggles relentlessly, even in death, protecting his vulnerabilities, and I did this for one reason, for one person. She deserved to hold onto the perception of him as her heroic figure. He deserved the dignity that extended beyond this chaos. Which is why Mr. Ortiz's relentless pursuit was nonsensical. This entire campus-wide uproar, spawned by the enigma of Ash's fate, was ridiculous. The most frustrating aspect was that, regardless of their stance, people placed some level of blame on Ember. As she returned, she'd be heading right into the lion's den. Marissa would have warned her about the rumors, but I wasn't sure she understood the extent.

I was ready to do whatever it took to keep her safe, not because I had to or because of any obligation, but simply because . . . damn it, I wanted to.

# EMBER

"How does it feel to be all moved in?" Marissa, who was wearing an oversized hoodie and a pair of leggings, sat on the brown leather couch that took up the entirety of my living room, but it made the perfect reading chair, so I didn't care how ridiculous it looked.

"I am happy that I got everything done before classes start tomorrow," I stated while opening two seltzers for us in the small kitchen and walking over to hand her one.

The apartment was small with everything in one area, but I'd furnished it with as little items as I could. I was going for comfort versus aesthetic. It was very college-kid vibe versus the warmth of my home in Dansport.

"You hear from your brother?"

I shook my head. He hadn't come home for summer break, and Dad mentioned he was getting more paranoid as the spring bonfire approached, but I tried to not talk about him because it hurt me to know that he could be involved.

"Does it feel okay being on campus?" she asked, and I had to take a long pull at my drink before I could respond.

As I entered campus and drove beneath the towering stone arch, an overwhelming wave of emotions hit me. I had to stop the car, tears streaming down my face. Yet, even in my pain, I reminded myself that Ash wouldn't want me to drown in sorrow. He'd want me to keep moving forward. So I wiped my tears, took a few deep breaths, and focused on the road ahead. I had to remember that life wasn't about seeing the entire forest at once. I needed to start by tending to the individual leaves, placing them where they belonged, and eventually, I could step back and appreciate the whole tree.

"Not really, but I haven't seen anyone either." Marissa had told me about the rumors. She also told me I wasn't the most loved person on campus.

People painted my brother as the culprit of Ash's death. There were lots of people, especially those associated with the Den, who blamed me. They believed I should have never gotten involved with him.

"It will be okay." She patted my thigh, and I grabbed her hand.

"I know this is hard for you with Pico not wanting to—"

"No, fuck that. For the record, it's not that he doesn't want to talk to you. He has been instructed not to."

I offered her a sympathetic smile. "But regardless, it's not great to feel like you're in the middle of something, so I guess this is just my way of saying thank you so much."

She gave my hand a little squeeze. God, you'd think it would be weirder to be friends . . . shit, my only friend is the girl who watched her boyfriend fuck me, but I loved Marissa.

"Hell no. Fuck everyone here. They're all insane for blaming you for Ash's death. I know for a fact if he . . . was still here," she said the last part slowly and deliberately, "he wouldn't have wanted to have people blame you."

Something tugged inside my chest. Tears loomed, threatening to spill at her words, but I took a deep breath.

"I don't understand why they are . . ."

"Because they're all idiots who think there is something bigger here. Everything coincided at a weird time, and everyone saw Ash as this all-powerful king of the Den, but I don't think anyone really saw him for who he was." I looked out the window, appreciative that I picked a complex similar to the last in one aspect only: the large floor-to-ceiling window.

I wasn't nestled amid the pines as my last apartment was, but I could see directly into the forest.

"I don't think I even saw him for who he was." I sighed, willing the tears not to come pouring out.

As if Marissa could sense the tension, she changed the conversation. "Tell me what classes you are taking this year?" She passed some of her homemade guacamole over, and I dipped a chip, then shoved it into my mouth.

"I took an easier semester. I finished most of my mandatory requirements last semester which meant this semester I could pick some electives. I decided creative writing and intro to film would be something different." I popped another chip into my mouth.

"Film should be fun. Do you have a camera?" I nodded and bounded off the couch into the bedroom to grab my old film camera.

"How retro is this?" Marissa said as I handed it to her.

"I'm super pumped." She put the camera onto the coffee table. "What are you taking?"

"Pico has been annoying me to be more like you and take more writing classes." Marissa's eyes narrowed on me. Another thing we discovered we had in common was our love for romance novels, but the kind you aren't reading about in your college classes.

"But you love your art classes?" Marissa was an art major. She specialized in painting, and because she was already a junior with all her requirements out of the way, she focused primarily on classes she loved versus classes she needed for graduation.

We spent the rest of the evening chatting, then there was a knock at the door. I checked my phone to see if Santiago had texted me, and nothing. Opening the door, I found him standing in the hallway.

"I just wanted to turn in for the night," he said, and Marissa was suddenly behind me, understanding he was kicking her out in a roundabout way.

"You don't have to leave," I said, and she smiled.

"I know, but I have classes in the morning, so I gotta prep. First day." She opened the door to the apartment next to mine. When she was tucked inside, I looked back at him.

"You need to stop kicking her out." I huffed. "I told you I was fine. If I am inside the apartment, everything is safe, you don't need to monitor me."

"But I do. It's literally my job."

"Santiago," I whined, and he laughed before going down the hall. He stopped and turned around.

"Remember to lock the doors." I did exactly as he asked after retreating into the apartment.

As I took a few strides back over to that window and looked outside at the forest, I wondered if I would ever have the courage to go to Ash's rock. To go where . . . Ash . . .

I glanced downward, my hand rising to my cheek where moisture had gathered. While pushing the tears away, my fingers brushed against the O etched below my ear. Sometimes, especially when the night embraced the world, I could feel a faint burn, a lingering reminder of what could have been.

Shaking off those thoughts, I shifted my gaze to where Marissa had left my camera. When I first spotted the film class on my school schedule, I thought little of it. However, curiosity compelled me to read the class description. Working in the darkroom to develop the film we captured intrigued me. It seemed to be a self-directed class, with lab times dedicated to processing the film.

As I picked up the camera, a sense of purpose settled within me. The film class seemed like a perfect fit for this semester, aligning with my desire for minimal interaction with others. The prospect of spending time in the darkroom, immersed in my own thoughts and work, felt oddly comforting. It was a way to channel my emotions into something creative without having to engage with the outside world more than necessary.

I slipped the camera into my backpack and made my way to my bedroom. Closing the door behind me, I exhaled deeply, letting the weight of the day settle. I placed the backpack on my desk and looked at the camera, a tool that would help me capture moments and express myself in a way that words often couldn't.

The room remained stark, aside from the one photo of Ash and me I'd put on my nightstand. I told myself I'd personalize the room, then remembered it wasn't my home. I had a few houses, but I felt lost. I didn't quite feel like I had a home yet, and maybe one day when I did, I'd think about personalizing it.

Climbing into bed, I closed my eyes, and sent a silent plea to the universe. Maybe tonight the nightmares would stay at bay, allowing me some respite from the torment that had become my nights. I hoped that tomorrow would start fresh and, maybe because it had been almost a year since everything happened, I could slip under the radar.

A girl could dream, huh?

# RAIN

"You need to come up with an elective, and fast," my adviser, an older woman with wiry gray hair and a bright floral top said as she shifted in her chair on the other side of the desk.

"Why?" I moaned, running my hands through my hair. On the first day of school the last thing I wanted to do was sit in here. I glanced around at the overly obnoxious colorful paintings of the beach and ocean which seemed ironic since we were in the forest. Truly, the happiness in this tiny room made me repulsed, but the frantic email this morning from Ms. Burns telling me I needed to be here STAT forced me up at the crack of dawn.

"You failed your classes and are only starting to catch up. You somehow failed your elective, so before you can register for any upper-class writing sections, you need to figure out an elective." She handed me a piece of paper, sliding it slowly like it contained the answer to all my problems.

"What is this?" I looked down at the paper, and everything seemed like gibberish.

"These are all the electives that are currently available. Since the semester started today, most things are taken, but there are some spots available." I looked more carefully at the paper.

"Introduction to Farming?" I narrowed my eyes at her and laughed. "This must be a joke."

"It most certainly isn't. I guess I am the only one thinking about your future here." She huffed, crossing her arms over her chest. I wondered how long it took for her to find a pair of earrings with matching bright-pink and neon swirls like her dress.

"Ms. Burns, please. I *am* thinking about my future, but as you know, my brother passed away a mere eight months ago. Sorry if Introduction to Farming is the one thing I read today that actually will bring me joy and not swallow me in a pit of despair." Her eyes grew wide.

I tried to keep the cool facade wrapped tightly around me, but something inside of me stirred at the mention of Ash's name.

"I-I'm so sor—"

"Underwater basket weaving sounds interesting," I interrupted, not wanting to hear any half-assed apologies from people who had truly no idea what I was going through.

"You'll have to go into Dansport for the final for that one," she explained.

Hard no.

"What about the film class?" she asked. "It is a very quiet class and usually the pace is at your own leisure. There is one small partner-based project that you have to work on, but otherwise, although the class has certain times, you can come and go as you please."

Huh. If I picked a partner who was smart enough, then maybe I didn't have to do any of the work and could focus on whatever Mr. Ortiz needed from me. It kind of sounded like a perfect fit.

"Why didn't you just say that from the start?" I laughed, and she started typing furiously on her computer.

"There is only one more spot left." There was a dramatic pause before she clicked her mouse. "Got it."

She clapped her hands. "Bad news is that the class starts today in roughly one hour, so you better get going. It's over by the English building in the basement." She handed me a piece of printed paper with the details. I grumbled before grabbing my backpack and heading off.

"Oh, and Rain?"

I turned back around. "Yeah?"

"You'll need to stop by the camera store down on Main Street and grab a film camera before class," she added. I rolled my eyes, regretting my decision to pick this class because it was becoming expensive as shit.

In the end, I realized enrolling in this class was essential for my graduation. It also carried the bonus of irking Mr. Ortiz, which, I must admit, brought a selfish sense of satisfaction. That man needed a place where he wasn't constantly barking out orders. In any case, I was determined to make it through this semester, no matter what it took, and finally graduate.

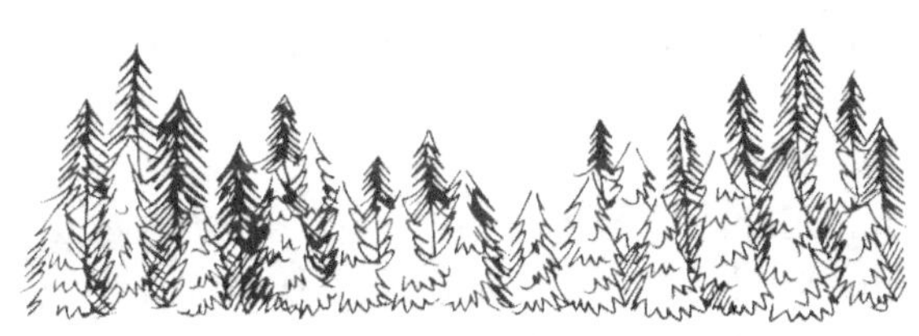

After grabbing my camera and the rest of the gear I needed from the shop off Main, I revved up my motorcycle and headed toward the English building. When I gave Ember my car, I never bought another one. A few guys rigged the engine of Ash's Jeep since we never found the keys and drove it back to the Den, but I couldn't bring myself to drive it, so it sat in the back of the long driveway under a car cover.

Knowing Ember was an English major and that there was a high possibility she could be in this building, put me on edge. Add to the fact that for some stupid reason the university decided to have the first day of classes this semester on a Friday, which meant I needed to prep for the first party tomorrow.

Thankfully, there were no initiations this weekend because, as the leader, I was expected to participate. I thought it was the worst and dumbest part of the Den. Eh, I thought most aspects of the Den and the Cartel were absurd, siding with Ember's complaints about how we were just grown-ass men acting like toddlers with guns.

I loved when she would come in and sit cross-legged on the couch while bitching about Ash being late because he was at another meeting with his dad. I loved the way she smelled delicate and feminine. When she spoke was what I truly admired about her because her words were so thoughtful and strung together better than any song I could ever have imagined.

But Ember was always Ash's. Even when she sat on my lap that first night at the frat with this exuberant confidence and shoved her tongue into my mouth.

"Fuck," I said as I realized I was now standing in front of the older stone building.

*She's not yours.*

It was a reminder I'd often had to tell myself because the way she talked, the way her body moved, and damn it, even the way she fucked my brother was the most erotically beautiful thing I'd ever laid eyes on in my entire life.

*She is not yours.* I repeated, over and over.

I walked into the building, following the signs for the basement. The descent seemed to stretch on forever, and the farther I went, the eerier it became. Unlike the rest of the campus, where the sunlight filtered through the dense trees, down here, it was an abyss of perpetual gloom. The only illumination came from the flickering fluorescent lights above, casting a stark, cold light on the narrow corridor. It was the kind of place you half expected to stumble upon a hidden passage leading to a mystery novel's clandestine lair.

Despite the surroundings, I found a strange comfort in the atmosphere. The basement's grim ambience resonated with my love for crime novels. The darkness down here, the relentless hum of the ventilation system, and the distant echoes of footsteps in the corridor all contributed to an otherworldly setting reminiscent of the gritty narratives I cherished.

I arrived at the small classroom attached to the darkroom, and when I glanced at my phone, I realized I was late.

"Story of my damn life," I grumbled. I used to be a top-notch student. Eight months ago, I was a contender for valedictorian of my class. I was well-liked by my classmates and generally kept to myself within the Den. Now, I was bitter, furious, and a shadow of my former self.

# EMBER

I was always early for class. If you told me a certain time to be somewhere, I would always be at least thirty minutes early. Especially for the first day of class, I thought it was imperative to arrive early because it gave me the opportunity to pick the best seat.

There was a science to this. Not sitting too close to the professor but not sitting so far back. I paused as that thought crossed my mind and felt the subtle sting behind my ear. This same thought crossed my mind when Ash first appeared in Dr. Connolly's class. A small laugh escaped me as I recalled how he fell asleep on me, his behavior catching me off guard. Remembering those seemingly inconsequential moments between us, now deeply ingrained in my daily life, brought me joy.

I blinked back to reality and looked around the classroom, selecting a seat in the second row. The room was tiny with only a handful of desks and a large door connecting it to the adjacent darkroom. Santiago had been texting me, plagued by worries, but I had insisted on handling my classes independently. I reminded him about the tracker, our shared location, and all the details at his disposal. Attracting more attention by having a bodyguard accompany me was a no-go. As a few other students filed in, their disdainful glances directed at me didn't go unnoticed.

I'd gotten here without being recognized, meticulously preparing all my meals at home and persuading Santiago to do my grocery shopping to avoid contact with anyone in town. I simply wasn't prepared for that yet. Being in a small class, where it was impossible to blend into the background, felt daunting, but at least no one had said anything thus far.

Our professor, a woman in her forties with brown curls fashioned into a high bun, dressed in black with oversized hoop earrings, entered through the connecting door. "Greetings, students," she began. "You'll find me listed as Ms. Broadbent on your syllabus, but I'd prefer you all call me Evie."

A chorus of "Hey Evie" resounded through the room just as the bell signaled the start of class.

"This class is quite straightforward. I won't burden you with numerous rules, and we have only one assignment throughout the semester."

Whoa. I wasn't sure if I liked that or if I needed the work to occupy my time and hands. A ripple of excitement flowed through the classroom as the door swung open. My gaze flicked to the empty seat beside me, the last vacant spot, and silently prayed the person would be the one student on campus with no inkling of who I was.

My attention snapped to the door, where a figure clad in dark jeans and a drenched black hoodie stood.

"Damn," I muttered, the realization that I'd walked to class sinking in.

The door creaked as it swung shut, and the shadowed figure stepped into the classroom. As he moved farther into the room, my heart thudded in my chest. The room's lights revealed him slowly, unveiling a silhouette that felt both foreign and achingly familiar.

His eyes, those penetrating orbs, were a shade of blue I could never forget. They were like a stormy sea, captivating and tumultuous. His every movement held a grace I had once known so intimately, and in that moment, time seemed to slow to a crawl.

The world faded into insignificance as his gaze swept through the room, searching for an empty seat, but there was a hint of uncertainty in his steps. Then it happened. As if guided by an unseen force, his gaze locked onto mine. The world stood still, and shivers shot down my spine.

For the first time in eight long, agonizing months, I was looking into the eyes of the one person I had desperately needed for answers—the one person who shared the same torment and grief that had clawed its way into my soul. The one person who, I knew in my heart, wanted nothing to do with me.

"Rain . . ." I whispered. It had been so long, I almost forgot how related they looked even though they weren't blood relatives.

Rain's hesitant steps carried him closer, and he mumbled an apology to our professor as he passed her desk. His presence was a magnetic force, drawing him inexorably to the empty seat beside me.

He sat down, his gaze fixed resolutely ahead, not daring to meet mine. His jaw clenched with an unspoken tension, and his hands, hidden beneath the dark fabric of his hoodie, gripped the edges of the seat as if it were the only thing keeping him anchored in a turbulent sea.

Every fiber of my being ached with the desire to reach out to him, to demand answers, to vent my anger and pain, but I couldn't tear my eyes away from him. I wanted him to see the turmoil in my gaze, the resentment, and the questions left unanswered. I wanted him to know how he had left me shattered, how his silence had been a weight too heavy to bear.

As Rain sat there, avoiding my gaze, a silent storm raged between us. Emotions, raw and unspoken, hung heavy in the air, a chasm of hurt that neither of us knew how to bridge. As Evie continued to describe the class's expectations, a speech I typically clung to at the start of every class, I stared at him.

His hair had grown longer, slicked back from his face, while his jawline sported a thicker stubble, and lines had etched deeper into his features. He seemed older, marked by the weariness that clung to him like a shadow.

A memory flashed before my eyes, the same fatigue etched on his face that night—the night everything changed.

"Rain," I whispered, trying to be discreet. His knuckles whitened as he tightened his grip on the desk, then he lifted his chin, pretending to focus intently on the teacher's words.

Normally, the old Ember would have taken the hint and let him be, but things were different. I had no patience for anyone's nonsense.

"Rain," I repeated, this time with more force.

A faint quirk danced on his lips, but he refused to look my way. Instead, he retrieved a notebook from his bag, feigning interest in taking notes.

Now, he was starting to irritate me. I reached into my bag, grabbed a notebook, and hastily scribbled him a message.

I tore the note from my pad and crumpled it into a small ball. My gaze shifted from the teacher to Rain, who continued to act insufferable. With careful precision, I launched the crumpled note toward his desk, where it landed squarely in his lap.

His eyes darted quickly in my direction, but he avoided meeting my gaze, instead focusing on the note he'd unfolded.

Evie approached Rain's desk, her curiosity piqued. She picked up the crumpled note from his desk, glanced at it briefly, then, with a bemused expression, read it aloud.

The class erupted into laughter, including Rain, who couldn't help but chuckle at the embarrassment thrust upon me.

Evie, after a hearty laugh, looked at both of us and said, "Well, it seems like you two need to work things out. You're going to be partners on the only assignment. Maybe you'll find some common ground."

I buried my face in my hands, mortified by the attention, as Rain flashed a playful grin in my direction, then I shook my head and looked down.

Evie continued to tell us the basics of how our camera worked, and I spent the rest of class determined to catch up on what I had missed and attempt not to embarrass myself anymore.

When the bell rang and class was dismissed, Rain tucked the little note into his backpack and practically sprinted out of the classroom, pushing a few kids aside in his determination.

I wouldn't chase him down though. If he wanted to act like the immature little ass he was being, then fine by me.

I slowly grabbed my things and realized Rain left his camera sitting on the desk. The first part of our assignment was due next week, so he'd probably need this before then. So I shoved it in my bag before heading upstairs.

Thankfully, the rain had stopped, so I walked back home, pleased to avoid anyone else and grateful that it was the start of the weekend.

"Please, come," Marissa begged, standing in my living room on Saturday. I shook my head.

"No." I laughed and fell onto the couch with her. Our friendship was something I cherished. It was a relief to have such an easygoing connection, a stark contrast to my strained relationship with Maddy, who hadn't reached out to me or checked on me since I'd returned to Isles. Given the town's small size, I was sure she'd heard something.

"I'm not going to a party at the Den tonight." I wrinkled my nose, both at the thought of it and the fact Marissa was even suggesting it.

I am not going to a place where people hate me and where I will see Rain. He hadn't made an effort to see me or even communicate with me, so I wouldn't go out of my way to see him.

"I think it's a good idea for you," Marissa insisted. "Show the boys you don't give a damn. Weren't you close with a bunch of them before all of this?"

"I was." I liked to play video games with them, mostly Rain though.

"So, go, show up, hold your head high, and remind them who's boss."

"I agree, Ember," a deep voice chimed in from the now-opened door, causing me to recoil as Marissa rushed toward it. I extended a hand to halt her.

"Who the hell are you?" Santiago, materializing from what felt like nowhere, demanded from behind the stranger, his wary eyes darting between Marissa and me.

Marissa dragged me aside and made her way toward the newcomer, brushing off Santiago's weapon and planting a kiss on his lips.

"Pico?" I asked, squinting. Sure enough, it was Pico, casually leaning against the doorframe and seemingly unfazed by Santiago's previous threat.

He looked so much like Rain it was uncanny. Both had gelled back long black hair. Pico was bigger than Rain and much stockier. He was wearing an oversized U of Isles hoodie with a pair of black joggers.

"You know him?" Santiago asked.

"Yeah, this is Marissa's boyfriend, Pico." I clarified, and Pico extended his hand toward Santiago, who regarded him warily before shaking it.

"Hey man. You graduated a few years before me, yeah?" Santiago seemed to agree as recognition flashed before him.

"Oh yeah, brother. It's good to see you." Santiago pulled him in for a hug.

"This is a totally normal reaction to someone you thought was about to murder me, Santi." I rolled my eyes as I walked over to Pico.

Santiago laughed, then waved me off, heading back to his apartment.

"I didn't realize that Ash hired him . . ." Pico paused, then slowly turned toward me.

"I didn't mean to—"

"It's okay." It was the truth. In some weird roundabout way, being in Isles and remembering Ash had felt better than not being here and wallowing in the sad memories.

I still felt lost most days, but there were glimpses of hope, like remembering the first day of class, where I'd felt not a profound sadness but a gentle reminder of what was.

"Seriously, though, I know a lot of the guys would want you to come to the party," he continued, and I narrowed my eyes at him, resulting in both of us laughing hysterically.

"Come in." I gestured and went to the fridge to grab another seltzer.

They walked hand in hand over to the couch and sat.

"We both know that not a single person at that house wants me to be there," I said as I sat opposite them.

"I want you there," Pico muttered. I looked over at Marissa who shrugged.

"Did she change your mind?" I asked, gesturing to Marissa. To my knowledge, Pico wasn't allowed to talk to me.

"Rules changed." Pico placed his hand on Marissa's thigh.

"So I'm just supposed to be all cool about it, like, 'Hey, it was awesome how you ignored me for so long because of these stupid club rules that got my boyfriend killed last year. But welcome to my house, and I'm super glad you're here?'" My words dripped with venom, a bitter admission of the past, something I hadn't said aloud.

I glanced between them, overwhelmed by a sense of shame. I'd let my anger consume me, blurting out truths which hurt everyone in the room.

With my emotions welling, I sprang from the couch and retreated to the bathroom, tears streaming down my face. The shame from making grief my entire personality trait and hurting those close to me washed over me.

A soft knock at the door startled me from my thoughts. "It's me." Pico's voice came from the other side. I wiped away my tears and slowly opened the door.

"I'm sorry. That was so mean," I said.

"It was." He gave me a little smile before opening his arms and wrapping me in a hug.

"He loved you so much, Ember." I couldn't speak, feeling the wetness back on my cheeks. "I failed him. I failed you." I tried to shake the feeling off, but then his voice cracked and it was game over for me. Sobs racked my body, and I shook in his arms.

Marissa rubbed my arms, soothing me while telling me everything was okay. I didn't know where she came from, but I was so oddly grateful for them.

"Everyone is right, though. It is my fault," I said as I pulled away.

"It's not. He had a lot of shit going on with him growing up with his father." I turned back toward the sink and let Marissa wipe my tears with a washcloth before we went back to the living room, then I poured us each a shot.

"This type of conversation requires more booze," Pico chimed in, and we all agreed.

After we downed the shots, I sat next to them before looking at Pico.

"Who changed the rules?" I asked, my curiosity piqued.

"The boss," Marissa replied. I wasn't sure who had taken over for Ash, but someone had to. I always assumed it was Pico.

"Who?" I pressed for more information.

Marissa exchanged a quick glance with Pico, then she whispered something to him. After a moment, she turned back to me and asked, "Are you sure you want to know the answer to that?"

I had asked out of mere curiosity, but now I felt a growing need to know. "Yeah."

Pico gave Marissa's hand a reassuring squeeze. "Rain."

"Of course it is," I grumbled. Deep down, I knew Rain didn't want this role. When I was initiated as Ash's girlfriend, Rain had distanced himself from the club's rituals. Ash had confided in me that he disliked these traditions, and I understood Rain's involvement had been more out of obligation than personal desire.

I continued my questioning, "And what did the boss finally say?"

Pico sighed. "He said it was cool if I reached out."

Of fucking course he did. My frustration with Rain's newfound authority grew, and I couldn't shake the feeling of anger. Who was he to suddenly create rules dictating when people could talk to me? I clenched my fists, struggling to contain my emotions.

Turning to Pico, I questioned, "Why is it okay now? Why is any of this normal?" My voice wavered with a mix of anger and confusion. "Just because he's grieving too, doesn't give him the right to act like an asshole."

Pico shifted in his seat. "You're right. It doesn't."

Anger welled up, and I wanted nothing more than to stick it to Rain. Grief might have clouded his judgment, but it didn't excuse his behavior. I had been through hell too, and I refused to let anyone dictate my life.

Finally, I turned to Marissa, my hands planted on my hips, and said, "You know what? I think I do need to go to that party tonight."

I did have his camera I needed to return.

"Am I on the list?" I asked Pico. He shook his head.

"You'll struggle getting in. Security is tight, and honestly, they'll know it's you the minute you show up with your bodyguard."

"He's not coming," I said. "I'll sneak out." I shot Marissa a knowing look, but I didn't give a fuck.

"What did you tell him you were coming to talk to me about?" I asked, knowing the rules of the club enough to know Pico had to ask permission to come here.

"Just checking in to see how you were doing after yesterday."

I didn't know why but that made me even more upset. He could have called me to ask. He could have come over, but no, he wouldn't dare do that. Like he didn't check in these last eight months, what made this any different?

I excused myself to my room and grabbed the camera from my backpack before going back out to the living room.

"This is Rain's camera he left behind in class. I guess it would only be just if I returned it to its proper owner." I shrugged. I would not let my trauma dictate my decisions. When I was in therapy, I learned I needed to overcome the pain, and this felt like something I needed to face on my own. I was just going to deliver a camera.

Marissa and Pico exchanged knowing looks before Marissa grinned and said, "Hell yeah you should."

It took me a minute to find the perfect outfit in my closet. I wanted something that felt comfortable, but also knew if I was going to one of these parties, I would need to blend in, so I grabbed one of the skimpy dresses I had borrowed from Maddy's closet, but it didn't feel like anything I wanted to wear right now. I glanced down at my ratty ass, comfortable sweats.

"Fuck that," I grumbled as soon as I heard a knock on my door. "Marissa?" I shouted from the hallway. Something sounded off. She had just left with Pico, and by the way they were all over each other, I assumed they wouldn't come back immediately.

I made my way over to the door and looked in the peephole, but found nothing. I shrugged it off, and then the knock happened again, so I rushed back to the peep hole but still found nothing.

My heart racing, the knocking sounded again, more insistent this time, but the peephole still showed no one. Doubt and anxiety gnawed at me, making me question my sanity. I couldn't ignore my gut feeling.

In a hurry, I dialed Santiago's number, my voice laced with concern when he picked up. "Someone is at my door. I don't know—" A door was slammed open in the hallway.

Santiago's voice took on a serious tone. "Stay inside. I'm coming."

I hung up and stepped away from the door, my heart pounding in my chest. The inexplicable knocking and the subsequent commotion in the hallway sent shivers down my spine, leaving me with a sense of impending danger I couldn't shake. The seconds felt like hours, and I was on the verge of panic. My mind raced with a thousand questions and scenarios, none of which made any sense.

Just as I was about to call Santiago back, my heartbeat intensified with a sudden rush of adrenaline. I could hear the struggle but could see nothing through the peephole.

My trembling hand hovered over the phone, torn between calling for help or staying hidden. Then the struggle subsided, replaced by a hushed conversation. Curiosity and fear swirled within me as I strained to hear what was being said.

I opened the door and saw Santiago with a female clutched to his chest, a gun pointed at her head.

"Get inside," he demanded. Just as I was about to close the door again, I realized I recognized the girl in his arms. It was . . .

"Beatrice." She was disheveled and bewildered. A shriek escaped my lips, a mixture of terror and relief as I recognized her.

Although I wouldn't have considered her close, I assumed she would have reached out since we socialized a few times and she'd been there the night Ale kidnapped me.

"Santiago, stop. It's Beatrice," I shouted, my voice echoing in the corridor. "I know her."

He released his grip, and they stood up, panting and bewildered. Santiago looked at me, his eyes wide and his cheeks pink. "I'm . . . sorry" he stammered.

Beatrice hurried over, her brows furrowed and her eyes darting around the scene. "W-what's happening here?" she asked, her voice tinged with uncertainty and a hint of fear, her hands fidgeting at her sides.

My emotions swirled—relief, anger, and an overwhelming need for answers. I turned to Beatrice, demanding, "Why were you incessantly knocking on my door and then leaving without a word? You scared me half to death."

"I was coming to apologize. I didn't mean to scare you. I was just coming to tell you that I was sorry, but then I got scared, so I turned to leave."

Santiago had let her go, and she gripped her neck where he'd had her in a chokehold. She was doubled over, her breath ragged.

"Who is that?" She turned to Santiago, whose face was blank as he stood tall in the hallway.

"Santiago, my bodyguard." I introduced. "Because of all the hate I've been getting on campus, he needed to come for my safety."

Beatrice winced, then took a hesitant step toward me.

"I came here to apologize. Do you think I could come in?"

I looked back at my empty apartment, then toward her and shook my head. "No," I said. She never once reached out to me in the last eight months to acknowledge my feelings or emotions. And unlike Maddy who outwardly spoke of her hate for me, her quiet disregard of what I was going through was just as bad.

"Oh, okay . . ." She shoved her hands into her pockets, looking down. "I just wanted to say sorry for what happened—"

I held up my hand. "I don't need an apology from you. I needed support when my boyfriend was no longer here, Beatrice. I don't wish you any ill will or harm, but honestly, you need to leave."

I was pissed off. The anger bubbling beneath the surface only fueled the need to see Rain.

Beatrice stepped back, her eyes heavy with guilt. "I understand, but I genuinely am sorry. I should've been there for you, and I wasn't. I have no excuses. I listened too much to the gossip. You deserve more than an apology, but I hope you can find it in your heart to forgive me someday."

My emotions were a tangled mess as I locked eyes with her. Part of me longed to hear her apology, and another part resented her for not being there when I needed her most. It was a battle that left me conflicted.

"I'll think about it," I said, my voice softer. "But for now, I need space."

Beatrice seemed to understand and turned to leave. Santiago stood there, and she gave him a quick nod before walking around him. She hesitated at the elevator, looking back at me. "If you ever need someone to talk to, please don't hesitate to reach out. I mean it."

I offered her a small wary smile. "Thank you, Beatrice. I'll keep that in mind."

Santiago gave me a silent nod before retreating into his apartment.

"Thank you," I mumbled as I shut the door, feeling the weight of the unexpected encounter. Part of me wanted to believe that her apology was sincere, but my trust had been shattered, and it wasn't something that could easily be mended. The turmoil in my heart only served as a reminder of how much I longed for Rain's presence and support, and I wondered if that was the part I needed to fix first before I could forgive anyone else.

# EMBER

This was a terrible idea.

Possibly one of my worst decisions yet, but honestly, I couldn't care less. Dressed head to toe in black, I stood out amid the vibrant colors of the frat party. I had my backpack with Rain's camera and a pair of oversized sunglasses—yes, at night. I knew it made me stand out, but I needed an excuse for leaving my house so late. The only logical thing I could think of was Marissa's suggestion to tell Santiago I had gotten my period and needed to run to the store. It had worked well enough as a cover before. Marissa and Pico had to take care of a few things first, so I decided to go before them. Marissa had given me a hug, confirming I was okay to go ahead of them.

"I'll be good. Thank you," I had responded softly before I headed out.

When I got there, I walked past the people waiting in line, and groans and annoyed murmurs came from behind me.

"Who does she think she is?"

"She can't just cut in line like that."

"You can't skip us."

I had never waited in that line before, and I wasn't planning to start now. Strolling up to the front, I half expected to see Rain since he usually manned this post, but it wasn't a face I recognized.

"I need to see Rain," I demanded, positioning myself in a way that blocked him in with my body, hands gripping the arms of his white folding chair. A searing pain shot from the back of my ear as memories of last year flashed before me. I blinked, trying to will back the self-assured Ember.

"Who the hell do you think you are?" The guy tried to pry my hands from the chair, but I held on tighter.

"Don't make this any harder than it needs to be," I said, pointing at his radio on his hip. "Just use it to call him."

"And say what? Some crazy chick is demanding to see you?" He chuckled. "Come on, girl, move along. No pussy is worth this mess."

I saw red. Without hesitation, I snatched the radio off his hip and flung my sunglasses at his face. As he screamed and grabbed my hand, I pressed the talk button.

"Get your damn ass out here," I growled into the radio, confident he would recognize my voice.

"What the hell?" The guy grabbed the radio, but I let it slip, along with my sunglasses, from my grasp before he glanced in my direction. "Ember?"

"Oh crap, that's the girl whose brother killed her boyfriend," someone shouted from the line. I winced, and my confidence evaporated. My chest was caving, feeling like the air was getting sucked from me.

"You shouldn't be here," the doorman growled, and for once, I agreed with him. The people in line were murmuring. I was trying to focus on the small task here.

"Just let me in," I pleaded, but he shook his head.

"No can do. It's the boss's rules." He shrugged.

"Fucking bitch. You killed your boyfriend," someone shouted from the line.

*Don't turn around.* I repeated over and over again.

"Look." I pulled the backpack off my shoulders and unzipped it so he could see the contents. "I'm in class with Rain. He left his camera. I'm just trying to return it."

The guy shrugged. "After what you or your brother did to Ash, God rest his soul, I am not letting you in."

The anger bubbled inside of me. The same anger I felt whenever *I* thought about his . . . passing. Because this asshole didn't realize I blamed myself, too.

I edged closer to the folding chair and leaned down so I was in his face.

"I was his girlfriend," I said through clenched teeth, my anger bubbling. "I loved him more than you can imagine. I did everything for him, spent eight months banished to Dansport because of how people saw me. But I'm tired of this." I turned around to face the crowd, standing tall. "I loved Ash Ortiz. I have his initials tattooed on me. He had my name tattooed on him. Do you think I don't blame myself, too? Because I do."

I walked back to the doorman, leaned down, and screamed into the darkness, "I loved him too, and he left me. I blame myself every damn day. Let. Me. In," I demanded, flipping his chair back. He scrambled to his feet, and the people in line fell silent.

"You little bitc—"

"Don't finish that sentence," a deep voice warned. He emerged from the shadows, as if he belonged in the woods all along.

I paused, my heart skipping a beat. He was a beautiful man, radiating an aura of mystery. Unlike Ash, whose aura was different, I could never tell if Rain liked me, hated me, or just felt indifferent about it all. Over the past eight months, I had called him, texted him, and begged for updates, all with no response. I assumed he wanted nothing to do with me and blamed me for what happened, but I had no way of knowing because he never talked about it.

"I just came to bring you your camera," I said.

"You needed to come to the house to bring my camera on a Saturday?" Rain asked.

"This obviously played out better in my head," I confessed while glancing over to the guy in the chair now nursing a broken nose from the fall.

"You're hurting my men, Ember." His voice was so low and gravely. He stalked toward me like a lion to its prey.

"I d-didn't mean to. I was just . . . fuck, Rain, what happened?" My voice cracked, close to crying, so I prayed I could hold it together long enough to give him the camera and go back to the safety of the apartment.

"Hey man." I turned around to see Pico, hand in hand with Marissa, strolling up to us. "Ember."

"I don't even want to go to this stupid party, I just wanted to bring this to you and look at the man who maybe shared in the same grief I felt about—"

"Get upstairs," Rain demanded, and I nodded, following his lead.

The man in front of me was different from the one I left last year. He was mad, angry, and in charge. The man I left behind shrunk beneath the shadows, but this man was . . . powerful. People listened to Ash, too, because he didn't give a fuck what weapon he used. Rain just had to use his words, and men bowed down to him, nodding without explanation.

Once we got inside, I paused, letting my surroundings sink in. I hadn't been here for eight long months and realized how much I missed it all. The music was loud, and the DJ played some pop song that had people crowding the dancefloor flailing their arms. In the corner of the room, were still a few people heavily making out; one girl had her top hoisted to her neck, tits exposed. Instead of cringing like I had the first time I was here, I gave a little smirk, knowing what may have happened earlier in the night.

Rain reached behind and grabbed my hand. I paused for a moment before he guided me through the crowd and upstairs where no one was allowed.

I expected since Rain was the president to be led upstairs, but he brought me to the room that he slept in last year. I looked up the stairs to the loft, then back at him.

"No one could take it this year. Didn't feel right." I wondered what happened to his stuff.

Rain opened the door to his room and walked in, a gesture for me to follow, but I took a moment before I followed him in. I hadn't been alone with a man since . . . *him*. I took a slow step in and looked around his room.

He had a small bed in the corner, but the room was filled with books and bookshelves. I grabbed a few of them and saw some crime novels. It was rather neat, too; everything had a place.

"I didn't realize you read?" It came out more of a question as I sat in awe of the bookshelves.

"I'm an English major, Em." My head shot over toward where he was sitting on the bed the moment the nickname came out. My heart dropped in my chest, the familiarity of it felt so good. His deep-blue eyes blazing into mine, his hands fumbling in his lap.

"Ember . . ." I didn't realize how strong Rain looked until now. He had definitely been going to the gym more. He was . . . bulkier. His presence commanded more of the space, too.

"You fucking hurt me after everything that happened with Ash," I said, crossing my arms over my chest.

"I didn't know what else to do. I was shoved into this fucking position." He threw his hands in the air before standing. "I didn't have a chance to breathe."

"No," I practically shouted, "you don't get to use that as an excuse. I, too, lost him, Rain. You are the only fucking person I had alive who is connected to him."

"I was trying to do what was best. I need to appease Mr. Ortiz."

"Why?" I demanded. "You literally don't have to. He's the one putting in everyone's head this rumor that it was my brother who killed him—"

"No. You don't know anything, Ember."

"That's because no one fucking bothers to tell me," I yelled.

"I'll tell you anything you want, ask me a question." He pulled out a small chair by his desk and sat on the bed while encouraging me to sit in the chair.

"No you won't. Just like whenever I asked Ash for something, it was always met with some type of mystery around it. I am tired of asking questions you won't be able to answer."

He tilted his chin to look up at me. "That's where Ash and I are very different. I am on your side. I think this whole war between our families is absurd."

He paused. "Ask. Me. Anything."

# RAIN

When her voice came through the radio, I sensed trouble brewing. My instincts told me before I even laid eyes on her. As much as I held her responsible for Ash's death, I also understood the deep pain she was going through. Our shared love for Ash was so fragile, and with that love came intense anger and frustration. We both carried the weight from questions about his death, and the idea that Ash might have taken his own life felt like a distant, implausible truth.

"Why are you here?" she asked as she settled into the chair.

She was undeniably beautiful, always capturing my attention, even though I had never had hers. Her affections had been reserved for my brother and best friend. It was hard not to notice she possessed a captivating figure, and in the past eight months, she had evolved her style, even though she was dressed casually tonight. Her hair was pulled up in a high ponytail, her lips full, and her eyes . . . God, they were fucking beautiful.

*She's not yours.* His voice echoed in my head. The moment he found out I was the one working the door and she made out with me, he punched me square in the jaw.

*"Are we going to have a problem with this, Rain?" Ash asked, squaring up to hit me once more.*

*I threw my hands up to shield my face. "No," I muttered through clenched teeth, my eyes stinging from the previous punches.*

*He sneered at me, a malicious glint in his eye. "She's beautiful, isn't she?"*

*I nodded, cautiously confirming his statement before he landed another blow to my side.*

*"What the hell was that for?" I hissed, trying to control my anger.*

*"Don't look at her again, Rain," he growled, his voice dripping with possessiveness. "Don't you dare kiss her. Keep your hands off her. She's mine."*

*I saluted him with mock obedience. "Roger that."*

*Exiting the room, I couldn't help but feel the weight of the sacrifice I was making. Despite the love I had for her, I owed it to Ash and his dad, considering all they had done for my mom. Even if it meant relinquishing the one girl who gave me the most earth-shattering kiss I'd ever had. The one girl whose taste on my lips could never be replaced. The one fucking girl whose body I'd never feel in my arms again. I was ready to let him have her.*

Being here with her felt wrong, like I was betraying a promise to a dead man. It just didn't sit right. I needed to address her questions, then get her out of here. Moreover, everyone downstairs seemed to harbor ill feelings toward her, blaming her in some twisted way for Ash's death. Many believed she had tipped off her brother about Ash's whereabouts that night.

"What do you mean?" I responded to her initial question, and she huffed, her lips curling in an unintentionally adorable pout.

"See! This is exactly what I mean."

"Ember, I genuinely don't understand your question." I almost rolled my eyes because I had no idea what she was implying.

In an instant, I regretted barking at her because over the last eight months, all I'd been doing was yelling, being angry and pissed off at people. She was the last person I wanted to be mad at or upset with.

"I'm sorry," I whispered, hoping she didn't hear me, but her long lashes fluttered in my direction, captivating me.

"Like, what are you doing as the leader of all this? You didn't want this role, did you?"

I let out a short laugh. "No, I didn't want it, but I didn't have a choice when Ash died."

"But you do have a choice. That's what I'm trying to tell everyone—"

"No. You're just being naive," I snapped, regretting my tone when her lip quivered. "I didn't mean it like that."

"It's fine. Do you like being the President of the Den?"

"Hell no." I despised it.

"Are you planning to work for Mr. Ortiz when you graduate next year?"

"Yeah, but I got held back, so I'll be in Isles through the summer."

"Why?"

"I failed the spring semester last year. After the incident, I never went to any of my finals." I shrugged like it was no big deal, but her big doe eyes gave me some sympathy, and I held up a hand. "Stop. You, of all people, know what it's like to have people feel sorry for you in this whole situation."

She laughed . . . but not like a normal laugh, no, this one was manic and crazed. "You think I know what it's like for people to feel bad for me?"

She stood, walked over to where I was sitting, then paused. "You have no idea what it feels like to have every single person blame me for someone's . . . incident." She couldn't say "death." "I am the single most hated person on this campus. No one, including you, felt sorry for me."

She raised her hand, then my cheek stung, and my hand moved to my cheek.

"Did you just slap me?" I asked, looking down. What the fuck?

"Yeah. You're being a . . . pendejo," she quipped, her tone serious. I scanned her face to ensure she wasn't joking.

Then, like a bolt of lightning, it all hit me at once, and I burst into laughter so hard that I had to clutch my stomach. "What did you just call me? Do you even know what that means?" I asked between fits of laughter. I couldn't contain myself, and there she stood, arms crossed, a hint of cleavage peeking out from her top.

"What?" She exhaled in reply. "Santiago says it all the time to the grocery store clerk who always clucks her tongue at him."

Santiago . . . her bodyguard. The one I had hired after Ash's incident, but I made him tell her it was Ash who arranged for her protection before his death. What she didn't know wouldn't hurt her. It had become necessary to ensure her safety, especially after everything that had transpired with Mr. Ortiz.

I pulled the waistband of her sweatpants so she was standing between my legs. With my other hand, I grabbed her jaw and pulled her so our mouths were a whisper apart.

"Call me that again, Em, and I am going to show you what an *asshole* I can really be," I hissed in her mouth. Fuck, I was so close to her thick, plush lips I could practically taste them.

She pulled away, then opened her bag and threw the camera in my face.

"If you want to act like one, Rain, then here." There was her lower lip again, quivering.

"Why are you here, Ember? Why does any of this matter to you? Can't you move on?" I barked out, clutching the camera and standing so I had her cornered against my bookshelves. The inner anger demon I kept trying to bury, suddenly awakened, and I wanted to fucking rage and punch something. Instead, I pushed her away. Whenever people got too close, like Ember or Pico, I was best at getting them to leave me be.

When Ash died, when my mother failed to protect me and married Mr. Ortiz, and when I was forced to do something I hated, I realized I had no say in the life I wanted to live. The quiet life where I got to write thrillers and horrors. That person wasn't allowed to exist, so I let the rage consume me.

Aside from the thumping of the music downstairs, a light pattering of rain smacked the windows.

"I am trying, Rain, but I just don't understand what happened. I don't understand why he would leave. I th-thought he loved me . . ." Tears streamed down her face.

Fuck, I hated seeing her cry because it reminded me of my mom and all the years I watched her sit in her room and cry over my deadbeat dad. The dad hooking up with Ember's mom because all he gave a shit about was getting ahead in the business and never enough about us.

I walked toward her, closing the distance between us, and I so badly wanted to reach out to her and pull her into my chest, but I couldn't because his voice was in the back of my head. All I could think about was if she was thinking about him when I comforted her.

"He did love you, Em," I said, hoping my words provided her the comfort she needed. "He loved you so much, but I told you he was complicated. Shit, I can't even figure out half the shit that happened that night, and I promise you I've been trying for these last eight months."

"Is he breathing down your neck?" she asked, her tears slowing. I could only assume she was talking about Mr. Ortiz.

"Yeah."

"Are you okay?" she muttered, and, for some reason, those words hit me hard because they didn't come with the same sorrow or sympathy other people had. Nor were they laced with a sad look or a let-me-fix-you vibe. No, it was a genuine question.

All I could think about was how much I would give to hold her, to touch her. How perfect she would feel in my arms while I glided my hands down her curves. God, I was betraying my best friend. These feelings were wrong and deceitful. I had to fucking stop. I needed to answer her question. The faster I did, the faster she'd get out of here.

"No," I confessed after a pregnant pause. She offered me a tight-lipped nod.

"Me neither." The words escaped her mouth as a sob rolled through.

"I know," I said, then she closed the gap between us, grabbed my shirt, pulled me in, and cried into my chest, just as she had *that* night.

She cried for what felt like hours into my shirt. I let my arms fall onto her back, my hands resting between her sweatpants and the hem of her shirt, relishing in the warmth of her skin. It was like we were the perfect fit. I kept my arm on her lower back as my other hand cradled the back of her head while she sobbed into my chest. In reality, it had only been a few minutes before that feeling of cheating crept back into the forefront of my mind. Before all I could think about was my brother. Before . . .

"Ember, stop." I pushed away from her, and even that movement killed me. "Thank you for the camera. You need to go. Santiago is downstairs in the back waiting for you."

She balked. "You—You called him?"

"Yes."

"Why? I am not a fucking child that needs to be walked home. You could have done it." She threw her hands in the air. "See, Rain, this is the fucking problem I have with you. It's a fucking headache being here. Aside from Marissa, I have no friends. The entirety of this campus hates me, so I can't even take solace in the library like I used to. I have a bodyguard my dead ex-boyfriend hired, and . . . you know what? Forget I said anything." She was pissed. She reached down, grabbed her backpack, and fumbled with the straps as she yelled at me. "I'll just see you in class."

Something was bothering her. Something more than what she was letting on. "Ember, I didn't mean—"

"No, you made it pretty fucking clear." She headed out to the door. "For the record, it's not like I'm here trying to hit on you or anything, so don't make this fucking weird. I'm just trying to figure out what happened to Ash, and fuck if I thought we were friends at one point, that maybe you'd like to team up together."

"Please wait." I tried, but she only held up a hand for me and glided down the stairs with her sunglasses on her head. I looked out the window, which overlooked the back of the house, and shrouded in the darkness, Santiago offered her a shoulder as she walked with him back toward her house.

"Fuck," I screamed, banging my hands against the door. This wasn't how this was all supposed to go down.

# EMBER

"I'm mad at you," I said mid-bite of my cheese pizza as Santiago and I sat on a curb at the edge of town. Behind us was the pizza place. It was run-down and open until midnight for all the after-bar-hours crowd, but the pizza was greasy and hit the spot. He insisted I needed something to eat, and we walked all the way to the edge of Isles without another word between each other. I didn't argue because I was starving.

"You left without telling me. When I heard from Rain, what was I supposed to do?" I took another bite and refused to look over at him, knowing full well I was acting like a child throwing a tantrum.

Santiago was a good-looking man in his thirties with thick brown hair, similar curls to Ash, and the same tanned skin most of the guys in the Den had. He wasn't married, a former military man, and honestly, in the last year, we'd gotten along well. I respected him, so not telling him where I was going when he was simply looking out for my safety was a crappy move.

"Plus, when I heard you were at the Den on a Saturday night, I thought it was just too early for you to be there without some protection." I had to agree with him there.

"We don't like Rain." I looked over at him, and he laughed.

"Oh really? We don't?" The corners of his lips twisted into a small smirk. *Asshole.*

I shook my head. "Absolutely not."

"Why not?"

"Because he's an asshole," I said while grabbing another slice from the box.

"He only cares about you, Ember."

"Nope."

"Ember, I know what happened to you was terrible. I know what happened afterward; words cannot even describe how you must feel. But before you came here, you were doing good in moving forward in your life."

I crossed my arms over my chest as he kept talking. "I lost a lot of men in Iraq when I was in the Special Forces. A lot of men that I knew personally. When I got back stateside, I was supposed to just imagine that life was better." I shoved the slice into my mouth. I needed to keep my hands busy and refocus my thoughts to avoid choking up. "But life wasn't easy. All I could dream and think about was the booms, the screams as people fell to their deaths, the stench that proceeded afterward. I thought I'd never move on, but I realized that doesn't mean that you need to be constantly sad and mad."

"What does it mean, then?" I asked, putting the slice of pizza down and hugging my knees while I looked at Santiago, who offered a small rub on my back.

"It's about acknowledging what happened, making peace with his death . . .with your death, and making the most of living before you meet them in the afterlife." I started to cry again. I'd probably beat the record of how many times I'd cried in one day if the night continued.

"What if I can't seem to find a way to make peace with it out here?"

"Then you need to do whatever it takes, Ember," Santiago continued, his voice carrying the weight of his own experiences. "It might not be easy, and you might never get all the answers you seek, but it's essential for your own healing and peace of mind."

I wanted to know what happened to him and to clear my name, but I also wanted to know that my brother had nothing to do with his . . . passing.

"I'll try." We sat in silence while Santiago picked up a piece of pizza.

"And for God's sake, forgive Rain, because he hasn't made peace with Ash's death either," he said as he shoved the slice into his mouth. "He's a good man, Ember."

"He never checked in on me . . . at all. He's the only person who knows what all of this feels like, and didn't bother to check in on me." Shoulders slumping, the pain seeped back into me. I felt second-string to everyone else and wanted to feel . . . supported. I wanted someone to tell me my trauma was normal and my reactions were fine. Going through something really fucking heavy alone sucked. He wasn't there.

"He did."

I snapped my head in Santiago's direction. "What do you mean?".

"He just was too scared to hurt you, but he checked in on you." This changed everything . . . literally everything. "Sometimes in grief, people don't know how to function. Everything was thrown at Rain all at once, being forced to figure out a death and come up with some alternate ending when it was clear what happened."

"Wait, how do you know all of this?" I asked. I figured Santiago had connections with the Cartel, but this felt like some top-secret shit he was confessing.

"I worked for Mr. Ortiz for a while. That's how R-Ash found me."

Hold on a moment . . . did he just say . . .?

"R-Ash?"

"Ash, Ember. Don't read into it. We were talking about Rain for a moment, I got it twisted," Santiago explained. I cocked my head in his direction. Something was awry here.

"Okay." I agreed, determined to figure out the solution to all of this.

"Let's go home?"

"Yeah, let's." We walked back to my apartment.

"Do you ever want a girlfriend?" I asked Santiago, and he laughed.

"No. Too tóxica."

"We are not," I blurted to defend womankind.

He narrowed his eyes at me, then laughed. "Ember, you were upset when we left the fraternity even though you snuck out on me. Could you imagine if I had a woman? The drama that would ensue?" I punched him in the elbow, and he let out a snicker.

"I bet there will be someone out there for you," I murmured.

"I'll take that into consideration," he said as we got to the building and took the elevator to the third floor. As the doors opened, the small foyer was filled with erotic noises coming from Marissa's apartment.

"They're back from the party, I guess." Santiago stuck out his tongue like he was gagging, and I giggled as I said goodnight and walked into my apartment, promising that I wouldn't sneak out again.

To be honest, I was exhausted, and it was well into the early morning hours anyway.

I stripped my clothes off, threw on an oversized T-shirt, and laid down in bed, staring at the ceiling and thinking about what Santiago had told me. Somehow, I got the feeling that Rain was far more involved in what had happened with me over the last eight months than I had thought. He had been keeping track of me in his own way, suffering in his own depths of grief, but I wished he'd take me up on my proposition. I wished he'd let me in, and together we could figure this out. Between his inside knowledge of Ash and how intimately I knew him, we could figure it out together . . .

One could only dream.

# EMBER

The next week passed pretty seamlessly. It was Friday, which meant I had to see Rain, regardless if I wanted to, plus it was the start of our group assignment, so we needed to figure out what the prompt was.

I drove to class because it was raining, and parked behind the English building. Early as usual, a book about fae bat boys falling in love with a set of sisters caught my eye in my backpack. It allowed me to escape the world for a little and pass the time. At about twenty pages in, I realized someone else had walked into the room.

I quickly snapped my head up and saw Rain sitting next to me, slung back in his seat with a book in his hand. He was reading a famous thriller book, *Gone Girl*, and was probably as engrossed in it as I was in mine.

"You're early," I said, resting my elbows on the desk and putting my book down to look at him. He turned his head in my direction, his deep-blue eyes burning a hole through my own.

"Em," he whispered as he grabbed the legs of my desk and pulled it toward him, the metal scraping against the floor. "I fucked up."

"Yeah, you did," I responded, not looking at him, but the warmth of his body seeped into me.

"Can you look at me?" I shook my head, being the stubborn ass I was, and sat back in the chair, staring ahead at the clock on the wall.

He grabbed my chin and gently lifted it so I was facing him. His eyes looked pained and sunken. He looked just as tired, if not more than, as he did when I saw him in this class last week.

"What do you want?" I whispered as he held my chin, even though at this point, I was willingly gazing at him. The place his fingers lay, burned through me, sending a rippling current of heat through my body.

"I need your help," he confessed, the words coming out slow.

"With what?"

"You were right." Well, wasn't that just music to my ears, but I would not boast with an I-told-you-so moment.

"About what? Stop being so fucking elusive, please."

"Okay." He shook his head a few times, pulling the hair off his forehead. "I need a teammate in figuring this Ash shit out."

Well, that is definitely not what I expected him to say. I was expecting him to demand an apology for last weekend, apologize for being an asshole, admit he was actually flirting with me, but definitely not this. He dropped his hand from my face and brushed a hair off my ear.

"And you want me to help you, I assume?"

"Please."

"But, why now?"

"I can't do it on my own anymore, plus, I think you're right." Rain cracked his knuckles before looking back at me, his hand going behind my ear to touch where the O was tattooed. "I think he killed himself, but I need to prove it to Mr. Ortiz. I need concrete proof that your brother or your family wasn't involved."

"Don't say it like that," I demanded, pushing his hand off me. I hated that everyone blamed Walsh or me. I hated that people couldn't see Ash's struggles. I hated that mental health struggles weren't a concept that people grasped. If Ash had cancer, there would be no one to blame but the cancer. Why was this any different?

"Say what?" he asked.

"That he . . . that it was his fault."

"I don't know how you want me to say it any other way, Em." I was about to tell him off, frustrated with the whole world, when the door swung open and a student walked in. They paused as they noticed how close we were sitting and how far out of my row I was.

I looked over at Rain and whispered, "Push me back." He chuckled before doing so.

Just then, a couple more students filed in, and I pulled out my notebook and camera, ready for Evie to give us instructions on the project. Rain leaned over as the bell rang and threw a small crumpled note on my desk.

I mouthed, *Why did you sign it*? He laughed, then I put the note inside my bag, not wanting Evie to read this one aloud.

"Okay, everyone, if you are not sitting next to your partner, please make your way next to them and go ahead and smush the single desks together."

Rain gave me a knowing glance before he smushed me back next to him.

"Long time no see, mi pareja."

"What?" I asked, scrunching my nose, not recognizing that word. I learned a few phrases after Ash passed, hoping it would keep me connected to him and his culture.

"Don't worry about it."

Evie interrupted us before I could press for more. "The project will commence this week, and before we go into the dark room, we will need to work on the actual shooting part," she explained. "The project is to take a series of photos of things that scare you."

Someone raised their hand and asked, "Like snakes?"

Laughter rippled through the room, but Evie hushed us with a gesture.

"In theory, yes, snakes could be something that triggers fear, but I want you to dig deeper. What I'm asking you to explore are your inner fears, the things that truly disturb and terrify you, things you may be avoiding confronting," she explained.

"For the rest of this hour, I want you and your partner to brainstorm. If you finish early, you're free to leave or continue your discussion elsewhere. However, I'd like you to spend this time talking and planning. Next week, we'll delve into darkroom basics."

People turned to their partners, engaged in conversation, but Evie halted us again. "As we covered the basics last week, I encourage you to practice with your film cameras by capturing subjects that evoke fear. It could start with something as literal as a snake, but it should evolve into deeper explorations." She gestured for us to go ahead as she essentially dismissed the class.

"What do you think? Wanna ditch this joint?" Rain asked.

"Absolutely." We grabbed our stuff and headed out of the basement.

"The basement is too fucking creepy."

He paused, scanning for any signs of life before agreeing. Part of me thought it was for my own comfort.

"Where to?" Rain asked. "I don't want it too crowded." I knew the implications of us together in public. I was out with my late boyfriend's brother who was the head of the organization that still blamed me and my family for his . . . passing. I wasn't jumping at being seen in public with Rain either.

"I have the perfect spot." I remembered as we headed toward the parking lot. "Where are you parked?" I asked.

"Right here." Rain gestured over to the motorcycle, and I stared back at him.

"Still a solid absolutely not, especially with sleek roads," I added.

"Where's the fun in that?" He chuckled, then inquired about my location, to which I pointed toward my car.

"You're still driving my car?" He seemed surprised, and for a moment, I forgot that it was actually his car.

"Oh yeah, you can have it back." I tossed him the keys, and he caught them.

"No, I'm glad to see you still driving her," he confessed before handing the keys back.

"I figured you had a tracker or something on the car," I half joked, feeling Rain's hand against mine.

"Em, I told you I was different from Ash. I don't need to track you. I know you're strong enough to take care of yourself," he reassured me.

His words triggered something within me, a sensation I couldn't quite label, but it felt like . . . attraction? No, that couldn't be it. I had always acknowledged Rain's enigmatic allure, but I had never considered being intimate with him even though my body was telling me a different story. I guessed I could count that one time I accidentally stumbled upon him with a girl while I was still with Ash. His mysterious demeanor had brought me a certain curiosity. What was happening inside of me right now?

I opened the door and jumped in the driver's side as Rain got in, and I drove us down toward the edge of campus.

Then I pulled up to the familiar diner whose sign was burned out. Since the last time I was here, it had gotten far more run down. Rain glanced at me sideways.

"Just trust me." I laughed before opening the car door and headed toward the entrance. Rain trailed behind me.

Walking in, I was shocked at how nothing had changed over the past few months. Although, I probably shouldn't have been, because this place likely hadn't changed décor in years. It emanated old-school-diner vibes with its large, red booths. I picked the small booth on the opposite side of the restaurant I typically sat in. I wasn't trying to replace memories of Ash, but I wanted to paint new memories in this life. Rain slid in on the opposite side of me.

"He found this place?" he asked, grabbing the straw, pulling off the paper, then fumbling with the paper between his fingers.

"Yeah," I managed to squeak out.

"I do the same thing." I cocked my head in his direction, and he lifted the paper up. "Yeah."

"Nervous habit." He chuffed.

"It is."

"I guess we should talk about what scares us, then?" Rain questioned. I fiddled with the straw, not wanting to make eye contact just as the waitress came over.

"We'll have two chocolate milkshakes and a burger to split," I added before the waitress took our order happily.

"Hey. You're that girl whose boyfriend passed away?" I winced, and Rain went to get up, but the waitress quickly followed up with. "I'm so sorry to hear that about him. You must miss him so much."

I offered a tight-lipped smile to avoid crying because if I said anything, it would be accompanied by tears. "I do, very much so."

I was sad, not because she asked about Ash but because she asked about him in a way that was gentle and forgiving. It was nice to feel some sympathy without being blamed for his death.

She walked away before I turned toward Rain and took a deep breath, exactly what I had learned through therapy.

Just as Rain opened his mouth, I interrupted him. "Tell me about him like when you guys were younger."

Rain smiled and sagged in his booth, which made our knees touch, and I jolted before leaning into it.

"I met him when I was little, in elementary school. He was so structured. I thought it was so weird because it wasn't how it was at my house."

I thought I remembered something that Ash had said about Rain's dad, but I couldn't quite pinpoint what it was.

Quickly changing the subject, he said, "You know Ash was always . . . sad."

I shook my head. "What do you mean?"

"His dad ran the house like it was the military. Ash had to make his bed every morning at zero five hundred before going to school. In high school, he was forced to attend meetings with Mr. Ortiz after school, so he didn't have any time for friends or extracurricular activities."

"That's terrible." I sighed, imagining what a dreadful life that must have been, especially for a teenager.

"He was essentially forced to grow up too fast. Things improved when my mom and I came into the picture, but my mom was a . . ." Rain ran his hands through his hair. I gave him space, letting the silence linger, unwilling to fill it with unnecessary words.

After a moment, he continued, "She let Mr. Ortiz control her, so she liked the structure. It made her feel secure."

"Are they still together?" I inquired.

"They got married last winter."

"Oh, wow . . ."

"I know. Me, too."

"Was Ash happy?" I asked, secretly hoping for a different answer.

"No, Em." He rolled his lips, like he wanted to tell me more, but he seemed forlorn, staring out the window.

"Were you?" I inquired. Rain locked eyes with me, and for a moment, I felt lost in the deep-blue pools. He seemed surprised by my question.

"Yeah, I think I was pretty chill. Mr. Ortiz never bothered me much, so I kind of became a wallflower, lost in books."

"Do you reread often?" I asked, changing the subject to something lighter. Readers often debated whether you should reread books or only read them once.

"Hell yeah. I have some serious comfort reads. When I need an escape, I pick them up."

I laughed, nodding.

As our food and milkshakes arrived, I put everything on an extra plate for Rain. "I've never had anyone share with me. I kind of blended in too much, I guess. People often didn't notice I was around."

"I always noticed you, Rain," I admitted, taking a bite of my burger. What came out of my mouth next was a shock, as if my brain hadn't processed it. "Even when you watched me during the initiation, I was watching you, too."

Rain's cheeks flushed, and he took a bite of his burger, trying to avoid the conversation. I chuckled.

"Did you guys ever share?" I asked, my curiosity getting the best of me. Rain twisted his lips into a frown, then paused before responding.

"Never," he stated. "I don't share what's mine. I never will."

"But what if you get a girlfriend this year? Won't you have to do the initiation?" Rain put his food down and leaned over the table, getting closer.

"Never. I don't care how much trouble it might cause; I will never share what is mine . . . ever."

Oh no, there was absolutely no denying the fact I felt something . . . down there. It was unexpected, catching me off guard. For a moment, I didn't even think of Ash, the grief, or the complicated situation we were in. All I could focus on was the intensity in Rain's eyes, the confident declaration of ownership, and the undeniable attraction that had surged between us.

My cheeks flushed with embarrassment and desire as I tried to regain my composure. I cleared my throat and shifted in my seat, attempting to hide my reaction. "Well, I-I admire your determination," I said.

Rain's gaze lingered, a knowing and almost mischievous glint in his eyes. "I'm a man of my word, Ember," he said, his voice low and filled with an underlying promise that sent another wave of heat through me.

I quickly changed the subject, feeling the need to break the tension that had enveloped us. Deep down, I couldn't help but wonder if this unexpected connection between us would lead to something more, something I hadn't anticipated in all my grief and confusion.

# RAIN

"I think I want to go over to his rock," Ember said as we walked out of the run-down diner and back toward the car.

"Are you sure?" I asked.

I had been there a few hundred times going over and scouring the entire place to see if there were any other clues. Since this was likely her first time back, I wanted to support her in ways I hadn't been able to before this.

"Yeah."

"Now?" I wanted to double-check that she was certain.

"Now." Her voice was unwavering.

"Are you sure you're ready?" I leaned back against the car we were standing next to.

"W-will you come with me?" she asked. I didn't want to. Every time I had to go back, I always felt him next to me, and I hated acknowledging that was the last place he saw. Obviously, I'd do it for Ember because, shit, if she wanted me to walk to the other end of the world for her, I'd do it without thinking twice.

"Okay," I whispered. "Want me to drive?"

"Please." I jumped into the driver's side as she went to the other.

"Wait," she exclaimed. "Where's Santiago?" She frantically looked around.

"He's back at his apartment. I told him you're with me." She narrowed her eyes on me.

"How did you know his number?" I laughed again. I should tell her the truth because she deserved to know and I promised I would be the only person to never lie to her.

"I texted him the other night when you were at the Den." I shrugged.

She grabbed my arm, and the moment her skin touched mine, a shiver crawled down my spine. I loved the way she felt and missed her taste from the one time I got to have her, and I tried so hard to replace the way she made me feel with others but hadn't been successful.

"Tell me the truth, Rain."

"I hired Santiago. When you left Isles last year, I hired him to watch over you." Looking straight ahead, I pulled out of the lot, not wanting to make eye contact.

"You . . . what?"

"I hired Santiago from the Cartel. He was looking for a job, something that got him out of the daily grind, and wanted an assignment. I told Mr. Ortiz that Ash had hired him before he passed, and who was going to argue with a dead man? It was the only way to keep him on payroll, keep you safe." I kept driving straight out toward the edge of Isles. It was silent for two blocks, and I didn't dare look in her direction.

"That's why he told me Ash hired him."

"Yeah."

"Thank you."

Then I glanced back at her because I was damn well expecting a verbal lashing. "Thank you?"

"Yeah, for telling me the truth." She folded her hands in her lap. "It's all I ask, and it seems like a task most people find utterly impossible."

"I'll always tell you the truth. Always." I promised, knowing it was damn well a promise I would uphold. Ash never told her the full truth because the truth underneath all those layers was terrifying even for himself. I'm not sure he even knew the full truth himself, because then he would have had to face it within himself. It's scary to have to look at yourself in the mirror and admit that the person looking back at you is a stranger you don't recognize.

I've been there. I'm there now. Because every damned morning, I look at myself in the mirror and hate the person staring back at me.

We exit Isles, and I check the mirror to make sure it's just us. The one good thing that came from what had happened was that the Alpha house and the Den seemed to come to an understanding that neither of us were hunting until we figured out what happened to Ash. The Alpha house insisted they had nothing to do with him, especially not before the bonfire. Yeah, they wanted him dead, but only in a way that was legit.

"Are we . . . safe?" Ember asked, and I snapped out of my thoughts and back to her.

"Yeah," I admitted, double-checking that I had my two Glocks tucked into my waistband just in case we needed them.

"Are you ready?" I asked.

"Ready as I can be," she replied as we drove down the windy roads and straight to the pull off I'd been to many times over the last eight months. So many times that even during my worst nightmares, I'd drive here, imagining what it must have felt for Ash in those last moments.

I pulled off where we found his car and got out before walking toward Ember's side. As I opened the door, she was white as a ghost and her hands shook in her lap.

"Is this what you want?" I asked again.

"Yes," she replied, so I did what I thought was right in the moment and laced my fingers with hers and pulled her from the seat.

She hesitated, but ultimately followed me. Fog hid the setting sun, so it was pretty dark already.

"I have a light in the trunk," she said. So without letting her hand go, I went around the back, grabbed the flashlight, then headed in the direction of his death.

"Tell me what you know," she murmured as we walked toward the edge where we found him.

"The rain has washed most of the evidence out, but we did take pictures. I have them back at the house." Over the times the rest of the Den and I had scoured this place, we'd cataloged everything we saw: what kind of plants were there, shoe imprints, and anything else that stuck out to us.

"Were the cops ever called?" she asked.

"Yeah. Isles had to, but it was a clean-cut case of—" I swallowed hard. "Suicide."

I leaned over, pausing us in our tracks, and wiped away a rogue tear that had fallen down her cheek.

Her breath picked up in pace as her chest heaved up and down. I gave her hand a quick squeeze, and she looked up at me with her big beautiful eyes.

"I haven't said that word since he . . . passed," she mumbled.

"It's okay not to, but that's what we are doing out here. We're trying to figure out what happened because I do think that *something* was out here, but I just can't figure out what."

"You don't believe what Mr. Ortiz did?"

"No. But I do think your brother not telling the truth is somewhat telling in terms of something else happening." I needed to figure out who else was there.

"I agree." When we finally got into the clearing, she took a deep breath.

"I learned this in therapy. Helps ground me."

"Can I do it with you?" I asked, willing to try anything to stop the nerves from jostling through me.

"You wanna take a breath?" I gave her a small twist of my lips, knowing it sounded ridiculous, but not caring either way.

"Yeah."

"Okay." She shrugged. "It's easy. You just inhale, hold it for three seconds, then exhale. Repeat until you feel more grounded."

I held her hand and did exactly what she asked. In all honesty, it seemed hokey, but after doing it a few times together, I felt more comfortable being out here. Either that or being here with Ember, holding her hand in a place where the one person we loved the most saw last comforted me.

"Tell me what this looked like that night," she asked. As we stood there staring out into the clearing, neither of us dared to go onto the rock itself.

"We knew Ash had been out here. I drove, saw his car from the road, and parked. There were two distinct sets of shoe prints. Although one of them had a steady forward motion, the other seemed frantic, like it was searching for the first person." I gripped her hand a little tighter to steady her.

"How many sets of shoe prints were on the rock?" she asked.

Huh. I hadn't thought to ask that, nor did I know the answer.

"I have no idea." She looked up at me, batted her lashes, then glanced over toward the rock.

"If he was pushed, it is always muddy up here, so you'd see the two sets of shoe prints on the rock. Maybe we can have a look when we get back to the house?" I asked, wanting her involved, desperate to spend more time with her.

"I'd love that." She gave me a slight smile. "I want to go up there."

"Okay," I said, stepping forward before she pulled me back. "Alone."

"Okay," I repeated, turning toward the car. "I'll just wait—"

"Can you just stay here?"

Looking around, I found a small stump on the side, pulling away before letting her go forward. She needed to see him, to feel his spirit, to feel what I did every time I came up here. She needed to know it was okay to live, that what she'd been doing in the city wasn't living; it was existing, and there was a difference between the two.

I may not have been a pro at offering advice, but I knew I had to heed my own wisdom. I was simply going through the motions in life, existing rather than living. Being here, after I got past the initial fear of solitude, was a form of healing. It felt good to see the last thing he did, to find beauty in the quiet, to see the birds gliding through the air, and to believe, in some way, that he had found peace here, no matter how it all unfolded.

# EMBER

A tranquil silence surrounded me, almost as if Ash's spirit had wrapped its arms around me, urging me to find closure and move forward. I found it imperative I unravel the truth of what had happened to him so I could begin healing and let go of the pain I had carried for months. That's what propelled me to keep walking toward the edge, pushing me through the fear of being in the one place so connected to who Ash and I were together.

As I ventured closer to the edge of the rock, memories of our happier moments seemed to materialize before my eyes. Standing where I imagined he once stood, taking his last breath, I couldn't hold back the tears that welled up and streamed down my cheeks.

A mixture of laughter and sobs escaped my lips as I became submerged in the vivid recollections. Amid the overwhelming emotions, an unexpected sense of tranquility settled upon me. I gingerly touched my tear-stained cheeks and perched myself at the edge of the rock.

"I miss you," I whispered, my voice barely louder than a breath. "Going through everything without you was excruciating. I felt so utterly alone."

Loneliness had been the most tormenting aspect. It had felt like an unending battle waged in a world of solitude, and the fear that accompanied such isolation was paralyzing.

"I hope you're watching over *her*," I whispered.

I buried my face in my arms, allowing the waves of emotion to wash over me.

"Want some company?" A dark yet comforting tone snapped me out of my thoughts, and I looked up to the deep blues I'd grown accustomed to over the last couple of weeks.

"Yeah." Rain sat beside me, leaving a sliver of space between us.

"I'm so tired, Rain," I whispered, surrendering to the overwhelming sadness that had descended upon me like an unyielding weight. If my life were a story, this moment would be the darkest, most heart-wrenching chapter. I desperately longed to break free from the suffocating grip of grief, but I was immersed in it, wading through its depths.

"I am so alone, yet I am so scared of letting someone in. It's fucking terrifying to imagine that someone else could take another piece of my heart and then leave me again. But I am tired of doing this . . . life." I sighed. "I grew up stuck alone in a house with no friends. I was alone when I came here, and Ash gave me something I needed. He showed me a way into the darkness but somehow I got trapped. And now I don't know what to do."

Losing someone unexpectedly in a manner so brutally unfair, coupled with the fact I had already grappled with two deaths within eight months, was akin to sinking into an abyss. I yearned for a lifeline, for someone to extend a helping hand to pull me out. In that moment, I realized someone was there. His hand was extended toward me, waiting for me to grasp it. All I needed to do was reach out and take hold.

"You aren't alone anymore, mi pareja." I glanced over at Rain, then rested my head on his shoulder.

"I think someone else was here, but I don't think they pushed him. What their role in all of this was, is beyond me, but I want to figure it out." I looked at the night casting its shadow among the pines.

"I agree," Rain whispered before resting his chin on my head.

"Em?" he murmured.

"Yeah?"

"Wanna go home? It's just that it's getting dark, and I don't like being out here in the dark."

"I agree," I said as he jumped up, carefully lifting me and turning on his flashlight.

"I don't know how to get unstuck," I muttered as we walked together, this time with the space between us.

"What do you mean?" he asked.

"It's just that there's been so much grief and sadness over the last few months. I don't know how to reach for your hand," I explained. There was a brief pause.

"My hand isn't going anywhere. I'll keep reaching out, and whenever you're ready, you'll take it." As we walked forward, I searched for his fingers and splayed out mine.

Without even looking down, Rain reached for my hand and pulled me close to him so there was virtually no space between us. He stopped just as we reached the car, using his free hand to tuck a strand of hair behind my ear.

"I'm so proud of you," he murmured, then lowered his head to rest his forehead against mine. We stood there for what seemed like a lifetime, breathing each other in. He was the lifeline I always needed. The one person who'd help me figure a way out of the grief. There was one more thing I needed to do—to tell him—before I could hold his hand. Before I trusted him enough not to let it go because I didn't think my heart could take any more heartbreak.

We pulled up to my apartment, and I was cold and exhausted.

"Santiago asked if I could walk you to your door," Rain informed me as he parked on the street. I responded with a weary nod, too drained to put up a fight.

Taking my school bag, Rain escorted me to my apartment door, where I stood frozen, my hand hovering over the handle. I looked up at him, seeking answers. "You promised you'd always tell me the truth."

"I did."

"Then tell me why you left me all alone for eight months. Tell me why you didn't call me about the funeral or let me know what was happening when I got to Dansport. Why are you suddenly the beacon of truth? Why now?"

Rain glanced around the hallway, visibly uncomfortable. "Can we go inside?" he requested. I pushed the door open, allowing him to enter first. He walked to the windows at the far end of my modest apartment.

As he stood there, staring out into the edge of the forest, he remained silent for a while. His voice, when it finally broke the silence, was both commanding and desperate, a tone I had never heard from him before. It piqued my curiosity, and I complied with his request to sit down.

Kneeling in front of me, he gripped my thighs for support. "I couldn't." He sighed heavily. "You were the one person who was so close to him. I envied him, Ember. I resented the fact that he had you because I wanted you from the moment you kissed me in front of the Den." My heart started to race again. I wanted to tell him I'd kiss him all over again, but that felt wrong to even think. The fact I was getting so turned on watching him kneel before me was like a knife in the gut. My physical body felt like it was betraying my mind.

"And then, suddenly, he wasn't here anymore, and I just couldn't handle myself. Maybe I didn't listen to him enough in those last few months, or maybe I should have told him he wasn't in the right headspace for a girlfriend."

Rain's eye twitched as he continued, "Perhaps I should have confided in more people that he was suffering and needed help. Initially, when you left, everyone was in my ear about your brother, and I was angry, thinking maybe you had led him on. But Santiago was sending me reports on how you were doing. When he told me you had spent months hardly leaving your house, Em . . . You spent three months confined to your bed. My whole world crumbled. I felt selfish and utterly despicable."

A single tear traced its path down Rain's cheek as he leaned his head against my thighs. Without thinking, I reached down, gently grasping his face and lifting it to meet my gaze.

"I was on the way to see you, to tell you about all of this when Santiago told me that you'd finally gotten out of bed. You were starting to look up, and I thought my presence would fuck it all up. I thought about how many times I'd just let Ash take control and tell me what to do and how shitty that made me feel. If I showed up and acted like a knight in shining armor that you'd somehow end up . . . like him." He coughed out the last part, and his head landed back on my thighs as he broke into a fit of tears.

"I-I-I didn't know." I couldn't come up with the words I felt for all of Rain's confessions. It was so heavy. Moving from the chair, I kneeled with my back against it and wrapped Rain in my arms. He blamed himself as much as I did. I felt horrible for assuming that he was upset with me the entire time. I didn't know he was checking up on me.

"You wouldn't have."

I paused.

I remembered the initiation and how Rain looked at me with disgust that night, but knowing all this now, it had to have been jealousy.

"Is that why you wouldn't participate in the initiation?"

He nodded into the crook of my shoulder.

"Why didn't you say anything?" I whispered.

He glared up at me, his body still positioned between my legs. "How could I, Ember? My brother was never allowed to have anything in his life. He was so damn depressed, drowning in that robotic role he was forced into by his dad. For once, he was finally happy. How could I rip that happiness away from him?"

I fell into a momentary silence. "I loved him. So much. I'm sorry that it wasn't you." My tone dropped to a whisper. "I still love him."

"I get it," he whispered as if he understood the pain I had gone through because he, too, felt the same. I wanted to know what would drive Ash to bring himself there. I wanted to know what happened so I could confirm I had nothing to do with it.

I didn't understand why he'd want to *you know* himself when he told me we were in love. The questions swirled around my brain, and I was desperate to find answers. Then adding onto the fact this confession from Rain was so much. I didn't realize he was into me . . . at all.

"It's not your fault," he said, his voice heavy with emotion. "I guess when I saw you come back to Isles, I did everything I could to stay out of your way. But then you showed up in class, and I saw you, and all bets were off. It feels like I'm screwing up by spending time with you. But I can't stop thinking about you. I want to know if you're okay. I want to know if you're getting out of bed, showering, or eating three meals a day. I want to be around you because you're addicting, but I can't because I feel like I'm breaking some unwritten rule about—"

"Stop," I demanded, pushing him off me and standing up. I ran a hand over my temples, the weight of this conversation pressing down on me, far too heavy and exhausting for the moment. This wasn't what I had expected him to say. I wasn't sure what I had expected, but it wasn't this. I didn't want a confession that he might like me, because I couldn't even wrap my head around that possibility.

"This is too much for one day. I-I can't do anything either, Rain. I don't know if it'll ever be possible for me to be with anyone else. I was so in love, and it was ripped from me."

Rain nodded, understanding what I was saying, but I knew I was hurting him.

"I'm not saying we should, but you asked me, and I felt like I had to tell you the truth."

He paused before getting up and walking toward the door. "If I didn't tell you how I felt, then, somehow, I think I'd never have the opportunity. I guess when I saw you in person it was hard to hide how I felt." He shook his head. "I'm going to go back to the house to check and see if there was another set of footprints on the rock."

"Okay," I whispered, then closed the door behind me. I pushed my back against the cold wooden door before dropping to the floor, hugging my knees with my hands and sobbing.

No one suffered with me, aside from Santiago, for so long, that it felt foreign to have someone to share this space with. Learning that Ash had been suffering from depression for much longer than I had existed in his life, both comforted and saddened me. I wish I'd seen it. I wish I'd been able to see it, but I was too blinded by our all-consuming love.

Ash always told me there'd never be a world in which he and I could exist together, and he was right. There wasn't. If he'd been suffering for as long as Rain could remember, then I wondered if he always knew that deep down he would not be here this year. If, somehow, he had headed to the rock because he had some intel.

"Fuck," I whispered, knowing exactly what I had to do as I picked up my phone.

Ember:

I think it's time we talk.

I waited only a minute before three bubbles popped up, indicating that he was typing back.

Walsh:

Anytime, Ember. I miss you. I hear you're on campus so please . . .

Ember:

I'll contact you.

My gut told me I needed to talk to him. He was keeping a secret, but after seeing the rock, I knew in my soul that whatever happened to Ash wasn't malicious. I needed to find out the truth so I could move forward and tell Rain the truth. Because after being with him today, I was lying to myself. I rolled over in bed and plugged my phone back in just as it pinged with a new message. I opened it one last time before sleep consumed me and saw a text from Rain.

Rain:

One set of prints on the rock. Two sets of tracks leading up.

# EMBER

It was Saturday, and Marissa was in my apartment, per usual, as I was debating whether I even wanted to go to the hair appointment she set up for me.

"This is dumb," I told her, shaking my head, insisting I could do my hair at home. We were sitting in the small bathroom of my apartment researching different hair styles I would like.

"It's not *dumb*, you haven't ever dyed your hair, and some highlights would be cute. You sure you don't want me to come?"

"I'm not even sure *I* want to go." I laughed, and she handed me the piece of paper she'd written instructions on. "I feel like you're my mom or something, handing me what to tell the hairstylist."

"Well, it's a pretty big deal to actually get your hair done for the first time." She winked at me. I had only ever done the box dye you get from the drugstore. She told me in order to feel good on the inside, you needed to feel good on the outside too. I'd be a rotten fruit, but at least I'd have fabulous hair.

We scoured Pinterest for styles and colors I liked and decided on some "babylights" and face-framing pieces. I told her I wanted to look as natural as possible with my dark hair.

"Santiago is insisting on walking me, so he'll be there. No need to worry." Her eyes narrowed in my direction.

"On another note, what're you doing tonight?" She grabbed an apple from my fridge and took a massive bite. I stared at her, laughing. I never had a sister growing up, but this was how I'd imagined having one would be.

"Definitely not going to the Den," I stated before grabbing my wallet and purse from the chair and making my way out the door with her.

"Ugh. Nothing I can do to convince you?" she asked, and I shook my head no.

"I need to finish my book and do some work. Maybe I'll convince Santiago to play another game of Scrabble."

"Ah, mija, so you can kick my ass? I think not." He chuckled as he closed the door to his apartment. I glanced toward Santiago, feeling the warmth he exuded toward me with that small comment. It made me feel like we'd developed a father-daughter bond over the past months.

"You got a big date or something?" Marissa asked, and Santiago swatted her. Marissa's older brother was friends with Santiago, so they knew each other from way back.

"Let's go?" Santiago asked before pressing the elevator button. I hugged Marissa, and she told me not to forget to show the hairdresser the note.

The salon was next to the Tipsy Tavern in Isles. There was a small nail salon attached to it, and quite a few people were already inside. It was a large street in the middle of town with the same cobblestone alleys the quad had. There were small buildings with students coming in and out. Truthfully, since this was the main street, there was a lingering smell of vomit from the night before, but the salon looked modern and inviting enough to pique my curiosity.

"Are you okay to go in?" Santiago asked. This would be the first real outing, aside from class and the occasional grocery store run. Apart from the one time at the Den, I tried to keep it as low key as possible.

"Yes," I responded before walking toward the salon and Santiago sat on a bench across the street in direct view.

"Hey. What's your name?" the icy receptionist asked. She had her arms crossed over her chest and barely looked up from playing a card game on her phone.

"Oh, um, hi. My name is Ember Solis. I am here to see Tana." The girl pointed to a set of chairs in the waiting area. There were large, oversized pillows on them that I presumed were there to make them feel more luxurious. I was standing in the front waiting room, and it was as inviting and modern as the outside felt. Beyond the receptionist desk was a drawn cream curtain where she'd just disappeared behind. Chatter came from back there, and I assumed that's where the heart of the salon was. She came back quickly and took her place behind the desk.

"You're the girl whose boyfriend died?" she asked, and I gulped the pain down.

"Yeah," I muttered, hoping she didn't hear. Shifting my gaze out the window, Santiago looked up at the same time. I shook my head because I didn't want him to come in, I was only making sure he was in eyesight. There was a comfort in having him so close by.

"Come back. She's ready for you." I stood up, following her behind the curtain where a few stylist chairs were set up with a small shampoo bowl in the back.

She pointed to a chair as far away from the window as possible, which made me slightly anxious, but I swallowed, reminding myself this was all about an experience I never got to have. This was all about the new me and feeling good about myself.

"What're we doing today, boyfriend killer?" I paused, making sure I understood what she said. My mouth hung agape as I processed the words.

"I-I'm sorry?" I must have misheard her. There was a smirk on her face when she looked back down at me.

"I said, what're we doing today, honey?" I swear that's not what she said, but being the innate people-pleaser that I am, I convinced myself she didn't say what I actually heard.

I shook it off and then reached into my pocket and pulled out what Marissa had written.

"I've never gotten my hair done before, so my friend suggested this." I gave her the piece of paper, then she looked down at my hair while smacking the gum she was chewing on.

"No."

"No?" I cocked my head to the side so I could look her in the face and not through the mirror.

"This will look terrible," she admitted.

"Oh?"

"Yeah, this is too neutral for your hair and your face shape. We are going to put large chunky lights in the front."

"Is it going to be very natural looking?" I swear I saw a glint in her eye before she responded.

"Of course, honey," she said coolly, and I sat back, trusting she was a professional and knew what she was doing. At any rate, Marissa and I were using Pinterest to find similar looks, we didn't really know what we were asking for, so I trusted the professional.

Tana excused herself to go get the color, and I sat in the chair, awkwardly looking around when the salon had gone quiet. When I arrived, there was a hum of chatter heard throughout the building, but the noises had dropped to a dull whisper.

*Huh. That is weird. I'm not sure getting my haircut is something I will do often in the future.*

My eyes darted toward the window, but I couldn't make out Santiago, so I sent him a quick text to let him know everything was okay in here. The last thing I needed was my big bad bodyguard bounding through the salon making a scene.

When Tana arrived back at the station, she started to put the color in my hair and wrap it in foils. I relaxed slightly because from what I'd seen on social media and YouTube, she seemed like she knew she was doing. Plus, this wasn't in someone's garage, this was in an actual salon. I kept trusting she was the professional and knew what would look best on me.

"So, what's it like with your brother on campus?" she asked, and again, I did a double take at her. *How does she even know my brother?*

"Walsh Solis?" I asked, double-checking she didn't have me confused with someone else.

"Yeah." She looked down at me while she added another foil to my hair. "Come on, Ember. Everyone knows who you are and what you did to your boyfriend last year."

My jaw dropped. *I am so fucking naïve.* I knew people would laugh at me in public but never while working intimately with me.

"Yeah, it's been a hard year." This was the phrase Santiago and I had come up with to deter people from asking more questions.

"I can't believe you actually came back to Isles. To what? Wreak more havoc on the Den?" I blinked a couple times, trying not to cry, but the girl kept going. "Hear you've been getting cozy with the best friend? You going to have your brother kill him too?"

"What the—"

"Wait here while the foils lighten." She walked away to the back room, leaving me blinking my tears away. *Don't cry. Don't cry.* I refused to let anyone else in the salon see she was getting a reaction from me.

Sitting at the chair underneath a large blow dryer, waiting as my hair lightened, I texted Marissa.

Ember:

> Remind me to never get my hair done here by Tana again.

Then I tried a technique my therapist had suggested when I became flooded with emotions. Searching for five objects, I named them, then smelled five distinct smells, then touched five items around me. It helped ground me and prevent the panic from taking over.

After I had gone through my grounding technique, Tana had come by, moved the hair dryer, and brought me over to the bowl.

She gave me the quickest and most aggressive shampoo while she talked to another hairstylist.

"Yeah, I cannot believe nobody checked the schedule before allowing her here."

"I didn't realize until this morning, yuck."

"Ha. You'll see what she's getting."

It was just soundbites of what I could hear through the water sloshing around the bowl. She threw a towel on my head and brought me over to the station where I sat in front of the mirror again.

She looked down at me, a sly smile creeping on her face. "You ready to see your big reveal?"

"Totally." She was a professional, there was no way she was going to—

"What the fuck did you do?" I screamed, jumping from the chair and running my hands through my wet hair.

Even though my hair was damp, it was streaked with large chunky highlights everywhere. It was nowhere near the natural look I had asked for. I hated it.

I hated it so much tears rushed from my eyes, as I was unable to keep them at bay this time. I didn't realize how much sadness and anger an unwelcome hair style could make you feel. All I wanted was to feel better about myself. I was trying so hard to patch myself back together, and that ripped everything apart.

"Why did you do this?" I looked at the hairstylist who stood stoically behind the chair, her hands gripping to the back. At this point, I didn't give a flying fuck that every person in here was staring at us. I was so upset. This was the exact reason I didn't leave the house. It was exactly what I had hoped wouldn't happen.

"The natural look you wanted just wasn't going to frame your face well, so the chunky highlights—"

"But this isn't what I asked for. I just wanted something small." I wanted to crawl into my skin. Everyone at the salon was silent. I searched around desperately and could see Santiago crossing the street from the large window in front of me. The curtain was behind us, separating us from the front area, but passersby could still see through. The moment we locked eyes, I knew he saw the tears falling like a freaking waterfall down my face.

"No one at the Den wants you in Isles anymore. You're ruining the entire organization," Tana barked, and everyone turned their heads in our direction. When I noticed someone pulling out their phone to record this interaction, I decided to eat my words and take the high road.

I threw a twenty at her, then started to walk out of the salon.

Tana protested, "You underpaid me." I couldn't help but let out a crazed laugh, the frustration and sabotage from this woman getting to me.

Santiago looked at me but said nothing, simply taking my hand as we walked down the street. He removed his hat and handed it to me.

Outside, I put my still-wet hair up into the cap, not wanting to risk getting sick from the damp air. I looked up at Santiago, still in shock from the ordeal.

"I-I don't know what to say," I began, feeling a heavy weight pressing down on my chest, the disappointment overwhelming.

"What happened?" Santiago asked.

"I asked for a natural hairstyle, and then she started talking about Ash, blaming me and telling me I needed to leave," I rambled on, choking on my sobs. I sat on the grimy curb, hugging my knees.

"She then added these horrible highlights in my hair as some sort of revenge."

"I'm going back in there," Santiago demanded.

"Please don't," I begged.

"Come on, mija. Let's go home," Santiago urged, trying to help me up, but I felt glued to the curb. Frozen in place, I couldn't move, overwhelmed by a deep sense of defeat.

"I-I can't," I murmured, realizing how embarrassing it was to be sitting on a curb in one of the busiest parts of Isles but not caring at all. "I want to go back to Dansport."

For the first time, the thought crossed my mind and I wanted to admit defeat. Perhaps, in some twisted way, Tana was right. Maybe I was a boyfriend killer, and getting close to Rain meant putting him in harm's way, too. My mom died because of what she did, maybe I was death's best friend.

I needed to talk to Walsh to uncover the truth behind what had happened so the overwhelming guilt could begin to ease and I could find some semblance of peace, but right now, I was frozen in place.

"I don't know how many deaths I can experience in one short time period and survive it, Santiago." I cried, and worry etched into the fine lines of his eyes.

"Please don't go back to that place." He begged. "What can I do to help you?"

I shrugged because I had no idea. I had no one to call. My family got tangled in this web of deceit and lies. I had nobody. Yet, somehow, all I wanted to become was a nobody.

The anger I felt toward Ash bubbled to the surface. I was mad he left me here to deal with this alone. It was irrational and I knew this was simply a trauma response to what had happened, but I was so fucking upset.

"My mom used to say this phrase to me: 'Into the darkness I'll go, and into the light I'll be' when I was younger and scared of the dark. Santiago, she lied. She lied about all of it, because I am deep in the darkness, and I don't know where the light is."

"No. You do have light and you know exactly where it is." He shook his head like I was saying something that didn't make sense.

I rubbed my eyes, and he walked away momentarily before returning to sit next to me on the curb.

"I am your family, mija. I love you like a sister, and I hate seeing you hurt. What can I do? Please let me in, Ember." His voice fell into a hushed tone at the end, and I looked out to the street.

"I just need to sit here." I sighed, letting my shoulders sag, and buried my head into my hands. Sitting there, not caring that the cars were flying by or the people on the street were staring at two people sitting on a curb. I just needed to sit in it.

"Ember," a familiar voice said from above me. I lifted my head, and Rain was towering over me.

I snapped my head over toward Santiago who shrugged before getting up. "I needed to call the one person whose hand you'd reach for. I'm not letting you go back to that place, mija."

"You tell him everything now? I bet you even told him about—"

"Never. That is not a story for me to share. But I was, no I am, worried about you." Santiago paused before turning toward Rain. "I'm heading back to the apartment. Let me know if you need me."

He walked away quickly, and I let out a deep sigh. I'd stopped crying when the fourth truck had passed down the road, however long that was, but I was emotionally spent.

"Do you want to talk about it?" he asked as he replaced Santiago's spot next to me.

I told him what happened, unfurling my hair from my cap, while holding back tears.

"I need to talk to the guys at the house. We need to clear Ash's name immediately. Whoever's been running your name is fucking dead to me."

"I texted my brother. I'd like it if maybe you'd come with me," I said, doing the one thing Santiago told me to, reaching for the hand of the person trying so desperately to pull me to him.

"I want to, but I don't know if I trust him fully. I need to make sure we do it in a safe way."

"Of course, it's a no." I rolled my eyes before his warm hands pulled my chin toward his face.

"I said I fucking wanted to, Ember, I just need to figure this situation out with your goddamned hairstylist first." He ran his hands through his long hair.

"You don't have to—"

"And for the fucking record, I am not going to leave, Ember. I cannot imagine a world without you in it, and I cannot imagine leaving you alone." He jumped up, not letting me process anything he said before offering me a hand, which I took.

It actually surprised me how quickly he helped me get out of whatever frozen response had me stuck to the sidewalk.

"You what?" I asked.

"Ah, fuck, mi pareja, it doesn't fucking matter what I said. Let's go."

"Where are we going?" I shifted the cap so it was covering my hair, and Rain's hand clenched as I did.

"To the Den."

We walked together in silence before Rain walked in front of a motorcycle parked on the street.

"Get on."

I stared back at him because he knew my thoughts on his freaking bike.

I crossed my arms. "No."

"Come on, mi pareja."

"Tell me what that means?" He scrunched his nose, and honestly, it was fucking adorable the way he looked like he smelled something foul, but then a small smirk formed on his mouth before he mounted the bike.

"One day. I promise."

"I thought you'd tell me anything." I huffed, arms still crossed over my chest.

"It's the one secret I'll keep from you, Em." He threw me a helmet. "Get on."

"You'll keep me safe?" I asked, thankful that the helmet would at least keep the ugly ass hair hidden.

"Always," he whispered.

Jumping onto the bike, my arms wrapped around his thick torso, and I leaned my head against his back. He revved the engine and pulled out into the street. He was going slow, but being on this bike for the first time was freeing. Plus, it helped that Rain looked so fucking hot driving it.

When we stopped at the first stop sign, he dropped one of his hands from the handle and clasped my hand with his.

I responded by lacing my fingers through his and pressing into his chest.

As the damp cool air whipped around my body, I felt exhilarated. Part of me wondered if all this grief I felt was part of some bigger plan for me. I was supposed to experience all this death in my life before I could actually live.

And maybe Santiago was right. I could see the one person offering me a hand, I just needed to reach up and grab it. Bringing the dead back to life was impossible, but I could live with the ones on earth until we meet again later.

Rain was right here. I just needed to let him in.

# RAIN

The thought of her visit to that salon, where one of the guys' ladies had dared to meddle with her hair, ignited a slow-burning fury within me. I yearned to exact retribution on them for what they had subjected Ember to.

"I'm calling for an emergency meeting," I asserted, my tone resolute. "You stay upstairs for now. We need to talk afterward." Ember scrunched her nose and raised her eyebrows. I noticed a subtle transformation in her demeanor. There was a newfound gentleness, a vulnerability that tugged at my heartstrings. It made me ache to draw her close, to be the one she turned to in times of need.

I reached for the baseball cap she wore, probably borrowed from Santiago. While I appreciated his support, a twinge of envy gnawed at me. I longed to be the pillar of strength for Ember, the person she confided in first. However, deep down, I couldn't help but feel I might never have that privilege.

I parked the bike in the driveway, and my gaze sought Ember's. Her face lit up with a mixture of emotions, and I couldn't help but be captivated by the delicate interplay of expressions on her features.

As she walked toward the front door, each step was a tantalizing, rhythmic pulse that echoed with the promise written in the stars. The gentle sway of her curves beneath the fabric of her dress ignited a fervent yearning within me, an ache that only she could soothe.

Then she stopped and turned around, her gaze locking onto mine with a magnetic pull that drew me closer. In that moment, she was the embodiment of all the light I needed after enduring the torment of unrelenting pain after his death. Her eyes, like twin galaxies of longing, held a promise of solace and redemption, a promise that everything I had endured was worth it just to be in her presence.

Ember stood there, bathed in the soft glow of the porch light, her form a silhouette of desire against the impending evening sky. She was not just a woman; she was a beacon of passion and hope, a vision of love and longing with the power to heal all wounds and ignite the most fervent of desires.

She was the embodiment of my person.

"What?" she asked, giving me a slight pull on the corners of her lips as they moved into a cross between a smirk and a smile.

"Nothing." I chuffed. "Come on." I gestured to her inside.

She tensed right away, but I offered her a comforting hand on the small of her back as I guided her through the house and upstairs.

"I think if it's okay with you, I may take a nap?" she asked when we got to my small room. I handed her a couple blankets from underneath the bed storage.

"Here." I gave it to her, and her hand lingered on the blanket while looking up at me.

"Rain?" she asked.

"Yeah?"

"Thank you," she said in a hushed tone.

"For what?"

"For being there for me. I didn't see it until now, but thank you." A soft smile played on Ember's lips as she gracefully took the blanket from my hands. She moved and settled on my bed as if it were her rightful place all along, a vision sent to soothe my wounded soul.

I stood there for a moment, simply watching her as she curled up on my bed. The way she nestled in, the way her presence seemed to light up the room, it was as though she had always belonged here, beside me. I hesitated, caught in the enchantment of the moment, before finally tearing my gaze away from her. There was an emergency meeting downstairs, one I couldn't delay any longer.

Something, some inexplicable force, tugged at me, urging me to make a brief detour before joining the others. My eyes were drawn to the small staircase, a ladderlike ascent leading upstairs. It had seen little use since the day Mr. Ortiz had cleared Ash's belongings and clothing from there. I had avoided it, fearful of what memories it might hold. Yet, watching Ember so peaceful on my bed, stirred a longing within me. Without conscious thought, I climbed the ladder and opened the door.

My hand hovered over the doorknob, a sense of trepidation washing over me before I slowly turned it. I half expected to see Ash on the other side, to hear his infectious laughter, to feel his warm embrace. He would have welcomed me with that ever-present smile, the one that never wavered, no matter what lay beneath. I had questioned him, asked him countless times about his well-being, but he never let me in on the battles he fought.

"Damn it," I whispered as I stood in that half-empty room, gazing out the windows at the encompassing forest of the Den. The gentle rain tapped against the windowpane, yet the room retained a sense of Ash, as though he lingered in its very essence. It felt foreign, out of place, and a lump formed in my throat.

"Why did you do this, Ash? What was your plan?" I cried out, the tears finally flowing freely. After months of being stuck in this seemingly emotionless state, they came like a waterfall.

"Am I supposed to love her freely now? You left behind two shattered souls, both of us blaming ourselves for your departure."

I cried, my hands buried in my hair, each sob racking my body. A sudden clap of thunder accompanied by lightning felt like Ash's spirit urging me to find my strength, just as he would have.

"I think I love her too, Ash, but is my love enough for her?" I walked over to his desk, my fingers tracing the remnants of his life scattered upon it.

"Why didn't you share your pain with me? I would have helped," I murmured to the silent room. Grief had given way to anger, a burning rage building within me. I was tired, exhausted by the masks I had to wear, and now I was left to heal yet another broken heart.

In a fit of fury, I seized a lamp from the desk and hurled it against the wall. The grief had transformed into a tempest of anger, threatening to consume me whole.

The door creaked open, and I swiftly drew the Glock from my waistband, a precaution I had taken before the meeting, anticipating the need for a show of force. Yet, all I heard was the light pattering of rain on the window behind me.

*I swear to God, Ash, if this is your ghost—*

"Rain?" Ember's voice, tinged with concern, pierced the room. I couldn't let her see me like this—broken and enraged. While kicking a few pieces of glass that had fallen to the floor behind the bed, she pushed the door in quickly.

"Get out of here," I rasped, "por favor." I needed to shield her from the wreckage of my emotions. This wasn't who I was supposed to be. I was to uphold this protective shell around me so she could break down.

Ignoring my plea, she entered the room, her eyes widening as they swept over the half-empty space. I recognized the void reflected in her gaze, a reflection of my own. Yet, she didn't dwell on the lifeless room. Her eyes met mine, and she rushed toward me, concern etched across her beautiful face. She grabbed the Glock in my hand and threw it on the bed before pulling me tight into an embrace.

"Rain," she whispered, her fingers brushing away my tears. "Why? How?"

She blinked back her own tears and cupped my face, her warmth wiping away my sadness.

"Are you okay?" she finally asked, her voice filled with genuine concern and care.

"No," I choked out, remaining true to my commitment to always speak the truth. Our gazes remained locked, and in that fleeting moment, even with her hair gathered in a simple bun, she exuded an enchanting grace that transcended the turmoil surrounding us.

"I need to protect you. You shouldn't see me like this," I demanded, trying to push her away, but she only placed her small delicate hands on my chest, gently tugging my shirt so I was closer to her.

"Oh Rain," she whispered. "You don't always have to be the strong one. You can break down and feel what you're experiencing, too."

"I don't understand any of it, Ember, including my own damned emotions. And, most of all, I don't comprehend what I'm supposed to do about you."

Ember paused, withdrawing slightly, her eyes casting about the room in contemplative silence. A solemn expression painted her lips, and she turned her gaze from the window to meet mine once more. Then with a sigh, as if releasing all eight months of pent-up tension, she uttered words that carried a weight beyond measure.

"I think he wants us to keep living our life. We should honor him *in that way*." Her breathing seemed to slow, as though finding a profound revelation. "We should share his story and then give him the peace that he was desperate to find." Her eyes once again flitted around the room as she took his . . . aura in. The room was so empty, but at the same time felt so full of his spirit.

"I've been trapped for so many months, but I believe it's time to uncover the truth and move forward, no matter what that entails." She returned to my side, her eyes falling upon my fingers, which bore small nicks from the shattered lamp.

"I don't have all the answers about 'us' either, but those emotions you're grappling with?" Her gaze bore into mine as she nestled her forehead against my chest, her voice barely more than a murmur.

"I feel them, too." My fingers found themselves tangled in the silk of her hair, and together, we stood in his room, two souls seeking solace amid the echoes of the past. Holding a silent promise that we knew that this moment, this quiet moment, would transform us.

"I need to get downstairs." I coughed while she pulled away from me slightly, looking in my eyes for something.

"Okay," she whispered. "Are you sure you don't want me?"

I laughed. "No. Don't get me wrong, pareja, I do, but this is something that I need to speak to the guys about first." She nodded and then walked downstairs. I glanced back at the room once before turning back toward her.

"I need you to stay in my room no matter what you hear. You need to promise me."

"Okay," she murmured, and I grabbed her hand, lacing my fingers between hers.

Ultimately, she was right. We couldn't forget or move on from my brother's death, but we had to move forward because we were still here, breathing and living.

Promising myself I'd return when I was ready to face the daunting task of cleaning up the mess around me, I closed my eyes, reminiscing about the first time I met Ash at his dad's house. It was a memory that felt bittersweet, given the circumstances.

*"Hey, what are you doing in my room? Who are you?" A little boy with floppy curls, who was about as tall as me, stood before me. His room was way cleaner than my other room. There was already a small bed on one side, but there was nothing else except what was in my backpack.*

*"I guess I'm living here." I shrugged. The little boy paused and looked at me all curious.*

*"How old are you?" he asked.*

*"I'm seven," I said.*

*"Me, too," the kid said. "What's your name?"*

*"Rain Fortin." I put my hands in my pockets and looked around the room, wondering if any of my stuff would be here. I really wanted my books.*

*The boy, who was the same age as me, walked over to me handing me a red car. I grabbed it, thinking it was cool and not something I'd have at my other house.*

*When my mom told me to pack my stuff earlier today, she told me we were moving in with her boyfriend. A guy she'd only been dating a couple weeks, but that was common with Mom. She would always date someone and then break up with them, but we were actually moving this time, so it was serious.*

*Still, I didn't wanna get too close to this kid because what if they broke up. It would suck to leave him.*

*"My name is Ash Ortiz. I think you're going to be my brother now." I smiled, but this felt . . . kinda weird. I'd never had a brother before or any siblings.*

*"Come on. Wanna play with my cars?" Cars were cool. From that moment on, I knew this guy would be my friend forever.*

"What the fuck's this about, Fortin?" one of the guys asked as Pico slid into the room. We were gathered around the dining room, and most of the guys were sitting while I stood towering over them. Pico stood behind me.

The night had fallen, casting the house into a shadowy realm illuminated only by a few dim lights. My feelings about being a leader and most of the people here were complicated, but strangely, I held a deep affection for this place. It was like a haunted mansion crossed with a horror film set, nestled right on the edge of the ominous forest. Typically, we kept the first floor tidy, especially since it welcomed most of the campus during the typical Saturday party.

As I scanned the room, I couldn't help but realize how little I knew about most of these guys. Honestly, I had no interest in getting to know them. They came across as sheep, reeking of desperation as they tried to climb the ranks through the Cartel. However, it wasn't my favor they sought; they were desperate to impress Mr. Ortiz, the head honcho. I just happened to be the direct link to him.

In frustration, I slammed my hands onto the dark wooden table, creating a thunderous noise that shattered the silence, making everyone turn their heads toward me.

"Who is fucking around with the hairstylist at the salon on Main, Tana?" I asked when the room quieted. There were a couple whispers of guys mumbling, but as I stared at each of them, no one confessed.

"I am not kidding." I tried to muster the courage to be the leader I needed to be. All of them still sat quietly, some even crossed their arms. These fuckers were being defiant, none of them wanting to rat on each other.

I gave a quick glance back at Pico, who nodded inconspicuously at me before moving from the shadows and standing next to me.

"Shut the fuck up, assholes," he bellowed as he grabbed his gun and slammed it on the table. That was the voice of a leader, someone in charge, who created order out of a room and had a presence that when he entered, you listened.

The exact opposite of who I was. This was not the person Ember saw.

"I will personally cut each and every one of your fingers off and render them useless until someone confesses who is fucking with Tana Hosthrop at the salon on Main Street."

No one was talking loud, but there were whispers with people looking around to see who I would pick out. Pico grabbed the guy, Roger, next to us by the shirt collar, lifting his finger to the knife.

"No one wants to talk?" He laughed maniacally, which only affirmed his leadership role. "I'm going around ripping off fingers then until someone does."

Silence.

"Tommy's girl," a guy in the back shouted, and everyone whipped around to a small little dude sitting at the front. Tommy glared at the guy who ratted him out while Pico stalked toward his chair. Bringing the knife to his neck, he seethed at him, his face practically on top of his.

"The fuck took you so long to listen to Fortin?" Pico asked, and I just sat there watching the scene unfold because that's where I preferred to be, blended in the background.

"Stand up," Pico demanded, and the guy shuddered, but stood, walking in front of the room.

I gave him a quick nod of gratitude for handling it for me. "Your girl fucked over Ember."

Tommy furled his upper lip at me but otherwise didn't show an ounce of emotion. "I don't know what you are talking about."

I shook my head, letting the corners of my lips twist into a smirk. "Get the fuck outta here. You planned this shit with her?" The silence from Tommy was more telling than his voice. "She purposefully fucked up my girl's—"

"Oh, so she's yours now?" he asked.

"No." *Fuck.*

"No. Ember's fucking hair." I grabbed my Glock from my waistband and pointed it to his head, not giving a fuck about anything else.

"What did you tell her?" I seethed, my voice laced with anger and suspicion.

"The truth," Tommy replied.

"Which is?" I tilted my head in his direction, the cold metal of the gun pressed against his temple a stark reminder of the seriousness of the situation.

"Ember killed Ash. She either drove him to his death or her brother—"

"No." My finger tensed on the trigger. "Shut the fuck up," I demanded, my tone taking on the weight of authority. This was for Ember, and I would do anything to protect her.

"Is it not the truth?" Tommy asked, his gaze fixed straight ahead, his composure unyielding.

"No," I stated, taking a moment to scan the room. "For the fucking record, if any one of you breathes a word about Ember to anyone on this campus or in this house, you are fucking dead and out of the fucking organization."

A heavy silence fell over the room as my words settled in. They knew the consequences of leaving the Den—a Cartel leadership role would be forever out of reach. This place served as a training ground for the organization, and leaving meant abandoning any hope of advancement.

"Ember doesn't deserve any of this shit, and I am determined to uncover the truth about what happened to Ash . . . *with concrete evidence.*" I made it clear how resolute I was about getting to the bottom of it. "I will do all of this before the spring bonfire. If, for whatever reason, it remains unresolved, then you all can continue to point fingers at their family and blame whoever makes it easiest for you to sleep at night."

No one dared to talk, and I didn't move my weapon from Tommy's forehead. Pico gave me a quick nod of approval, and I knew I was on the right page with how I was treating this situation. I knew, as their leader, regardless of my feelings over being in this position, I could show no weakness. Allowing these fuckers to rag on Ember was the line for me.

"Do I fucking make myself clear?" I asked again, and everyone gave a resounding "Yes" before I stared at Tommy, who remained as still as a statue staring out into the dining room.

"You all loved Ash? Appreciated him as a leader, no?" A murmur of "Yesses" were heard throughout the room. "He wouldn't have wanted you to touch her. You all know it. So if you are not doing it for me, then do it for him."

"Tommy?" I asked. "Do you understand why telling Tana about Ember and having her fuck her hair up on purpose was wrong?" I seethed through gritted teeth.

He slowly moved his head in my direction, but I didn't move my gun from its position.

"Yes, Boss. It is crystal clear what your position is on this . . . situation," he snarled. Grabbing the gun, I tucked it into my waistband and, in one swift movement, retrieved the knife next to it.

I held his hand to the table and stabbed it right through the middle. Gasps reverberated around the room as Tommy screamed in pain.

"I don't think I made myself clear. You are to stay the fuck away from her," I gritted out. Then I glared at everyone else, whose eyes had gone wide and mouths had dropped to the floor. They needed to understand I was their leader and I needed to be respected. I was doing this for Ember and Ash. The two people who mattered most. My brother and his—mine—ugh, fuck, Ember.

I left the knife in his hand as I snapped at Pico to help me clean this up. Before we pulled it out and walked away, I looked back at Tommy.

"Call your girl. I need the products that will get her hair back to normal delivered to the house in the next ten minutes. If they aren't, then I am doing this to your other hand, too."

I headed into the kitchen, past the door to the basement, a.k.a torture chamber, and out the back.

I choked on the air in my lungs while staring at my hands covered in blood splatter and shaking profusely. I'd never acted like that before. Yeah, I'd been around a lot of fucking death, but always as the person watching, cleaning up, managing the cops, et cetera. I'd never actually been the one to deliver the blow, and even though I hated Tommy and Tana right now . . . I hated myself more.

I was turning into the one person I swore I'd never become because that person was ugly, horrible, disgusting. He was the devil in an Armani suit, and he also happened to be stepdaddy dearest. The one person no one was blaming for Ash's death, yet they all should be because he was responsible.

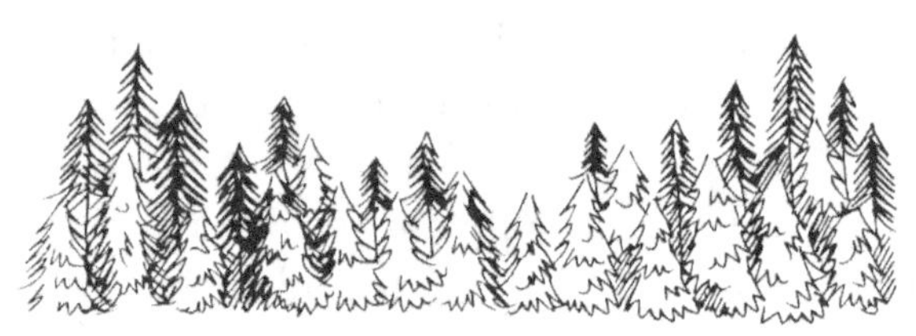

*"Hey, Ash?" I called out as I roamed through the house, but the silence was deafening. Normally, we would be home right after school, but I had gotten stuck at the math club, unlike him. Mr. Ortiz had strict rules keeping Ash away from after-school activities. Instead, he often had to shadow his father during business dealings. However, with Mr. Ortiz and my mom away on a trip since yesterday, Ash should have been home.*

*My phone displayed no texts from him, which only fueled my growing sense of unease. I couldn't explain it, but something inside me screamed that something was amiss.*

*Climbing the stairs that led to our rooms, I reminisced about our newfound freedom as sophomores in high school. It meant we finally* got our separate rooms in the west corridor of our mansion in the city. Although we had to share a bathroom, it was a welcome change. I could have my own space for books without enduring Ash's early morning routine, which started at the ungodly hour of five.

Reaching the corner where our rooms connected, I noticed no signs of movement or sound. "Ash?" I tried again, but there was no response. I gently knocked on his door, pressing my ear against it in case he had company, a common occurrence when his father was away on business trips. Ash's popularity at school, thanks to his striking appearance and charming demeanor, made him quite the ladies' man.

With a growing sense of dread, I pushed Ash's door open. What I saw on the floor shattered my heart into pieces. There lay Ash, surrounded by empty pill bottles, with tears streaming down his face. My breath caught in my throat as I rushed to his side. For the first time, my brother looked broken. I'd looked up to him the entire time we'd been brothers, but he didn't look like the person I knew.

"Ash, what the hell is going on?" My voice trembled with fear and disbelief.

He looked up at me, his eyes red and swollen, and let out a choked sob. It was the first time I had ever seen my brother cry. It was a heart-wrenching sight that tore at my very soul.

"I . . . I didn't take any," he said between sobs. "But I wanted to. God, Rain, I wanted to."

I sank down beside him, feeling helpless and overwhelmed by the gravity of the situation. The reality of the moment hit me like a ton of bricks. Ash, the person I had always seen as unbreakable, the one who presented a façade of strength to the world, was hurting, and he was hurting badly.

For the first time, a chilling realization washed over me. I was scared for my brother. Terrified that the pressure, the expectations, and the suffocating grip of his father's control had pushed him to the brink of despair. I had never seen him so vulnerable, so lost.

*Tears welled in my eyes as I held him, to let him know he wasn't alone. We were in this together, whatever "this" was. And no matter how daunting the journey ahead, I was determined to help my brother find his way back from the darkness that threatened to consume him.*

*I held Ash in my arms as he continued to cry, his body trembling with the weight of his emotions. The room felt suffocating, as if the walls themselves were closing in on us. The bottles of pills strewn about served as a stark reminder of just how close we had come to losing him.*

*Holding him, I whispered soothing words, promising we would get through this together. I didn't know how, but I couldn't let my brother down. He had always been there for me, and now it was my turn to be his rock.*

*After what felt like an eternity, Ash's sobs began to subside, then he pulled away slightly, wiping the tears from his face with the back of his hand. His eyes met mine, and in that moment, I saw a raw vulnerability I had never seen before.*

*"Rain," he croaked, his voice hoarse from crying, "I can't do this anymore. I can't keep living like this."*

*His words sent a chill down my spine. I knew he was talking about his father, about the suffocating control and the relentless pressure that had been crushing his spirit for years.*

*"We'll figure it out," I said, my voice filled with determination. "We'll find a way to get you out of here, away from him."*

*Ash nodded, and a glimmer of hope shone in his eyes. It was a small spark, but it was enough to reignite my own determination. I needed to get us out of here. It was the one hard truth.*

*"When we get to Isles, everything will change, but I need you to hold on until then." Ash looked up at me, his eyes locked with my own gaze.*

*Although we shared no blood, we'd spent every single day together dodging the responsibilities he had, and when he got in trouble, I'd help pick up the slack. Because of my position, or lack thereof, in the family, I knew I had to help him when he needed it because his dad would never suspect it was the two of us. We spent countless Saturday mornings remaking his bed over and over until it was to Mr. Ortiz's satisfaction. At the end of the day, it was Ash who helped me. He kept me company—gave me a brother. Gave me a purpose in this life, and after today, I knew I needed to give him that back. I needed to protect him. I would not fail him.*

"Earth to Rain," a familiar voice said, and I blinked away the thoughts I was lost in.

"What's up?" I asked Pico, turning my full attention toward him and away from the memories that had plagued me for the last eight months.

"You did good in there. I was fucking impressed."

I chuckled before giving his shoulder a slap. "Thanks, man. Your help at the start doesn't go unnoticed. You are far more fit for the leadership role than I ever will be." I laughed.

"Nah. After the stunt you pulled today, I am fully impressed with you. Congrats."

"Thanks."

"I heard your slip-up. Not to change subjects or anything." Even in the night, only illuminated by the small porch light in the back of the house, I could see Pico twist his lips into a slight smile. I looked back at him, my mind still on Ember.

"It was nothing more than a slip-up. Exactly as you said." I tried to cover my tracks because calling Ember mine felt so right, so natural, but she would never be mine . . . at least not fully. Not until we resolved what happened with Ash.

"Of all the people walking on this earth today, he'd want it to be you." I swallowed hard at Pico's confession. He would have wanted it to be me. I knew Ash. He put so much already in my hands, he'd want it to be me, but I couldn't let it be. Because I still saw her as his.

"Growing up with the two of you was wild." Pico chuckled and ran a hand through his hair before leaning against the back of the house and lighting a cigarette.

He handed me a pack, and I grabbed one from him and let him light it. I didn't smoke until high school, and even now, I didn't like smoking, but it kept my hands busy. I needed something to keep them busy because there was so much to process, not to mention the fact Ember was just upstairs sleeping in my room.

"Why?" I asked as I inhaled the tobacco.

"Because you two were like fucking twins, if I hadn't known any better. Ash bossed you around, and you always followed him. But man, if he didn't want to do something or you weren't involved, he used to fuck people up."

"Wait, what?" I asked, not knowing this.

"You didn't know?" I shook my head, and Pico laughed before he took a deep pull of his smoke.

"Okay, you remember when we were in eighth grade, and we were invited to Trey Thompson's house? It was like our first real party since his parents were going to be out of town?" I gave him a smirk, remembering my first real party invite.

"Well, he didn't want to invite you. He called you a weirdo because you liked to sit in the back of class and at lunch with your book." I narrowed my eyes at him, which only made him laugh. "Come on, you were kinda a loner." I shrugged at his confession. "Anyway, Ash went over to his house and fucking beat the shit out of him until he personally came up to you at school and invited you."

"Shut up," I said, laughing.

"Nah, it's totally true. He fucked him up good, too. Told him that he was going to get his dad to personally murder each one of his family members, too. He was a damn eighth grader and was acting like his fucking dad already."

This made me feel sad because to everyone else, he was a born leader, but what no one saw except for me was that Mr. Ortiz groomed him to be this way. He literally broke him down and tried to remold him into this born leader.

"Damn, that's impressive," I responded, letting the cigarette dangle from the corner of my mouth. My hands twitched at my sides as the anxiety creeped into me.

"It's all to say that you guys had a bond like I'd never seen. I definitely don't feel the same about my sister."

Both of us were now propped up at the back of the house, looking into the depths of the forest.

"I went up to his room," I said, not directed at Pico but more so at the darkness that threatened to consume us.

"And?"

"I'm trying to figure out what happened to him that night, Pico. I just cannot believe that anyone else was out there, but that doesn't explain the two tracks." I purposefully left out the fact that I knew there was no mud on the rock with the second pair of boots. I trusted Pico, but I wanted to keep this between Ember and me, at least until we could get the whole picture.

"You'll figure it out. If you need anything, too, I'm right here ready to help." He paused, then turned his head toward me. "I know it doesn't help much, but I am on your side, Rain. I'm right here."

"Thanks man," I responded, and then slowly dragged the smoke from the cigarette before looking back toward the trees.

"Is smoking at the edge of a forest really such a good idea? Won't the trees, like, set on fire and suddenly we'll have a forest fire?"

A delicate voice melodically drifted our way from where the door stood, and Pico and I turned our heads in its direction.

"The ground's wet, Ember. No one is starting a fire here, just two guys indulging in a bad habit," Pico said before he pushed off the wall and gave me a friendly pat on the shoulder.

"See you later. I'll go check to make sure everyone's cleaned up." Pico winked at me before greeting Ember, then heading back into the house.

"I have something for you," I said, and her eyes looked up at me with awe and mystery. She was beautiful, but that word felt too mundane to describe her. The moment she entered a room, my breath escaped, and it was as if she were the only one who could fill my lungs back up.

Ember Solis had stolen my heart the first night she walked into the Den.

"What is it?" she asked, her voice breathless. She was different from last year, in a way that made her even more captivating and enticing. Ember stood there in an oversized hoodie and leggings, her hair still up in a messy bun. Her large brown eyes held a mixture of curiosity and concern as they locked onto mine. She was curvy, her figure captivating even in the oversized hoodie, and every glance at her left me utterly speechless.

"A surprise," I said as I dragged the last bit of the cigarette smoke into my lungs.

"That's a gross habit." She crossed her arms over her chest and looked up at me. Her tone, although serious, had a joyful lilt to it.

"I know." I chuffed.

"So why do you do it?"

"I don't often, just needed something to keep my hands busy after the meeting tonight."

"It didn't go well?" She took a few steps toward me and stopped in front of me, watching as I brought the cigarette back up to my mouth.

"It did, actually. I just hate being in front of a big crowd. Makes me anxious," I confessed.

She grabbed the cigarette from my hand and tossed it to the ground, stomping on it extra hard. Then we looked up at each other at the same time.

She took another small half step toward me, then interlaced her fingers with mine before bringing both of our hands up to her cheek. The softness of her cheek against my hand sent a jolt through my body, but her eyes didn't falter from mine.

"You can keep your hands busy with me anytime," she whispered before taking that last small step toward me. As her hands left mine, I felt the need to keep the close physical connection we had, so I squeezed her hips. She caressed the stubble on my face.

We stayed there, our chests heaving in sync—up and down. Our gazes pulled deeper into each other as if trying to bring us closer even though our bodies were touching.

Playing with my chin, she ran her forefinger up and down from the bottom of my hair to the tip of my jaw. She was so fucking close, I could just drop down and taste her now, but it wasn't the right time. It wasn't . . .

I stopped her by looking up and saying, "I really wanna show you what I got you."

She took a deep breath and sighed, her eyes locked onto mine, our fingers intertwined because I wanted to feel her touch to let her know how much I needed her.

We walked back into the house through the kitchen, away from the dining room and toward the main foyer of the expansive home. I picked up the bag at the bottom of the stairs before we headed upstairs.

"What was your meeting about? Did you figure out—"

"I told them that from here on out, you won't be targeted for any more attacks like today," I replied.

"You . . . you did?" Her voice held a hint of surprise.

"Yeah. You don't need to be subjected to any of that shit again," I said as I brought our hands up to my lips and pressed them gently against her fingers. We stood in the middle of the staircase, the intimate gesture giving me pause. It wasn't so much a kiss as it was a way of showing her how much I cared.

I pulled away and continued our ascent toward the bathroom. Ember didn't say anything, but she didn't need to. There was only one other person in this lifetime to whom I felt this connected, and he wasn't here anymore. But Ember . . . She felt like she had always belonged.

# EMBER

I was so tired and had been sleeping on and off in Rain's bed before I went to go find him. I found him behind the house talking to Pico while smoking a cigarette. The patio light cast him in a glow that had him shining so brightly in the darkness of the night.

There was something so familiar about him, too. I was drawn in his direction. It was so different from when I first felt captivated by Ash. There was so much push and pull between us, but with Rain, in some weird cosmic way, I knew I was supposed to be here with him. Maybe not even in a romantic way, but that we would take this journey together.

"Where are we going?" I asked as he guided me upstairs toward the bathroom, which was across from his room.

"Hold on," he mumbled before disappearing into his room and bringing out a stool. "Sit."

He brought the stool to sit in front of the counter in the bathroom and shut the door behind us. He emptied the contents of the grocery bag which included a mixing bowl, paintbrush? It was some tool I'd seen at the salon. And some other tubes I didn't recognize.

I shook my head, not understanding what was happening but trusting him, regardless.

"What's happening?" I swung one leg over the stool, but before I could sit, he grabbed me by the waist and spun me around, instructing me to lean back.

"Why?" I questioned, but complied, and he gently placed a towel around my neck. My head was tilted over the sink, and he ran warm water over my hair. "I'm dying your hair back to its original color. If I were an expert, I'd give you any color you desire, but I hope your natural shade is okay?"

I paused, lifting my head abruptly to look at him. He was busy mixing something in a bowl, his eyes on a piece of paper. "What are you doing? Get your hair back in the water," he instructed.

Instead of obeying, I continued to stare at him in disbelief, my mouth hanging open. I wasn't sure if I fully comprehended what he was saying. "You're dying my hair?" I asked, seeking confirmation.

"Yup," he replied, still not looking at me. My heart pounded in my chest.

"Wait, do you even know what you're doing to get it back to normal?" I asked once more, still in shock. For a moment, he glanced up at me, then back at the paper and laughed.

It was the sweetest melody filling the small bathroom—deep yet filled with joy, and if I thought my heart was going to burst earlier, it was now on the verge of exploding.

I couldn't help but think how much I appreciated him for his care, laughter, and for simply being him.

The shock of the situation lingered, and the thought of even liking him in this way scared me. What he was doing for me, shocked me in the best way possible. It was a simple, gentle gesture, yet it was changing my life in a profound way.

As he continued to mix the dye, I couldn't help but reflect on how much I had hated my hair. My once lustrous locks had become a mess of mismatched colors.

And here he was, offering a solution, taking the time to fix what had been broken. He wasn't just repairing my hair, he was mending something deep within me.

His focus never waned. It was as if he had done this a hundred times before, though he claimed not to be an expert. As the minutes passed, I relaxed into the unexpected intimacy of the moment. There was an unspoken understanding between us, a connection that seemed to grow stronger with each passing second.

When he finally finished mixing the dye, he looked at me with a small satisfied smile. "All done," he announced, as if he had completed a masterpiece.

I couldn't help but smile back, feeling a warmth spread through me that had nothing to do with the dye. "Thank you," I whispered, my voice filled with genuine gratitude.

He met my gaze, his deep-blue eyes locking onto mine. In that moment, I felt like he could see right through me, as if he knew the tangled mess of emotions I had been carrying, and for the first time, I didn't mind. It was as though he was peeling away the layers, revealing the real me underneath.

As he put the dye on my hair, I closed my eyes and let myself embrace the sensation. It was like a cleansing, not just for my hair but for my soul. This simple act of kindness was changing everything, and I was no longer scared of where it might lead.

He slowly painted the dye all over.

"Your neck okay?" he asked, and I laughed because even though I was in a shared fraternity bathroom, this was the experience I was supposed to get at the salon.

"Yeah." I closed my eyes as his hands worked through my locks. The peacefulness was calming while he concentrated on working on my hair.

"So according to these instructions, you gotta let it sit on your head for twenty minutes."

I pulled my hair up into a bun on top of my head and lifted off the bowl while sitting on the stool.

"Okay," I said in a hushed tone. There were a few silent beats between us as he closed the bottles on the countertop and then looked back at me.

"Rain?"

"Mm-hm?" he murmured. There was no thinking right now. No thoughts in my mind other than happy ones. Because for the first time in eight really long months, I felt . . . loved. I grabbed his hands and placed them on my thigh.

"To keep your hands busy," I whispered.

"Leave them here?" He chuffed, awkwardly leaning over with his hands on my thigh. He cocked an eyebrow, and I chuckled.

"I guess you can move them around or something . . . if you need it."

His hands rested on my thigh, and the sensation sent a shiver of anticipation down my spine. The warmth of his touch through the fabric of my shirt was both maddening and exhilarating.

He hesitated for a moment, as if deciding what to do next. Then, slowly and tentatively, his fingers traced delicate patterns on my thigh.

"Like this?" he asked breathlessly.

"Yes."

My breathing quickened as his hands moved higher, inching up beneath the hem of the dress. He was so close to my core, but he didn't venture there. Instead, he continued to trace those tantalizing patterns, watching me while moving his hands.

As the minutes passed, the room seemed to close in around us, and I was acutely aware of every sensation: the heat of his hands on my thighs, the rapid beat of my heart, the electric charge in the air. It was a touch I hadn't experienced in what felt like an eternity, one that awakened a deep, primal longing within me.

As our gazes locked in a silent understanding, a potent current of longing flowed between us. In that intimate moment, we shared a profound desire that simmered beneath the surface, unspoken yet palpable. It was a yearning that echoed in the charged air around us, leaving me both exhilarated and trembling.

"Rain," I breathed out, my voice sounding more like a moan than the initial warning I had intended it to be.

"Do you want me to stop?" he asked, locking his gaze on mine.

That was the question. Did I want him to stop? No. Did I need him to stop . . .?

He paused, as if reading the conflicting thoughts in my head, before pulling my dress back down. I didn't realize I could feel like this again, that my body and mind had the ability to feel wanted, turned on, and desired by someone who wanted me.

But this was Rain, and Rain was so close to *him*. I was disappointed in myself for not having a definite answer to give him.

"It's . . . it's complicated—"

He held up a hand. "I get it, Ember," he whispered before turning away from me and adjusting his pants.

"Wait—" I giggled like an immature teen. "Are you . . . hard?" I asked, and he tossed a look over his shoulders.

"Of course I am, mi pareja. Jesus Christ. I just have to look at you and I am fucking hard." He threw his hands in the air when he finished. "That's the fucking problem."

I laughed with him, and then he came back over to look at my hair. "Where did you learn how to do this?"

"The guy Tana was fucking admitted to what happened. I . . . convinced him to give me the instructions."

"You hurt him?" I was surprised, because while Ash used physical force to get what he needed, Rain never struck me as the type.

"I did," Rain confessed.

"It's refreshing that you actually tell me the truth when I ask you a question. I never feel like I am digging for something from you."

"I think that's how it should be. My mom was always kept in the dark by Mr. Ortiz and my dad that when I was younger I promised myself I'd never become that way. I just feel like there's no point in keeping secrets from you," he whispered, and I grabbed his waist, opening my legs so he could stand between them.

I grabbed his chin, bringing him toward me, and something in the air shifted between us. It was hard to put into words or even explain, but I felt . . . safe.

"Thank you for making me feel this way." I gestured around us, hoping he'd understand what I meant.

I didn't know what was happening between us, but I knew there was something. I just didn't think I was ready just yet to do anything about it. There was so much stuff left unsaid about Ash and so much I needed to tell Rain that it still felt too fresh.

"You deserve to feel this," he murmured, and grabbed my jaw, tilting my head up. He pressed his lips against my forehead. It wasn't a kiss, it was an intimate gesture, but it awakened something deep within me.

There was something to be said about the fact I had met Rain first. I'd kissed Rain already last year. I knew what he tasted like, what his lips felt like against mine, but it wasn't what I felt in this moment; this was so much more tender.

"I need to wash the dye out of your hair." He pulled away from me and shook his head before I laid back into the bowl of the sink.

"Does it look okay," I asked as I could see the dark brown water falling into the bowl out of the corner of my eyes. He stood next to me, his fingers threading through my hair, taking care to clean it.

"Think so," he responded but furrowed his brow as he rinsed my hair.

After a few moments, he gave me a towel and I lifted off the bowl, then he dried me off and turned me around so I could see myself in the mirror.

"I know it's wet still, but I think we got most of the . . ."

I was in shock as he rambled. My hair felt more alive. The bright pieces were gone, and nothing felt out of place. Marissa was right. A good hair color could make me feel like myself, but little did I know that I needed my own prince charming to come to the rescue.

"This is perfect. I feel . . . good," I whispered, realizing how transformative this entire night had been. It was something I knew I needed for me to heal, to move forward. With grief, there was no moving on, but I needed to learn to live in the present again.

"Of course." Rain agreed before opening the door. It was well into the early hours of the morning, and I didn't realize how exhausted I was until I let out a large yawn.

"Come on," he whispered, and I jumped off the stool and followed him to his room.

"Are you going to take me home?" He looked over at me while I took a seat at the edge of his bed.

"No," he said quite matter-of-factly.

"Oh?"

"Stay with me?" he muttered. His shoulders slumped forward as he reached out for my hand. His eyes had deep circles underneath them and as much as I wanted to stay here for him, sleeping in the same bed was so personal.

"Okay."

He took his shirt off, leaving every curve and etch of his torso on full display. His skin was flawless, free of tattoos, just golden hues of beauty. We stared at each other, unmoving.

His hands moved up toward the waistline of his jeans in an erotic way, and I swear I stopped breathing as he unbuckled and unzipped his pants.

"Do you like what you see, Ember?" he asked in a raspy voice. I gulped. The only thing I could do was nod.

"You don't have the cave tattoo," I whispered.

He shook his head then shrugged. "Everyone is supposed to get one, but I never felt like I fit in. Mr. Ortiz never hounded me to get it."

He slipped out of his jeans, and his abs rippled as he bent down to pull them off. He stood in front of me in his boxer briefs, his entire golden body on display like that of a statue. My eyes closed, imagining my hands circling around his tight chest.

I took a deep breath before I exhaled and opened my eyes, staring as he pulled on a pair of gray sweats.

"N-no shirt?" I asked before he chuckled.

"Do you want me to wear one?"

"I mean, that is not my decision, it's totally up to you." He laughed again, and I sounded like a fucking idiot blubbering away.

"Turn around and scoot over," he demanded, and I did what he instructed before he slipped into the bed and laid next to me.

As I gazed at the wall, he encroached upon my personal space.

"When we were younger," Rain began, his voice tangled with the weight of his memories, "Mr. Ortiz would chastise Ash about not making his bed properly. We shared a room until we were teenagers, so I'd often sneak into his bed late at night when I heard him crying, facing the wall." My heart ached at the thought of a young Ash enduring such beratement from his only family member.

"You were strong too, Rain," I remarked, a heaviness in my own words. "He was forced to grow up fast, but you were thrust into a caregiving role when you were just a kid yourself."

Rain chuckled, though it held no mirth, more like a sigh of disbelief. "Yeah, I suppose you're right." A somber silence settled between us, with only the patter of rain against the window providing a soundtrack.

"I'd lie down with him," Rain continued, his voice softer now, "and just stay there in silence until he eventually calmed down and drifted off to sleep. It was a tough household for him . . ."

I turned around slowly, my eyes inadvertently locking onto his bare chest. "I can't even begin to imagine how tough it must have been for him, and how much love you felt compelled to give him."

Rain nodded, and I thought I glimpsed a tear tracing a path down his cheek.

"You were mine the moment you laid your lips on me," he whispered, his voice thick with emotion. "Until he met you."

Suddenly, it hit me. I, too, had become that person in Ash's life, though I hadn't fully comprehended it until now. Rain must have grappled with a whirlwind of emotions when I entered the picture.

"And then, suddenly, you had to share that role." I realized, the pieces of the puzzle falling into place.

"Yeah," Rain confirmed, a hint of resentment in his tone. "I resented you for a while, but there was also this inexplicable connection between us. I felt the need to protect you, too. It's one of the reasons I couldn't participate in the initiation."

"Really?" I responded, as Rain rarely spoke about such matters.

"It just felt too intimate," Rain explained. "Aside from the fact that I find it utterly ridiculous."

"I know Marissa and Pico enjoy it, but I don't think I could ever do it again," I admitted.

"If you were mine," Rain murmured, his fingers gently tilting my chin upward. "I'd never share you." His possessiveness startled me, as I had always envisioned myself with someone equally possessive, not someone who could share.

"Do you regret it?" Rain asked, his voice laced with hesitancy.

"No," I replied without hesitation. "I consider it a life experience, but honestly, it's not something I'm eager to repeat. I think I have other . . . preferences," I confessed, my cheeks warming at the admission. It was a word I wouldn't have uttered years ago, but I had evolved since then.

The corners of Rain's lips twisted slightly. "You have other preferences, mi pareja?"

"I . . . I don't know," I stammered, feeling my cheeks flush even deeper. "Yes," I finally admitted.

"Oh," Rain responded, not pushing further. "Me too," he whispered into my ear, and I turned to face away from him. I sensed his hand hovering near my waist, and then he shifted so his back pressed against mine. He lifted the covers, enveloping us both. Sleep began to claim me, but amid my drowsiness, I couldn't help but reflect on everything Rain had done for me today—the risks he had taken, the confessions he had shared, and the deepening connection between us.

It was a revelation I hadn't anticipated, but it kindled a fire of affection and desire within me that I couldn't ignore.

# EMBER

I woke up to a warm hand against my stomach and my body pressed tightly against a chest. It also felt like one of those weird déjà vu moments, where it felt so familiar yet so different, and I couldn't quite place where I was.

I blinked in the morning light, realizing I was in Rain's bed and his arm was wrapped around me. Rolling over, I faced him. His chest rose and fell, and his thick lashes rested on his cheek. His body was hard . . . all over. His boner poked my stomach, and he moaned.

"Are you going to stare at it or do something about it?" he murmured.

"Ew," I exclaimed, playfully punching him on his rock-hard abs. He chuckled, stretching out and opening his eyes.

"Mornin'," he mused. "What're you doing today?"

I rolled over, lying on my back and gazing at the blank ceiling above me.

"I think I'm going to see Walsh," I murmured. "But then I figured if you're not busy, we could walk around campus and work on our project."

"I know you want me to come with you to see him . . . I just can't right now."

I pressed a finger to his lips. "I know."

As much as I wanted him to join me, I also understood the reason he couldn't. Any movement toward the house would alert the others that we were investigating what was happening, and not in the way that Ash's dad wanted us to. We were searching for the truth, trying to uncover the evidence.

I jumped out of bed, got dressed back in the same clothes I had worn yesterday, not caring I wasn't dressed up, and shot off a text to Walsh, asking him to meet me at the coffee shop in town, away from the center of campus.

I grabbed my purse and looked at Rain, who was still watching me, propped up on his elbows.

"What?" I asked, shaking my head at him.

"You just got dressed in front of me." I playfully slapped him on his chest again. "Come on, mi pareja, don't fault me for being a man and looking."

"Yeah, yeah." I laughed and then started to leave the room before he grabbed my hand.

"Wait . . . you're not waiting for me to walk you down?"

"Uh, honestly, I don't know how this is supposed to go?" His hand held mine as he got out of bed.

"At the end of the day, Ember, I am your friend. If you were at a friend's house, would they walk you to the door?"

"Yeah." I remembered Marissa often walked me to the door.

"Okay . . . friend." He let go of my hand before laughing, knowing my comment carried a weight of untruth.

Once Rain got dressed and we got downstairs to the foyer, I realized the last time I'd been in this foyer without a party and walking out of the front door, it had been under way different circumstances.

"Are you okay?" he whispered. We didn't hold hands walking down the stairs, and I didn't feel this compulsion to reach up and kiss him, but being with Rain felt safe. All those anxious thoughts threatening to surface didn't spill over. In fact, I remained calm as I stood in the empty room.

As if Rain could sense my emotions, he encouraged me to walk outside, trailing behind me. That's when I noticed Santiago at the end of the gate.

"You called him," I stated.

"If you're going to see your brother, which I am not telling you not to, I understand why you do. But you need to have him come with you if I cannot be there."

"Okay," I said, not wanting or seeing a reason to fight. I kinda agreed with him.

We paused at the end of the walkway, and I gazed up at Rain, whose hair still had that messy, slept-in look. His eyes seemed a brighter blue today, and the lines on his face seemed to have disappeared overnight.

I glanced over his shoulder at the house where some of the guys would be waking up. A pang of guilt took over. It felt like I was doing something wrong and dirty, as if I were cheating on Ash even though I knew he wasn't around. The whole situation made me uncomfortable.

"Is it okay that we're seen together?" I asked him, my voice tinged with uncertainty. Indecision and the whirlwind of thoughts flooded my brain.

"Ember, we're just friends, remember?" Rain reassured me, but I knew he felt the turmoil in my mind.

"Yeah," I murmured before nodding goodbye. I turned my back to him, exited through the gate, and headed toward Santiago.

"Don't even." Santiago laughed as I approached him in my day-old clothes. "Nothing happened."

"I didn't say anything, mija." He wrapped his arm around my shoulder as we walked down the block to where I had arranged to meet Walsh.

"Tell me about the plan for today?" Santiago asked as we turned the corner, leaving the Den behind. I couldn't help but glance back, and Rain was still standing there, hands in his pockets, in the front yard.

It didn't feel fair, what I was doing to him. We were more than friends and understood the unspoken emotions between us, but acting on them was a colossal step, one I wasn't ready for. I just hoped that today, my brother would cooperate.

"I just need some answers," I explained, "and it's been almost a year since Ash's . . . well, whatever happened. I need him to finally tell the truth."

"Do you think he's going to tell you now? What makes today any different from yesterday?" Santiago asked, a hint of skepticism in his voice.

"I don't know," I admitted. "I'm hoping time, the approach of the spring bonfire this year, and the fact that I'm finally willing to confront him face-to-face will make a difference."

"I hope it works out in your favor," Santiago said, and his face dropped, his eyes soft as he looked in my direction. Even he didn't want to believe that Walsh would share the truth with me.

"And after?" he inquired.

"After Walsh?" I confirmed.

"Yeah."

"I guess I'll hang out with Rain for a little bit." Santiago stopped in his tracks and shot me a knowing look.

"Hey, it's not like that," I protested. "We're in the same class and have to do a project together."

"Whatever you need to tell yourself, mija." Santiago chuckled as we continued walking, heading past campus and toward the center of town. I had chosen to meet Walsh off campus so someone like Tana wouldn't see us together and report it to someone at the Den. I didn't want it getting back to Mr. Ortiz and ultimately, then getting Rain in trouble. This seemed like the safer option.

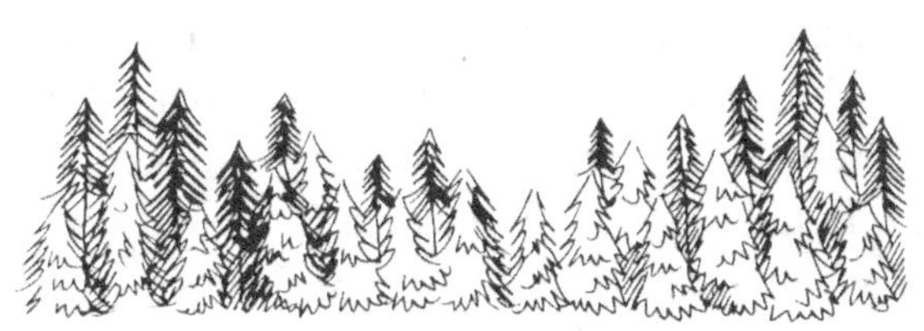

I grabbed a coffee for Santiago and me at the counter, then sat at a booth in the back corner so we were somewhat hidden from anyone who walked through the front door. Santiago sat beside me at an adjacent table.

"You didn't have to pay for me," Santiago clucked. "You pay me enough in salary."

Another thing that Ash had left me in his will was a portion of his fortune, which is another reason his dad had it out for me. Only Santiago knew, but now that I thought about it, I needed to ask Rain about it.

My thoughts were interrupted when someone cleared their throat from above me.

"Hey sis," my brother said. He looked different. His hair was cropped short and gelled back, but he looked as put together as he'd always had, wearing designer threads and polished, slick black boots.

"Walsh," I responded coolly, gesturing to the seat next to me, not bothering to get up. He gripped his cup of warm coffee as he slid into the booth next to me before his eyes darted over to Santiago who was not so hidden.

"Your bodyguard?" he asked. I knew the implications of the question. Santiago wasn't part of the Mafia, and Walsh knew it.

"From Ash," I whispered. Santiago was a gift from Rain, not from Dad. Based on the wince on his face, Walsh understood I was not accepting the family's help.

"Not from Dad . . ."

"I didn't need any protection from Dad. Because the person that I needed protection from is sitting in front of me," I stated, not letting Walsh see my hands shaking under the table. I was no longer the little girl who needed to be locked in the closet while he and Dad did the dirty work. Because I was a different Ember than Walsh knew growing up. Even from what Walsh knew when he brought me to Isles with Dad last year. I didn't need saving, I needed answers.

"Are you ready to tell me what happened?" I asked, folding my arms across my chest.

"Nope."

"I figured that's what you were going to say which is why I came prepared." I pulled out some of the photos that Rain had given me before I left.

"There are clearly two prints in the mud, Walsh."

"That doesn't prove shit, Ember." But I saw through his mask. I saw him crack, just slightly.

"Walsh, I am your sister. We went through hell and back together and you won't tell me what I already know. You were there, Walsh."

"You don't know that, Ember." Walsh fidgeted with the cup in his hand.

"I do, but no one else does," I whispered so I was out of earshot from Santiago and anyone else in the restaurant. I leaned in, pointing at the second pair of boot marks in the mud photo.

"Walsh, you are the only person around who has these specific sneakers. These are the GG imprints on them." I pointed out, knowing my brother's obsession for designer items and that he would be the only person to wear designer sneakers out in the woods.

"Those are not specifically made for me, Ember. Just because I own the same brand of shoe, doesn't mean shit."

"But no one else knows this, Walsh. You can tell me without saying anything else. I won't tell anyone."

"Except your new boyfriend," Walsh mumbled, and I slammed a hand on the table.

"Excuse me?" I barked at him.

"Nothing, sis."

"No, I need you to repeat what you said to me," I demanded, my voice edged with frustration.

"It's just that I've noticed you've been getting cozy with the new leader of the Den." His words only fueled my anger.

"Stop having me followed, Walsh. You're my brother. If you've got something to say, pick up the damn phone and say it," I yelled, not caring who might overhear our heated exchange.

"I've tried. You don't answer," he replied, leaning back in his chair and taking a sip of his drink.

This time, I felt myself breaking down. Why he wouldn't share what I already suspected and knew was beyond me. I wanted desperately to cry, to rage, to beg Walsh to tell me the truth, but I kept it in because I didn't want to fall apart in front of him. I had done so much falling apart that it felt like it was finally time to hold it together.

Part of the reason for all this, was knowing Rain was right there with me, desperately seeking the truth. Knowing I could go to him after this, felt reassuring and only fueled this need to hold it all together and be strong.

"Please, tell me the truth, Walsh," I begged as he fiddled with his hands. When he was a kid, this was always the first sign to our parents that he was anxious and didn't know what to say. "I'm your blood. Dad and you always preached to me that blood was thicker than water. I just don't get why you're doing this now."

Walsh closed his eyes and then finally opened them, gazing directly at me. All I could see was our mother, the way she used to implore us to stay close because in the world we lived, people would always try to pull us apart.

"I will tell you what I've told everyone, including Dad. I don't know what you are talking about or what happened that night. I *cannot* tell you what happened because I am *protecting* you."

I lifted my brow. "If I find the truth, will you eventually tell me?"

"If you find out what happened *at the rock* with Ash, then I will be able to tell you." He said his words deliberately, which made me realize I needed to go back to the rock . . . without Rain because I was meant to figure this out alone.

I hesitated, still upset with my brother for not sharing the truth, but I knew what he wasn't telling me might hold clues to unraveling the mystery of that fateful night.

"I have to go," I said as I slid out of the booth and stood.

"Can I see you again?" Walsh asked, his voice filled with uncertainty, and I shook my head.

"Not until I can figure out what happened, then I can find peace in our relationship," I explained.

"Ember." Walsh grabbed my hand. His face twisting in despair. He was suffering. I knew my brother. I'd grown up with him and knew he would do anything to protect me.

"You don't need to protect me anymore," I said one last time. Santiago stood until I gave him a gesture that I was okay.

"I do, sis." He whispered so softly that if I hadn't been looking at him, I wouldn't have been able to hear. "I promised him."

I ripped my hand away from his, shocked. Without telling me what I needed to know, he told me what he knew.

"You-you *were* there?" Tears formed in my eyes, but Walsh slid out of the booth and stared straight at me before giving me a kiss on the cheek.

"I'm telling you, sis, I would do anything to protect you." He turned to walk away before he paused and looked back. "Dad told me what happened. I realized from that moment on, I needed to do this for you. It's my duty."

*I can protect myself* was what I wished I could have expressed to him, had I found the words. Instead, I stood there, fighting back tears. Sniffling, I watched him exit the coffee shop. Overwhelmed by emotions, I slumped back into the booth, signaling to Santiago I needed a moment to collect myself.

I could rely on myself. It sounded like something Ash might have said or asked my brother to do because Ash always felt the need to protect me. Maybe last-year Ember needed his protection, but today, I needed no one to shield me. I was entirely capable of unraveling this mystery on my own.

As I sat there in the booth, a mix of emotions flooded over me. Walsh's evasiveness about that fateful night, my brother's secrets, and the burden of the questions all weighed heavily on my shoulders. Yet, a newfound determination surged within me.

Over the last nine months, I had grieved, and I had done it mostly on my own. I had learned to stand on my own two feet in the face of adversity. Ash's absence had forced me to become more resilient, to become Ember Solis, a woman who could confront her fears and pursue the truth, no matter how elusive it seemed.

To find the answers I sought, I couldn't rely on anyone else. It was a journey I had to undertake alone, a path of self-discovery and resilience. This quest for the truth wasn't just about finding closure for Ash's sake; it was about finding closure for myself, too.

I wiped away a stray tear, took a deep breath, and stood from the booth. Santiago's brows furrowed as his eyes locked onto mine, silently conveying their unwavering support. A gentle hand reached out, offering reassurance and solidarity in that fleeting moment of connection. "You okay, mija?"

"Yeah," I replied with a newfound determination in my voice. "I'm more than okay. I've got some leads to follow up on. Thanks for being here, Santiago."

I left the coffee shop with a renewed sense of purpose. It was time to unravel the mystery of that fateful night, to find out what had happened with my brother, and to prove that I could stand on my own two feet and face the darkness that lay ahead.

# EMBER

As I strolled down the street with Santiago, heading back to my apartment, I couldn't help feeling anxious as we got closer to campus. After Tana's incident, I wished I had a cap or a hoodie to hide my face. Santiago noticed my unease and tried to distract me with his random questions.

"What year was the university created?" he asked, and I narrowed my eyes at him.

"How am I supposed to know?"

"You are a reader. I figured maybe you'd have been curious about where you were living, so you studied it." I laughed and kept counting the cracks inside the sidewalk as we walked forward. There were only a couple more blocks to my apartment.

I paused momentarily when I looked up and recognized the same patchwork tattoos I'd seen hundreds of times last year.

"Ember?" The familiar voice echoed in a somber tone. It was my old roommate.

"Hey," I responded, trying to walk around her, but she got in my way.

"I heard you were back on campus, but I guess I couldn't quite believe it." Santiago tightened his grip across my shoulder.

"Here in the flesh." I offered a tight-lipped smile, hoping the answer would satiate her and she'd leave me alone.

"Why?" she asked, not bothering to step out of the way.

"Why, what?"

"Why'd you come back?" she hissed; there was the Maddy I knew. The person who could pretend to be your best friend one moment, yet was constantly preoccupied with her own needs, wants, and desires.

"Because I deserve to be here like anyone else does, Maddy Kensington." I didn't owe her an explanation, but I wanted to give it to her because I was so tired of people dragging my name.

She shook her head. "It's Madison Ryan. I went by my mother's name for so long." She shrugged before turning the conversation back on me.

"I can't believe you told your brother to go after him the night before the bonfire. You couldn't give him that time to prep." My jaw was so wide, I swore I could feel the cement with my bottom lip.

"I'm sorry . . . but kindly step the fuck out of the way." Santiago started to step in front of me, but I threw up a hand, wanting to face her myself.

"No . . . I see you fixed Tana's mistake."

She paused for a moment before adding in, "And looks like you moved on to his best friend pretty fast, too."

*Crack.*

Without a moment's hesitation, I struck her square in the nose, the sound of a little crack filling the air, and Santiago snickered next to me. My clenched fist dripped with her blood, and an unexpected fierceness coursed through me.

"What the hell, Ember?" she muttered, her hand going up to her bloody nose.

I was taken aback myself, impressed by my own sudden action. There was no contemplation; it was a pure, instinctive reaction.

"Oops." I shrugged.

"You're a bitch," she yelled onto the otherwise empty street.

"Yeah, just like when you left me alone at the party to get drugged, tattooed, and kidnapped. I'm simply returning the favor." With that, I took an extra-large step around her and continued walking, not bothering to look back.

I kept moving, my feet propelling me forward, but I couldn't shake the shock of what I'd done. Santiago quickly caught up to me, and once we were at a safe distance, he erupted into a wild symphony of cackles.

"Ember Solis," he taunted, pulling me into a side hug.

"I can't believe I did that," I confessed, still reeling.

"Me neither."

"I think I was . . . no, I *am* just sick and tired of people assuming the worst about me, about Ash. I was simply done with it, to be honest."

"No, don't mistake my laughter for thinking you did something wrong. I'm genuinely proud of you."

"In a strange way, I feel like I understand how upset Ash would be about all of this. He'd want to protect me and shield me from it all. But I think I needed to stand up for myself, to learn that I can protect myself, that I deserve that."

"I agree."

"It's kind of ridiculous, considering I'm saying this with my bodyguard right next to me. But I swear, I think this is part of my personal growth journey."

Santiago grabbed my shoulders, stopping me. His expression was thoughtful. "No, mija. Your path of personal growth is like a winding road, full of unexpected turns and challenges. Embrace each twist and turn, for they lead you to the person you're meant to become."

"And Maddy was a bump?"

"She was someone in your past who wasn't good for you. She probably never was if you really looked back, but it is only now with your eyes wide open that you are able to see her true colors."

I sat on this statement and then giggled. "Are you sure you aren't replacing my therapist?" Santiago laughed as we arrived at the apartment complex and walked inside.

"Are you staying here?" he asked as he opened the door to his home across the hallway.

"That's the plan. I'll let you know if I decide to go to Rain's later." I wasn't being truthful. I had every intention of heading to Ash's rock, even though I didn't want Santiago to join me or list all the reasons it was risky to be off campus, especially during the spring semester. While Ash's . . . situation technically was allowed because he was off campus, I'd assumed that people would show some restraint this year regarding the bonfire. Of course, that wasn't the case, and the leader this year was Rain. He would be put in the same precarious position that Ash was in that led to whatever turmoil he'd encountered.

"I've got to make sense of this before then," I muttered to myself. I didn't want Rain to know what was going on or have him worry unnecessarily. After getting myself cleaned up, I spent an extra half hour in the bathroom, waiting until it was safe to slip out of the apartment. I quietly descended the stairs and reached my car, starting it up without a second thought. Pulling out of the driveway, I headed toward the outskirts of town, my mind focused on finding answers, even though I couldn't quite figure out what exactly that meant.

As I drove away from Isles, I glanced over my shoulder, following the cautionary lessons Ash and Rain had imparted. When no one was tailing me, I turned onto the road leading to Ash's rock. Even though I wasn't officially part of the Den or the Alphas, I couldn't shake the feeling that I, too, might become prey like Maddy's roommate had two years ago.

The route to the rock was etched into my memory, and as I navigated the winding mountain road toward the clearing, I couldn't help but imagine the fear and torment Ash might have experienced in this very place. Whether he was battling his own demons or someone chased him, I imagined as he took this route here it was not easy.

As I approached the clearing, I parked on the dirt path, grabbed the flashlight, and embarked on my journey down the path leading to the rock that overlooked the forest clearing. A vivid memory resurfaced, one from when I had run away from Ash after he refused to tell me about the tattoo. He had kept me in the dark about many things. I touched the tattoo behind my ear, reminiscing about the day it had become a part of me. I had been so scared and naive at the beginning of that year.

But . . . I had also been deeply in love. Maybe it was more of a lustful infatuation, but I distinctly remembered how captivated I had been by Ash. He was the first boy to ever show interest in me. He was my first boyfriend, my first love, my first sexual experience, or at least, the first that mattered. I had perpetually been on cloud nine, oblivious to the harsh realities of the world. Looking back, I wondered if I should have paid more attention to Ash's underlying depression. Perhaps I could have noticed that Maddy was treating me poorly, or maybe I could have been more honest with myself. I didn't want to share Ash, nor did I want to share myself, but I had been so consumed by the intoxicating spell of love that I could see none of this.

My steps faltered as I realized I had walked in a circle and now stood atop his rock. A pang of guilt coursed through me for harboring these thoughts. I sat down, my feet hanging off the edge, and contemplated how different life might have been if I had never met Ash.

Because without Ash, I wouldn't have had the opportunity to find . . . myself.

It was one of the most important lessons I'd learned. Through the darkness and loneliness, came a significant wave of self-awareness. I chuckled as I remembered the phrase my mother used to tell me when I was a kid.

*"Into the darkness you'll go, and into the light you'll be."*

That maybe it was all a metaphor for what life was. I'd spent so many months upset at my mom, too, blaming her for Ash. If it hadn't been for the realization that she'd cheated on my dad, then maybe Ash and I wouldn't have had to break up.

But as I took in the serene clearing, I knew it wasn't about my mom or even Ash. This was the outline for the journey I was supposed to take. They were the words to the story I was writing.

Just then, I glanced to my right where Rain had pointed out the . . . incident . . . happened, and got up, stalking over to the area. Walking around, I noticed there was something hidden behind some bushes next to a fallen tree branch.

A wave of anxiety hit me, and I had no idea why. I moved the branch that seemed to have fallen recently and was providing some sort of a shelter or protection for whatever laid beneath it. As I cleared away the branches, my eyes widened. It wasn't just *his* hoodie.

Carefully, I picked up the abandoned hoodie. It was damp but had shielded whatever was beneath it from the relentless rain. My fingers brushed against a hard, cold object, and I realized it was a phone. No. It wasn't just *a* phone.

"Holy shit," I whispered as the matte-black iPhone was so familiar.

This discovery left me baffled. As I examined it more closely, I noticed it was still in good condition despite the constant rain that frequented this place. I tried to turn it on, but it was dead. I mean, how ridiculous to even think the phone almost a year ago would turn on, but there was hope.

My heart raced with a mixture of intrigue and apprehension. Could this phone hold any clues about what had transpired here? Questions swirled in my mind as I held the phone in my trembling hands.

Pushing branches aside, I searched for anything else that could be down there. I was desperate and knew I needed to go see Rain. After I felt like the area had nothing else mysteriously lying around, I jumped off the path and ran to my car where I had a charger.

My hands trembled the entire time, not knowing if anything would be on the phone or if it would even turn on, but there was something there. I just knew it deep down.

The stomping echoed as I ran as fast as I could through the woods. The quicker I could get to the car, the faster I could plug the damned phone in.

"Please, Ash." I prayed I'd find any answer at all.

Just as I reached the Jeep, I jumped inside and shoved the charger into the bottom of the phone. My fingers crossed that it would turn on and reveal the answers to Rain's and my biggest problems, but it was a long shot and the phone likely wouldn't even turn on.

I switched the dial to heat to warm the icy-cold shiver basking in my bones. Time stood still as I waited to see if the phone would turn on.

By some miracle, after ten minutes, the phone turned on and wetness greeted my cheeks as the familiar photo of the two of us together lit up his lock screen.

It was taken at this exact spot on the day of our first date when Ash surprised me with a picnic after class. He had also forced me to take a photo, and I was staring at him, entranced by everything about him. That feeling sent me back to that place again. It was like being hugged by your favorite childhood stuffed animal or doll as an adult. That feeling washed over me like the warmest blanket, and I welcomed it in because I was desperate to feel close to him.

I wiped away the tears now pouring from my face. This wasn't cute or sweet crying. I swiped the home screen, but the phone was password protected.

"Fuck," I wailed because just when that small string of hope was given to me, it was snatched away.

I tried his birthday, but it buzzed, warning me that was not the correct password.

"Think, Ember," I told myself, and then tried my birthday but was surprised when the phone notified me that was also the incorrect password. *What else could it be?*

"Rain," I whispered aloud, surprising myself at knowing Rain's birthday was November tenth. I typed it in, and the phone greeted me by opening to the home screen.

It was bittersweet being reminded of Rain through all this. I was desperate for answers, but Rain's presence was still very much here with me.

I went to his Notes app, hoping that he would share something there, but most of it was just random instructions and meeting notes from the Den.

Then I went to his messages, and there was an exclamation mark next to one to show he'd attempted sending a message, but it never sent.

As my finger brushed across the screen to open the message, a surge of emotions rushed through me. There it was, a text meant for me, even after our breakup. My chest tightened.

It was one simple phrase. Three small words that changed my entire life.

*I love you.*

I buried my hands in my arms and wailed, deep sobs bursting through my very core. As I sniffled, I stared into the darkening forest sky through the front window of the car and whispered, "If you are up there with her, I hope you're teaching her how to ride a bike." I laughed, inhaling the snot that was also unattractively pouring out of my nose. "You're probably teaching her how to shoot a gun or something, honestly."

I took a few deep, centering breaths as I caressed the unsent text message.

Fuck, I am so grateful this phone was cosmically saved by the branches through all the storms. I lifted the damp hoodie to my nose. Although it smelled nothing like I remembered Ash to be, the faint smell of pine from the forest wrapped around me. I imagined the way his arms felt holding me.

Finally, when I had enough courage to go through the phone, I skimmed through the most recent texts, then realized I would need a tech person to do a dig through this phone. Nothing else seemed out of the ordinary, so I went over to the Call app.

I clicked through his recent phone calls, and there were a bunch from Pico and hundreds of missed calls from Rain and his dad. A few voicemails pinged through as service to the phone was restored.

I clicked on the voicemails and pressed the first one from Rain from the night of the accident.

*Hey man. I am worried about you. I haven't heard from you in a while, and I know you were going to your rock, but this isn't cool. Where are you, man? I'm going to have to find your GPS from your car soon if I don't hear from you. I know as you listen to this you probably are laughing at me because you're going to tell me to stop overreacting, but I am legit worried. Okay, love you, brother.*

Then another, a little after his . . . passing. He was in tears while leaving the message.

*Ash. Don't do this. Why did you do this to me? I keep calling you even though I know you'll never get this. We cannot seem to find your stupid ass phone either, so good luck to some random hiker or forest person finding this. Your dad thinks someone else was there. Fuck, Ash.*

Another.

*We found another set of tracks on the trail before the rain washed them all away. Who the fuck were you with? I always knew you suffered, and when I found you in the house when you were in high school with the bottle of pills by the floor, I told you I'd get you out. What am I supposed to do about Ember? She's in Dansport but . . . fuck, I was tucking away all the emotions I felt about her for you. Because you were my brother and because of what happened in high school, you deserve someone who made you feel special, but now all I want to do is go down and comfort her, but I'd be hurting you if I acted on my thoughts.*

And another.

*Ash. Your funeral was today. Everyone was crying, but I forgot how to. I can't seem to shed another tear. I'm so lost without you. I feel so empty inside. Your dad is saying I have to replace you at the Den. I don't want to. I want nothing to do with this godforsaken organization. I always knew there was a possibility this would happen, but I had no idea you'd do it to yourself. I wish I could have changed things. I wish I would have been a better brother to you—protected you more. I wish I was more like you.*

Finally, I tapped on the most recent message, which was a couple of weeks old, dated the day after I'd seen Rain in our photography class.

*I saw her, Ash. I know precisely what drew you to her; she's stunningly beautiful. Her curves, her luscious lips . . . I couldn't help but fantasize about every way I wanted to have her right there on that desk. But I couldn't ignore your voice echoing in the back of my mind. How the hell am I supposed to protect her while resisting these urges? I think we're both lost souls, but I need your permission somehow. I need you to tell me it's all right to pursue her. From the moment I laid eyes on her, from the sweet words that flowed from her lips like a melody, I knew she needed to be a part of my life. However, you wanted her more, so I handed her over to you, as I always did. I wanted to ensure your happiness. After the affair between her mom and my dad, which ignited the feud between the Cartel and the Mafia, as you always reminded me, I took a giant step back. Your dad was the one who pulled the trigger on Ember's mom but it was her father who killed mine. I know Mr. Ortiz was looking for revenge, thinking he's the savior here, but there was a lot of shit from all sides. God, I pushed her away, even going as far as being a total jerk to her because I had to remove her from my life completely. But, Ash, I think I might love her. Not as you did, but in a way that I want to see her smile again, hear her laughter, and have her spirit around me. She's more than just Ember; she feels like . . . she's mine.*

Then there was a long pause.

*Damn, this is unbearable. Please tell me what to do.*

As the message ended, the phone went dark, and the air inside the car became oppressively hot. I pulled my shirt collar away from my neck, as it was becoming increasingly irritating and itchy. My eyes shifted toward the door handle, and I grabbed it, trying to open the door but nothing happened.

*Get me out,* I cried to myself.

Panic coursed through me as I struggled to escape. Silent pleas for help reverberated in my mind over and over again, and just as I forced the door open, I tumbled out, landing on the branches below. My face met the dirt, and I raised my hands, my legs still feeling as unsteady as jelly beneath me.

I took a deep breath, inhaling the familiar warm scent of pine, and tried to sit upright on the dirt.

Holy shit. If Rain's dad was the one who was having the affair with my mom...

I cannot believe it was Rain's dad, Franco. I wasn't sure how I didn't put two and two together. I should have known when Rain told me in the diner.

*I should have known.*

I needed to get home. I closed my eyes and when I reopened them, the forest floor was dark, as were the trees around me. I'd been gone for far too long, and if Santiago hadn't already gotten wind that I'd left, he would soon.

I jumped into the car, leaving Ash's phone charging, before I pulled my phone out and checked the messages. There was nothing, which meant I could take my time on the drive back to Isles.

I couldn't believe Franco killed my mom. He's the person they were after. My dad was the reason Rain didn't have a dad and got roped into this. Rain had to have known, so why didn't he tell me? So much of his message hit me in the face like a slap.

He-he loved me?

# RAIN

When Ember left this morning, all I wanted to do was go to the library and finish some of the work I needed to get done for my classes, but Mr. Ortiz had a different idea.

Just as I was reversing down the driveway, his familiar entourage of cars pulled to the front of the Den, which was a surprise because none of us were notified of his departure from Dansport.

Pico came running out the front door before glancing over at me as I dismounted the motorcycle, letting out a large exhale.

"I can entertain him if you need to go somewhere," Pico offered.

"Nah, I was just going to study because I'm still failing, but he'll tell me this is more important and I need to sit my ass down." I cracked my neck, the tension rippling through me.

As I parked the bike, took off my helmet and walked over toward him, he exited one of the middle cars.

"Rain." His smooth voice echoed throughout the property, and a few more guys rushed to the front door. He looked so much like Ash it was uncanny. He had the same brown curls framing his face, and although there were far more lines etched in his face than Ash would ever have, there was something so sinister about Mr. Ortiz. Ash may have looked like the villain from the outside, but he was always warm and fuzzy when you got to know him. Nothing about Mr. Ortiz gave anyone the warm fuzzies.

"To what do we owe this pleasure to?"

"I need to talk to you." He glided past me with his gazillion bodyguards, which he believed made him impenetrable, but it was more obvious than just going under the radar.

"Oh-kay," I grumbled once he was out of earshot and striding into the house. I stood there on the porch of the house and took a deep breath before I walked in.

"Sit next to me," I told Pico because, little did anyone know, I had a plan for next year and part of it required Pico's help.

Once inside, a few guys brought Mr. Ortiz his cigar cutter and a glass of whiskey on the rocks before we all gathered in the formal living area. He settled into one of the oversized mustard chairs in the corner while Pico and I took the couch.

As I sat down, I couldn't help but think of the last time I was in here the morning after we found Ash passed away and I made Ember sleep on this exact couch and stayed up watching her. That night. It haunted my dreams. It kept me up when I thought about the way I saw him. The day I lost a part of my heart.

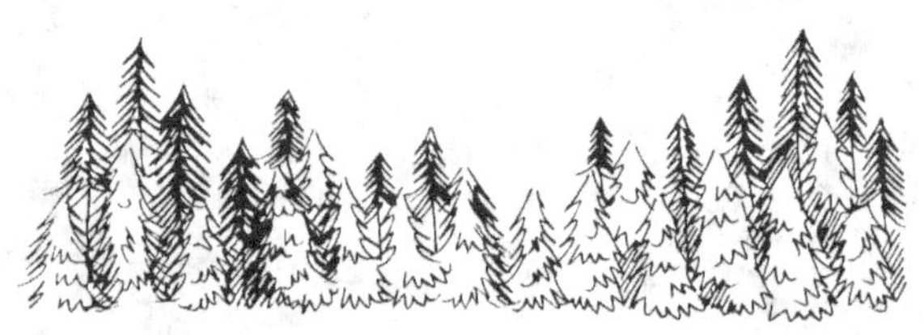

*"We found him," one of the members of the Den told me as I paced around the house waiting for this call. None of them would let me go look. They feared something with the Alpha house because the bonfire technically was supposed to happen tonight.*

*"Where is he?"*

*"We sent you coordinates. You need to come here now." I nodded, hanging up, and then realized where they wanted me to go was off campus.*

*I looked to Pico. "Come with me, but leave everyone else here. I don't want to risk anyone being off-campus."*

*The implications of finding Ash off-campus penetrated through my brain because I knew this would not be good. I'd been calling him for hours, but this couldn't happen. He tried ending it all when we were in high school, but I thought he was doing better. I thought he was okay.*

*Yeah, I knew he and Ember were going through a rough spot, but I thought with being away from Mr. Ortiz and the confines of the house, he was doing good. Fuck.*

*I jumped on the bike, and Pico hopped behind me before we peeled out of the driveway and followed the directions that the guys sent us. Why would Ash have even been found off-campus?*

*As we veered off the road into the darkness, I quickly scanned our surroundings to ensure we were alone before heading toward the location he was last seen.*

*Upon arrival, the first thing that caught my attention was his car. I swiftly brought the bike to a halt and dismounted, discarding my helmet on the ground. As I circled the vehicle, I realized the car was in pristine condition. There were no signs of it being rammed into this small clearing along the woodland path. Instead, it seemed deliberately parked here, hinting at one unsettling possibility.*

*"Please," I muttered as Pico raced down the path, maintaining a stoic silence, refusing to confront the looming dread. As he bolted toward the other members of the Den, I followed the trail, meticulously documenting the track marks on the dirt road, capturing photos obsessively as I pressed forward.*

*Thankfully, we were blessed with a brief spell of decent weather in Isles, which prevented the total obliteration of crucial evidence but a lot of the mud was washed away already. As I traced his path leading to a clearing, my breath caught in my throat. Even in the dimness, an eerie tranquility hung in the air, and a dreadful certainty settled over me.*

*My gut churned with an attempt to betray me as I approached what I already knew. I looked down over the ledge.*

*"Retrieve the body," I whispered to Pico, who had his hands over his eyes, kneeling on the ground, seeking solace from a god who couldn't change the grim reality before us. However, I needed to distance myself, otherwise I would be ensnared in the same anguish as he was despite my knowledge. I didn't want to accept it, but he had suffered in silence for far too long.*

*"I'm going to handle this," I vowed, for ultimately, there was no one to blame but Mr. Ortiz. He had forged the monster that had taken residence within Ash. He had coerced him into leading a life that was a charade, void of authenticity.*

*"Do you want—" Pico began.*

*"I said get the damn body," I screamed, then scanned my surroundings. Mr. Ortiz wouldn't react well to the revelation that he had played a role in his own son's death. None of us could have rescued him, not even Ember.*

*Damn it.*

*I ran my hand through my hair. What was I going to say to her?*

*As I meticulously inspected every inch of the rock, with the others retrieving the body, Pico joined me.*

*"She needs to know," he murmured.*

*"I intend to tell her," I asserted, halting him in his tracks. Then I realized I could no longer live in Ash's shadow. I needed to carve my path outside of it. This had to be avenged for him. Ensuring this tragedy never recurred, that this senseless ritual ended, became a necessity. The senseless feud between these two underground organizations had to stop. They were too blind to realize that by joining forces, they could be stronger.*

*However, none of this was pertinent at the moment. Right now, it was about my brother—the one person I would protect to the ends of the earth—who was now gone, leaving a void in my heart. Something so irreplaceable I didn't know—*

*"Fuck," I cried out, the tears threating to come as Pico placed a gentle hand on my back. It was a gesture so foreign to us, neither of us ever feeling this emotion.*

*"Someone came after him . . ."*

*"No," I whispered. "No one but his own demons . . ."*

"Rain Fortin." My name snapped me back into my current reality of sitting on this godforsaken uncomfortable chair in a house I had no desire to ever be a part of.

"There is a significant amount of money that was intended for my son that is missing—you told me you were looking at this. Where is it?"

I knew where the money was. It was built into a business that Ember owned. A fake business with only one owner that was basically impenetrable by anyone except the IRS, but even then, I could probably pay someone off to get them off her back, too.

"I'm still looking into it." I paused.

"Remind me, who gave Ash the money?" Pico did a double take at me, knowing exactly who had the money. It was in Ash's will. The will that also had mysteriously gone missing.

"Ash's mother left him a fund that was dedicated solely to him. I had no access to it unless he died and gave it to someone else." Mr. Ortiz's eyes glared into mine.

"Where is the will?" And now Pico could understand why it took me so long to figure out what happened to Ash. I could see him, brows furrowed, as the puzzle pieces suddenly came together.

"I'm still looking for it. I told you that I have to figure out what happened that night and that particular piece of information is coincidentally missing."

Mr. Ortiz took a slow pull from his glass of whiskey before setting it down. This plan was fucking stupid, to say the least. I was trying to one up the biggest head of the Cartel. This man dealt with people far larger than my pay grade, but I had one thing on my side. He maybe had a small soft spot for his child and desperately wanted to know where the millions he had thought he would make were going.

"I am still figuring out what happened." I repeated.

A resounding sound of glass hitting glass echoed throughout the house, and I winced, but Pico stayed stoic. He really should have replaced Ash. He had all the qualities of being the one in charge—a true leader.

"I need to know what happened to my son."

I couldn't help but stifle a laugh. The only other instance in all the years I'd known Mr. Ortiz refer to Ash as his son was during the funeral in front of everyone. Otherwise, he simply called him either the leader of the Den or Ash. It was undeniably disheartening.

"I know you do, and I've been tirelessly working to unravel what happened—"

"Is that why you've been getting close to the Solis girl?"

It was like a punch to the gut. I had always been aware that Mr. Ortiz had eyes and ears everywhere in Isles, but I foolishly believed that we had maintained our discretion. I should have anticipated that bringing Ember to the house would inevitably expose her, and by making the entire meeting about not interfering with her, I had essentially laid it all out.

"She's a valuable asset in all of this, sir." Pico interjected on my behalf, and I silently thanked him once more. He was a born leader.

"How so?"

"Because she was close to Ash and Walsh. She's just as determined as we are to solve this mystery."

"Is that why I have one of my former associates tailing her at all times?" Mr. Ortiz responded with an air of composure that made me struggle to remain still in my seat.

"Exactly. Now you're grasping the essence of what we mean. We're merely safeguarding our asset here."

Mr. Ortiz cocked his head to the side, sporting a smug look that made me wish I could rip the words right from his mouth. "So, where did the funding originate from to employ this Mr. Santiago Torres?"

"From my trust. Before my father passed away, he set up a trust fund for me, so it's coming from my resources." It was a half-truth. Santiago's annual salary was covered by Ash, but the majority of the initial funds to hire him had come from my pocket.

Honestly, it all seemed absurd because Ember didn't even require the money. Her father had amassed enough wealth to provide for her comfortably for the rest of her life. However, I desired to give her the life she deserved. I yearned to be the one to protect her, and that's why I had made it my personal mission to do so.

"And you are doing this all for the betterment of the organization? Because after the little stunt you pulled this week by gathering all *my* men, I needed to come by to make it very clear what was happening, and I think maybe you needed a reminder of who is in charge." That was it. I fucking lost it. The rage I'd been working hard on repressing in my soul was finally coming out to play.

I leaped to my feet and turned to leave the room. Nobody left Mr. Ortiz unless they were properly dismissed, but I was changing that rule because I didn't give a fuck about what this man said, I was thoroughly pissed off.

"You think I asked to be in this position?" I bellowed as if I was trying to awaken the spirits inside the walls. "Yeah, fuck you man."

Shit, I was on a roll, because rule number two was that no one screamed or dared tell Mr. Ortiz he was wrong. The man was never wrong . . . until today.

"Excuse me?" Mr. Ortiz said while folding his arms across his chest. His demeanor hadn't changed. While I was throwing my version of an adult temper tantrum, he was stoic.

"I never wanted to be a part of this family. I shouldn't have to pay for the sacrificial lamb you used my father in some greater scheme at getting back at the Mafia. I shouldn't have to atone for him getting caught and your whole operation fucking sinking. I didn't want to fucking live with your tyrant ass nor did I demand it." I shoved my hands in my pocket.

"Therefore, when Ash passed away, really you should be taking a fucking mirror and looking back at yourself when you speak about him or want to figure out what happened to him." That was a low blow, but the words came out before I could register and pull them back in.

Pico stared at me and cocked his head to the side in a gesture I didn't quite recognize, but the bubbling rage and anger grew from inside me like a demon desperate to claw its way out. There was no stopping it.

Call it whatever you wanted—a product of the trauma I had to endure growing up, the guilt and shame I carried over Ash's life, or my own insecurities, but the deep-rooted pain was on the surface. There was no way to tuck it back now.

"Rain, you need to watch what you are saying because words are irreversible," Mr. Ortiz stated.

"Good because I mean every damned thing that I am saying. I don't want this life. I never fucking did. I want to live in a small house, write thriller novels in the country, and live peacefully away from all of this shit." My breath was harsh, my breathing ragged, and the pain in my chest was exploding throughout my entire body.

Pico was coughing, and it took the time of my entire body regulating back to normal before I shot a look in his direction. He was cocking his head to the side, but still trying to play it cool, and while Mr. Ortiz stared at me, I attempted to look in the direction he was silently gesturing to.

And that is when I saw her. Standing in the dark shadows of the room, was Ember. I looked behind me. It was dark, and I hadn't checked my phone because I was too busy prancing around with Mr. Ortiz to even know. She had tears glossing her eyes, and I so desperately wanted to shove this motherfucker out of the way so I could run to her and ask her what was wrong.

"I'll figure out what happened with the . . . account," I stated, uncertain of how much Ember had overheard. I wanted to fill her in later, but also needed to leave calmly to avoid alerting Mr. Ortiz to our guest.

"If you'll excuse me, I need to go," I mumbled, but his hand shot up toward me, grabbing right underneath my elbow and squeezing tightly.

"You do not go until I give you permission to," he grumbled.

"No." I stood my ground this time. "I need to leave. I've done enough of hosting for the evening. I have classes that I need to finish."

"Listen to me, boy. You sit your ass down . . ."

"Or what?" I shrugged. At this point, anything was better than staying here, and this fucking asshole wasn't dumb enough to shoot me in the living room of the Den, so I didn't give a fuck what he was threatening.

"Listen," I calmly added, regaining the normalcy throughout my body, with Ember's presence grounding me further. She felt . . . safe. "To be honest, whatever plan you have concocted to figure out where the money went, the schematics are going to go over my head. Pico here is a better person to understand all of this. In fact, dare I say he probably is the better person to lead this entire fraternity, but I don't think you're quite ready to have that part of the conversation just yet."

Mr. Ortiz rose after I concluded my little speech before looking at Pico. "Is this why you gave the girl the tattoo? I know my son didn't agree with my command, but you were the one who gave it to her."

Swallowing hard, I felt ashamed. Giving Ember the tattoo wasn't my choice; this place forced me to do it. But I also knew that by doing it, she would be safe. He'd protect her. I'd protect her. She was ours in some twisted way.

"I gave it to her because it was a command my higher up demanded. I gave it to her because I couldn't imagine her being drugged and worse happening to her so at least if she was with me, then she was safe."

"You had one thing that my son lacked," he said as he reached his hand out toward mine. "And I can respect that."

"Which is?"

"Brains."

My eyes darted into the corner of the next room over Mr. Ortiz's shoulders where Ember was breaking down. She was walking in this direction. As if Pico noticed the same thing, he moved me out of the way, and I grumbled a goodbye, and Pico changed the topic, talking about matters that likely interested Mr. Ortiz more. Money.

I glided into the back of the house, where I caught Ember midstride, and I shoved my hand to her mouth, begging her to be quiet. If she said anything, it would make things worse for the both of us, so I didn't want to startle Mr. Ortiz to look in our direction.

"Come on," I whispered in her ear as I gently wiped away some of her tears.

Just as we got outside, I paused but not before shoving her up against the house.

"What do you think you were about to do?" I barked. "Run up in there and suddenly be involved in the fucking Cartel business?"

Fuck. I didn't mean to scream at her. Regret churned in my stomach, making me feel nauseous.

"I-I—"

"I'm sorry. I was . . . pissed." I admitted, interrupting her to genuinely apologize. "When I am around him, I become a different person, someone I don't recognize at all, and I hate that it happens, but it does, and I am only human."

Her delicate fingers pressed against my lips before her free hand wrapped around the small of my back, pulling me tight into her.

"Shh," she murmured. "It's okay. I get it." God, the way she spoke felt like feathers tickling the back of my spine. It was melodic and beautiful, yet safe and comforting. How a voice could create those emotions from within me was beyond my understanding.

"Rain—"

"What did you hear?" I asked, my voice softening as I gazed into her eyes, my possessive instincts flaring, a deep longing in my chest.

"Everything," she whispered, her voice trembling, her lower lip quivering. The moonlight painted her delicate features with a silvery glow, making her look ethereal in the dark woods surrounding us.

"I'm so fucking sorry, Ember." Her fingers went up behind her ear as a single tear fell.

"Y-you did this?"

"Yes." I would not start lying.

"Why?"

"They already had given you medicine to make you tired and pass out. It wasn't a choice I had. Ash didn't want to do it, but we knew without being marked you had a bigger target on your back especially when you went back to Dansport. I did it because you needed it and I was trying to do the right thing."

She shook her head. "I-I cannot believe it. I always thought Ash did."

"No. I was the one with the tattoo machine. I did it because he couldn't. He gave the directive."

"Why didn't he ever tell me this?"

I shrugged because I had no idea. "The only reason I can think of is to protect me. He wanted us to get along. We were both so important to him."

I paused as she processed the information she'd learned. "I'm so fucking sorry, Ember."

My raspy tone was full of the pain and guilt I held onto.

"Our parents..." She trailed off.

"I know but we are not our parents. We do not live by their rules. We are not history repeating itself."

She nodded. "No," she whispered softly. "We are not."

I pulled her closer, unable to resist the warmth of her body pressed against mine, my heart racing at her softness against the rugged backdrop of the forest. The ancient trees towered around us, their branches creating a canopy of secrets.

"Come with me," I said with urgency, our connection palpable, the moonlight casting enchanting shadows on her face. I looked up at the stars, and it felt as if some of them were twinkling down at me.

*Good one, brother.* In some alternate universe, this was Ash's permission, all the assurance I needed to take Ember there.

"Where are we going?"

"A place that is special to me," I said as I handed her a sleek, blacked-out helmet, its matte finish seen faintly in the night. Without hesitation, she mounted the bike, her arms wrapping around me, her body fitting perfectly against mine. It surprised me how much I loved holding her close, the possessiveness bubbling within me, a fire I couldn't contain. I pulled out of the driveway without a second glance at the house because I had everything I could ever want right here.

# EMBER

I didn't know what came over me, but when I heard Rain, an inexplicable urge surged within me. I longed to stride up to him and assure him everything was all right. Forgiving him tugged at me, but I also yearned for him to display a bit of humility. There was something unmistakable between us—something substantial and distinct from what I'd experienced before. It felt steady and grounded, lacking the usual whirlwind of emotions. Our connection was built on mutual respect.

If I had to describe it to someone, I'd say my love with Ash had been immediate and passionate. I loved Ash wholeheartedly, but what I had with Rain was growing. It felt like we were constructing a foundation, as though we were nurturing the roots of a flourishing tree. I wanted to explore where these roots would lead us, to witness the beautiful blossoms they might bear. Assuring that our connection wasn't merely a result of the trauma we'd both endured was crucial. I longed to delve deeper into each other's lives, to uncover our shared interests and differences before I could fully commit.

However, as I entered the room and saw Rain standing up to Mr. Ortiz, I realized he was venturing into forbidden territory. You never spoke disrespectfully to the boss. Yet, in that moment, my curiosity for him deepened. I hungered to unravel the intricate layers of our emotions.

I closed my eyes, my head resting on Rain's back as he guided me through the woods. Partially because I was terrified of this stupid motorcycle, but also because it felt . . . secure.

As I drifted off into a nice lull, we pulled up to a little portion of the woods where an ATV was parked behind a large tree trunk.

Rain pulled the bike behind the tree before helping me off.

"Wait . . . you got me into this death trap but now you're saying I have to go into that one?" I pointed to the ATV, and Rain only chuckled.

"Come on, mi pareja. I will even let you drive." He tossed me the keys, and I caught them midair.

"How will I know what or where I'm driving to?" I asked.

"I'll guide you." He answered simply, which only piqued my curiosity more.

Fuck it. Tis the season for change, I may as well give this thing a try. I mounted the ATV, and Rain helped turn it on for me. He got on behind me and leaned so his chest was pressed tightly against my back.

Languidly, he placed his fingers atop mine and rested his head against the shell of my ear.

"Drive," he demanded, and the way he spoke the word slowly, yet with a hint of a command to it, sent a shiver through my entire body. I swallowed, and I swore the cold air permeated into my lungs as I peeled out of the small clearing and drove forward.

I wouldn't lie, this was much harder than it initially looked, because I had to dodge massive pine trees, and the deeper we got, the closer together we became.

"You are doing so good, mi pareja." Rain praised as his hands did most of the work, navigating us through the forest.

"We are close now," he whispered, and sure enough, a small light illuminated the porch of the world's tiniest little cabin.

"Lift up on the brake, let go of the accelerator so we can slow down," Rain instructed.

I did, and we came to a halt. It was far darker and cooler in this part of the forest, but the nervousness I felt through my body wasn't just because we were in the forest.

"What is this place?" I asked, my breath catching in my throat.

"My hunting cabin," he replied, and suddenly, everything fell into place. This was the spot where Ash was supposed to spend the night during last year's bonfire.

"This is yours?" I asked, and he confirmed it with a nod.

"I bought it when I was a freshman, using some money my . . . dad had given me." He paused briefly, and I sensed a deeper story there. "I needed a getaway from the Den, so I, along with a few guys, pretended it was a hideout for everyone. We even installed a septic tank in the back for plumbing and running water. And here it is."

I gazed around in wonder. The cabin exuded a charming and rustic aura amid the towering pines. It was a humble abode, yet the fact Rain had constructed it himself made it even more endearing.

"It's incredible," I murmured, my admiration evident as I approached the front door.

Rain walked in front of me and unlocked the door.

"How are the lights on already?" I asked.

"I was here yesterday." Then he pushed the door open so I could see what was inside. We stepped in, and I was pleasantly surprised at the vintage and quaint little cabin. It was literally one room with a small bathroom, but there was a small full-sized bed in the corner, two reading chairs in the other corner, and a small kitchenette.

"Wait, I love this." I exclaimed, surprising Rain and myself.

"I have some of my rarest books here." He motioned over to the built-in bookshelf above the chair, and I was shocked when I thumbed through some of the copies.

"Holy shit." He had rare first editions of Agatha Christie, Stephen King, and some other authors I didn't recognize because I liked reading about faeries ramming into each other.

"Cool, yeah?"

I paused in the center of the room. "Why'd you bring me here?" I asked, but my voice sounded softer than usual and much more timid, so much it almost reminded me of the old Ember.

He shoved his hands in his pocket, and in this light, I saw him for who he really was. He wasn't the born leader that Ash was. He wasn't the villain in the story everyone was demanding he become.

I took a slow step toward him before he could respond. "You're kinda cute when you geek out over books."

He chuckled, running his hand through his hair and avoiding eye contact with me. "I guess. I know our book tastes are different, but I've always been obsessed with horror and becoming published as a writer is really a dream of mine."

He paused momentarily. "Before the accident, and now everything's a mess."

"But is it?" He cocked his head. "From what I overheard, give it all up. You have your own money from your dad. Mr. Ortiz will let you out—"

"No, he won't, Ember, not until I tell him where the money went."

The part of the conversation I'd overheard and knew immediately where the lump of cash was.

"It's in Dansport in my house." Rain nodded.

"It's in my bank account. The millions of dollars that were suddenly wired into my account when I was . . . mourning." Another silent nod.

"The night he died, I put it all in your name. I'd gotten the house for myself but in the moment, it made more sense that you'd need it. When you were sleeping, I put it all into the house."

I-I thought Ash had gotten me the house. I could feel my chest cleave into two.

"I don't need that money," I whispered, and then Rain reached inside the backpack he had brought and pulled a document out.

"I know you don't need it, but it's yours," he whispered, handing me the paper labeled "Last Will and Testament."

I scanned it, not understanding most of the legal jargon until Rain came over and pointed to a highlighted section.

"Ember Solis is the designated beneficiary of the complete allocation of my estate, held within an offshore account domiciled in Switzerland, specifically identified by the account number: 08429. It is hereby affirmed that she is the exclusive recipient of the aforementioned inheritance."

I paused, realizing what I had just read. He planned this. He knew this would happen, so there was no way someone else could have pushed him, because he wouldn't have had time to—

"I know," Rain whispered as if he was reading my thoughts.

"I-I found his phone." I pulled it from my purse, and while showing him, it turned on straight to the photo of the two of us together.

Rain winced.

"Did you . . . Were there . . ." He paused, turning away from me. His hands ran through his hair, and I came behind him and wrapped my arms around his thick chest. I laid my head against his back between his broad shoulders.

"I heard your voicemails. All of them." My voice was nothing more than a hushed whisper.

He grabbed my fingers with one hand, but didn't turn around.

"Did you find anything else?"

I could barely say the next sentence, but I swallowed, managing to get the words out. "He sent me a text message that never went through saying he loved me."

"Can you turn around?" I asked.

He slowly moved me so that his chest was pressed against mine.

"I didn't realize you felt that way about me," I whispered. "I didn't realize you felt that way about all of this." I gestured around the little cabin, remembering his confession about how he wanted to live in the tranquility out in the countryside.

"I hate this. I hated watching how it untangled the one person I loved, Ember. Because I loved him, too." He stared at the photo in my hand.

"Can I take this with me? I have an IT guy who works for me, not the Cartel. He can see if there are any other pieces I can untangle." I handed it over to him.

"Did you send yourself what you needed from it?"

"Yes." I'd sent screenshots and voice recordings that Ash left me and that I'd left him, too.

"Are you okay? Finding this?" Rain paused and laughed for a second. "I can't believe you actually found it and it works. Pretty fucking wild with all the weather all this time."

"I understand," I replied, sharing a chuckle of disbelief. "Rain, I need you to stay on the topic."

"About what, Ember?" He took my hand and led me to one of the cozy reading chairs in the corner. Then he headed to the kitchenette and retrieved two pineapple-flavored seltzers from the small fridge.

"You like these?" I asked.

"No." He shrugged and settled into the chair beside me. "But you do."

I narrowed my eyes at him, recognizing that we needed to address the looming feelings between us. Rain always seemed to provide the answers I required, so his avoidance of the topic was telling.

"We really need to have this conversation," I insisted. "We can't keep avoiding it like we have been."

He let out a heavy sigh. "Ember, I just don't know where to begin. It's . . . complicated." He ran his hand through his hair before he popped the top of his seltzer and took a long pull.

"I want to get to know you. Aside from your love of books, what makes Rain . . . well, Rain?"

He smiled, then paused, the corners of his mouth twisting into a frown. "I don't know, and I think that's the problem with everything. I have spent most of my childhood and then my adult life living for Ash and making sure he was protected and at peace at home and loved. That his death has ripped a hole through the atmosphere. I don't know how to fill it."

I leaped out of the chair and slid onto his lap onto the chair he was now sitting, across from me. His hands pressed firmly on the curves of my hips, and our bodies melded together like we always belonged to each other—like it was the perfect puzzle piece fit.

"Start with something small," I murmured, reaching up to play with the soft stubble growing on his chin. "Like, what is your favorite color?" I murmured.

"Why are you like this?" he asked quietly.

"Like what?"

"So . . . caring? Why does it matter to you so much, anyway? You'll always be in love with him."

The pang in my chest grew to a degree so insurmountable I didn't have the words to say.

"I think that's what I learned this last month though," I murmured right into the shell of his ear. "I loved Ash. I will always love him, but I think there is space in my heart to move forward with the life I am living now."

I dropped my voice even lower and then pulled away so that my hand was still on his face, and our eyes locked.

"I cannot imagine my days without you in them either, Rain. Even after all of this goes down, I don't want to lose you," I said, biting my lip. "But I want to figure out what happened that night. It's important to me."

"So do I."

"And I don't want to rush or label whatever this is right now. I don't think I'm ready for that because that would mean involving the others, the initiation—"

"No," he growled. "That will never be a thing between us." Rain pulled my waist tighter to him.

"Mine," he whispered in my ear. "You're just simply . . . mine."

He caressed my cheeks and I melted into his touch. "I like the color blue."

I pulled back, the corners of my lips twisting into a smile. "Blue? I would've pegged you for a depressive gray."

He chuckled. "No, we have more than enough of that color in Isles. Now it's my turn."

"Alright." His fingers continued to trace the contours of my face.

"What do you envision yourself doing after graduation?" he inquired. "If you could choose anything."

"I would write his story, our story, so it would be forever memorialized," I replied, hesitating slightly after his recent confession about wanting me to be his and our mutual honesty about our feelings.

His hand never stopped moving on my face, even when I spoke of Ash. He pulled my head so I was leaning to the side, and whispered in my ear, "I think you should do that."

"I wish," I commented. "I know my dad has some plan for me, to marry me off to one of his buddies. We never really talked about it, but it was always just assumed."

A low growl could be heard throughout the room.

"I've been through so much, Rain," I whispered. "I guess all I want now is to live quietly in the countryside." I paused.

"Maybe we could be neighbors in our future life." I chuckled before his warm tanned hands swiped the hair off my forehead.

"What you've been through in life wrote your story. It made you stronger," he added, but I only chuffed because that's what I'd read constantly, but it wasn't true.

"No," I demanded, shifting so I was still on his lap but now my eyes fixated on  him. "What I've been through in my life nearly wrecked me. It gave me nightmares. It stole my true identity. It made me feel deeply alone and a pain that nearly wrecked me." He stared back at me with his deep-blue eyes.

"I was handed something that I didn't ask for. In fact, I was desperate to live a life that was different from my parents, from Walsh's, from Ash's, even now, but it's the trauma that helped me learn to live. It was in this shit that I trudged through where I learned so much about myself—my strength, my power, and the ability to overcome pain."

A cleansing breath escaped my lips as I paused, gazing through the room's dimly lit expanse and out into the densely wooded forest beyond the windows. "So, please don't tell me that I'm stronger because of the hardships I've had to endure in this life. No, I made it through all of this because I unearthed my inner strength I had all along."

There was an eerily quiet that passed between us before his fingers crept up to my lips. A shiver passed through my spine as his fingers traced the outline of my lips.

"The words that come out of this mouth are like being wrapped up with a good book on a cold day. You know that feeling?" I thought my heart was about to explode with how fast it was beating. Unable to  string together a complete sentence, I just nodded.

"Ember?" he rasped as he brought my forehead down onto his, his thumb still circling my mouth.

"Yeah?" I could hardly talk between my heart racing a mile a minute and my lungs slowly losing breath.

"I need to kiss you, but I am trying to be respectful of your boundaries." His finger parted my mouth, and I slowly bit down as I shifted on his lap. He was very . . . hard. His free hand wrapped around the back of my neck.

"Ugh," he groaned, pressing our foreheads together.

In the cocoon of our shared silence, I could practically hear the thunderous rhythm of my heartbeat. His thumb continued its mesmerizing exploration of my lips, a slow, deliberate caress that sent shivers through my body. I couldn't help but nibble softly, aching for more, as a pool of desire welled inside my core, its intensity growing with each passing second.

His strong hands gripped me by my hair, pulling me back with a confidence that exposed the vulnerable expanse of my neck. The heat of his breath, a warm whisper, teased its way up from my chin, each languid movement feeling like an exquisite form of torture. His fingers, once tenderly tracing my plush lips, now held my chin with possessive intent, guiding me down until our mouths hovered atop each other. The air around us seemed to crackle with electric tension, our locked gazes revealing a profound connection neither of us could deny.

Another pause.

"Fuck it."

In that fraction of a moment, his lips seized mine, igniting a blaze of longing that consumed every ounce of resistance. His mouth, warm and full, felt like a seamless fit, as if it had been crafted specifically to meld with mine. Yet it wasn't just the sensation of his lips against mine that had me surrendering so completely, but the way he moved, each calculated stroke and flick of his tongue sent me spiraling into a heady abyss of need. His assertiveness, a stark departure from his usually reserved demeanor, commanded my surrender, skillfully parting my lips and leading me deeper into the kiss.

"Like everything I've dreamed of," he murmured between pants. I could only respond by letting out the smallest moan.

"Do that again and I might fucking come in my pants, mi pareja."

I shifted again so I was straddling him and my knees were tucked in the cushion of the oversized reading chair. We were the same height from this position, but his mouth never left mine. I only responded by moving my hips in slow circles.

"Fuck." He was the one moaning now as his hands dropped from my face and slowly caressed the sides of my body. "Every curve."

His fingers delicately circled my tits as they heaved in my shirt. I had leggings and an oversized shirt on, but the heat between our bodies made me feel like I was sitting in a thousand-degree sauna and I needed to strip.

"Every inch." He leaned up to whisper into the shell of my ear.

"Every dip," he mused as his hands trailed toward my hips and landed on the curve above my ass.

"You are my perfection." His lips traced mine as his tongue found its way back into my mouth. My hands cupped his face as if I didn't want him to disappear. I didn't want this kiss to stop.

I was wrapped up in every moment of it. The way his mouth was fucking mine with a fevered heat that only intensified my own.

"Are you getting wet for me, Em?" he murmured.

"Mm-hm." Apparently I'd lost the ability to speak a coherent sentence.

"Use your mouth, Ember. Tell me, if I reach down here"—he tugged at the waistband of the leggings—"will I find your wet little cunt just waiting for me?"

"Mmmm" was the only sound I could make.

"Use your breathtaking words, Em." His finger traced my navel, and then he opened my leggings, shifting so his hand rested against the top of my lace boy shorts.

"Yes. I'm soaking," I cried with a need so heavy. "Please."

It had been so long since anyone had touched me like this. The desire my body harbored for this man was insatiable. It was a primal attraction, and I found myself intensely drawn to every facet of his being.

"Stand up," he said as he lifted me off him. I could barely hold myself up, as my knees were wobbly. It was as if his stance somehow grew larger in the last hour. "Take them off."

My eyes followed his as he zeroed in on my pants. I shimmied out of them without thinking about it.

He watched as I stood there with no pants, my shirt hitting right above the curve of my ass.

"What?" I asked as he stood there and shoved his hands in his pocket, taking a half step backward.

"I-I'm just admiring the view," he growled.

"Stop." The flush of my cheeks burned.

I attempted to push down my shirt when he reached out and grabbed my wrist.

"No. Nobody, including you, touches what is now mine."

I was a fucking puddle and desperate for more of him. I needed his touch against my throbbing cunt so desperately I would do anything.

"Take off your underwear, Em," he demanded, and I obliged. His hand lifted the hem of my shirt, and he pointed over toward the bed.

"Walk to the edge of the bed. Turn around, face the wall, and hold the frame." The mattress was perched atop an antique spiral frame, boasting a quartet of intricately designed spirals that curved gracefully. He gestured for me to hold onto the lower part of the bed.

I approached the bed, bending at the waist to reach the spirals, my fingers extending to grasp them.

"Spread your legs." I obliged as his fingers made their way to my needy little cunt, desperate for more of his touch. He shoved two of his fingers inside before adding a third.

"Oh fuck." I moaned so loudly I was convinced the animals in the forest would hear us.

His fingers were fucking me, and I bounced on them, matching his movements with my own. We were in sync with each other as his other hand caressed the cheek of my ass.

"So fucking beautiful," he growled. I turned and his hand jerked his freed cock with frantic movements. Its size enamored me as it pulsated. It was a fucking . . . dinosaur, and the thought of it coming near my cunt sent a thrill of unease and curiosity down my spine.

"Turn around," he demanded as he drove his three fingers into my core, using his thumb to flick at the top of my clit, sending me in a spiral.

"I'm not going to last." I moaned as his strokes picked up in pace. It was embarrassing how quickly I would come all over his fingers, but I hadn't been touched by anyone in almost a year, including by my own fingers, so I was so close to sinking into a deep oblivion.

More flicking.

More wetness pooled around me as he stretched me until I was enduring pain and pleasure. My hands could barely grasp the frame, as I thrust onto his hands and exploded atop of him.

"Oh my god." I moaned, sinking deeper into my orgasm, riding out the wave as I went slack, his hands left my now very satiated cunt before I finally turned around.

His cock was still hard and there were no signs of cum anywhere on his hands, my body, or the ground, so I parted my lips and dropped to my knees.

"It's only fair?" I murmured in what came out sounding more like a question. A smirk danced across his face as he took a few steps toward me, opening my jaw with his hands. His pleasuring hand rubbed my cum over his cock.

"Open wide, Em," he demanded. "It's going to hurt so you need to go really slow."

His instructions sent an electric shock to my core, and my desperate little pussy was ready for round two. *Calm down.*

I opened my jaw, relaxing the back of my mouth as much as I could.

"I'm going to go slow."

I nodded as I flicked the tip of his massive cock with my tongue, licking the combination of my wet pussy and his pre-cum off and swallowing it down whole.

"I love the taste of us." I moaned as he pressed his cock deeper into my mouth, and I gagged.

"Holy fuck," I mumbled through a mouthful of dick. "So big."

Rain let out a chuckle and pressed farther into me. He was so fucking big and kept hitting the back of my throat, so I tried to open my mouth, allowing him in deeper.

"You are doing so well taking me in." He praised as my free hand reached up to help guide him in.

Once he was finally in, he whispered, "Now, very slowly go back and forth. Don't try to go too fast at first."

I did as he instructed and slowly sucked on him, using my free hand to stroke the parts my mouth couldn't get off.

"Yes, Em. Your mouth was made for me." Fuck me. His possessiveness was all I could have ever wanted.

"Such a good girl," he rasped, and grabbed my neck so our gazes connected but only momentarily before he looked up and slammed his cock inside my mouth.

Alternating between sucking and flicking my tongue around, I reveled in taking him in, then he let out a tormented wail as warm heat exploded in my mouth. He grasped the edge of my chin as he pulled out.

"Swallow" was all said, and with an audible gulp, I obliged.

He walked through the little door in the corner where the bathroom was, and before he shut it, he glanced back where I was still on my knees, my back against the spindles of the frame of the bed.

"Get up. Get dressed."

The door slammed shut . . . And my heart with it.

# RAIN

The guilt hit me like a tidal wave, overwhelming and crushing. I couldn't bear to meet her gaze, fearing that her eyes would expose the lies I'd been telling myself.

I had conjured the idea that she would be mine, and now she stood before me, well, knelt before me, offering herself, but I couldn't follow through. All I felt was a searing shame as her eyes lit up with anticipation when she took me into her mouth so perfectly, only to watch that spark fade as I walked away after coming in her.

If I weren't so consumed by my own self-loathing, I would have been disgusted with myself, too.

"Fuck," I yelled, aware she was just on the other side of the door, hearing every word.

I grabbed some water and splashed it on my face and cock in a futile attempt to clean up the cum still dripping down my thigh. Perhaps wiping away the physical evidence would erase the pain carving into my heart.

There was a faint rap at the door, followed by her gentle voice. "Are you okay, Rain?" I remained silent, convinced she shouldn't be the one asking about my well-being. I needed to be strong in this situation, to find the courage to apologize for being a complete asshole.

Her concern only intensified the guilt gnawing at me.

"You don't have to talk to me, but just know that—" I opened the door and found her standing there wearing that oversized shirt that concealed her curves yet heightened her mysterious allure.

"I am fine," I demanded, pushing past her to go get my pants. Her steps tip-toed against the floor as she followed me, and suddenly, I was regretting bringing her here.

"Talk to me?" she asked, and I glanced over my shoulder before shaking my head as I pulled my pants up.

"I'll be waiting outside," I whispered. I could barely string words together in my own head, so saying them aloud took me by surprise.

I rushed out of the small cabin, as the walls felt like they were closing in on me.

Once outside, the same shame dripped slowly back into my veins. In the same very veins that shared the love I had for him. I was tangled in a web of deceit . . . or at least that's how it felt, and my lungs felt so fucking tight. Why was the air so cold up here?

I couldn't take a deep breath as I hobbled down to where the ATV was parked. Fuck. I grabbed at my chest and pounded on it as if that would will it to take a deep breath. So many thoughts swirled in my head.

*You are a liar.*

*You betrayed him.*

*You will never be enough for her.*

Why couldn't I breathe?

Clutching my heart, I looked up in the sky and kept tripping over my feet. I felt like I was drunk, but hadn't had anything but the fucking seltzer earlier. What was happening?

"Rain?" a cautious voice mumbled through the droning of the ringing now playing in my ears.

"Rain?" the voice said again, and I turned to look at who it was, but fell to the ground. The footsteps quickened toward me, but I couldn't get over what was happening. My vision was blurry . . .

"M-my chest . . ." Then the world went blank.

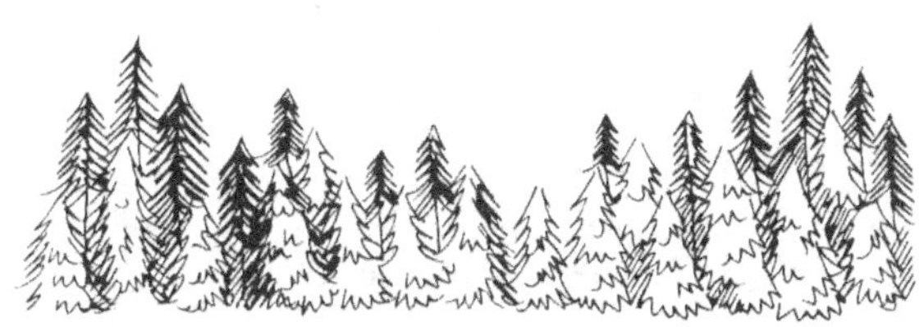

The next morning, I woke up and stretched to my side. My head was pounding as I realized I was in my own bed in my room at the Den.

"What the fuck?" I could barely remember what happened yesterday, besides passing out in front of the cabin.

Pulling the covers off, I jumped out of bed, grabbed my phone charging next to me, then my black backpack I'd brought to the cabin.

There were a slew of texts from Ember.

Em:

> You probably won't remember this but just talk to Pico.

Em:

> I am worried about you. Text me when you wake up.

Em:

> Please don't shut me out.

"Shit," I groaned as I threw on a pair of gray sweats and a shirt, heading toward Pico's room a few doors down from mine.

I rapped slowly in case he had Marissa over. Why they chose to not go to her apartment instead of the frat house was beyond me.

The door opened, and an exhausted-looking Pico dressed in only a hoodie and sweat shorts looked me up and down before giving me a smirk.

"Your ass is heavy, dragging you through the fucking woods and back here." He slung his arm over my shoulder and then walked me down the stairs toward the kitchen table. "Glad to see you're up. Let's get a coffee and chat."

I nodded, and as we got downstairs, he handed me a hot cup of coffee, then we sat at the dining room table. It was Monday, so most of the guys were in class already.

"How'd the rest of the conversation with Mr. Ortiz go?"

"He's a fucking dick. He also knows Ember has the cash somehow, but isn't admitting he does." I nodded, not caring how this conversation went but more so wanting to fill in the pieces of what happened last night.

As Pico took a big gulp of the hot coffee, I asked him to fill in the missing pieces.

"Ember caught you, and we think you were having a panic attack. You kept saying that your chest and your heart felt like it was constricting." I was so fucking embarrassed after we did what we did, but the insurmountable shame I felt in this moment was even worse. "She called me in a tizzy. I managed to get you onto the ATV, then Ember drove you here in my car and we called the doctor who said everything checked out in terms of your heart. It was probably a panic attack." He leaned back in the wooden chair and then looked up at me.

I dropped my gaze to my hands gripping the mug so tightly to prevent them from shaking.

"I-I- don't know what to say." I glanced back up at him. "Thank you."

"Do you want to talk about what happened?" It was a question he'd posed countless times in the past eight months. "I lost a friend, too. I know it's different, but if it helps, I miss and think of him every damn day."

"What makes you think it was about Ash?" I gritted my teeth, feeling a surge of irritation coursing through me.

"Well, wasn't it?"

I sighed. I could either deflect Pico's attempts to connect or open up to someone who had tried to be a friend. I chose the latter and nodded before taking a long sip from my mug.

"We hooked up," I said, urging back the tears welling in my eyes.

Pico offered a simple, encouraging "Hmmm," urging me to continue.

"I called her mine. She was incredible, but I couldn't look her in the eyes. I don't know, it felt so close and so . . ."

"Hard," Pico finished for me, and I nodded. "I get it. She was your brother's, but now she's yours."

"Yeah," I replied, finding solace in the fact someone understood my turmoil.

"But your brother isn't here anymore. He left us. She is yours, Rain. You should have seen her last night. She thought she was going to lose you, too, and she was panicking," Pico added, turning his gaze to a corner of the room.

"For hours, she paced back and forth while Marissa tried to calm her down or at least make an attempt. She's really something special. The whole thing made her feel terrible, and you're an asshole for telling her she was yours, hooking up with her, and not even being able to look her in the eyes."

Tears fell onto my cheeks before I even realized I was crying. Growing up with Mr. Ortiz in the Cartel had ingrained in me that *real men* weren't supposed to cry or show emotion, as if it made us less of a human.

"Don't do that," Pico mumbled. "You should feel sad about all of this. Maybe letting these feelings out will actually help you."

I swallowed hard. "I didn't mean to scare you. I didn't mean to make her feel like just a means to an end, because she deserves so much more than that. She texted me last night, worried."

"She does. You need to talk to her. I think both of you are harboring secrets, and it's about time you shared them."

He paused for a moment, then stood and walked over to me, kneeling next to the chair I was in. "I'll handle the meetings here. I actually like this stuff." He gestured around. "You go finish school and figure things out with Ash, and then sort things out with Ember."

I nodded. "Thank you."

"I'll keep Mr. Ortiz at bay, but this needs to be resolved by the spring bonfire. I can't hold him off any longer," he added.

I nodded again. "Go get dressed and go to class or something." I laughed, grabbing him by the shoulders as I got up.

"Thank you," I whispered, giving him a hug. He embraced me tightly before stepping back.

"Anytime, man." Pico nodded.

"Besides, I agree with you. I think if we finally took the time to sit down and use Ember's relationship with her dad, we could become a more formidable force. This ridiculous feud has done nothing but cost both sides lives," Pico added before taking a sip of his coffee. He started back upstairs, leaving me alone with my thoughts in the dining room.

I pulled out my phone and texted Ember back.



Three dots alerted me she was texting back.

Ember:

You really want to wait a week? Fine. I was just really fucking worried about you.

Me:

You shouldn't have been. I was an asshole.

Ember:

. . .

Ember:

I don't care about any of that. I was just worried about you.

Me:

I have midterms this week. Please give me until after class?

Ember:

K.

Whenever a girl types the word 'k,' I assume that she is horribly upset, so I knew Ember was pissed, but I needed this week. I needed to manage my thoughts because the shame and guilt I carried needed to find a new home. The panic attack I'd had last night was enough, and I didn't want to go back to that place.

I sighed, grabbed my bag, and headed to the library to study. I just needed to get my thoughts straight . . . right?

# EMBER

I was genuinely trying to be understanding, but an entire week had passed without hearing so much as a single text from the guy I had hooked up with over the weekend, and it felt awful. The memory of our passionate encounter still lingered in my mind, yet the silence that followed it was deafening. That night, he couldn't look me in the eyes and was behaving like a total jerk, which was out of character for him. The confusion and hurt I felt were festering, and I was genuinely pissed off. He should have spent the whole week groveling for my forgiveness, but instead, he withdrew, much like he did when Ash passed away.

The amount of guilt coursing through me after that night we shared was insurmountable. Ash was my boyfriend who . . . passed away, and I slept with his best friend. When Rain left, it only accentuated my thoughts that I was doing something wrong—we were wrong together. It was the guilt in those quiet moments that pushed me over the ledge. Coupled with his silence, I was utterly alone, experiencing a flood of emotions reminiscent of the aftermath of Ash's death, where I felt abandoned by everyone.

Yet, when he had his panic attack, I thought I was going to lose him. I was terrified. He was complaining of his heart hurting, but was incoherent when I tried getting an answer from him. I called Pico and Marissa out of desperation, and thankfully, Pico knew exactly where we were.

When the doctor mentioned that it was a stress-induced panic attack, I connected the pieces easily. He couldn't look me in the eye because of Ash. He was an asshole to me because he was unable to manage his emotions in that moment. It didn't make what he did or how he reacted okay, but I knew where he was coming from. I'd had my fair share of panic attacks. Yet, instead of using his words and talking about his feelings, he retreated.

Walking down the stark and eerie basement toward our photography class that week, I hoped beyond hope that we'd be dismissed early because I had zero desire to be in the same room as him. Even though he told me he wanted to talk after class today, I was regretting even coming. As each day passed and the silence got louder, my irritation and pain deepened. Every scenario of why he hadn't reached out yet played through my mind, stressing me out.

I entered the class late, my heart pounding with a mix of frustration and longing, hoping to avoid sitting next to him. However, as I walked in and apologized to the teacher, the only available seat was next to Rain. He removed his backpack from the empty seat, and I reluctantly took it, a surge of complicated emotions swirling through me.

Leaning toward me, he whispered, "Can't escape me today, mi pareja," wearing a smirk that I desperately wanted to wipe off. How could he come here and act like everything was normal while my heart ached with unresolved feelings and questions left hanging in the air.

I snapped a look in his direction, and he only laughed.

Evie coughed. "Thank you for showing up, Ember, but if the two lovebirds can work out whatever they need to after class, that would be ideal." My cheeks went red. Next to me, a low chuckle sounded, which only infuriated me.

"I got all of your preliminary drafts on what really scares you guys, but I was overall pretty disappointed," Evie said as she propped herself up. "I really want us to now dive deeper into what scares you. Instead of thinking at surface level, I want you to imagine you are knowingly at the end of your days, what would scare you the most?"

Rain reached over and caressed the small of my back. If that statement didn't hit home, I'm not sure what else would.

"Let's rearrange our desks so we are in a circle together, please." Most of the class moved effortlessly, but as I shifted my desk, Rain's gaze never left my eyes.

"Sorry, Evie, but respectfully, what does this have to do with photography?" Rain asked.

Evie sat atop her desk, facing us as I stared at some of the ceiling lights flickering above us. If I stared at them long enough, maybe I'd blink and class would be over.

"Because photography is an art dedicated to tickle the creative part of your brain. I think in order to tap into that part, it's imperative you look deep within yourself. You have to really *feel* to get the effect of the art."

Just. Keep. Staring. No thinking.

"Okay, so for this objective, I need everyone to go around and share one thing that scares them the most."

This was cruel and unusual punishment. What did I deserve to have this happen? I refused to stop staring at the lights, but Rain's gaze burned a hole through the back of my head.

I swallowed, hoping that since I was in the middle, class would end before it got to me and I wouldn't have to share.

"Alright, we are going to start with the lovebirds in the middle. Rain, why don't you go ahead and start us off?"

I snapped my gaze to his as the panic inside of me increased.

*It's okay,* he mouthed before turning his attention to the center of the room. He must've been panicking too.

"Go ahead, Rain."

His chest rose once before the words came. "I am most scared of failure."

"Dive deeper into that," Evie encouraged.

"I'm terrified of failing the one person who truly deserves better, of becoming someone I never wanted to be and hurting them in the process," Rain confessed, his voice quivering with a mix of anguish and fear.

*Please*, I silently begged, *don't let the tears start now.*

"I want to be strong, but it feels like I'm stumbling, failing," Rain continued, and I could not hold back the tears anymore. "I just wish I could show them that I deserve even a fraction of their heart. It would be an honor to have just a small part written into their story."

The tears flowed freely, and I couldn't stop them.

"I'm scared of living a life filled with constant lies with this person," he admitted, his voice choked with emotion. "We both hold back so much, especially our feelings for each other. We hide behind the lies about moving on from last year, when in reality, I'd give anything for just one more moment with her—er, I mean, them."

His gaze never left mine as he gently wiped away the tears that fell onto my cheeks. In that vulnerable moment, he whispered, "I'm so sorry," and the three words felt like a balm to my aching heart.

I nodded because I couldn't talk, especially not in front of the entire class. There was a resounding applause, and my attention turned toward Evie giving Rain a standing ovation.

"Bravo," she exclaimed. "That is the type of vulnerability I was hoping for."

She paused. "It is only fair the second part of the love entanglement to go second, although, a hard act to follow."

I pointed to myself, and she nodded eagerly. On the inside, I wanted to fucking melt away. I could very well lie my way out of this.

"You don't have to do this," he whispered, and I simply offered a twist of the corners of my lips. I didn't have to, but I owed him something—both of them.

I swallowed hard, my gaze sweeping across the room, where curious eyes were fixed on the two of us. Most probably knew who I was, or at least had some inkling.

"I'm terrified of letting myself fall in love again, only to have it cruelly ripped away," I began, my voice trembling, and tears welled up at the corners of my eyes.

"I-I—" I took a shuddering breath, my focus unwavering on Rain, who seemed eager to whisk me out of that room, but I couldn't let him. "I'm afraid of death and love simultaneously, not concurrently. Terrified that my heart is capable of loving two people in one lifetime. How am I supposed to reconcile the idea that the person I loved so deeply and intensely would be okay with the person I love, er, like, now so comfortably and protectively?"

My chest tightened, and I struggled to get the words out, each one a heavy burden. I locked my gaze onto Rain, determined not to falter.

"I've loved so many people who've just abandoned me," I continued, my voice wavering. "My mother died when I was young. My boyfriend . . . he . . ." It was the first time I'd uttered the word death aloud.

"Ember," Rain whispered, his voice laced with sympathy. "It's okay." I shook my head because nothing about it was okay. I wasn't okay.

"When he died, I thought my world had crumbled. I blamed myself for the illness that consumed his mind, for his not getting help. He fought an inner battle and lost, yet selfishly, I continued to blame myself for his death, just as everyone else on this campus did." I scanned the room, noticing a few tear-filled eyes. "After his . . . death, I thought that would be the end of the pain I'd have to endure, but it was far from over."

I paused there, realizing that some parts of my life were too raw, too exposed to share in a classroom. None of this was school-appropriate, but here we were.

"So, part of me is scared to open my heart again, to risk another person leaving," I admitted, gaining momentum. "In this lifetime, I just want to know that my heart can love two people because . . . whether I want it or not, I think . . . I think I might be falling in love again." My voice barely rose above a whisper as I finished speaking. I blinked back a few tears, then hastily grabbed my bag before anyone could respond and bolted out of the class.

I ran.

My bag moved up and down with every pounding step I took on the cold tile of the basement.

I ran up the steps and pushed the door open and was greeted by the cool drops of rain as I looked up into the gray abyss above me. His presence was felt before I heard the shuffle of his steps.

"Em," he croaked, but I continued to look up and let the rain droplets hit me.

"Don't come a step closer," I told him when I finally turned around, and he stood there on the sidewalk. "Your speech in that classroom doesn't make up for the fact you said some really mean shit to me last weekend and then ignored me."

"No, it doesn't," he added. "In fact, it probably makes it worse."

"Yup." I rolled my eyes. "Before your attack, you were still planning on leaving me. You were the one running away."

"What can I do? To make it up to you?"

"Start by not remembering anything you heard in that classroom." He shook his head.

"That is going to be hard to do because—"

"Then I have to go." I folded my arms across my chest and walked over to where my car was parked.

"I see you're still driving . . . *my car*." I turned around and stuck my tongue out at him, which only produced a chuckle. "Gimme the keys."

"Why?" I demanded.

"I am taking you on a trip." I shook my head and narrowed my eyes.

Rain walked over to the other side of the curb where a black vehicle had pulled up. The driver's side door rolled down, and Santiago started to hand Rain a bag when I ran over there.

"You are in on this, too?" I looked between them. "No."

I stomped on the sidewalk. "What if I am unsafe wherever he is taking me?" Santiago laughed now.

"Mija, you will be okay. I know where you are going. It's safe . . . trust me, no one wants to visit that place." Rain only punched Santiago in the arm.

"Who packed my underwear? Did you rifle through my stuff?" I grumbled as I opened the bag and realized everything was meticulously packed, including a few sets of sweaters, pants, jeans, and a dress.

"Marissa helped. I don't touch that stuff, out of my job description." Santiago gave me a wink, and then Rain looked between the two of us before he backed away, slinging my bag over his shoulders. I shot him a venomous look.

"Be nice. He is trying to make up for what happened last weekend." I'd told Santiago what happened because I needed someone to help Pico carry Rain into the house.

"Blindsiding me with a surprise trip to God knows where in the spring semester that already gives me a lot of anxiety freaks me out."

"There is plenty of security there." He chuckled as if he was remembering something. "I promise you no one wants to be there."

"Okay." I paused, walking away before looking back. "Thanks for the bag . . . and, you know, everything else." I quickly ran back toward *my* car.

Rain was already on the driver's side, the massive smirk still plastered on his face.

"Come on, mi pareja." I jumped into the Jeep before he pulled out and headed outside of Isles.

"You better do some groveling." I huffed as the rain hit the windows over and over again.

He reached over and grabbed my thigh. "I will."

# RAIN

I bought another house. I suppose when I said I should focus on schoolwork this week, it didn't also mean to buy a house in the countryside outside of Dansport, but that is what I fucking did. At twenty-two, the last thing I imagined was owning a hunting cabin, buying Ember's house with Ash's money, and now a place out in the countryside. I was on my way to show Ember the house . . . hopefully, our house.

Instead of taking the exit into the city, I veered right onto the smaller highway leading to the countryside. We were secured by a few bodyguards trailing behind us.

After an hour of driving, Ember finally broke her silence, asking, "Wait . . . where are we going?" During the entire drive, she hadn't uttered a word, rendering this whole attempt to make it up to her quite challenging. I might be a writer, but I was terrible with words in situations like this.

"I told you, it's a surprise," I reassured her, giving her thigh a gentle squeeze. My hand had remained on her the entire time; I didn't want to let her go.

"How much longer?" she inquired.

"About an hour," I replied, and for a moment, it seemed like we'd turned a new leaf because she didn't argue with me.

When we finally turned onto the long driveway, the house I had recently purchased came into view. It was a modest farmhouse-style home with a spacious wraparound porch. What made it special was the breathtaking view, especially at sunset when the rocking chairs on the porch provided the perfect vantage point. The house sat in a clearing, surrounded by farmland on the left, apple orchards on the right, and the characteristic pine trees of the area at the back of the property.

Inside, the house had been recently renovated, but the previous owners had preserved its old-world vintage charm. The interior felt cozy, and the best part was that I had bought it with all the furniture included.

As we continued down the driveway toward the property, with our bodyguards following, we slowly approached the guesthouse at the front of the estate. The guards pulled in toward the guesthouse and I continued forward toward the main house.

Ember turned around, noticing their departure.

"This is it?" she asked, and I came to a complete stop in front of the house, and her door opened.

"What is this?" she asked as the gravel crunched underneath her feet. I slowly climbed out of the car and went to the other side of the Jeep.

"A house." I shrugged and grabbed her bag from the passenger side before I walked toward the house.

Ember was chasing behind me, yelling and flailing her arms around.

"I can clearly see that, Rain. What are we doing here? Whose house is this? Is this like a vacation rental?"

I chuckled and used the key to open the door, holding it open for her.

"It's not a vacation rental, mi pareja. It's yours."

"What?!" she exclaimed, stepping into the foyer of the house. The wooden floors creaked but were still in pristine condition, and the furniture exuded a welcoming and brand-new look, styled for selling the house.

"This must be a joke. I have a house in the city," she said in awe, continuing down the narrow hallway leading to the family room where the housekeeper had added a roaring fire in the fireplace that morning. On the other side of the room sat the small, but modern kitchen.

"Are those apples?" she asked, making her way toward the window.

"Yeah, orchards," I confirmed.

"What on earth is this place?" She turned to look at me just as the sunset was about to grace the scene.

"Come here . . . Hurry."

I grabbed her hand, and we walked out the back door to the porch where I sat in one of the oversized rocking chairs, lifting her by her hips and placing her on my lap. Just then the sky exploded in a hue of purples, yellows, pinks, and blues.

I wrapped my hands around her hips as she leaned her head back against my chest, staring out into the sky.

We were silent for a while before the sky finally settled into dusk and the darkness took over.

"I can see why you bought this house now," she whispered, and I nuzzled my head into her long black hair.

"I bought it because you encouraged me to." She turned so she was facing me. "You told me that I should follow my dreams. This place? When I saw it this week, I realized that this is my dream. Living in a small place like this, with these sunsets, raising kids . . .with you?"

As if the words finally registered in her mind, she jumped off my lap.

"I don't want kids." She crossed her arms and looked around as the night settled in around us. "I didn't ask to be here."

She walked inside as I jumped out of my chair to chase after her. With how she emphasized only a portion of what I told her, I could feel something was fucking wrong.

"I thought this would make up for treating you like shit last weekend." I trailed after her as she grabbed her bag and headed upstairs. So much for giving her a tour.

She was huffing and refusing to let me in. I needed for her to tell me what was wrong, but she kept stomping around upstairs until she reached the long hallway of doors.

"What did I do wrong?" I demanded as she slammed open the first door she saw, which was one of the hall bathrooms. Not a peep from her, and it was now starting to get under my skin.

"Nothing." She huffed, but didn't give me a single glance back. Well, good. I was glad she was talking to me at least.

She shoved the second door and third door before settling on the smaller guestroom in the back corner. Damn. I wasn't expecting her to fall at my knees again and say what she did, but this wasn't the reaction I was expecting, especially after she'd been so hot and cold all day.

I needed her to talk to me. I needed her to let me in.

Why wasn't she letting me in? I was becoming frantic.

"I don't get this," I practically screamed at her from the hallway as she shoved her bag on the bed.

"Get what?" She shuffled around inside her bag, trying to make herself look busy.

"You told me that you were fucking falling in love—"

"I did not." She crossed her arms over her chest, and I leaned against the doorframe, watching her. My eyes narrowing at her because she confessed it in front of the whole fucking class.

"Ugh." She threw her hands up in the air before falling to her knees and burying her head into her hands. I rushed to where she'd fallen, dropping down to reach her level.

"I didn't mean that . . ." I said before her hiccups and sobs carried through the room. There was a painful ache inside my chest because I didn't want to be the one to hurt her, but I didn't understand what was happening either.

"It wasn't . . . You wouldn't understand." Her sobs slowed. "This is so beautiful. It was a precious moment earlier and I completely ruined it."

"You didn't ruin anything, Ember."

"I always ruin everything," she mumbled, and the wails began again. I held her as she rocked in my arms, letting her warm body fold around my hands.

# EMBER

This was the ideal way to make up for the embarrassment he had caused me last weekend. It felt like the perfect moment as we sat together, his hands gently holding my waist, watching the sun dip below the horizon.

And here we were, sitting in a house where our dreams resided. He said the house was mine, but I also was smart enough to know I signed nothing. Although, it wouldn't surprise me if my name ended up on the title.

Then he mentioned a future with children, and my heart constricted. A familiar feeling of helplessness and profound loss washed over me. My chest was so tight, I thought I would have a panic attack like Rain had last weekend.

This led us to the moment where I hadn't planned to break down, yet here I was, in his arms once again. He carried me downstairs to the cozy fire, where tears racked my body, placed me on the couch under a thick blanket, and settled in behind me, tracing soothing circles on my back.

"I'm sorry," he whispered, and I knew he wasn't apologizing for anything he had done. Instead, it was a heartfelt apology born from empathy, an apology for reliving this pain repeatedly.

He sat with me, his hands moving from my lower back to my hair, his touch a comforting dance around me. Leaning back into him, I closed my eyes, recognizing that it was time. I needed to share this with him, to move forward, which had been my guiding principle all along.

I leaned farther back so my back was supported by his chest and took a deep breath, preparing to open up.

"Ember, it's okay," Rain muttered. "You don't have to tell me."

Closing my eyes, I knew I had to tell him. It was time, no matter how hard it would be. I owed it to myself because there was more than one story I was trying to write today. I wanted to explore *our* version too.

With my eyes shut, I whispered, "I was pregnant."

The circles stopped, but only for a moment before they continued. I kept my eyes shut, willing the tears to stay in. He stayed quiet, but I had no idea what his face looked like because I refused to look back.

I think that's why it hurt me when I needed Maddy, my friends, my dad, my own brother the most because I was going through a simultaneous loss, and no one was there for me. They were all wrapped up in the blame game trying to figure out who was at fault for something that was so obviously no one's fault.

All I needed was comfort.

"I-I found out the night after the accident. I thought I was throwing up constantly because I was under so much stress, but I realized that my period was late, and I took a test, and sure enough, I was pregnant."

"Em . . ." He grabbed my shoulders, and I turned around to his deep-blue eyes that held a world of care and concern. I didn't need his concern now, I needed it back then. Now I was a different person than I used to be.

"Let me finish," I whispered. He nodded, and I shifted so my feet were draped over his lap, and his hands continued the comforting circles around my thighs. I inhaled as much as my lungs would allow me to.

"I was twenty weeks pregnant when I lost the baby. I'd just found out it was a little girl." I swallowed, remembering the day I found out she didn't have a heartbeat. I'd gotten her a little shirt in the mail that day and was so excited to put it in what would be her nursery. It was my first real purchase because coming to terms with being a single parent while grieving was so fucking hard. For a month, I was in denial I was even pregnant, but the more I had to go to ultrasounds, the more real it became for me. I remember thinking she would be my little sunshine in all the darkness.

"I was going to name her . . . Sol." I could barely breathe as the words came out of my mouth. The only other person I'd ever told this to was my therapist. I wanted to give her a piece of her dad in her name, and it felt so fitting.

"I went to the doctor's office." My voice cracked, and the wetness padded the tops of my cheeks. I stared diligently at the circles that Rain kept rubbing on my leg. "I was all by myself, Rain." I closed my eyes, unable to remember what happened because of the pain that I could feel surrounding me like an unwelcome hug.

"They told me that her heart stopped beating and I was going to have to deliver her . . . sleeping. I had to get so many ultrasounds to confirm what the doctors knew; her heart just no longer worked. It was unexplainable. No one knew why it was happening." I swallowed so hard that my throat felt raw as the words tried to come out. "The next day, I needed to go in for them to start the labor process." I paused as my breath quickened, and I knew I needed to get this out quickly before the pain consumed me.

"It was a sterile room. Santiago was there. He was the only one who knew what was going on and held my hand the entire twenty-four hours. I-I wouldn't be here without him. After I gave birth to my sleeping angel, I went home and spent those four months alone in my room, and I couldn't get out of bed." The wetness gathered on my cheeks as Rain's hold on me tightened.

"I knew that she had to go meet her dad first because of how special he was. She was just ready to rest with him before she had the chance to meet me. But right after it all happened? I couldn't understand that. I was really fucking depressed. That's when my dad started to come around a little because Santiago was worried and both of them encouraged me to talk to someone about what happened, especially because I refused to talk to my dad about it." I sighed.

"Ember, if I had known—" I looked up for the first time since I told my story, and Rain had tears flowing freely, wetting his cheeks.

"You would have what? Come and rescued me?" I chuffed. "We both know at that time you wouldn't have done anything."

I sighed, realizing that sounded shitty and I didn't mean it. "There was a lot of healing we needed to do internally in order for us to find each other again."

He paused, then slowly brought his fingers up to his face, rubbing away my tears. "I haven't been able to feel this intensely since he passed away."

"Is that a bad thing?" I said, wishing I had the same problem, no, instead I did too much crying.

"Yes. I just want to . . . feel," he whispered.

I wasn't ready to dive into the arms of anyone right away, even a couple months ago when I first came back to Isles. If you told me I would fall in love with my late boyfriend's brother, I would have laughed. He wasn't there for me, and he needed to do a lot more groveling than just one weekend could allow for me to forgive him.

I learned so much about Rain these last few months. The foundation we'd built was steady, strong, and protective. Ash was always meant to be my first love—the one who would take me on a wild ride of sexual experiences and emotional rollercoasters. With Rain, it felt more consistent, and we shared a deep connection. But those were things I couldn't see until I saw him break down last weekend in front of me.

Sitting on that couch and witnessing him crumble, I yearned to tell him that everything was all right. I had endured and come out stronger, thanks to the resilience I had discovered within myself.

"I'm okay . . . now. I've had a long time to process what happened." I gave him a slight smile. "Like I said, Ash was just that special. She needed to hang out with her daddy first."

Reaching up, I wiped the tears freely falling down his face. "Shh, it's okay," I whispered. "What I said in class earlier, my biggest fear is that I am not able to open my heart anymore to expose myself for more loss because I truly cannot take it after all of this."

He paused, sighed, and looked up as if the ceiling would rain down all the answers he needed.

"He's up there." Rain's voice was nothing more than a whisper.

I looked up at the ceiling, matching Rain's movements, as if we could see Ash. My foot shook uncontrollably.

"He's up there with his daughter—your daughter— taking good care of her."

Thinking of what it would look like if I saw the two of them again, kicking a soccer ball together or something a dad would do, the corners of my lips twisted into a sad smile before I muttered, "Yeah, he is."

We sat with only the crackle of fire from the hearth around us as I gained control of my chest, the air slowly making its way back to my lungs.

"I bought this house for the two of us. I-I don't want to leave you, Ember." He paused, and as I started to speak again, he quieted me. "I want, er, no, I hope that you are able to write me into your next chapter, because I so desperately want there to be one where we get to live our story together."

He sighed. "You know, sometimes when you read a book, you have chapters, sure. But there are some books with entirely distinct parts, right? Like, you'll have Part One in one section, and then you skip a couple of years, and there's a Part Two?"

I understood his analogy completely.

"I imagine that's what's happening with your life story," he continued. "That you're capable of loving in two different ways with two different people, and they are just parts of your life. Each section contributes to the whole story, which, in your case, is still unwritten. Somehow, we're in Part Three now."

I couldn't help but ask, "What was Part One?"

"The story of what it was like growing up with your mom and dad." I chuckled a little, realizing how well I could visualize his comparison.

I shifted so I was on my knees still on the couch and leaned over so our chests were touching. "My mom used to share this saying with me when she was alive. 'Into the darkness I'll go, and into the light I'll be.'"

"Mm-hm?"

With tears still staining our faces, I spoke softly. "I believe you're my guiding light." I caressed his face and then rested my forehead against his. "Everything I said in class, I meant it."

He let out a slow, longing sigh as I lifted my head to meet his gaze, our eyes locking. "I think we need to stop running away from each other. Stop resisting this thing between us."

I gestured to the house around us. "This is a pretty big grand gesture."

He chuckled. "Yeah, I suppose it was."

"Was this with the money Mr. Ortiz wants?" I asked.

"Nah." Rain shook his head. "I bought this house with my own funds. I needed some separation so if anything ever happened, you'd be safe."

"So, the house is in my name?"

"Yes and no." He stood up and walked over to the kitchen where he pulled out some papers and set them down on the coffee table next to us. I leaned over as he sat next to me.

"You'd have to sign these to officially make it yours, but it is if you want it. I guess . . . I didn't want to scare you off again," he murmured.

My hands grazed along the stubble on his cheeks. In the dimly lit room, the air was heavy with anticipation, thick with a desire that had simmered between us for far too long. Our eyes locked, the connection between them intense, and the world seemed to fade away, leaving only the two of us.

"I don't think you can scare me off," I mused.

My breath was caught in my throat as Rain's hand, warm and gentle, cupped my cheek. His thumb traced a featherlight path along my jawline, sending shivers of longing down my spine. I leaned into his touch, my heart racing, and my senses heightened.

Rain's gaze flickered to my lips, his desire mirroring mine, and then he moved closer. Our lips brushed tentatively at first, the contact as delicate as the first snowflake of winter. But the spark ignited something fierce within them.

Finally, our kiss deepened, becoming an addiction neither of us could resist. It was consuming, as if we were trying to taste every ounce of longing and desire that had built up between us. I responded in kind, running my fingers through the hair at the nape of his neck, tugging gently, urging him closer. Our mouths moved in perfect harmony, a tantalizing ebb and flow of passion, each moment building upon the last.

As our tongues continued their sultry dance, a soft moan escaped my lips, mingling with the low, sensual sound that echoed from Rain.

We broke the kiss momentarily, our lips parting but hovering mere millimeters apart. Our eyes met again, the intensity of our desire reflected in the depths of our gaze.

"I don't want to do anything you aren't ready for," I murmured.

"No. I want this. Us." He looked me up and down, drinking me in. "I was scared last time because I felt like there was so much unsaid between us but . . . I am really trying."

"I know you are."

"Please, Ember. Kiss me."

Then we came together once more, our lips crashing together in a fiery embrace. The kiss grew more urgent, more passionate, as if we were trying to capture every single moment we'd missed out on. Rain cupped my face and deepened the kiss even further.

Our bodies pressed against each other; the heat of our desire nearly palpable. It was a kiss that felt like a prelude to something extraordinary, a love story written in the language of our intertwined souls.

When we finally pulled away, our lips were swollen, our breaths ragged, and our hearts pounded in unison. We gazed at each other, both lost in the lust.

Rain leaned his forehead against mine, his warm breath fanning over my lips. "Ember," he whispered, his voice husky with desire, "I've been waiting for this moment for so long."

I smiled, my heart overflowing with emotion. "Me too."

The words came tumbling out like the true confession they were. I felt every bit ready, nervous, and filled with a deep want for this man. A desire from within my core that stretched throughout my body. A need that was so . . . primal and carnal, yet full of sweet lust and love. Our lips met once more in a lingering, sweet kiss, sealing our fate.

But quickly, our mouths were doing more than just kissing. Our tongues found their place intertwined with each other as I grabbed his neck and pulled one of my legs over his other thigh so I was straddling him.

My hands dug into his coarse dark-black hair as I ground my hips into his, deepening the fevered need that I had exploding throughout every part of my body.

He carefully pulled away, but his hands found their place along my hips.

"Are you sure?" They were the only words he murmured, but with the way his tone sounded raspy, I knew he was starving in the same way that I was.

"Yes," I whispered.

Our mouths met again, and I grabbed the hem of my shirt, peeling it over my head and exposing the lace bralette I was wearing. I was . . . well endowed, so this choice of undergarment was chosen for comfort, not for being shuffled to a country house where I was going to fuck my . . . friend, or whatever we were calling him nowadays.

I huffed in a laugh, imagining if I called him a friend out loud. What kind of punishment that would get me—or, wait . . .

"What's got you so distracted?" Rain asked, and I pulled back, a smile twisted on my lips.

"I was just thinking how we've been at each other's throats." He nodded. His rough, thick lips met the delicate warmth of my skin as he grazed down my neck, leaving in his wake a trail of sloppy kisses.

"Mm-hm?" he murmured as he continued to indulge.

"And I was thinking of how much we've had to work to get to this point." His tongue joined in on the kissing, and I let out a moan. My chest heaved up toward his as my nipples perked with the quick brush of his skin against the delicate fabric that was between us.

"Yeah?" he murmured.

"And I think . . ." I paused because I didn't know how ballsy I wanted to be in this moment, but then the part of me growing hungry for him was like *fuck it*.

"I need to be punished for being a bad, naughty girl."

His lips stopped moving, his breath quickened, and his pulse was so fast it was practically jumping out of his skin.

I looked down at him with a glint in my eye, and the man in front of me was different from the man who held me tenderly just moments before.

"Stand up, Em," he demanded, and I obliged.

I was in my jeans and red bralette with my very hard nipples while his blue orbs drank me in—devouring every single ounce of me from head to toe.

"Is that how you want this?"

"Yes."

That was why Rain intrigued me—drew me in. He was this perfect concoction of gentle, sweet, and protective outside the bedroom, but inside, his possessive and dominant side raged.

"When you caught me fucking the girl in the room last year, you were a curious little one who watched?"

I nodded.

"And you want me to do that to you?" he asked, and I nodded again.

"No."

I moved to take off my jeans—Wait . . .

"What?" I barked out. The corners of his lips twisted up, and there was a mischievous glint in his eyes, but that was the only tell he wasn't being serious.

"What do you mean, no?" I demanded, shoving my hands into the pockets of my jeans.

He got up from the couch and closed the gap between us. "Because when I am with you, I want to show you every part of me, mi pareja. I want you to reach down and pull out my deepest desires and temptations."

I was so wet it was pooling in my panties, and I didn't give a fuck how shamelessly I melted into a puddle for this man. "Come here," he whispered in the shell of my ear, and I obliged, letting his hand slide onto my lower back and wrapping tightly against me.

"You wanna know what I crave deep down inside?" I nodded, yet again.

"You like running, Em?" I narrowed my eyes on him. "You like to make a big spectacle in class and leave, knowing damn well I was going to chase after you?" His face was filled with wanton desire, but his words were laced with a truthful venom.

"You liked leaving me at the house last weekend? Running away instead of staying because you knew that I was going to have to come groveling back? You knew I'd come back on my fucking hands and knees and beg for you?"

He was right. Brutally right. What this had to do with wanting him to dominate me in the bedroom though was where I was struggling to draw the connection.

"That wasn't my intention—"

"No. I never said that. Maybe you didn't even realize it until right now, but deep down inside, you love the idea that I have to chase you, don't you?" I ran my tongue along my bottom lip. "You want to know what fucking turns me on the most? What I crave? What makes the darkest parts of my deepest desire?" His hand glided over my chin as he pulled me up to him.

"Answer me," he demanded. Fuck, I loved this version of him. I loved how powerful he was.

"Y-yes," I breathlessly let out.

"You like running away from the feelings you have for me? Do you like denying that you have always been a little curious about me, mi pareja?"

"N-no."

He leaned down so that his mouth was hovering over mine. "Ah, but you do, princesa. You like the chase, don't you?"

I mean, he wasn't wrong. The more groveling he did, the more I fell for him, but I wasn't about to admit this to him right now, especially when my knees felt like jelly and were about to fall into the puddle my pussy was making.

"Because I fucking love chasing you. I love it when you want me to beg. I love when you watch as I grovel my way back to you." My lungs constricted. The want growing. "How does this relate to this moment, you ask?"

I didn't, but I was curious.

"Yeah?"

"Because I don't want to just turn you around and fuck you like I'd done hundreds of times, Em."

I gulped. "Wha-what do you want me to do?"

He looked at the door behind us that led through the apple orchards and out toward the edge of the pines. Well, that is what you would've been able to see if it was daylight, but in the dark, it was eerily quiet and dark.

His eyes darted back to mine. "I want you to do what you do best, Em. I want you to fucking run, and don't stop." My brows were furrowed. I was standing in the freaking living room, in my bralette and jeans. It was cold outside, and the last thing I wanted to do was run around the freaking orchard and forest in the dark. That seemed . . . terrifying.

"Don't think about it, Ember." His eyes filled with a lustful sin, not faltering from my face. "Go and whatever you do . . . don't let me catch you this time."

I stared blankly at him, not sure if he was being serious, but the moment he opened the door, a mischievous glint shone in his eyes.

And without a second thought, I ran.

# RAIN

Watching her creamy tits bounce in the moonlight as she ran through the orchard was written in every fucking fantasy I'd ever had since I met her. Shit, I'd probably imagined this a thousand times over when I wondered what my life would look like when I grew up—chasing after the most beautiful woman I'd ever laid eyes on as she ran away from me like I was some big, scary monster.

Ever since I was a horny teenager, I had this fascination with the thrill and chase of catching a woman. The harder the challenge, the more turned on it made me. It's probably why I was so sickly attracted to Ember because she made me work for it.

When I was in high school and Ash pulled girls constantly, I hated how easy they became. Then after puberty, the girls started to fawn over me, and it was so . . . boring and vanilla for me. There was something to be said about the fact that I loved the chase.

Because I knew what Ember loved, and if this was what she'd wanted, then I'd happily oblige. I gave her a head start while I jumped from the back porch and walked through the orchard slowly, as to not rustle the leaves on the ground below me.

"Mmm, mi pareja. Sal, sal de dónde quiera que estés."

The only things around me were the moonlight overhead and the sound of crunching as I stepped on a fallen apple. Yet, I could sense her presence, feel her moving among the rows of trees, as if there were an instinctual connection between us.

As I ventured deeper into the enveloping darkness, my senses became finely attuned to the nocturnal world around me. The rustling of leaves, akin to a whispered secret, reached my ears, serving as a breadcrumb to her presence. Ember was somewhere ahead, dashing down the aisle of the orchard, and I pursued, my heart galloping with anticipation.

In the velvety night air, a faint and intoxicating trace of her perfume lingered, a sultry blend of floral and musky notes. It hung like an invisible ribbon, drawing me further into the labyrinth of trees. My pursuit intensified, spurred by the bewitching allure of the chase—merely a seductive dance between us.

The moonlight filtered through the apple branches, casting intricate, shifting patterns of light and shadow. It conjured mirages of her, a phantom gracefully navigating the orchard's hidden pathways. The thrill of the hunt saturated the air with a palpable charge, each moment heavy with a magnetic pull that surged between us.

Her laughter, soft and teasing, tickled my ears. The tension between us thickened, a web of desire spun in the obsidian embrace of the orchard. Every rustle of leaves and crunch of the apples beneath me, heightened the burning need I had to find her.

As I exited the orchard, she ran through the break of grass that separated the apples from the pine trees behind us.

I quickened my pace, my cock throbbing inside my pants.

"There is no more running, princesa. I see you,"

I stretched, cracking my knuckles, knowing what I wanted to do with her would not be delicate or gentle. No. I would make her mine.

"I am not going easy on you." I ran, trying to avoid as many leaves on the ground, then her black hair glinting in the moonlight glow gave her away. She was crouched behind a tree.

I turned the other way so I was approaching her from behind and, almost at a crawl, I made my way toward her.

She was peeking out over the trunk of the tree when I threw my hands over her mouth.

"There you are," I whispered into the shell of her ear. "I found you."

# EMBER

"Fuck," I whispered as I turned around, and his deep-blue eyes manically searched mine. He gripped my hips, pulling me tight into him.

There was dirt all over the bottom of my jeans and mud on my feet, but I didn't give a fuck because all I needed was to feel him inside of me. This game of cat and mouse we were playing was . . . God, I had no fancy words to describe it other than just addicting.

"I need you," I begged as his hands tangled into my hair.

"I caught you, princesa. Are you going to keep running?" He pulled on my chin so I was looking into his eyes.

I shook my head. "No."

"You're all mine, Em." I knew I was.

He ripped off my bralette, and my breasts bounced free as he rolled my nipples between his fingers. I cried in pleasure.

"I am yours," I murmured as he ripped off my jeans and tossed them aside. He lifted me up, and I wrapped my legs around his hips as he walked me back out of the woods and dropped me on the cool, damp grass.

He tore off his shirt, pants, and boxers, and I stared at him breathlessly. He was a fucking god. His abs rippled in the darkness, his body a golden-tanned beauty. His . . . cock was standing tall, thick and huge at attention, slick with arousal.

"Please," I huffed in a breathless moan.

"Tsk, tsk, princesa, wasn't it you who asked me to punish you?" Shit. I'd forgotten about that because all I needed was to feel him inside of me.

"B-but—"

"No." His eyes were a cruel shade of blue as he leaned down and opened my legs, lifting my hips up so they weren't directly on the grass.

"I want to taste you. I want to brand you with my tongue, making you mine and only mine." He placed my legs so they wrapped around his shoulders and peppered delicate kisses onto my throbbing mound.

"Fuck," I wailed, desperate for his tongue to taste my cunt.

"Such a wet girl—so desperate and needy for me."

Then his mouth reached my cunt as his tongue explored and lapped up the wetness that kept growing. I was so fucking needy, and there was a fire burning inside of me. But the moment his tongue licked up, alternating between flicking at my clit and sucking me dry, I was a symphony of sobs.

His mouth was desperate. His tongue explored my clit as his fingers played with my opening, gently sliding in and out. I was grinding into his mouth as the sobs became more vile the faster and deeper his tongue explored me.

Just as he came up for a breath, he paused, shoving two fingers inside of me.

"Look at me," he demanded, but between thrusts, I knew I was being edged. I was right there about to orgasm, but his fingers grew slower, more languid in speed.

"What?" I barked back, angry that I couldn't fucking come.

"Tell me, princesa, are you planning on running away after this? Let me fuck you, then run home after tonight?"

"Yes," I said because the thought of falling in love again scared the shit out of me, but my heart wanted to desperately. In fact, I think it was already there.

"Then I guess I'll have to continue to punish you," he whispered, ripping his fingers out of me and getting up.

"What the fuck?" I said, wondering if the same thing that happened last weekend was happening now.

He only laughed, his naked form walking toward the illuminated house.

"Why did you stop?" I demanded.

"Because, Em, I am not fucking you in a wet field the first time we have sex. I am not fucking you like an animal the first time my cock touches your pussy. As much as I am desperate for it, I know that you'd use it as an excuse as to why we weren't meant to be together and then run away in the morning." His whole demeanor softened.

"I don't want to do anything you don't deserve or need and right now, none of this feels . . . right." He paused, turning toward me. "And that kind of running away is not the kind I fucking like."

He continued the trek back to the house while I stood there frozen in a cold apple orchard with a rotten apple under my foot.

He was right though. He was always right, which drove me up a wall. I would have found some excuse tomorrow morning and rationalized in my head this wasn't right for us. But I also wanted him to know that I could see what he was doing. I wanted him. I wanted to be there in the morning when we woke up. I wanted both of us.

"You're wrong," I said. He paused in his tracks but didn't turn around. "You are so fucking wrong, because I like you."

I huffed, in disbelief that the words were even pouring from my mouth. "I don't know how to yet. It's fucking messy inside my head, but I fucking like you a lot, and I don't want to leave. I see you."

I walked over to him and wrapped my hands around his naked waist, then leaned up to his ear, whispering, "Catch me."

I sprinted past him, then heard his steps behind me. I dodged between rows of trees, running toward the house where I saw the glistening blue pool in the distance. I was sweaty; I was not the person who enjoyed running for pleasure. Sure, maybe since it was from a tall handsome, brooding man behind me, I'd do it, but you want me to run around the block for exercise? Hard pass.

I was dirty from the trees and immediately knew where I needed to go. I ran all the way up the deck toward the back steps, then jumped into the hot tub.

I let the warm water envelop me when the bubbles in the oversized hot tub fizzed, alerting me someone else was inside.

As I popped my head up, he dropped down into the heated water. His hands touched my cheek as he drank my face in.

"Found you," he murmured. I knew he saw the hot tub bubble, letting me know someone was inside, but I wanted him to have this win.

Our lips collided. Something pivotal changed in this moment for the two of us. Both of us running, but this time, it was toward each other.

"I mean it, Rain," I whispered, drifting my body toward his and wrapping my legs around him to keep me anchored.

"Why?" he croaked as I kissed his cheeks, his nose, his lips, his eyes. I wanted to feel every part of his body—memorize every single curve.

"It's unconventional. I can't explain it, but I just . . . feel it inside of me." My mouth landed atop his and we kissed, our tongues fucking each other. His cock twitched underneath me as I stopped us, got out of the hot tub, wrapped myself with a towel laying neatly on one of the chairs on the deck, then ran inside.

He chuckled as he followed, but just as he walked into the threshold of the door, I dropped my towel.

My entire body was on full display in the warm glow of the fire.

"Fuck me," I begged the words barely coming out of my mouth before his body collided into mine. Lifting me up, he carried me upstairs.

"Are you sure?" he asked before he opened the door in front of us.

"Very." I was more than sure—more than ready.

Instead of going to the room that I'd thrown my stuff into earlier, we went into the primary bedroom. It was insanely huge with a full sitting area in the corner and a four-poster bed in the center.

"This is our room," he murmured into my ear as he dropped me onto the bed.

"I found you, mi pareja." He slithered his body up toward mine, then he spread open my thighs.

Our gaze connected, and he searched my face.

"Are you sure?" I asked.

His lips twisted into a smile. "The only thing I've ever been so sure of was how much I need to feel you underneath me."

His pre-cum mixed with the heat of my own needy cunt as the tip of his cock slid between my thighs.

"Fuck," I cried.

My heart felt so open it could explode with desperation.

"Take a deep breath," he encouraged as he slid into me. His cock slowly pushed into me. I cried out because the pain of him stretching me was so intense mixing with the pleasure of finally feeling him inside me.

He paused. "Am I hurting you?" His brows drawn in concern.

I shook my head and demanded he dive in deeper. He obliged and just as he got all the way in, I let out a carnal moan. It was not sexy. It came from deep within me. A noise of undulating pleasure as I unwrapped every single piece of myself in front of him.

"Holy shit. Keep making those noises, princesa, and I won't last long." He fucked me. Thrusting inside of me as he alternated between a slow pace and then quickened as the need pulsed through both of us.

I grabbed his neck and spun us around so I was on top of him, because I wanted to watch him underneath me. I needed to see the look on his face as I took him in like the good little slut I was being.

His fingers pinched at my nipples as I ran my hand through my hair while bobbing on top of him.

"Your cock was made for me," I told him, reaching up into the air as if I was grabbing onto an invisible bar to hold me up. I was in my own little world now—giving and receiving pleasure.

"I've never seen such a perfect woman in my entire life." He moaned as his hands trailed down my skin. We were the perfect combination of darkness and light—both existed within each other.

His fingers circled the entrance to my cunt, and I could feel the build-up inside of me.

He then lifted me off him like I was a feather, and I was startled by the sudden stop.

"This again?" I heaved, and he only laughed.

He walked over to the oversized chair in the corner where he splayed out, then patted his lap.

"I want to watch you as you come on top of me."

I huffed, but obliged as I stepped over to him. His hand went up immediately to stop me.

"Nuh-uh. On your hands and knees." He said leaning down so he was eye level with me. "Crawl to me."

I gave him a smirk as I dropped to the floor, my gaze never leaving his. Languidly, I moved one arm forward and my knees followed.

"Like this, Daddy?" I asked, pursing my lips for him. He groaned, something so deep within him as I crawled all the way to where he was sitting.

"Yes," he murmured. "Now show me what a good girl you are and take my dick like my dirty little slut."

I huffed and opened my mouth as wide as I could, letting his cock touch the back of my throat, gagging at his mere girth and length as his thrust impaled me.

My eyes couldn't help but look up at him. When our gazes met, there was a fire burning so deep from within him, he didn't move them from me.

"Perfect seems like a waste of a word to describe the way you look right now, on your knees in front of me sucking me down so well." I licked the pre-cum around his cock as I continued to bob up and down. My hands circling around his balls, giving them a small tug.

Right as he clenched inside of me, on the precipice of exploding, I edged him by pulling my mouth away. He let out a disappointed moan, but I stood up and wrapped my legs on either side of his body.

"Fuck me," I begged. He looked around frantically.

"What?" I snapped.

"A condom?" I let out a laugh because all of a sudden he was worried about that?

"I'm on birth control and my last screening was negative because . . . well . . . yeah."

"Same—" I stopped him, letting the tip of his dick touch my clit.

"Not now," I demanded because I needed this release more than anything. I was getting grumpy from not being allowed to come all night long, so I was going to take what I needed from him.

I lowered myself onto him, grabbing his shoulders for stability on the way down. I thrust onto him as I rolled my hips back and forth, letting his entire length fill me up.

"I need this," I demanded. God I was so fucking close after being edged, chased, and fucked all night long.

I could feel the build-up happening as I dove deeper with my body, his hands holding me at my hip-dips as his mouth sucked and tugged on my nipples. My back was arched, aiding in his cock slamming against my G-spot.

"Rain," I cried aloud. "Oh god, Rain." I repeated as my orgasm rolled through me.

"Mi pareja," he sobbed as we came at the same time, exploding into our own pleasure.

As the wave of bliss powered through me, I fell against his chest and he pulled out while lifting me up and placing me over onto the bed, which felt like a cloud.

When I didn't feel the weight of his body next to me, I got up, then heard the familiar sound of the bath running.

That's when I saw him in all his postcoital blissed-out state. His hair was disheveled all around him, the muscles in his body were tense and his veins were pulsing as if he'd done an intense workout.

"Come," he murmured, gesturing to me to follow him into the connected en suite. The bathroom was unlike the rest of the house. It was modern, spacious, large, and covered in quartz.

"Whoa. This house must have cost a fortune." He laughed as he stopped the tub from filling any more.

"That's the first thing you're going to say?" he asked just as a smirk exploded onto my face, or maybe it'd been there a while.

I dropped into the tub as he leaned over the side, cupping his hands to fill them with water and splash it over me.

It was a huge tub, made for two, so I asked him if he wanted to come in.

"There's plenty of room?" I added.

"Mmm?" Rain mused. "You want me to come in?"

I simply shrugged.

"Scoot up." I felt Rain's hard—literally—body everywhere, sloshing the water around before he settled in behind me. I leaned back on him, and he wrapped his arms around me.

"I, er, thank you," I whispered.

"For what?" he mused and pressed wet kisses along my collarbone.

"Understanding," I said, as if that one word held the weight of a thousand in my hands.

"We don't have to use labels, we can go as slow as you need, and I can't promise I won't fuck up along the way, but I just want you in my life, Ember." He sighed, pausing before whispering, "The eight months I didn't have you were the scariest of my life. I asked

Santiago for a daily update to make sure you were okay and now knowing what you were going through I think I'll spend my entire life trying to make it up to you."

"But you were suffering, too," I whispered. "And we grieved in different ways. I am good at running away from my problems, hiding in a closet, whereas you experienced sadness by taking control to please others." He seemed to agree.

We sat there in the warmth of the bath, Rain pouring some water over me.

"Are you going to run away?" His voice sounded so different, so scared. "They all run away from me . . ."

"What do you mean?"

"I wasn't enough for Ash, not enough for my dad who felt like he needed to protect his family so much so to get involved with Mr. Ortiz and . . . er, your mom."

I nodded.

"Everyone fucking leaves me, Ember. Why wouldn't I assume you would, too?"

I turned my head so I could look him in the eyes. "I don't want to leave, Rain. I am fucking terrified, but that doesn't mean I want to run away."

I jumped out of the bath, surprise washing over his face as I wrapped myself in a towel.

"Give me the papers," I demanded.

"The . . . what?" His face scrunched at my sudden outburst.

"The fucking papers." I huffed, irritated he didn't know what I was asking about.

"Ember, I don't know what you're talking about," Rain said as he got out of the bath and grabbed a towel from the rack, wrapping it on his lower self. Momentarily, I got distracted by his fucking abs, but my attention snapped back to him when he chuckled.

"The house title," I demanded, but it was *really* hard not to stare at his chest.

"You can touch, princesa. You don't have to continually stare."
I rolled my eyes.

"Just take me to them."

He walked downstairs ahead of me, his shoulder blades flexing with each step he took. Damn, who knew shoulders could be so hot.

He went to the coffee table where he'd set the papers earlier and handed them to me. I looked them over and then back up at him.

"Gimme a pen," I demanded.

"Ember, you shouldn't sign something like this without talking to a lawyer. Why don't you sleep on it—"

"Did I fucking stutter?"

He chuckled.

"No, ma'am," he said, and then came back from the kitchen with a black pen. His hand grabbed my wrist just as I was about to sign on the dotted line, and I looked back up at him. "Are you sure?"

"I don't want to run away anymore," I whispered and then just as his hand released me, I signed the title of the house.

"We have to get these notarized, but otherwise this house is yours now as much as it is mine." He smiled . . . like a genuine happy smile, something I hadn't seen in a while. He crossed the distance between us, and his left hand slid over the small of my waist.

"There you are," he murmured, his fingertips lifting, touching the edge of my smile. "I missed this."

And in that moment, I realized I hadn't smiled like this in so long. Nothing had felt this right in a year. Absolutely nothing. It finally felt like I'd found the puzzle piece I'd lost along the way. The last little part of me I needed to get in order to complete myself. Now, if only I could figure out where it fit into the bigger puzzle.

"Come on, let's go to bed," Rain whispered, and we walked upstairs.

Rain gently tucked me into his bed—our bed—before sliding in next to me and wrapping me in his arms the same way he'd done a couple weeks ago. This felt far more intimate than letting him chase me around naked in the orchards.

Yet, it also felt so much more at home.

# RAIN

Weeks had passed after we'd gotten back from the house in the countryside, and Ember had insisted we legalize all the title documents for the house. I wasn't going to argue, but little did she realize she was making my dreams come true. I also spent most nights at her house, but it was one of those things we didn't really acknowledge what we were or what we were doing so it wasn't true. Everything was better left unsaid, and I was okay with that.

It was time to put my plan to action because I knew what I had to do to finally close this chapter we had and move forward with our life. Plus, Mr. Ortiz has been on us at the Den to see if we'd gotten any new information.

Pico was walking me to the edge of the town at the small diner that Ember had taken me to weeks ago. It was a run-down little place, but the food was probably the only decent thing in this town.

"What're we doing at this shithole?" He looked up at the sign flickering and furrowed his brows.

"Hey, don't knock it until you try it. They actually have legit burgers." I laughed before he narrowed his eyes at me.

"Ash took us here. I disagree." I laughed thinking of Pico being forced to come and do couple-y things with his girlfriend. He loved Marissa deeply and had since I could remember from back home, but he also played the tough-guy act a lot and was a stubborn piece of shit most of the time.

"Can you believe that next year we will be outta this place?" Pico asked, looking behind us where Isles was being greeted by the shadows of the evening.

"No," I said flatly because I had no fucking idea what that meant for me, no clue what my so-called future would look like.

"Anyway." He pushed open the door, and the little bell jingled. "Are you going to tell me why we're here or are you going to make me guess?"

I laughed slowly before looking around the diner and finding the familiar head of hair in the back of the corner booth before I gestured him in that direction.

Pico reached for his waistband before I shook him off.

"This is peaceful," I told him, trying to convince myself of it. I reached out to him when Ember told me she was going to meet with him. After debating it for a while, I figured the worst thing that could happen on neutral territory was we make a bigger fight for the spring bonfire than last year.

As I walked in front of Pico and approached Walsh, Ember's brother, it was uncanny to see the resemblance between them. They resembled their mother. I'd only ever seen photos of Ember's mom briefly when I was in her room. She kept a photo of them when she was a baby tucked behind her desk inside her bookshelf. As if she was ashamed, leaving her in the shadows, not ready to face that yet.

"Walsh." I swallowed, and he stood up and shook my head.

Walsh looked at Pico and then back to me.

"I thought we were coming alone." He eyed Pico one more time, giving him a once-over. "Not bringing our dogs."

"Pendejo." I placed my hand on Pico's chest before he pressed.

"He is an important part of this conversation," I encouraged. "Plus, he, too, had no idea who we were meeting with."

I slid opposite Walsh on the other side of the bench.

"Are you going to explain why we are here?" I knew Pico wanted to ask the same question, but would never question me in front of

Walsh. That's why I knew what I was doing was the right step with what I was about to do.

"Yes—"

"What can I get you guys?" The familiar waitress came over with a pad of paper and pen in hand, ready to take our orders. It always fascinated me that the people who actually lived in Isles had no idea what this place stood for. I mean, they had to have known with how the place reeked of blood and war every spring, but none of them ever said anything if they did suspect.

"Chocolate milkshake," I told her, the corners of my lips turned into a smile.

"Who the fuck orders milkshakes for this type of conversation?" Pico said, and I chuckled. Walsh was also laughing.

"What? They're fucking good. In fact, you all need one."

I looked back at the waitress. "Make that three chocolate milkshakes."

She nodded and rushed away before I gave them a smile, thankful that ordering milkshakes had broken the thick ice pulsating between us.

"We are all graduating this year. Well, I am a bit behind both of you, but nonetheless, we are respectively going to be heads of our new worlds."

Walsh gave a quick confused look at Pico, furrowing his brows. I was technically bound to be the leader of the Cartel in the US. When Ash died, everyone knew it.

"I don't want to be in the organization," I confessed, and this time, Pico broke his stoic stature.

"What?" he balked.

"Listen, I was never meant to be a leader. It was always supposed to be Ash, and without him here, I realized I am a shit leader."

"Why are you saying this right now?" Pico pressed his lips together, and I could only read between the lines of what he really meant. He was calling me an idiot for confessing this in front of our enemy, but that was my whole point.

"Because I am tired of having this decades-long fight between us. Our parents are stupid, stubborn assholes."

"What the—" Walsh slammed both hands like I offended him personally.

"Come on, Walsh. You and I know that your mom and my dad were the first people to get sucked into this whole shitty ass world and then somehow a pawn for a larger war that was at play between our two organizations."

"My mom was innocent."

"My dad was fucking power-hungry, but was innocent, too. At the end of the day, we need to make sure Mr. Ortiz steps down nicely. In order to do that, we need to all sit down together, end this fucking . . . tryst between them, and show them that there is strength in power and numbers versus constantly fighting over each other.

"And when the time comes for it, I need both of you to know that I will not be taking over. In fact, with Pico's permission, I want out of the organization altogether."

Pico looked at me and gave me a small pat on my shoulder. "Of course, brother," he said sincerely, as if he'd forgotten that Walsh was sitting across from me.

When he pulled away, he coughed before regaining his composure back into his ice-cool stance in front of Walsh.

The waitress came back and dropped our milkshakes off. They all had bright-pink straws in them and some of those cocktail umbrellas you get at fancy restaurants.

"I like the extra flair, Sue." I winked, and she laughed the entire way back to the kitchen.

I plucked the umbrella out and took a sip of the creamy shake.

"Come on," I encouraged. "They're fucking good."

Walsh and Pico did the same thing, and getting two mortal enemies to drink umbrella-style milkshakes out of pink straws had me feeling pretty fucking invincible.

I waited until they tried their shakes and then asked, "So?"

"I can see why she likes you," Walsh said, and it sobered my goofy mood.

He knew.

"How did you..." I asked, cocking my head.

"You put her name on a house. I am not stupid. I have dings on my sister if she buys anything new or whatever just to make sure no one is taking advantage of her."

*Note to self: remove the tracker he has on her.*

He raised his hands. "I'm not upset. I just wish she'd see I want what's best for her."

We all took a pregnant pause.

"I think it's a good idea," Walsh added, breaking the awkward silence. "I think we need to sit down with our parents and tell them about this. There are a few things I also want to tell them together."

"I agree. It's time to end the feud," Pico added. "But I have one request if we are going to work together."

I waited to see what Pico had to add because I was curious.

"Yeah?" Walsh inquired.

"I want to stop the spring bonfire tradition for good." I swallowed, thinking of what this could've done last year.

Walsh looked at me and nodded to respond to Pico, but his gaze never left mine. "I agree."

His tone was suddenly far more somber, and I knew he knew more.

"Pico"—I turned toward the man next to him—"I think we can hash out the details on how to get the guys together later. If you wouldn't mind letting Walsh and I have a few personal words."

Pico agreed. "I'll just be waiting outside."

Pico slid me one of his Glocks, and I slid it behind me on the booth just in case this conversation took a turn.

If Walsh was nervous, he didn't show it. As Pico walked away from us, he extended his hand to him. "I look forward to hearing from you."

Pico looked down at his hand and then back at me, and I shrugged.

"You too, man," Pico finally said, and shook his hand before heading out of the diner.

"How is she?" Walsh muttered, and I leaned back in the booth, because talking about a business I didn't give a flying fuck about and talking about Ember were two different things. I felt protective, fearless, and I also knew that Walsh was withholding a secret from both of us. A secret that he'd tucked in for a while.

"You should ask her," I said.

"I tried. She came to see me—"

"I know." I refused to cede control of the conversation. Leaning across the table, my elbows supporting my weight, I locked eyes with Walsh.

"Walsh, don't misconstrue my attempts to end this as kindness or gratitude. I'm doing it so that I can move forward with your sister. Because I fucking love your sister and I want nothing but her happiness." His expression tightened.

"But let me be crystal clear. I'm well aware you're keeping something from us. Ember knows it, too. Your silence speaks volumes. Neither of us understands why you won't open up, but we have his phone now. Our IT team is looking into it. If you're involved in any way, I'll find out."

Walsh audibly swallowed, mirroring my posture by leaning over the table.

"Tell Ember that she only needs to know that *I* can't tell her," his voice barely above a whisper, "but the answer is there."

I rolled my eyes. "You need to figure this out before our meeting with our parents. It will resolve a lot of problems for all of us. It will also give them the look that we are a united front. There should be no secrets moving forward.."

This time, desperation laced his tone, as if he clung to a deep secret he wanted to bury.

"I can't."

"Just answer me, were you there?" I pressed, my hands tightening on the table.

After a moment's hesitation, he nodded without uttering a word.

"Did you do it?" I asked again, my fingers now gripping the table's edge, waiting to see what he had to say because part of me wasn't even sure if I wanted to know the answer to the question. I didn't want to because had he done something, I'd have to fucking kill him.

There were two people I would kill for, and one of them was no longer here.

Slowly, he shook his head. I let out a sigh of relief, but that was brief before the anger washed over me yet again.

"Damn it," I muttered as I rose from the booth. I appreciated that he'd answered the questions I'd already known the answers to, but his mysterious and ominous behavior grated on my nerves.

Before exiting the restaurant, I cast a final look his way. "If you'd lost Ember in the same way, wouldn't you search for answers to understand why?"

"I would," he replied through clenched teeth.

"Ember and I lost a lover, a brother. Both of us lost a deep friend. We're seeking closure, just like you would. Your evasiveness is infuriating, Walsh. You hold the missing piece of this puzzle."

He swallowed hard. "I promised him."

I was certain he'd said that, but before I could respond, he abruptly left the booth, shoved his hands in his pockets, and exited the restaurant.

"Fuck," I screamed as I grabbed the gun and shoved it in my pocket before throwing a couple twenties on the table for Sue.

As I stormed out of the restaurant, Pico pulled me aside before I jumped onto the bike.

"You good?" he asked. "Why didn't you tell me you wanted me in your spot?"

He looked pissed, but I just didn't have the fight in me left.

"Because you deserve it. Come on, you see how I can barely control the Den for our meetings or I pass them along to you. Hell, you know how to manage Mr. Ortiz better than I do. It's something you're good at, and from what I gather, you fucking like it."

He nodded. "I do . . . like it." I offered him a tight-lipped smile.

"Listen, for what it's worth, I won't let him down."

"I know you won't. That's why I think you're perfect for this." I paused. "Walsh didn't shoot Ash. He told me so much tonight, but he also admitted he knew something. I am fucking pissed and exhausted, so I am taking Ember to the lodge tonight if you need me."

"Cool." He winked at me before he turned away laughing. "Use a condom."

He was shouting so everyone in the deserted parking lot could hear him. I revved the bike, trying to drown his shouts.

"Be safe."

"Remember you can't spell class without some ass."

"What the fuck?" I shouted, and both of us broke into a fit of laughter before I headed toward her apartment.

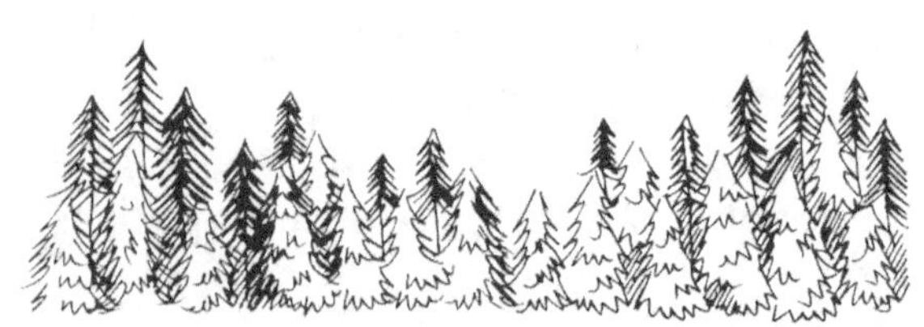

*"We are finally getting out of here." I was laughing as we started to pack our clothes into bags, separating whose was whose in Ash's room.*

*I turned over to look at him, and his tone didn't match the same excitement as mine. No, he was much more somber and sadder.*

"What's up with you?" I asked, shoving him a little, but he looked up with me in the same face.

"Dad wants me to take over as leader junior year, which means the spring bonfire,. I'll be a target starting next year."

"Damn," I commented. Mr. Ortiz sat both of us down to explain the bonfire earlier this year. It was the most dumb and chauvinistic use of force that I'd heard in a long time, but the fear in Ash's face was intense.

"I got your back, though," I told him, grabbing the shirt from his hands and folding it, forcing him to sit on the bed.

"I know, but you won't always be here for me, Rain. You've done so much for me, and I feel really fucking guilty."

I furrowed my eyebrows. "Ash, that's what brothers do for each other. We weren't born brothers, but you're the closest thing to me. You are my family." Ash feigned a smile before he laid back onto the bed.

"We aren't going to let anyone get in between us. No pussy, no beer, no fucking dads," I added, which only produced a little chuckle from A sh.

"Like you and I would ever go for the same girl, anyway. You like them quiet and meek." I rolled my eyes, throwing a pair of socks in his face while he laughed.

I was worried about him. He'd battled with his mental health for so long that I could only hope that going to Isles would help him and give him some separation between his dad and the life he had here.

"It'll all be okay in the end," I whispered to myself, hoping that he didn't hear me.

"In the end . . . I'll always take care of you too, Rain. Love you, brother."

# EMBER

For the past month, we had spent every single night together, but it didn't have a label. I was okay with it just being . . . us. The thought of having to put a name on whatever we were, terrified me.

During those nights, we talked about Ash, sharing happy memories of him. Neither of us felt shame or constant anxiety about the life we were living and the memories we held of him. It felt . . . good. Almost too good to be true.

Just as I was getting ready to make us dinner, his familiar Doc Martins thudded against the floor, followed by the click of the key in the doorknob. I took a seat on the couch and gazed out at the distant pines.

"Come on, Ember," he said, storming over to me. "Get up. We're leaving."

I quickly stood up, feeling a rush of questions. "Why? Where are we going?" I demanded, but he only scoffed and started gathering sweaters from my room, stuffing them into a duffle bag he found under my bed.

"Stop," I cried, closing the gap between us and grabbing his trembling hands. "What happened?"

My words tumbled out faster, driven by my desire for the truth, something I loved about Rain. "I had a terrible meeting," he lamented as my hands moved to cradle his face. "Please, don't ask me questions, Ember."

I swallowed my curiosity, rare in our relationship, because I could see he needed this.

"Okay," I whispered, and reached up to give him a small kiss on the cheek. Something for him to carry with him, knowing the burden he carried on his back was strong. Because he always spoke the truth, I would not push him.

He sighed and collapsed on the bed.

"I went to see your brother," he said as he stared up at the wall. It took a moment for those words to actually register with me.

"My brother?"

"Yeah," he replied blankly.

"What? Why?" I questioned for the second time in the five minutes he'd been home.

He sighed before pushing off the bed and holding my hands in his.

"I feel so much pressure for what's going to happen next. I am supposed to graduate this summer, go to Dansport, and start doing business dealings for the Cartel, for Mr. Ortiz. The last thing I want to do is that. I want to write . . . damn it." He exhaled a large breath. "I want to live in our country house . . . together."

"I don't graduate for another year," I whispered.

"I know. I want to stay here in Isles with you until you're ready to come with me, or go wherever you want to." He paused and then his fingers slid so they were cusping my chin. "I'd do whatever you want, Ember, because I cannot imagine a world without waking up to your smile everyday."

My heart started to race so fast it felt like it was going to practically jump-scare out of my chest. "Rain?" I could barely whisper his name aloud, but his fingers caressed my face as if he knew exactly what I wanted to say but the words weren't quite there yet. As if he understood the pause between us was more intimate than the eight little letters could ever combine.

"Wait," I snapped out of my daydream. "What does this have to do with my brother?"

"Well, Pico was there, too."

"Okay, and that answers absolutely nothing." I crossed my arms and rested so I was between his legs.

"It does though, mi pareja." His fingers were still trailing down my cheek and gently tucking my hair behind my ear. "I needed Pico and Walsh to get along and finally have a sit-down to end this war between our families. Pico is going to take over for me. He agreed."

"What?" I balked.

"Yeah. He's a born leader. He enjoys fucking around with people, and everyone respects him. I just need to find a way to sit down with your dad and Mr. Ortiz together. As soon as I piece together the evidence I need as to what happened last year with Ash."

"I can help." I stood up taller.

"Of course you can," he responded. "This was, after all, your idea."

My brows furrowed, not understanding what he meant.

"You told Ash when you first met him that words were a more powerful tool than running around with guns and hating each other." I laughed.

"He told you this?" Rain smiled as he remembered.

"He told me he'd thought it was the silliest thing he'd heard. Because what was more powerful than words? Words were just something that came out of your mouth, but brute strength was obviously something bigger and better."

He chuckled as if he was remembering the conversation. "But damn, Ember, did you prove him wrong."

I gave a breathless huff. "I did, didn't I?"

His lips came crashing down to mine while he whispered, "You absolutely did."

"Wait," I pulled away. "So, what did Walsh say?"

"He agreed to it, but then Pico went outside to wait for me, and Walsh essentially did the same run around he gave you except this time he acknowledged that he was there when Ash died, but that he cannot say anything other than that."

Of course he couldn't. "I don't fucking get it. He was never like this. Why was he keeping a secret that wasn't even his to keep?"

"I don't know, princesa." He sighed, clearly frustrated, and I decided not to press because it was obviously agitating him.

"Anyway, he said that the answer is in front of us like he was delivering some words of wisdom or something, but anyway, you can see why the whole meeting really just irked me." He grabbed my waist and pulled me tighter into him as his head nuzzled into my neck.

"Mmm, I am sorry for taking it all out on you. I just want to go away for the night."

My ears perked up. "Oh, yeah?"

"Come on, Em," he whispered as his lips came across mine. "Help me erase my day."

My lips were dancing atop his. "Okay."

I pulled away from him and grabbed a few extra sweaters and jeans, knowing where we were going without him even saying.

"Let's go," I whispered as I interlaced my hand in his. I looked up just as we walked out toward his bike and could have sworn I saw a little star above dancing in the night sky.

*Hi Ash and Sol.*

I glanced back at Rain on his bike handing me my helmet as he looked at what I was staring at.

"Are you ready?" he asked, and I looked at the man standing before me.

"Yes." I got on the back of the bike and wrapped my arms around his waist. He caressed my arms before he started the engine and peeled out.

When we got off the ATV and pulled up to the familiar cabin, I went inside because it was far colder in the middle of the pines than back in town.

"It's freezing," I exclaimed, and Rain laughed as we were welcomed by the warmth of the cabin. But there was something . . . red?

I looked around the cabin and realized it was blanketed in red rose petals around the bed.

"Did you—"

"What the—"

We both said at the same time and then a sly grin raised on both of our faces.

"Pico."

"Marissa," I told him, and he agreed. I walked over to the kitchen where there was a bottle of champagne, my favorite seltzers, and already popped popcorn because this place did not have a microwave.

"Netflix and chill?" he asked, and I giggled, feeling a little out of place in the cabin because the last time we'd been here it was so hard for Rain to look me in the eyes. Almost as if he could read my mind, he walked up toward me and brushed a hair behind my ear.

"It's different this time," he murmured.

"It is." I agreed. "Also, this is a little too cheesy for me."

This time he burst into laughter that rang like a melody throughout the room.

"I couldn't agree with you more." His lips were on mine, and I was fucking starving for his kiss. I wanted to fuck his pain away. I wanted to take away the pressure that brewed deep within me from my head to my core.

"Let's make a mess of it, then, shall we?" he asked.

"Is this why you brought me here?" I rasped, a small chuckle escaping my lips.

"Maybe?" A mischievous glint twinkled in his eye, which only made me drown into his deep blues.

"Show me what you got, then." I winked, and he closed the gap between us.

"You want me?" he growled into my ear, and I let out a moan, not able to contain it. "Good."

His voice was so harsh and raspy that I barely recognized it. "Play a little game with me, princesa?" I nodded as his lips pressed into the delicate skin on my neck.

"I want you to do what you do best." I paused, pulling away slightly to catch the glint of desire pooling in his eyes.

I knew what he wanted me to do. I looked around the room for my shoes, but he let out a symphony of groans as his mouth came back down onto my neck, and in this moment, I didn't care I was about to run out there without them.

Because I wasn't scared of the darkness anymore; I'd found my light.

I yanked away from him and glanced toward the door before running as fast as I could out of it. I swore I could hear him laughing as I triumphantly continued trekking deeper into the woods.

It was freezing as I unpeeled my jeans, leaving them in my trail and dodging behind the large trunks of the trees. I was breathless as the oxygen left my lungs with every pound of my feet against the cold, wet floor underneath me.

"Sal, sal, de dónde quiera que estés, princesa." I heard him whisper through the pines, knowing he was right on me as I slowly moved to the next big tree trunk and hunched underneath it.

There was mud everywhere, which was truthfully my only saving grace because it meant my footsteps were somewhat muted in the otherwise eerily quiet forest.

"Such a little mouse today," he growled, and by the way his voice echoed, I could tell he was closer.

I frantically looked around, but the thick pines covered most of the moonlight from the night.

"Shit," I muttered under my breath before I walked forward, crunching on the earth below me as I went. I was being so loud, there was no way he—

"Fuck," I screamed when two big arms wrapped around me and lifted me off the prickly ground, then he threw me over his shoulder and slapped me on my ass. He was my predator and I was his prey.

I yelled and thrashed, frustrated that I couldn't break free from his grip. Yet, as he hoisted me over his shoulders, I couldn't ignore the palpable sexual tension between us, intensifying the chilly atmosphere. When he tossed me onto the soft, muddy ground, I found myself melting into him, disregarding the dirt now covering us.

His mouth captured mine as I responded, my entire body succumbing to him. I was ravenous for him, never remembering how starved for a human I'd ever been like. We'd built our relationship on such a solid foundation that the trust that I'd managed to have for him was more than I'd ever experienced, and that scared me.

"I . . . need . . . you," I croaked out as our tongues clashed against each other in a frenzied demand.

"You have me" was all he responded with, his hands pulling at my lace panties, tugging them aside to fit his fingers into my soaking wet core.

My back rolled against the earthen floor beneath me as I writhed with each thrust his fingers made.

"Mmmm," I murmured as his thumb touched my clit and his other fingers fucked me. By the way he dominated me, he knew he was mine too. My ray of light in the life that was so full of sadness and despair. He was it for me.

As if suddenly I'd had an epiphany, my body responded to his touch in a way it'd never had before. I was needier—more desperate, if that could have even occurred.

"You are so wet for me," he mused. His eyes stayed fixated onto mine the entire time as his fingers continued to assault me.

"I need . . ." I froze.

"Tell me," he groaned into my mouth before pressing his lips onto mine. I was fucking drenched in mud, especially with how much I'd been moving beneath him, and all I could do was beg for his fucking cock inside my needy little cunt.

"Fuck me, Rain."

My sweater had ridden up so the bottom of my breasts were peeking out.

"So fucking beautiful," he murmured, his jaw clenched as he drank me in. "Like my little prey that I get to devour."

The sound of his pants being unzipped was the only forewarning he gave me before his cock sprung free from his boxer briefs.

"I love how wet your cunt responds when I come close, like it knows who is its home," he mused as the tip of his pre-cum cock touched my opening.

"I love how fucking dirty you look after I chased you around the forest like the fucking little minx that you are." He pushed inside of me. I was in a state of complete bliss. My brain floating above my body until his voice brought me back to reality. The pure raw and feral fucking between us as I locked my ankles behind his back. He was ramming into me the pressure building at my core, and I was at the edge of a release. I needed him so desperately inside of me—to feel his warmth collide with my own.

"Please," I begged. I was so fucking close as his hands gripped my neck, adding a little pressure.

Suddenly, my breath slowed as he pressed down, not painfully, but just enough to make sure that my orgasm slowed slightly as his muddy hands slid around my sweater and my stomach.

"Tell me who is yours." His voice was thick with pleasure as he demanded more from me.

"Y-you." He released my neck enough for me to respond before he added a little more pressure, cutting off the air from coming in.

"Not good enough," he commanded. "Who, Ember?"

"Rain," I cried out, and then he released my neck as the rush of pleasure exploded through my core.

"Rain . . . Rain . . . Rain," I repeated as I writhed beneath him, letting the release roll through my core and sending a shiver down my spine.

I collapsed on the cool mud, suddenly remembering we were in the woods. I was hesitant only because I was worried the wave of shame would creep back into my life, but it didn't happen.

Rain lifted himself up, covered in a mess of mud, leaves, and tree bark. I burst into laughter. It wasn't even the cute, giggly type of laugh either, no, it came from deep within me from a joy hard to describe.

"Come on, princesa." He offered me a hand, and as I sat up and looked at it, I couldn't help but plaster a smile on my face.

"Rain?" I questioned.

"Yeah?"

"Can we grow old and still chase each other in the woods like this?" His fingers shook as he still held his hand out toward mine.

I knew my words held a deeper and heavier meaning. They implied I wanted to be with him forever. Aside from the house in the countryside I'd signed for, neither of us spoke of a future outside of Isles. It scared both of us to live in a future where he and I could exist together.

Because sometimes it was beautiful to dream and romanticize what your life could look like. I wanted to curl up by the fireplace and escape to faraway cities and talk about what our future would and could look like with him. I wanted to exist in the present, future, and even in the past. Because I never wanted us to lose the love we shared for Ash, either.

"It would be my honor," he finally whispered after a long pause. I grabbed his hand as he lifted me up.

"Let's go home?" he asked, and I nodded, then we ran together through the forest. In my mind, it felt like we were simply frolicking in a field, but we were naked from the bottom down, covered head to toe in mud.

Rain grabbed my jeans on the way back to the cabin where we exploded through the door into a fit of giggles as he guided me into the small bathroom.

He turned on the shower as hot as it could get, and we both tumbled in. The grass, leaves, mud fell into the tub as he rubbed soap onto my body. We were both silent, but his hands never left my body. They continued to wash and clean me.

"Do you feel better?" I asked after the silence became too deafening.

"From fucking you?" He asked and I giggled.

"No." I reached my now clean hands up to his face to wash a streak of dirt. "This is the first time we are here after what happened last time."

"My panic attack?"

"Yeah," I responded.

"I started to see a therapist."

"You did?" I asked in shock.

"Fuck yeah. After you told me you did and felt better after, why not? I have a lot of shit to work through. Obviously, I cannot tell her everything, but it feels nice to have a time set aside to talk about all of this."

"And it helped with your . . . panic attacks?" I asked as the warm water kept trickling down my back and he worked meticulously to wash me with the little bar of soap.

"Yeah, I think I just realized that you are your own person, you know?"

"No, I don't," I answered honestly.

He looked down, washing me but not looking up, as it seemed like he was trying to come up with the right words.

"I just always assumed it was Ash and Ember. Without Ash here, you were still Ash and Ember in my mind, and I needed to separate the two of you. Like you could exist with him, but you also weren't with him anymore," he explained, pausing. "It's selfish of me, but I don't know if there was anyone else other than you. I sacrificed for him to protect him, but in my heart, I watched the one person I felt an immediate connection with fall for my brother, and it was so damn hard."

"Rain," I offered empathetically, trying to ease his inner turmoil.

He pushed my hand away and stepped back in the shower. Both of us stood under the water as I blinked rapidly. "It's okay, Ember," he continued. "I think that's what I needed to know. It's okay that you were his. I'm glad he got to know what it felt like to love you."

His voice choked up as he continued, "Because loving you has been the best thing to ever happen to me. If he even felt a fraction of what I feel right now, he's an incredibly lucky man. Loving you has been the greatest honor of my life."

I knew he was crying now, even through the droplets of water from the shower. "Rain, I think I—"

He brought his fingers to my lips again, stopping me from speaking. "No," he said silently, his voice raspy, and he washed the soap off me in silence.

"Turn around," he whispered, and I obliged, his hands trailing down my body.

Once he finished, he turned off the water, handed me a towel, and gave me one of his oversized t-shirts. He helped me put it on, guiding one arm through, then my neck, and the other arm.

It was a slow, familiar routine we'd established over the last month of being together. "I don't want anyone else," I whispered, tears flowing freely. "Please, be mine," I pleaded as I turned toward him.

I was in his cabin, standing there in only his T-shirt. He was toweling off his hair lazily while putting on my favorite pair of gray sweats, which for some inexplicable reason, made him look incredibly attractive.

We walked out of the tiny bathroom and headed toward the bed in the center of the room. "Get in, mi pareja," he said, lifting the covers after he'd jumped onto the bed. I slid in next to him as he wrapped me up into a warm cocoon.

After a few minutes of silence, with only the sounds of the forest filling the cabin, I shifted so I was facing him. "Rain?" I asked for the third time today.

"Mmm?" he murmured. His eyes heavy with sleep.

"I love you," I blurted, not wanting him to stop me from saying it. I knew it wasn't technically the first time I'd confessed that I was in love with him because I had said it in class, but I'd never said it to his face.

"Em—" This time, it was my turn to stop him with my finger.

"I love you, Rain. I know you weren't always there for me, but you were. You were always there in your own way before we learned to love ourselves. When I was with Ash, our love felt so frantic and consuming." He gulped.

"I loved it because I needed it to learn that life wasn't about living in this closed-off world that I had been forced into my entire life." I smiled, thinking of falling in love with Ash and the beautiful memories we shared. "I loved him so much, Rain. But I also knew that falling in love with you would be different, which is maybe why I kept the door shut for so long. Your love scared me because it didn't consume me in the same way."

"I'm sorry—"

"No," I interrupted him. "I'm not saying that to upset you. Quite the contrary. That all-or-nothing type of love isn't sustainable for a long period of time. I can't tell you that I wouldn't be with him right now, but I also know that being with you feels safe, protective, supportive. You aren't the villain in this story; you're my hero, my savior. You brought me back from the dead."

"I'd crawl from hell to come back to you," he whispered.

"But you'd never be there. You'd be in heaven playing with Ash and Sol," I said, my chest constricting at the thought of them. "Loving you is like being wrapped in one of your hugs. It's warm, safe, and comforting. It gives me a steady surface when I still feel wobbly on my knees."

"Ember?" I looked up through blurred vision.

"Yeah?"

"I love you, too."

Our lips met in a frenzied kiss. As I sank deeper into Rain's arms, I realized that everything would be okay.

*Into the light I'll be.*

# RAIN

*I peeled open the curtains outside our dorm and noticed the car was waiting for us to take us back to Dansport. The Den, our new fraternity, was in the distance, and I couldn't believe that we were finally done with freshman year.*

*I walked into the connecting room to mine. There were two small bedroom areas, a living room, and a small bathroom in our dorm. Mr. Ortiz opted for more of the private rooms versus the open dorms.*

*"Holy shit, man, we actually did it!"*

*I was elated that we were finally on summer break. I'd decided to have creative writing as my major and was feeling good about starting those classes in the fall.*

*I expected to open the door and find Ash quickly packing his things but was welcomed by the darkness that blanketed the entire room.*

*"Ash?" I asked, my tone shifting to something more ominous. I looked around and found him tucked in the corner of the room next to his wooden desk across from his barren bed.*

*"What are you doing down there?" I asked, sitting on my haunches so I could get a better look at what was happening. He looked so sad—almost like a little kid scared in the corner. The entire year he'd actually had friends, survived his first spring bonfire where they weren't targeting him.*

*"Are you okay?" I asked when I noticed that his entire body was shaking. I dropped to my knees. The only person I'd ever get on my knees for and not in a sexual way.*

*"Ash?"*

*"I cannot go back to him, Rain. I feel so fucking lost."*

*"Then let's take summer classes and stay in Isles."* The words came out almost immediately, as if I'd been thinking about this for a while.

*"I cannot do that to you. You want to go home to see your mom."* I shook my head.

*"I don't. I want you to be happy."* Ash offered me a small smile as his sunken red face gazed in my direction.

*"You are always sacrificing for me, Rain. When are you ever going to do something for yourself?"*

*"I do a lot of things for myself,"* I told him. I thought about how I was able to pick a major that I wanted, I was able to have the friends I wanted, and I was able to have the choices that had been taken away from Ash.

I was also given the opportunity to live without this illness that burns through Ash, and I hated to see him like this. I'd give him the entire world if that's what he wanted.

*"Why?"* he croaked.

*"Why, what?"*

*"We aren't even related by blood. Why do you care?"* he asked, his voice so broken and sad that it pained me to even hear him speak.

*"Because you took me in when I needed someone the most. I lost my dad. My mom was floating around this world. I needed some stability, and you brought it to me. You gave a kid who liked to sit and read in the corner of classes the opportunity to have friends—a life."*

He gave a low chuckle. *"I gave you life?"*

I knew he thought this sounded ridiculous. Because what nineteen-year-old talks about giving someone life, but that's what Ash will never actually grasp. He gave me life because without him, I was a wandering spirit. A kid without a family. He let me understand the definition of family—of brotherhood.

"You did." I shrugged it off so nonchalantly because it was the truth. "What's it going to take to get you out of this?" I looked down at the floor.

"A beer and some pussy?" he asked, locking his eyes with mine, and I laughed so hard that I fell onto the floor with him.

"You got it, brother." I grabbed his hand and let him get up. "I'll cancel the car, too. I'll call your dad and tell him that I need to take an extra class this summer semester."

"You sure?" Ash hesitated. "I hate asking you to pause your life for me." I shook my head.

"This is what family does. But Ash? I need you to get better. I need you to talk to someone about this. There has to be someone on campus—"

"Stop." He held up a hand, straightening up and pulling down his shirt. "I am bound to be the leader of the Cartel in the United States. I was born to do this, so I cannot be talking to some shrink—"

"Mr. Ortiz doesn't have to know. It is all done in secret."

He scoffed at me.

"Let it go, Rain." He sighed and then walked to the living room. "I was just having a bad day. Everybody has bad days."

They do, but not all their bad days look this bad. That is what I would have told him had I said anything. But I said nothing because I never did. I just . . . let it go.

# EMBER

I woke up gasping for air, as if someone was suffocating me. I pushed up into bed and glanced around the room. It was early morning and dawn was about to crest around the trees. Rain shifted beneath me.

"What's wrong?" he murmured through sleepy eyes.

"I know what my brother was talking about. I need to go to his rock."

I didn't know how, but it hit me all of a sudden. The panic bubbled through me, but this time it wasn't because I was scared.

"Now?" The morning light was barely making its way into the room when I leaped out of bed and searched for some clean clothes in the duffle.

"Immediately," I demanded, and Rain only agreed before following, although far slower than I was.

"What's gotten into you?" he grumbled.

I didn't know how to answer it, but something in my dreams alerted me. My brother's words caressed my mind. He said that he promised to keep Ash's secrets. My brother was highly calculated in everything he did. The way my brother hesitated before telling me he couldn't tell me anything was a confession in and of itself.

My brother wasn't at fault here, but he was there that night, and I needed to figure out what he knew. I think the answer had been staring us in the face the entire time, I just needed to prove it.

"My brother told you that I just needed to open my eyes, right? That the answer was right in front of me?"

"That's what he told me, too," Rain said, still in a sleepy tone.

"It was either my mother or him, but when I was sleeping, I had this weird premonition that told me to go back to his rock."

"Okay."

"So, I need to go back there right now because I think we forgot something."

"Okay." Rain repeated.

"I know I probably sound crazy right now," I said as I shoved my legs into some jeans and then grabbed a clean sweater.

"Can we come back for the muddy clothes?" I wrinkled my nose because they smelled awful, and I didn't want to drive all the way to his rock with them in my bag.

"Of course." A smile finally spread across his face. "And you don't sound crazy. You sound confident. I love that about you," he mused.

He grabbed my wrists just as I finished shoving them through the sweater, and my eyes met his deep blues.

"Hey," he whispered, "I love you?" It was a statement but the way his tone lilted at the end made it sound like a question. Like everything we'd dreamed of last night was not true.

He was unsure—hesitant.

"Why are you worried?" I asked.

He scoffed. "It's hard competing with him." I wrapped his arms around me and pressed my body against his chest.

"There is no competition. You are right here. I love you."

I gave him a kiss on his soft lips before pulling away. "I love you," I repeated over and over again, and peppered him with kisses between the words.

"Okay, okay." He chuckled as he pushed me away softly. "I get it." I gave him a grin before I zipped the bag and headed toward the front door.

"We'll be back soon though, right?"

A mischievous grin lit up his face. "Why, princesa? You want me to chase you in the woods again?" A laugh echoed as I slammed the door in his face.

"I wouldn't be opposed to it," I bellowed as I walked to the ATV and hopped on the back. Rain laughed as he locked up the little hunting cabin, then jumped onto the ATV before grabbing my hands so I could wrap them around his waist.

As the wind whipped through my hair, my arms tightened around Rain, and I couldn't help but feel a sense of relief. Like somehow the answers I was desperately searching for were at the tips of my fingers.

# EMBER

We drove so fast toward Ash's rock. As we pulled into the clearing, I practically leaped off the back, grateful that my fear of riding this metal contraption has somewhat dissipated since I met Rain.

"Come on," I said, sprinting down the path toward the rock. Just as the morning light made its way into the clearing, lighting up the view, I was grateful it wasn't raining.

"What're we looking for?" Rain asked, and I loved that he didn't call me names or think I was being absurd, especially after both of us, his whole team, and so many people had combed this area a hundred times over trying to find the answers.

"It is right in front of you," I repeated my brother's words over and over again as I stared out at the clearing.

Rain came up next to me and said, "Tell me about what you guys did up here." My brows furrowed because I wasn't sure if this was the time to start talking about what we did.

"It may help jog your memory." He shrugged. "Come on, mi pareja, tell me."

"Okay," I whispered, standing there and staring out at the clearing. "After class one day, he took me here."

"The class with the fucking creep professor," Rain muttered.

"Yeah." I huffed. "But the thing was he had this whole picnic set up right on the flat part of the rock and then—"

"Wait," I shouted, and ran to where he'd pitched the tent originally and where we had the picnic. It was the only part of the rock that was flat so there was nothing underneath us as we were . . . intimate.

I ran over to where I swear the spot was, but there was a huge boulder in the corner we used to set up the blanket for our picnics.

"This was it, Rain," I demanded. "We need to move this rock."

I attempted to move it, but he only side-eyed me. "Ember, this rock didn't suddenly come from the heavens to this spot. Are you sure?"

"I swear. He must've come here beforehand to move it, but there is something not right about this." I looked at the boulder with determination. "Do you think we can move this?"

"Let's do it," he said with one of his charming grins before grasping the bottom of it so his entire body weight was pressed into the boulder.

"You push it while I lift it up."

I nodded, and as soon as he had it millimeters off the ground, I pushed the boulder forward giving it a little momentum and it slid down the clearing.

"If it was here this entire time, wouldn't you have noticed it was more stuck to the earth?" I asked.

"I'm not sure that's the proper term, but yeah, I assume if it was always here I'd expect to see more moss growing from the bottom."

"And it wouldn't have just slid forward this easily," I added, and he chuckled.

As Rain straightened, I spotted two plastic Ziploc bags where the boulder once was.

"Look," I pointed, silently thanking the world for making sure moving this boulder wasn't for nothing. "I knew it."

I reached into the little nook and pulled out the two plastic bags. Inside the bags were two letters with our names addressed right on the front in large, black Sharpie.

"I knew it," I repeated, the tears streaming down my face. "This is it."

I held the letters tight to my chest as if holding them closer meant I was holding *him*. I sniffled and then finally came back into the reality I was standing on this freaking rock yet again, but this time, with all the answers I'd begged for.

I looked up and Rain was tearing up. "It's okay," I whispered through my own sobs as I closed the distance between us, and he wrapped me in his arms.

"There are two letters."

"Yes," I said frantically, handing him his little Ziploc bag. "This one is yours."

He lifted it up before doing the same thing I did and clutched it against his chest with one arm while the other held me tightly. The two loves of his life.

"I think I need . . ." I didn't leave his side because I knew if I did, my legs would buckle from beneath me.

"I want to go read this, too." He went back to the bike down the clearing. Just as he was about to be out of sight, he turned back around and drank me in, his gaze pausing on me.

I had the same thought as him. I'd wondered if what was written inside this letter would change us. It shouldn't, but Ash had that power. "I'll be there when I'm done, I promise."

He hung his head low and turned back on his path.

I swallowed a few times before settling on sitting atop one of the trunks of the trees near the view where I'd found his phone. It made me feel closer to him.

I peeled the bag open with my sweaty hands. It was so hot even though it was well in the forties, inside, I was burning with nerves.

I took a deep breath.

"You can do this," I whispered to the trees before I pulled the letter from the bag and smelled it. It smelled like pine which I knew probably was a mere coincidence because we were in a pine forest, but I wanted to pretend like it was Ash. His familiar scent. His words. His script.

I slowly opened the letter, and it was handwritten to perfection. God, this is the closest I'd felt to him in so long. Even with his phone in my hand, he wrote this. His last letter.

Dear Ember,

By now, your very intelligent brain has already figured out that the boulder, which was a bitch to lug up here alone, did not belong in OUR spot, so you've now found my letter. At least, that is how I imagined this going in my head, but who knows, maybe this letter sits here for thousands of years until someone else happens upon it. Anyway, unless you are Ember Solis, please stop reading because this would make no sense, otherwise.

Mi sol, I understand that everything must appear bewildering to you. You've likely craving answers, and now, I can finally provide them. I expect you to be angry with me for making you work to uncover the truth. But you must understand that the most precious things in life often require effort. These were secrets I had to keep, not just from you, but also from Rain because revealing them would have placed you both in danger, and that was something I could not allow.

So, before you dive into these words, I implore you to open your heart and try to see things from my perspective. Every action I took has always been, and will forever be, for your sake. However, I need you to grasp that I, too, was trapped under a thick blanket of my father's protection.

After you read this, you must show this letter to your brother, Walsh. He holds all the proof you need. I had to ensure that he was the only one with this information, and only when you and Rain had gathered all the pieces, could you gain the upper hand. Please do not be angry with him for keeping this from you. Your brother and I both agreed that you should remain in the dark until you were ready to handle the truth.

I've been talking to Walsh for a while, but he never knew this was my plan. To be honest, until this morning, I didn't either. I snuck out early morning before the guys were awake, day before the bonfire, to move the boulder. As I write this, I still don't know if or when but I know when the time is right, it's my turn to go. I'll have a sign.

I'm chuckling now, Ember, because you were absolutely right. I now understand the immense power of words over force. I spent these last few months carefully arranging everything for you. Now, I need to tell you some things that may explain why this letter started the way it did.

To address the more difficult subjects, I had to leave because my role in this world had come to an end. I hope you won't blame yourself, as this decision had nothing to do with our separation. While I was heartbroken, it oddly helped me put together the final pieces I needed to feel free from the shackles which bound me to this earth.

The day I saw you in the elevator, I knew my task at trying to ruin you would be much harder. I went up there to spy on you—to see if you'd moved in but then I saw you come in and tell me I was hot. I laughed, genuinely laughed, for the first time…ever. I was told to park there to keep an eye on you so that I could get around your guards, but then I kept my car there just to feel closer to you. I loved you the moment I laid eyes on you.

So please refrain from blaming yourself. Let me emphasize once more: do not blame yourself. In fact, whenever you feel that urge, read this part of the letter repeatedly. I had been unwell for a long time, Ember. Rain knew it — ask him. Contemplating my departure was not a new thought. You've finally helped me see that my purpose was not aligned with the burdens I was forced to bear under my father's influence.

I am so tired, Ember. So fucking exhausted. But I want to leave you with everything you'd need to live your life because I need you to do that for me. Promise me you are living in a beautiful, happy way? I want you to go on and become the most amazing writer the world has ever seen. Heck, maybe you can write our story one day because the world deserves to hear about how you've blossomed in the last year. You are beautiful, Ember, and I hope you show the world that beauty.

Which brings me to the last point. Depending on when you find this letter, I guess it kinda makes this point either valid or moot, but I need you to know whether you want or need it. You need to live your life, Ember. Live it for the both of us. Fall in love with someone who isn't sick like me. I want you to fall completely and totally in love with someone who loves you more than I ever could, but first you need to promise you'll fall in love with yourself. Because self-love takes hard work and determination. It's something you need to work on every single day.

Love yourself over and over again.

Then fall in love with a person who will protect you fearlessly. My brother loves you, Ember. I cannot predict what the future will bring, but I see the way Rain looks at you. He'd protect you. He'd love you. He'd provide a life for you that I can't. I hope that you end up with him . . . or at least someone like him.

God, Ember, I'll miss you. I'll miss you so fucking much. But I need to go now. Go to Rain. Talk to Walsh. Go, mi sol.

You will always be the sunshine to my dark day. I just need to rest now.

I'll see you up there.

I love you always and forever,

Ash

# RAIN

Dear Rain,

I know. It finally happened, and you weren't there to rescue me. I can almost picture how you've tearing yourself apart inside, though I bet you won't let anyone see how utterly shattered you are on the outside. But you need to let her in, Rain.

Don't feign surprise right now. You've been in love with her since the very moment she kissed you in front of the house. I saw the way you looked at her, the hesitation in your hand as you tattooed her, the disgust in your eyes during the initiation because you knew what I was putting her through. Love her, Rain. I'm begging you. Just because I'm not here doesn't mean you should keep subjecting yourself to being away from her. I know you so well, Rain. We've been brothers for years, and in some cosmic way, I've felt we were always destined to be brothers. It just took us a few years to find our way to each other.

It's ironic because I can attribute the one good thing my father did to bringing me closer to you. If you weren't around, I would've left this place a long time ago, but you saved me in more ways than one. Reflecting on it now, it was always you protecting me. I had to do this to protect you. I've told Walsh that he mustn't say anything, to protect Ember, until you find these letters. I needed both of you to find your way back to each other, and I hoped that by giving you these letters at the same time, it would help you to piece together this final portion.

Stop. Blaming. Yourself.

There's nothing you could have done differently. I always knew this was what I wanted to do. Right now, I am at peace.

If I could envision your future, you'd be getting out of this place and living a secluded life in the countryside with Ember. Promise me you won't abandon her, even if she's happily married or something by the time you both retrieve these letters. Always watch over her for me.

Now, onto the business side of things, which I know you hate discussing, but it's crucial. You'll find the evidence Walsh has given you. Please don't be angry with him either. He was merely following a dead man's orders. Well, not entirely, but I'll explain further.

He possesses all the information you need to take down my father. Over the last few years, I've become quite adept at collecting information about him that the Cartel won't find acceptable. I don't want to get him killed, but I need someone you deem suitable to replace him. I won't detail what they are in this letter, but you'll find everything in a lockbox accessible with a key Walsh has.

Use this evidence to facilitate a meeting Ember had been wanting to arrange. It was supposed to happen, but I'm sure this event may have disrupted their plans. Have Ember call her dad, Walsh, and mine; they all need to be in the same room.

Use your words, Rain. They are so fucking powerful. Don't resort to physical force because that's what they'll expect. With words, you can accomplish so much more.

And Rain? I am incredibly proud and honored to call you my brother. You've done far more for me, sacrificed beyond my wildest expectations. It's time for you to unfurl your own wings and shine. Don't let them coerce you into something you don't want. You've always had the ability to hide within the shadows; now, it's time to soar and pursue everything you've ever desired.

Oh, and before I finish this up, I left Ember money in my will. Do not let him take that. Please. It's for her. And you.

You are my brother. See you soon.

I will always be there for you, Rain—in spirit.

Always and forever,

Ash

I felt.

I was feeling.

My body quivered, and the paper in my hands seemed as fragile as my trembling grip. Clutching it tightly to my chest, I closed my eyes and looked up to the sky, as if searching for a connection to him once more.

The sound of her boots reverberated through the forest as I dismounted the motorcycle, my face still drenched from the unrestrained tears. I carefully placed the envelope containing the letter inside the compartment on my bike for safekeeping.

Walking toward the sound of her footsteps, we locked eyes when we finally met, both of us pausing, as though aware that reading these letters might alter the course of our lives. And they did, but in ways we could never have foreseen.

"Ember?" I whispered, my voice quivering with emotion.

She sprinted toward me with unwavering determination, and I opened my arms wide as she crashed into me. Her sobs racked her entire frame, and she crumpled under my embrace, consumed by tears and exhaustion.

"It . . . I . . . Walsh . . ." She struggled with her words, so I held her closer. Swallowing hard, I allowed myself to feel, acknowledging the sadness of losing my brother, the pain I had carried for months until her return, and the guilt that had plagued me for a year.

"It's all over," I whispered through my own tears. "It's all okay now."

It wasn't over per se, but the pain we felt finally had some closure to it, and I knew that deep down inside it was our turn to live and we could close this chapter. But closing a chapter of a book doesn't mean it ends. It was a part of our life, but we could move to the next part of our story.

As our tears gradually subsided, I continued to cradle her in my arms, her head nestled against my chest. She slowly pulled away, and our gazes locked. Her eyes were rimmed with red and swollen from the mixture of physical and emotional pain, intermingled with the catharsis brought on by these letters.

"We need to find Walsh," she whispered, and I nodded. "I need to figure out why he was there that night."

"Are you okay?" I asked, refraining from prying into the contents of her letter, as I understood that it was her story to share or withhold, her choice.

"Yes . . . no." She chuckled as if her answer surprised her. "I just want to finally be able to get the last clue that we needed."

I shook my head in agreement. With one last deep inhale, the smell of pines wafted through my nose. I looked around me as warm fingers wiped the wetness from my cheeks.

I took one more deep breath before I gestured behind us where my bike still stood. "Let's go find him."

Ember looked down, clutching her letter to her chest, and I turned to walk away.

"Rain," she shouted, and I turned toward her. She closed the gap between us and reached for me.

I looked down at her hand and then back up, locking my gaze with hers. Her eyes told such a different story than the rest of her. They were soft and gentle. I grabbed her hand, we walked in silence toward the bike where she tucked the envelope next to mine and put on her helmet.

I revved the engine, but right before she leaped onto the back, she looked at me and whispered, "I love you."

The words could have been heard through the pines, ringing out like a melody before settling into their rightful place—my heart.

"Together," I whispered back.

# EMBER

We pulled up to the Alpha house and parked in front. Rain hesitated while I practically stormed off the bike, so I had to gesture to him to follow me.

"I guess it's been so ingrained in my head that this house is bad and dangerous it just feels weird to pull up here." He sighed before shaking his head and then opening the compartment where our letters were stored.

Our letters. It was hard to even say it to myself, let alone talk about it with Walsh, but I wanted to see the proof Walsh held and why he of all people had it.

I bounded toward the house, pounding onto the door until one of the members answered it.

"Where is he?" I growled at the guy. Poor guy didn't realize he was in the crosshairs of an angry sister.

"Up-upstairs," he mumbled before looking over my shoulder, then quickly straightened. "Oh no, absolutely not. He is not coming in here."

"Yes, he is. We need to see Walsh." The guy stood in front of the door, blocking us.

"No. He's not coming in unless there is an official meeting." The guy's eyes softened at me. "Come on, little sister, you know I cannot let you guys in together."

"Call him down. Make the meeting official. I don't care what happens, but we need to see him immediately."

"I don't know—"

"Let them in," my brother's familiar voice echoed from behind the guy at the door.

"Thank fuck," I muttered before reaching behind me for Rain's hand. Rain didn't hesitate. My brother would figure this out, anyway, and I needed Rain's support as much as he needed mine.

Walsh guided us to the office or converted meeting room in the back of the house where most of his business dealings took place. He closed the door behind us before sitting atop the desk and gesturing to two chairs in front.

I shook my head before I held out the letters in their Ziploc bags and shoved them at Walsh.

"Open it if you need to, but I think you already know what these are." My tone was bitter.

Rain came next to me, wrapping his arm across my lower back and giving my hip a comforting squeeze.

Walsh coughed. "Ah, I see you guys finally found them. I was hoping you—"

"Did you know where they were?" I barked.

"No, Ember. I swear he didn't tell me their location."

"Fuck," I cried. I would not let the tears come, but the anger was coursing through my veins deeply.

"Show us what you have," Rain added, and I snapped my attention toward him. His eyes met mine with some softness and comfort in them, but I didn't want to give my brother any mercy.

"Why?" I bit back while Walsh rubbed his hands together in his lap over and over again.

"Because he begged me to," Walsh said after waiting a beat to reply.

"No." I threw my hands in the air. "Absolutely fucking not."

"Ember," Rain warned as I slipped out of his grip and stormed toward my brother.

"You do not fucking get to give us these evasive answers like you've been doing over the last year, Walsh," I screamed in his face.

"You need to tell us what happened immediately, without leaving out a single shred of information in order to redeem yourself."

He sighed and then looked down at me. For a brief second, all the torment and the months of pain and waiting surfaced on his face. He looked tired from holding onto this weight of secrecy for so long.

"He came to me a few weeks before you guys broke up. He set up a private, formal meeting and wanted to give me this envelope. We looked at it together. You can imagine how it must've felt to get this information about my enemy and mostly my dad's archnemesis." Walsh looked up at Rain.

"Yeah, why did he do that?" Rain chimed.

"I had the same question, but then Ash told me that he was originally supposed to use Ember to get closer to our family. I was livid, but he convinced me that he was in love with her. He wanted to protect her and was worried something was going to happen to him." Walsh swallowed, his Adam's apple bobbing.

"I assumed it was from the Cartel initially, which I guess was fucking stupid, but he was acting so calm, so he handed me the envelope of this shit that would put away his dad forever and honestly, get the fucker killed." He paused. "Then he told me he was going to be possibly leaving for a while and needed to make sure that neither of you guys had this information until you got your letters."

"Did you ask him about the letters?" I asked.

Walsh shrugged. "I did and he said he was going to deliver them to you while he was gone. I didn't press him any further."

Walsh's hands were stark white from grabbing the sides of the table. "Over the time when you broke up with him Ember, he started to get more frantic and concerned that I was going to show you this. I promised I'd wait like I told him I would until the right time, until he got back."

I wanted to melt into the floor. My heart was shattering all over again thinking of the trauma and pain that Ash must've felt in that moment. "The night before the bonfire, I was worried about him. I heard from him earlier that morning. He told me he was going to leave that afternoon. He made me promise that until you guys gave me these letters that gave him permission I wouldn't share this with you. He made me." He took in a deep breath. "I was worried, so I followed him that day."

"He was running," Rain said, and I looked over to him standing in the back of the room closer to the door. I didn't hear him walk backward, too lost in my own pain, but I crossed the room and grabbed his fingers, interlacing mine with his. Our sign that we were in this together.

"He was escaping," my brother corrected. "I followed him to the woods. At first, I wanted to scare him a little bit because he was technically off-campus." Walsh winced. He added softly, "I am sorry."

I shook my head. "What happened next?"

I thought I was just scaring him, but then I realized he wasn't leaving the woods. He was hiding, so I sat quietly waiting to see what he was going to do. I wanted to be sure he got back to campus safely. My heart was beating out of my chest and I can't explain it but I just had a bad feeling about it all."

Walsh closed his eyes. "After a few moments I watched him walk to the edge of that damn clearing. When I realized . . ." This was hurting him. I closed my eyes, willing myself out of this nightmare, but I was in the room with the one person who saw Ash before he died.

"You were there," I repeated.

"I was. I was worried about him, but when I saw him standing on the edge, I called his name. I screamed no. I told him to stop. He stopped to look back at me." A tear ran down Walsh's face. Rain coughed, and I saw he was crying too.

"I begged him to step away from the clearing. I took a few steps closer toward the rock when he yelled at me, telling me that everyone would be looking in the area. That I would trek the mud onto the rock and they would think I pushed him because of how close we were to the bonfire."

"W-Walsh." Rain held me in his arms, my back pressed against his chest as he sobbed. I couldn't look up because if I did, the dam would explode within me, too.

"He looked so peaceful, Ember. He looked so at peace with this choice, which only made it harder. After he yelled at me to stand where I was, back in the mud of the path, he begged me to show you this, but not until you found your letters." He paused. "I begged him to tell me why we needed to wait, and he just said the answers were in the letters. You guys needed time to find your way to each other before you were ready."

Walsh swallowed back his own pain. "I screamed no again but then just watched as he...tumbled." A lone tear ran down my brother's cheek.

"That asshole" Rain said through tears, his chest heaving. "We may have never found them, then what?"

Walsh shrugged. "I wouldn't have shown you this. I guess life would have looked like it had." My brother glanced back toward me. "Ember, don't you think it was hard for me to keep all of this from you? You are my only sister, but over the time that I got to know Ash, I realized his intentions for you were built from the love he had for you. He was protecting you, and in some wild way, I thought that by complying with his asinine instructions, this would bring us closure."

His voice quieted. "Dad told me you were grieving hard."

"I was. I still am." My voice matched his soft tone.

"Ash loved you. He spoke of you so deeply and fondly. He knew that you were going to be the one to help push this all together. I just wanted to protect my sister. You're my only sister, and I spent my entire life protecting you, so I wanted to give this to you."

I was trying to be strong. I was really fucking trying, but my entire being was cracking in half as if the world was cleaving open.

"I told you I don't need protection," I whispered.

"I've seen a lot of fucking death in life, Ember. But I have never seen anyone . . . do that before. It was fucking traumatizing," Walsh whispered. "I just wanted to protect you from feeling the pain that I felt."

I wanted to curl up in a ball and melt into the floor and disappear. I wanted, no, needed an escape.

Rain coughed a few times before he looked down at me. "I have to—Give me a minute," he murmured.

He shook his head at me before he walked out of the door behind us. The weight of the room intensified as Walsh got off the desk and closed the distance between us.

"I was just trying to protect him and protect you, and maybe I fucked up, but I made him a promise, Em." His voice was quiet.

I knew that was what he was trying to do, and at this point, what's done was done, but it hurt that Walsh kept this secret for this long. We could have resolved this long ago if he'd have just given us the envelope.

"After what I saw, I couldn't help but keep that for him. I felt like I owed him that promise, so as crazy as it sounds I kept this from you. I know I should've told you but if you saw what I did–"

I stopped him, holding up my hand. "I probably would've done the same thing." Walsh let out a sigh of relief.

"Can we go back to talking to each other?" he asked, and I shook my head.

"I don't know how to move forward between us. We have a lot of learning and growing to do, but right now my focus is trying to figure this out. We're going to need your help with facilitating meetings between Dad and Mr. Ortiz."

"Of course, Em."

I paused, taking a deep breath. In that moment, I realized the trauma that my brother must have endured in this. Vowing to keep a secret to a dead man's last wish was something heavy, and truthfully, I was not sure I'd be able to share it either.

"I understand why you did what you had to, to respect Ash."

"Thank you," Walsh said softly, the red beneath his eyes growing as the tears flowed freely. "I've never seen anyone talk about you with so much love in his heart. I thought, stupidly, that Dad and I were all you were ever going to need, but when he spoke of you, Ember, it was with such a light. You brought him probably the best year of his life—even with the battle he was fighting inside his head."

I nodded because I was choked up. My brother closed the distance between us, and I let him hold me. Both of us were two broken, tattered souls, and I'd lost the last year with him.

"This isn't how you expected my college experience to be, did you?" I sob-laughed into his chest, and he held me tightly. After a moment, I pulled away and looked at his tortured face.

"I need you to know from here on out, I need to care for myself. I don't need anyone to protect me. I can protect myself."

"I understand." Walsh looked past the door where Rain had walked out a few minutes ago. "Is he . . . are you?"

"I don't know, but yes?" It was a question, not because I wasn't sure of Rain but mostly because I didn't know what we were. "I fell in love with him."

I swallowed because it was an uncomfortable thing to talk about with my brother for many reasons, but mostly because I felt guilty for having these thoughts of Rain while we were talking so intimately about Ash.

"He wanted you two to be together. He told me that Rain's letter was in there for you to find. He wanted it to be him."

I nodded because, again, if the words came out, they'd be replaced by a bucket of tears.

A slight knock at the door shook me out of my thoughts, and Rain came back into the room.

"Sorry," he muttered before coming next to me and pressing a kiss to the side of my head.

"It's okay," I replied, my hand lingering on his bicep so he knew I was there for him if he needed it.

"Okay. Let's talk about this meeting. Ember already knows about Pico and my wishes there."

"Right, yes. Let me go get the envelope. It's in a safe in my room. I'll be right back." Walsh excused himself from the room, and I turned toward Rain.

"Are you okay?" I whispered, getting up on my tiptoes so we could face each other.

"No. Are you?" I huffed an exasperated breath.

"No."

"Good. Now, let's take this pain and turn it into something else."

"I agree." His fingers caressed my cheeks as he brought my face to his, our noses touching.

"Together," I whispered, hovering over his mouth.

"Together." He kissed me in a way that was consuming. In the way he always kissed me.

Moments later, Walsh came in, and Rain and I sat in the two chairs we'd pulled up next to the desk. Walsh dropped the manila envelope onto the large wooden desk in front of us before retreating to the back of the room, giving us the space we needed.

"You do it," I encouraged Rain. "You'll know more about what's inside of this than I'll understand."

"Are you sure?" Rain asked.

"Yes."

His fingers hovered over the clasp of the envelope before he opened it. As he pulled out the papers, there was a loud gasp.

# RAIN

There were hundreds of photos, bank receipts, and transcriptions of what looked like phone calls in this envelope. All of which incriminated Mr. Ortiz. I quickly opened each paper detailing exactly how badly Mr. Ortiz fucked up.

Every. Single. One.

I inhaled deeply as I took the first one out and read it over. It was a bank statement that detailed Mr. Ortiz was skimming from the Cartel by quite a large percentage off of his large properties. He managed most of the legitimate businesses in America so they could funnel their drugs and launder their guns.

What Mr. Ortiz was doing was also taking a percentage of what they were laundering and keeping it for himself. If Ash had access to these, then others must've been close to figuring out what he was doing, too.

I pulled out one of the photos and was shocked at what I saw.

"Holy shit." Ember peered over my shoulder to see the same thing I was looking at. "Didn't they get married recently?"

"Yeah."

"What is the date on this?" she asked.

"A month before Ash passed away." I held the photo, and it was Mr. Ortiz walking out of a strip club next to the same person fucking him in the back of his vehicle.

"I am so sorry—"

"I'm not." I chuckled, which was highly inappropriate, but I didn't give a fuck, to be honest. "My mom has always had this happen to her. She picks the wrong fucking men all the time, and she stopped listening to me a long time ago."

Frankly, my mom and I never had a relationship.

"You never talk about her."

"There isn't much to talk about." My mom stopped raising me a long time ago. I relied on Ash to get through the day most of the time, especially when I was younger and he would help me get the basic necessities I needed to eat, sleep, and shower. My mom stopped parenting when she lost my dad, but honestly, who knows how much she did before that.

"You can always talk to me—"

"Ember, seriously. I am fine." It was the truth. Looking at these pictures of my stepfather cheating on my mom should have ignited some pain and hurt within me, but nothing happened. I felt absolutely nothing about it. He was a bad fucking man and not in the villain-gets-the-girl-bookish sort of way. No, he was a horrible human.

She squeezed my arm before I opened a few more bank statements.

"Walsh?" I said, turning around to where I knew he was still standing. "Can you come here and help me go through these?"

"Oh, uh, yeah."

I needed to excuse myself, to process the grief I was feeling, the pain I kept hearing in her voice, but the reason Walsh kept this to himself, I understood. It was all part of a bigger plan that Ash orchestrated. If he'd asked me to keep a secret before he died, I would've gone to my grave with it, too . . . especially if it was for Ember's protection. What Walsh had to see, experience, and do this last year had to have given him as much heartbreak as I had to endure, just in a different way.

"These are bank statements," I began, spreading the papers before them. "Mr. Ortiz has been embezzling funds from the

Cartel. There are also photos of him being unfaithful to my mom." I set aside another stack of documents. "These contain confidential Cartel information, like transcripts from the strip club."

"Holy shit," Walsh exclaimed, his jaw dropped. "This is really bad." He was thumbing through the transcripts from the club. They all described Mr. Ortiz as discussing confidential Cartel information at the club in front of the strippers. There was also a recording device on a USB with the actual transcripts, according to the note next to it.

"Good," I replied firmly.

"This will enable Pico to assume control swiftly," Walsh said.

"Yeah, right after graduation," I added.

"Pico?" Ember inquired.

"Yeah, mi pareja," I confirmed. "Remember I told you I thought he'd be—"

"Oh, right. I think he'd make the best leader," she said.

"I agree," I responded, giving her a warm smile. Her desire to be involved and included warmed my heart amid this otherwise somber day.

"What's our next move?" Walsh asked.

"I'll go back and speak with Pico, but we need to gather everyone together," I explained.

"Isles is the best place for the meeting, right? Doesn't the neutral territory extend to the elders, too?" Ember asked. I leaned in close to Ember's ear, feeling immensely proud of her.

"There you are," I whispered before pressing a kiss onto the shell of her ear.

"That's correct," Walsh replied on my behalf. "However, there's no way Dad will come down here for a sit-down with Mr. Ortiz without insisting on security, armed guards, and everything that could sabotage the meeting."

"You have a point," I admitted.

"What if we tell Dad to meet us at the diner? We can say that we've finally reconciled and want to talk to him about it. He'll probably come with just his bodyguard if he knows it's only us," Walsh suggested.

"I can inform Mr. Ortiz that we need to discuss what happened with Ash. I've pieced it all together now. He'll want to know about the missing money," I added.

"What money?" Walsh asked.

"Ash had a will that was done by a lawyer. It gives his entire trust to Ember. The whole reason Mr. Ortiz is so fucking hell bent on figuring out or thinking it was you at the woods that day was because he wants that money."

"I wonder if he knows someone is onto him, which is why he needs the trust to replenish the Cartel funds," Ember added, and Walsh and I turned toward her.

"Holy—" I was shocked.

"Shit." Walsh finished.

"Ember, that is it." I gave her a huge kiss on her lips before practically leaping off the chair and walking over to Walsh. I paused in front of him before I grabbed him and gave him a hug.

"He is using the trust to replenish the funds," Walsh repeated.

"In the meeting, we are going to fuck him by not outing him to the Cartel. As much as I'd like to see the fucker dead, I don't know if that's the best endgame right now. We will just use our evidence as blackmail and to get Pico to the top spot right after graduation this summer."

"Then we use the information to make sure Ember gets to keep her portion from the will."

"Yes."

"Okay. I'll have him come in tomorrow."

"Tomorrow works because I need to prepare Pico."

"Okay, I guess I'll see you guys then?" Walsh questioned. We both nodded before piling up the letters and bringing them back to the bike.

Once we got outside, I tugged on Ember's hand, encouraging her to meet me outside the gates. She looked between Walsh and I, unsure, but eventually agreed.

"I know it's an inappropriate time to talk about this, but I just wanted to let you know that I understood why you did that with him."

"Kept the secret?" Walsh questioned.

"Yeah." I sighed.

"I didn't want to hurt my sister, but I was so conflicted—"

I stopped him. "I know. I get it."

"Thank you . . . you know, for understanding."

I pursed my lips, my jaw clenching as I shoved my hands in my pocket. I was standing on the stoop of this massive mansion behind me while Ember waited just outside the large gates.

"About Ember," I began. "I just wanted you to know how much I really care about her."

"I know," Walsh added quickly. "I see it. I think Ash saw it, too."

"It didn't start until she came back to school, but there is just something about her." I looked out at the distance, watching her jet-black hair fly in the wind.

"She's special," Walsh agreed. "I know you don't need it or anything, but you have my permission to fall in love with her. To be with her forever." He chuffed.

"You know about the house, Walsh."

He shook his head, a smile creeping on his face. "Come on, of course I know."

I gave him a quick twist of my lips. "Thank you. For the permission. I do love her." I gave him a quick handshake before walking toward the bike where Ember was standing.

"Is everything okay?" she asked as soon as I'd gotten past the large wrought iron gates.

"Perfect, mi pareja." I dropped a kiss onto her lips. "Let's go home?"

She laughed one of those beautiful melodic laughs where her entire body shook. "Which one?"

The corners of my lips twisted up. "Very funny, princesa."

We'd decided to go to Ember's apartment.

"It's not even five p.m." She whined, and I looked at the clock for confirmation and laughed.

"It feels like it's freaking two a.m." Her weary smile was so bright, even in the dimly lit apartment.

"I like you here," she said, standing on the other side of the apartment where the small kitchen was. I was over by the windows watching as the rain lightly hit the window. The sound was something that existed in one of those sleep machine sounds to help people sleep. The *tap-tap-tap* from the rain hitting the cold glass was soothing.

"I like being here," I whispered, "but there's nowhere for you to run here." I gave her a little wink before she rolled her eyes at me.

"Unlike at our house." Fuck, the way she said *our* made me so fucking hard and desperate to taste her sweet little cunt.

"Come here," I demanded, and she stalked toward me.

"Take off your shirt," I growled back at her. She stopped midstep, about halfway to me before she looked down and pulled her sweater off her head.

"It is pretty dirty," she mused.

"So are your pants." My lips were slick with anticipation as I rolled my tongue across my bottom lip while watching her step out of them. "That's it. That's my good girl."

She was standing in the middle of the living room in a matching dainty lingerie set with all her curves on display. Every nook and cranny, perfect places for my hands to grab.

"Fuck," I moaned, thinking all the ways I could fuck her in this room. I needed her.

I crossed the room in two large steps, and my hand went to her neck, lifting her up, with a little pressure so she was forced to look in my eyes.

"So fucking beautiful," I mused. "Show me what a good little slut you are for Daddy."

The shock in her eyes was so apparent, but I think that's the part I loved most about Ember. "Don't act surprised, princesa. You know you want my dirty tongue all over you."

"Yes," she groaned as I let go of her throat and dropped down into the big armchair in the corner of the room.

"Get on your hands and knees." She dropped to the floor. Her black hair cascaded over her shoulders as her lips puffed in anticipation. How she could stir up every emotion inside me was incredible. But I mostly loved how she let me play this game with her. Let me be the predator for her.

"Crawl to me," I demanded as I splayed out in the chair. Even though my jeans were still on, my cock was throbbing. It was so hard I could have fucking come just watching her tits bounce as she happily obliged like the good little slut she was.

"Come on, my little princesa. Ven aquí." Her eyes enraptured me as they sparkled at the Spanish tongue that rolled out so easily in the bedroom.

My entire body pulsed with need as she crawled toward me. I bent down, looking at her from where I was sitting.

"Tell me, what do you want?" I demanded from her.

"You."

"And who am I to you?" I grabbed her chin, forcing her to look up at me.

"Mine." It rolled off her tongue with such ease that even I believed it was true.

"Yes, you are." I whispered. "Stand up. Take off my pants." I loved barking out rules to her.

She got up and helped me remove my jeans. Her little fingers toyed with the hem of my shirt as she slowly lifted it over my head. There I sat, displayed in all my glory for her to see. She let out this sweet little sound from her little fucking dirty mouth like she always did when she saw me naked. As if I was some god she watched, undressed. It was such a sweet and delicate little noise that rattled me to my absolute core.

"Can I suck your cock?" she asked. That was it. The head of my cock twitched as it leaked pre-cum. It would probably turn into me coming all over myself if she continued talking like that.

I looked down at my aching dick and then locked eyes with her deep-brown ones before she dropped back down to her knees, and I scooted toward the edge of the chair.

"Open up, really wide." I encouraged. Her big, beautiful round eyes looked up at me, clouded in a haze of carnal pleasure right before she took me into her mouth. Her jaw relaxed, pulling me in. The tip of my cock touched the back of her throat, and the warm sensation washed through me.

"You are doing such a good job." I moaned as she bobbed up and down, wrapping me up with an indescribable salacious sensation that only pressed me closer to exploding in her sweet, little mouth.

"Yeah? Am I doing good?" she asked, looking up at me with that same doe-eyed expression I wanted to fuck off her sweet face.

"Such a good girl. You know how to make Daddy feel so good. Keep going, princesa," I encouraged as she continued to take me deep down her throat. She massaged my balls, and I let out a noise that was a cross between a moan and a growl. It was not at all sexy, but it was felt deep down inside of me—something so primal.

She sucked me off until I almost exploded into a pure state of bliss. I leaned back in the chair, like the fucking king I felt, and closed my eyes while her sweet little mouth and tongue explored my needy cock.

The cool air blasted on me, and the immediate sensation of being released from her moist mouth shocked me back into reality.

"What the—" I exclaimed, looking to where she was supposed to be but instead she stood in front of me.

"Don't like being edged on the brink of an orgasm, huh?"

Oh, that little fucking minx was giving me a little taste of my own medicine. Well, if that's how she wanted to play the game—

"Come here." I grabbed her waist and hoisted her onto me.

"No." She tsked. "Watch me." One side of my mouth lifted as I leaned back in the chair.

She unclipped her lace bra, then shimmied out of it. Her voluptuous tits bounced freely, and her nipples pebbled in her cool apartment, although everything on my body was hot and bothered.

"So fucking beautiful. A work of art in human form."

The corner of her lip twisted in a smile, but only for a second before the fevered desire pooled in her eyes, getting hazy as her hands languidly trailed down her creamy skin.

They stopped at the top of her panties just as she leaned in toward me so her tits were falling in my face. I grabbed her nipple, quickly rolling it between my forefinger and thumb.

The noise that came from me touching her sensitive nipples was so carnal that my cock couldn't get inside her fast enough. She was working me up—knowing exactly what she was doing by giving me a performance.

"Tsk, tsk," she mused before pulling back and slipping out of her panties.

"Goddamn woman, I think you are trying to kill me." I was not beneath begging.

She turned around and then dropped down to her hands and knees again.

"Hold my legs," she demanded as she hoisted her legs up. It looked almost like I was about to wheelbarrow her with her ass in my face.

Her ass shook as it got into position, and I couldn't help but give it a little slap, letting the resounding noise echo in the quiet apartment.

"You like that?" she asked from the ground, and I responded by grabbing her hips and thrusting her onto my cock.

She was up on her hands in a modified handstand as I held onto most of her weight and slowly slid inside of her.

When I said I hated fucking in the same missionary way over and over again, this was what I meant by needing excitement. It was a combination of Ember being fucking perfection for me and her curiosity to explore. The fact she found a haven in me—in us.

"I love you, mi pareja," I whispered before I gave her ass a few little slaps, loving the way my hands left red hand outlines on her as my precum dripped into her opening.

"Ohh, fuckkk me."

I laughed. "That is the intention, princesa." My cock was twitching, a desperate little fucker, who needed to feel her tight little cunt wrapped around it. I pushed in deeper and was welcomed by the familiar tight, warmth and knew I would not last long.

She was losing balance as her body gave into her pleasure, but I gripped tighter into the dips right by her hips and let her ass slap against my stomach.

"Breathe. Go slow," I instructed, and her body responded to my demands. She propped herself up on her elbows for a little more stability as I slammed inside of her.

"Yes. Yes. *Yes*," she cried, the last one came out a strangled sob as she bounced on my cock, slamming over and over into her tight, little cunt.

"Fuck me, princesa," I demanded, and held onto her as she thrust up and down on me, moving her hips in sync with my body.

Each thrust was followed by a moan, and at a certain point, sweat beaded down her head, as she was upside down still fucking me.

"Rain," she cried before my own explosion crept up onto me.

"Rain," she moaned.

"Rain," she wailed over and over again.

"Yours," I replied right before exploding inside of her. My entire body released everything that was stress and tense.

She fell onto the floor, and I carefully dropped her legs before lifting her up and walking her over to the bathroom.

"No," she groaned. "Too tired."

I chuckled. "Come on, Em." I stood her up in the bathroom while I turned on the water, waiting for it to get warm before I lifted her into the shower and joined her.

"I have never sweat more in my life." Her eyes met mine, and we broke out in a laugh that exploded throughout the small bathroom.

"Ouch." She touched her red butt cheeks.

"You okay?"

"Just a little sore," she mumbled before grabbing some soap and rubbing it all over her and then jumping out. I hurried, too, so I could follow her.

"I am so tired," she mumbled before throwing on one of my shirts that I left tucked in the corner of the bathroom since she liked to wear them after she got out of the hot shower. She always took a shower before bed, claiming she hated to get into her bed feeling dirty from the day. She also liked the warmth of the shower and savoring each second in the humid air, so she liked putting on her pajamas inside the bathroom instead of going to her room.

It was the little things that I'd learned about her over the last few months. Things I pieced together that added to the entire picture of who she was.

She hobbled over to the bed before collapsing.

"So. Tired." She rolled over and grabbed the sheets before escaping into a deep slumber.

This was what I would love about our future—Ember would always be there at the end of the day. I'd get to fuck her all I wanted, feed her, cherish her like the damned queen she was.

Porque ella no era una princesa, era mi reina. And I was a humble servant to her kingdom, bowing down to my true ruler.

I tucked in next to her as I pulled the covers tightly over her.

"Turn around," I instructed, and she mumbled something that made little sense in her sleep-induced postcoital haze, but obliged by shifting her body to the other side. I lifted the shirt and slowly warmed up the lotion I found in her bathroom in my hands before running it over the parts that I'd slapped earlier.

"Mm-hm," she groaned out in pleasure. "That feels good. Thank you."

The smile that came afterward nourished me. It fed my soul. Because hearing her breath inside our bed, watching her want me, care for me, was something I wished I could write about. But between the words, the emotion that came out of the quiet moments were more powerful than all the ways I could describe how and why I loved Ember.

"I love you," I whispered before pulling her back tightly to my chest. I gave her a kiss by the shell of her ear as she murmured in pleasure.

"I love you, so much. Thank you for being there for me."

# RAIN

The next afternoon, I was so fucking nervous because while everything went according to plan and Mr. Ortiz was on his way here to meet at the diner, I knew confronting him was going to ultimately change the way our entire life would be—the map of my present and future.

"Does this look okay?" I fussed with the sweater, annoyed with how itchy it felt against my skin.

We were standing in Ember's apartment in Isles, but she'd packed a lot of my stuff in boxes already, getting ready to move to the house in the countryside after graduation. I was standing in her little bedroom staring at the floor-to-ceiling mirror in the corner.

"Just wear a shirt, Rain. This looks so uncomfortable," Ember said sweetly as she pulled on one of her dresses and a blazer, opting to look more professional for this meeting, claiming that it gave her more of a leg to stand on.

"I want to look like you." I gestured to what she was wearing before she laughed, walking out of the room.

"It's not you. Just be you," she encouraged. I fumbled with the sleeves of the sweater, ultimately deciding she was right and taking it off, replacing it with one of my long-sleeve black shirts.

I came out of the bedroom before she shoved a piece of toast in her mouth.

"SeeItoldyou," she said with food in her mouth.

"Chew your food," I grumbled before she flipped me the bird. I laughed in her wake, grabbing the envelope and the letters along with a copy of Ash's will that I had the lawyer fax over with his signature on the bottom, confirming it was all legitimate. I also had bank information on Ember's account on it.

"Why did you and your brother decide the diner was the best place to meet?" I asked again.

"I told you. He rented the whole thing out. It is on the very edge of town and in neutral territory."

"The irony." I interjected, and she huffed.

"You ready?" I asked her, grabbing the bag with all the documents and our helmets.

"Wait. One thing," she said, disappearing back into the bedroom.

"We're going to be late," I called out, looking at the clock as it counted down the hours to three. I knew I was being an asshole, but my shaky leg told me that my anxiety was taking over. I didn't want to go into a panic attack again, so I did exactly what my therapist suggested.

I allowed the panic to wash over me, for I had learned that denying it only intensified its grip. The push and pull of a panic attack often fed the fear, so I welcomed it in.

"Come in, you little fucker," I murmured, punctuating my invitation with several deep, grounding breaths.

"I think I should add this to the envelope." I snapped out of my thoughts as Ember circled back toward the door where I was standing.

"What is it?" I asked her, looking down at a folded black piece of paper in her hand.

"Just something, in case." There was a knock at the door that I ignored.

"I'm not in the mood for surprises, Ember. I'm fucking anxious as shit," I grumbled before her expression contorted to something I couldn't recognize.

"It was stupid," she balked before turning around. I grabbed her elbow.

"I'm sorry," I muttered, feeling like a total asshole. "I am just trying not to have a panic attack and lashed out."

Her eyes looked down, still clutching onto the piece of paper. "I'd love to know what it is, and of course you can bring it."

"I-I just think that maybe appealing to the very little human side that he had would help."

"It absolutely would," I said, feeling like a dick for snapping at her.

There was another knock at the door.

"Hold on," I yelled. Better to yell at whoever the fuck demanded our attention than my sweet beautiful . . . girlfriend? Although, honestly, that word seemed so trivial for what she meant to me. Still, now was not the time to debate what she meant.

"What is this, mi pareja?" I looked at her trembling hand and dropped the backpack to the floor and grabbed her wrists. "What's wrong?"

Frantically scanning her face, she handed me the piece of black paper. Slowly unfolding it, a lone tear dropped from the corner of her eye, tracing its path down her cheek. I diverted my gaze downward to see what I had unfurled.

I swallowed when I realized what it was.

"Is-is this . . .?"

She nodded.

"Sol," I said so softly before pulling her tightly into my chest. I inspected the little ultrasound. It was crazy how realistic and clear it was.

"She has Ash's curls." I pointed at the little hair atop her head floating around in little ringlets. There was so much hair, too. I laughed when I realized she had the fucker's big nose, too. "His large nose too."

"Hey," She slapped my chest, and we let out a small chuckle together.

"I think this is perfect and if you are ready, then you should bring it."

"I'm ready."

"Does anyone know?" I asked.

"Aside from Santiago, no."

I scanned her face before dropping down to give her a small kiss on her lips. "I'm so proud of you."

The door immediately pounded open, and there was Santiago on the other side.

"I was getting worried," he said before seeing Ember in my arms in tears. "What's wrong?"

He scanned the room before looking at the paper in my hand, immediately recognizing what it was.

"You told him?" he asked.

"I did."

He gave my shoulder a quick squeeze before bending down to look at her in my face as she buried her body in my chest.

"Good, mija. You need to talk about it. She needs to be talked about." It reminded me how grateful I was for him and how happy I was for hiring him.

"Are you guys ready?" he asked. It was my idea to have Santiago come with us to the diner. I'd informed him this morning of the plan. He would wait for us outside in case anything went astray, then he'd be able to remove Ember from whatever fight broke out.

"I still don't agree with this," she argued. "I don't need protecting. It's my family."

"Just in case," Santiago encouraged as he grabbed her in his arms, laying a brotherly kiss atop her head.

As we took the elevator outside, opting to use the Jeep instead of my bike, we went to the parking garage.

"So, does this mean I am out of a job now?" Santiago asked as we rounded the corner to our Jeep.

"What?!" Ember screamed, her voice echoing in the concrete parking garage. "Why would you say that? You cannot leave me."

Sensing the panic in her voice, I wanted to alleviate some of it for her.

"Not unless you want to be. We have a lot of property out in the countryside. In fact, so much property we might need you to stay in the guesthouse, if you wanted." I gave him a little wink.

"Of course, I am staying with you guys now." He laughed before jabbing her in the side. "Maybe now I won't have to play Uno until one in the morning with you while you cry over Swiftie music."

"*Hey*. She is a lyrical genius. Don't tell me you didn't love her new album." She puckered her lips at him, and he only chortled before getting in his car.

"Are you going to be okay?" she asked when we pulled up to the little parking lot behind the diner, not wanting to alert anyone we were coming. The plan was that I was meeting with Mr. Ortiz, and when Ember's dad came through, Walsh would guide him inside. Ember would be with me at all times.

"No, but let's get this over with," I said as we walked in the front door. The front sign was losing even more coverage and now only the D was lit up welcoming us in. The bell jingled and we walked toward the back booth. Sue was behind the counter today. We'd bought her entire day out, and I tipped her generously to come by only when needed.

Mr. Ortiz didn't know that the diner was bought out, because who would expect a shithole like this in the middle of the day to be full of patrons, especially if it was a meeting requested by his stepson.

We piled into the back booth and gave Sue a wave. I let Ember climb in first because I wanted to be able to protect her if something were to happen.

Sue brought us two chocolate milkshakes and gave a quick wink before making herself scarce.

"We got this . . . together," Ember said as she wrapped her puffy, pink lips over the straw, taking a sip. Her mouth let out a little whimper, and I narrowed my eyes at her.

"Make that noise again and I'm calling this meeting off so I can fuck you over this table."

The shock on Ember's face only made me laugh when the bell of the door caught both of our attention.

I stood up.

"Sir," I said, nodding at him, my body blocking Ember, at least until I moved aside and he had a full view of her smiling right up at him.

"Mr. Ortiz," she said so confidently, her voice not shaking even an ounce, and even I was impressed because my own tone couldn't say the same. Just as he was about to say something, she gestured to the other side of the table. "Please sit down."

He looked between us, and I shrugged before sitting next to her, giving her thigh a little squeeze underneath the table. She took her hands off the table and crossed them.

"We have some things we need to discuss about your son."

"Why is she here?" He directed the question to me, ignoring Ember completely.

"Ember can tell you." I snidely remarked so the conversation could go back to her. She deserved a voice, maybe even more than I did.

"No," Mr. Ortiz simply responded. "I have nothing to say to the woman who used my son so that her brother could kill him."

"Ah, now that is where you are completely incorrect, and we cannot wait to show you today," a new voice chimed in, and we all snapped our heads up. I was impressed that Walsh walked in here so stealthily, he must've come through the kitchen entrance.

"What the fuck?" Mr. Ortiz barked out as I stood and slipped next to him while Walsh piled in next to Ember.

"We're here to show you our innocence." Walsh took out the photos of the woods the day that he was there. "There is clearly one set of tracks on the rock based on the mud prints."

"That proves nothing. You could've washed your own footprints out." Mr. Ortiz made a swipe motion with his hand as if he didn't want to hear anything else.

"It does though," I encouraged, probing him so I didn't have to whip out the other paperwork, even though that was a far cry from what would happen, with his track record.

"Come on, Rain." Mr. Ortiz tsked. "I should have given you more lessons because your leadership skills are atrocious."

He said it in such a smug way that for a moment, I even believed it.

"No," Ember said, and Walsh placed a hand on her shoulder to stop her, but nothing would deter her from speaking her mind now. "You don't get to say that about Rain. He has spent the last year tirelessly working to find out what happened to Ash. So you don't get to call him a bad leader."

"Why are these peasants here?" Mr. Ortiz looked at Ember and Walsh and scoffed.

"Sir," Walsh began. "I am trying to tell you—"

"Ash killed himself." I straightened up. It was time for me to stand up for Ember—for myself. "Whether or not you want to believe it and you want to acknowledge your role in his mental health struggles that's up to you, but I will not have you speaking to Ember like that."

Mr. Ortiz narrowed his eyes at me before the corner of his lip twisted and he huffed in anger. "I see what is happening here."

"Which is?" I couldn't help but roll my eyes at his fucking disgusting face, grateful that he will no longer be in power for that much longer.

"You are fucking the whore. She wants to know what two stepbrothers feel like, so she took you—" Still sitting, I pounded him in the face—consequences be damned.

Mr. Ortiz stood up, the table in the center of us went flying toward Ember and Walsh. Out of the corner of my eye, I watched Walsh jump over to shield her body.

"Stop," another powerful voice with a deep low timbre echoed from the other side of the diner. "Sit down, Ortiz."

"Dad?" Ember said from beneath Walsh's body.

"Get up, Walsh," Mr. Solis demanded, and he jumped off Ember, who exploded out of the booth.

"I didn't need you to do that." She huffed, and I couldn't help but smile.

"We will not be referring to the children as whores, especially mine," Mr. Solis barked at Mr. Ortiz, and I couldn't help but to see how immediately the attitude shifted on him . . . like he was scared?

Seemed so impossible because his entire life Mr. Ortiz made everyone cower around him. He was tall, broad-shouldered and his strong jawline that looked like it could literally eat anyone who walked his way only added to his menacing presence.

"Sit down." Mr. Solis pointed to a table in the center of the diner.

"What're you doing here?" Mr. Ortiz demanded before Mr. Solis held the chair out again. Ember walked toward the table where she sat next to her brother. I sat on the other side of her and only squeezed her thigh, making sure she was okay.

She gave me a quick nod, as if confirmation that everything was all right between us—with her.

"Please listen to him," I begged, and Mr. Ortiz glanced at all of us before obliging and sitting in the empty chair next to Mr. Solis.

"You are in on this little reunion?" Mr. Ortiz asked.

Mr. Solis shook his head. "I had no idea that this was happening. I was told to come here to meet my children for dinner, but I suppose that isn't happening." He glanced around at the empty restaurant. Even Sue had scurried away from us.

"What is this about?" Mr. Solis asked, looking between both of his children before landing on me. I could have sworn he lifted his chin at me, a gesture that looked so similar to the one I gave Ember. I responded with a nod.

"It's time," Walsh told me.

I reached into my backpack to grab the infamous paperwork before I first laid out the bank statements on the table. Knowing I was presenting this in front of Ember's dad would make it worse for him because someone bore witness to what was happening, his enemy, nonetheless.

"What are you showing me?" Mr. Ortiz grabbed the papers and looked at them. Walsh, Ember, and I all remained silent as Mr. Solis picked up another document.

The large clock behind the waitress stood *tick-tick-tick* as the noise seemed to somehow grow as the silence did in the room. Seconds passed before realization washed over Mr. Ortiz's face. His mouth attempted to remain in an unscathed flat line, but his jaw kept ticking.

"Ortiz," Ember's dad warned as soon as he realized what he was looking at. "Mexico is going to fucking kill you if they find out about this shit."

Mr. Ortiz coughed as if he was trying to clear his throat. "Where did you find these?"

"I didn't." I laughed because Ash had set this all up for us. This was exactly what he predicted would happen, and it was all coming to fruition. "Your son did."

"What?" Mr. Ortiz balked.

"When he died, he wanted me to keep this paperwork safe. I didn't know what it was until they found letters that Ash had left behind." I noted that Walsh left out that he wasn't there that day, keeping that for Ember and me.

Ember pulled out copies of our notes that Ash had left before Mr. Solis quickly looked them over and then back at his daughter.

"Ember," he whispered. "I'm so sorry. I didn't—"

She held up her hand. "Now is not the time for apologies. I just want to get this over with."

I understood her, so I quickly said the last piece of information. "You're skimming the business. After graduation, Pico will be taking over. None of us are going to say anything outside of this table, but you will step down."

"The hell I will." He scoffed, and I pulled out the rest of the evidence I had in my bag.

"I know you don't value human life or relationships much, but this is evidence you've been fucking around on my mom. To make matters even worse, you're discussing sensitive business information at a fucking strip club with strippers. I don't think anyone will appreciate what you've been doing."

There it was. The utter wrecking ball I served him like it was a cold sandwich on a platter. A pure slap in the face without ever hitting him. She was right. Words could somehow resolve so much more than brutal force.

"H-how?" His voice shook, knowing I had the power in my hand. It felt so fucking good to play my cards, too.

"Ash," I said slyly as the grin exploded on Ember's face.

"If I do this, he is going to say something. Why would I trust him of all people?" He scoffed, putting the papers of his indiscretions down before slowly taking a deep breath and looking up at us.

"Dad?" Ember asked Mr. Solis.

"What're you asking for, Rain?" He looked over his daughter's shoulders.

"I want Pico to take over for the US operations instead of me. You were right about one thing, Mr. Ortiz, but it's not because I am not cut out to be a leader, I am choosing not to be one."

"Pico?"

"Yes."

"And I am to step down?" I nodded again at Mr. Ortiz's question.

"I don't know, Ember . . ." Mr. Solis started to say.

"Well," Walsh chimed in, "we will also be removing the spring bonfire ritual. We both agreed it causes more pain than pleasure, especially after Ash's death."

The two older gentlemen looked between each other, knowing their parents' generation created this neutral territory.

"Okay," they said at the same time.

"I just don't know if I can keep this a secret, Walsh. This is some serious shit, and his leaders have a right to know." Mr. Solis told him.

Ember's body vibrated next to me. I could feel the frustration pulsating off her.

"No." She stood up, her chair flying behind her. She pulled out the photo in her bag before I held my breath.

"You don't have to," I leaned over to whisper in her ear.

She shook her head. "No, I want to."

# EMBER

My hands were shaking as I shared the one thing I kept close to my heart for a full year. As I took a shaky breath, time stood still as Rain's hand gave my thigh a little squeeze. I didn't have to do this. No one forced my hand, but I also knew it would pluck at the last of my dad's humanity heart strings. It was the answer to solving all this.

I slowly, and with shaky hands, laid the ultrasound photo I had of our beautiful baby on the table. It was so clear because it was one of those 4D ultrasounds. I remember the day I had it done, it was the last appointment before they'd told me she passed. I remember going home and hanging the photo up next to the one of Ash and I sitting on his rock the day of our first date.

I struggled to find the words, closing my eyes to shield myself from the reactions around me. "This," I began, "is the reason I need you all to keep this a secret. I can't bear the thought of growing old knowing that my daughter's only living relative on her father's side is no longer with us. It would be too painful."

Rain's comforting touch, his fingers tracing circles on my thigh, eased my anxiety. He placed his hand on my lower back, drawing me closer to him. I welcomed the closeness; I needed to feel his warmth and support, especially in this chilling moment.

I mustered the courage to speak the truth. "I was pregnant," I confessed, emphasizing the past tense. "I had to deliver our child, who was born sleeping when I was well over halfway through the pregnancy. No one knows what went wrong, but she chose to join her father in heaven earlier than I expected."

I inhaled deeply, needing to continue before anyone else could respond. "I understand she's not with us on this earth, but I don't want anyone else close to me to leave or be threatened to leave again. There has been far too much sorrow and loss in the few decades I've been alive. I know you both may not value human life the way I do, but as your daughter"—I pointed to my father and then turned to Mr. Ortiz—"and as the woman who deeply loved your only biological son, so much that we created a life together, I implore both of you to please . . ."

My dad's usually stoic face shattered. His mouth shaking, his eyes watery, his lips turned in what resembled a cross between a frown and worry.

"I need to keep him alive so that I can remember Ash. God—" I chuckled, almost manically. "Of all people who don't deserve to be on this earth, it's you."

Now my words were directed at Mr. Ortiz. "The way you treated your son throughout his life, the way you disregarded his struggles and crippling mental health because it didn't align with the future you had planned for him, was utterly despicable. 'Foul' isn't even a strong enough word. I never wish for anyone's death, but if there's one person who deserved it, it's you, not him."

As my fingers gently traced the ultrasound paper, my face softened at what could have been, what should have been. "But I need to protect this small piece of history for her—for him," I added, turning back to my father.

"Please," I begged, reaching across my brother, my hands outstretched toward my dad. Walsh grasped one hand while my father held the other.

"Of course, precious. I didn't—God. Fuck." My dad was struggling to hold back tears. "I didn't know. Why didn't you tell me? Who was with you?" He fired off a series of questions in a frantic manner.

"Santiago was there. He was the support I needed at the time. I just didn't want to tell anyone, but it happened, and you were around more, so you were helping in a way, you just didn't realize it." I sighed.

"We can't change the past, but we can change the course of the future by making just this one decision. Please think wisely," Rain chimed in behind me, his hand giving my lower back a reassuring squeeze.

My father's head bobbed before the words tumbled out in rapid succession. "I know. Yes, of course. I'm so sorry, Ember. You have my word. I won't tell anyone. How can I?"

We all turned to Mr. Ortiz, who had remained silent throughout the entire conversation. His stoic demeanor softened, and the corners of his lips downturned in a frown. It was hard to discern his thoughts from such a subtle expression.

"You hurt my pregnant wife, Solis."

My jaw dropped. When I thought I knew the entire story, there was always another surprise. "She died after giving birth to Ash."

"What?" Rain and I shouted in surprise.

"You didn't know?" I asked him.

"No. I had no idea."

"Ash didn't know either," Mr. Ortiz added pointedly.

This meant everything Ash did to take down his dad, he had no idea what my own father did to his mother. I wonder...

My dad's voice shook that thought out of me. "She was at the spring bonfire one year. It was all...an accident." My dad hung his head. I couldn't believe this, but this is what Walsh was saying last year when he said that dad hurt someone who Mr. Ortiz loved. "I was looking for Mr. Ortiz because he was the leader of the Den. I went to try and find him and one of my men accidentally hit her car as she was pulling out of the house. It was truly an accident."

"That is what started the ploy to get Mr. Solis' wife wrapped up in the Cartel?" Rain asked for clarification.

Both men nodded.

This was so incredibly messy I could barely follow. The old Ember would have gotten up, stormed off and never talked to anyone ever again. I was no longer that version of myself though. I had found the power and strength to keep walking forward on a path that was full of bumps.

"We are not the mistakes of our parents," I said to both Walsh and Rain. They both tilted their chin in agreement.

"You," I pointed to Mr. Ortiz. "Whether it was a mistake or not, there has already been so much life lost. Your wife, my mom, Rain's dad, your son and...my daughter." The last word came out softer.

"Please," I begged. "We need this violence to stop."

There was a long silent pause in the room.

"Okay, then." Mr. Ortiz finally responded. I hadn't expected some grand revelation from him, where he'd suddenly confess to being the worst father. I had to accept what we could get.

"Pico will take over after graduation. I'll need one month to train him, but then he'll take over. I'll remain on the advisory board," Rain added.

"There is one more thing," Rain whispered as he pulled out the will that was notarized by the lawyer. "This is the will that Ash left. He had an account with money that he received from his mother's death settlement. The money won't leave the account, so whatever debt you have to pay back, you'll need to figure a way out on your own. This money isn't yours."

Mr. Ortiz ripped the paper out of his hand, scanning over it quickly.

"What the fuck?" he demanded, his voice now high and mad.

God, this man was a fucking joke. Talk to him about his son's death and he is emotionless, but when you start discussing the money that was never even his, he starts to go ape shit.

"It's mine," I conceded coolly. My dad and Walsh wanted to jump to my defense, but I held up a hand. "Period. You fucked yourself. Got yourself in a hole. Now you'll figure out how else to get the money back into the pots you skimmed."

"Fuck," he growled.

This time Rain stood up.

"This conversation is over. You are to leave." He was so fucking sexy I could have ripped—

"Now." My panties were one hundred percent soaked. I was so hot and bothered, and while I loved my independence, my feminism ran out the door while watching Rain stand up for me.

Mr. Ortiz grumbled something about how he'd get with us about the change in leadership because there was some traditional event they needed to hold, and then walked out the front door. The little bell rang in his wake. A blanket of silence swept over the diner before Walsh started to slow clap.

Rain grabbed me by my waist, hoisting me out of my chair and spinning me around rapidly.

"We did it, mi pareja," he announced.

He set me on my feet while I glanced over at Walsh and my dad before turning back to look at my favorite pair of deep blues.

"We . . . did it," I repeated.

Walsh came over and I turned, only to get wrapped up in one of his big, bear hugs. Something that I admit I missed so much over the last year. Right as he dropped me to the floor, I locked eyes with my dad.

"Ember . . ." his voice trailed off in a quiet, saddened way.

"It's okay, Dad." I went over to him, letting him wrap me up in my arms. "My little baby girl had to go through that all alone. You felt like you couldn't come to me, let me help you, let me protect—"

"No. I am tired of having the men in my life protect me." I turned so I was speaking to my dad, Walsh, and Rain. "You all need to stop. I begged Ash to stop. I am now desperately asking you all the same. I am perfectly capable of defending myself. This entire day should prove I don't need anyone in my life. I am strong. I am resilient, and if you are just recognizing it, then I am sorry you haven't been able to see it for a while."

I paused, closing my eyes before exhaling. "But please do not ever protect me from the truth again without my explicit permission. Just because I am a woman doesn't mean I need a man in my life. I choose to have you all because I love you."

They all shook their heads slowly. "You were right, Ember. I remember when you told me that you wanted to facilitate a meeting with the two dads right before Ash's death. I thought you were crazy because there for sure was going to be someone dead by the end of it. But you were right—"

"Words are a very powerful weapon," Rain finished for him. He knew exactly how powerful they were as an aspiring writer himself.

"They are," I added for effect before I gave my dad and Walsh a quick kiss, promising them I'd see them soon.

"Sir?" Rain spoke up as they headed toward the front door.

"I . . . I just want you to know that I love your daughter." The words emerged raw and throaty, accompanied by a swallow. "This past year has been the toughest of my life, but falling in love with her has been the easiest thing I've ever done."

My dad's gaze shifted between us, transforming into a surprised grin. "I know," he whispered. "I know. Thank you for loving my daughter the way I do. She truly deserves it." He sniffled. "I am sorry about your dad."

Rain shook his head. "Like I said, we are not our parents."

My dad gave him a tight-lipped smile. "That you both are not. I am proud of you."

There was another pause before he cleared his throat. "And thank you for honoring his presence in your lives," my dad added. "I didn't know him, but I know what it's like to lose someone you love unexpectedly."

Tears welled up, but I'd kept them at bay, and I would not break down now.

Dad turned to leave, his arm draped over Walsh's shoulder, leaving the two of us in the quiet, dimly lit diner.

A prolonged silence settled between us until he extended his arms, and I practically rushed into them, bridging the gap swiftly. This was where I belonged. This was safe.

"I'm not running away anymore," I murmured into his chest, eliciting a soft moan as he buried his face in my hair.

I pulled back slightly, locking eyes with him. "Well, maybe just in the bedroom," I jested, and we shared a light chuckle as his hands moved to lift my chin, tilting it upward. He leaned in until our foreheads met.

"I'd cross the earth, traverse heaven, and brave the flames of hell if it meant chasing you, because you are mine," he declared.

"And you're mine." I sealed my declaration with a kiss, and in that moment, the world melted away.

Rain gathered our belongings, stashing the copies of evidence in the backpack he'd brought. He paused to gaze at the ultrasound photo printed on the black crinkly paper before tucking it safely into his pocket.

"I want you to write about her when you're ready. I want you to write about him. Tell their story, Ember," he requested. "Your story."

I fought back tears threatening to escape, determined not to cry.

In silence, we left the diner hand in hand. The rare sunlight in Isles illuminated our faces, as if sending a sign from above.

I stopped right at the entrance to smile as Rain looked at me. "I'll meet you at the Jeep," he said, recognizing I needed a moment alone.

He walked toward the car, and my thoughts wandered to Ash, to us, but most of all, to Rain. He had been an unwavering pillar of strength during the most challenging period of my life, believing in my ability to conquer anything and everything.

I loved Ash with every fiber of my being, yet something had always felt incomplete between us. He was often distant and inconsistent, fostering a relationship shrouded in secrecy. With Rain, there was unwavering honesty. He saw me for who I was—a fusion of the sheltered, frightened girl I used to be and the woman I'd become in Isles.

Pausing as the sun bathed my face, I glanced over at the Jeep where Rain was settling into the driver's seat.

There was one thing I lied about—I wasn't done running.

I'd keep running, chasing him every single day of my life, pursuing him to the ends of the earth, too. He found my scattered pieces and helped me stitch them back together, becoming an essential part of my entity. I'd never cease chasing that feeling.

"Hey, wait for me," I yelled, a smile returning to my face as he grinned. "Let's go to our house in the countryside."

# EMBER



*Three Months Later*

I was running late for the final exam, which was unlike me. I stayed up late last night, meticulously editing the photos I needed to present in class. As I pushed open the massive wooden door to the building in Isles, the rain and gloom outside didn't match my internal rush I was feeling for being late. I blamed it on the adviser meeting I had to have this morning, but ultimately, I knew it was my own fault.

My academic adviser had encouraged me to take the required summer classes, which would allow me to graduate a year earlier than planned. Despite all the challenges I'd faced, I was still on track to achieve my original goal.

Clutching a large envelope containing my final assignment, which was a collection of images, I entered the building and quickly sent a text to Rain, asking him to save me a seat.

I practically sprinted down the long underground hallway to the classroom. When I burst through the door, I was met with an immediate rush of embarrassment. I'd arrived late, and our professor was already present and starting the final exam presentation.

"Sorry," I whispered, my face burning with embarrassment. I hastily scanned the room, searching for Rain. I didn't need to look for long; his distinctive long black hair made it easy for me to spot him in the crowd. In some cosmic way, I could always find him, even if we were in the most crowded place. I was drawn toward him.

I hurried over to Rain and took the empty chair next to him. Concern filled his blue eyes as he looked at me.

"You're never late. Are you okay?" he inquired. I lifted the envelope containing my final assignment, then settled back in my seat.

It was hard to believe today marked my official last day of school. The spring bonfire event had come and gone, and despite Rain and I being present, we'd shared a quiet night with no significant developments. The Den held a vigil the weekend after for the one-year anniversary of Ash's passing. It was the first time that Rain and I had publicly acknowledged that we were together.

Rain still maintained his leadership status of the Den until graduation, at Mr. Ortiz's request. A lot needed to take place behind the scenes, contacting Mexico and other countries so they were aware of the leadership change. It felt like the right decision. Plus, most of campus seemed to move on to the next big gossip thing and most people were back to being sociable to me. I was sure there were still a dozen questions people had, but I learned to ignore them. Because what mattered was us, and I had learned to drown out the noise.

We spent the last few months living mostly at my apartment during the week, and on the weekend, we alternated between the hunting cabin and the house in the countryside. I even drove him to my house in Dansport. God, what twenty-one-year-olds could tell you they owned or rented four properties. Every time I thought of it, I giggled a little, understanding how ridiculous it sounded.

We loved each other hard. We fucked each other hard. We sat on the couch, naked most days, being absorbed in our books or pieces we were writing. I'd even gotten the courage to start plotting the story I wanted to write. It was a long process, so I was taking each step with ease and focusing on school.

"Rain Fortin," our professor announced, and my thoughts retreated to reality as Rain leaned over, giving my knee a quick little squeeze before walking up to the front room with his portfolio envelope.

He turned off the lights so he could project the images onto the screen. As he grabbed an array of black-and-white images, hanging them on the board behind the screen, we could barely make out the images. Then he took a handful of filmlike photographs with a grainy, vintage look to them and placed them on the projector, but my eyes were stuck on the man standing before the class. Clad in his black jeans and signature black T-shirt his golden skin almost illuminated in the dungeon of a basement we were in. His gaze locked with mine.

"My name is Rain Fortin, and this is my final project entitled The Girl Who Scares Me. I know Ember and I were supposed to do the project together, but we decided it would be best if we split it up." Shit. I knew where this was going without even looking at the images, but my eyes pulled away from Rain to look at the projector.

The screen displayed hundreds of black and white photographs of me. I gasped when I saw my feet resting delicately on Rain's lap, his hand caressing my toes. There was another image of me wearing an oversized sweater, grinning ear to ear as I realized how it swallowed me. Then there was one of me in the driver's seat of the Jeep, my hand outstretched toward Rain, a radiant smile on my face.

I shifted my focus to the area behind the projector screen, where a dozen selfies of us together adorned the board. The first one showed the back of my hair as I nuzzled into Rain's shoulder and he looked down at me with pure adoration. The next featured both of us with our feet resting on Ash's rock during one of our visits to honor him. Another showed us sipping milkshakes at the diner. The one next to it was us walking through our orchards at our countryside house, and one snuggled next to the fire in the hunting cabin. There were countless snapshots of our shared moments.

"This is Ember Solis. We live together. We officially own a house now." Rain smiled while announcing, which prompted cheers and laughter from the room. He gestured toward me. "She is the strongest human being I've ever met, and she's incredibly beautiful, too."

"Hell yeah, she is," a voice chimed in from the back of the classroom, provoking more chuckles.

"Hey, hold on, pal. She's mine," Rain quipped, smiling at me.

He continued, "Ember brings me immense joy, yet she terrifies me. I could lose her. I'd be shattered without her, lost in a world of numbness, unable to find the words I so desperately chase in my head and commit to paper. I'd be drowning in my own despair. Because without Ember, you'd all be witnessing me scorch the very ground beneath our feet just to get back to her."

"Wha-what do you need to know I am not going anywhere?" I murmured forgetting we were surrounded by our entire class. A class that probably thought this was getting ridiculous as this was the second time this had happened in front of them.

"I need you, Ember," he rasped out. In a way, I knew what he was saying because I'd given him most of me but never allowed him to label what we were. "I want to be able to take you out in public in Dansport like a real proper date so that I can ask you to be mine . . ."

I swallowed audibly before the tears streamed down, wetting my cheeks. "You should've just asked," I choked out in an attempt to make a joke, but I was doing a poor job.

"Please?" He begged, and I could have folded right there in front of the entire class.

"Yes, of course," I assured him. "I'd love to go on a proper date with you. But I also want you to understand that these moments"—I gestured to all the images behind him—"are the moments that feel even more intimate to me than parading around a fancy restaurant in the city. You've always been mine, but if you want to make it official, use whatever label you need, because I'm yours too, Rain."

He beamed, and applause erupted around us.

"That is absolutely beautiful, Rain." Our professor grabbed the images from the projector before bringing him in for a hug and whispering something before he took his seat next to me.

"What'd she say?" I asked.

"That I aced the project." Leaning over our seats, I planted a kiss on him before hearing my name. Feeling more confident after going after Rain, I made my way up to the lit projector. There, I shared polaroid's along with some of the digital images I had worked on editing.

"My name is Ember Solis, and I am probably going to fail this final because I did not answer the prompt and I did not work with a partner." I giggled while glancing over at Evie and then meeting Rain's gaze.

I showed a variety of photos of myself on the screen. There were pictures of me studying, at Ash's rock, at the cabin, and doing mundane tasks like brushing my teeth. Dozens of photos I took of myself floated on the projector.

"I did not answer what scares me because right now, nothing scares me," I admitted, my voice filled with a newfound confidence I had never known before. My gaze shifted from Rain to my classmates, their faces reflecting anticipation. "This past year, I've overcome so much, faced unimaginable grief, and wrestled with the fear of moving on. But I did it. I opened my heart and let someone in, and now, it feels so damn good."

Rain's eyes sparkled with pride and affection as I continued, "I've found a life I've always wanted, a life that feels normal. Now, our biggest arguments are about whether Rain used my toothbrush." I chuckled, and the room shared in the laughter.

"It's the little things, the everyday joys, that I cherish the most," I said, my voice filled with ease. "The feeling of waking up next to Rain, his warmth beside me, and realizing that I'm no longer alone.

Sharing morning coffee, navigating the day's ups and downs, and falling asleep next to the person I love. These simple moments, this life we've built together, that's what truly matters."

I walked over to him, my eyes bore into his, and extended my hand to invite him to join me at the front of the classroom. He rose from his seat and came to stand beside me, our fingers interlocked.

Taking a deep breath, I continued my speech, "You see, when I look back at the person I used to be a couple years ago, I was scared of everything—scared of the darkness, scared of the secrets, scared of the world I lived in. I thought that was my only reality."

I glanced at Rain, his hand squeezing mine, providing the support I needed to keep going. "I've learned that fear is only as powerful as you allow it to be. It's a choice. I chose to embrace the love I found with Rain. I've learned that it's okay to be scared sometimes. It's okay to love and be loved in return. And that's the life I want, a life where love and happiness conquer fear. A life where my heart stayed open, overflowing with love, enabling me to cherish a tale blessed by two of the deepest loves I've ever experienced."

As the applause filled the room, I leaned in and kissed Rain, savoring the taste of love and contentment on my lips. "This is what feels right," I whispered, my heart brimming with gratitude.

Our professor applauded the loudest as she came toward me. "You aced this assignment," she whispered as I felt the flush return to my face. We walked back to our seats where we watched the rest of our classmates dive deep into what scared them. I'd be remiss to say I was actually listening to them because I couldn't help but watch Rain.

He kept looking at me as he reached over the table to hold my hand, giving me a squeeze every so often. When class finally finished, we gathered our stuff before we walked outside. It was still raining and gross, but I sat outside the class building looking around. Both of us would still be here all summer to take our classes, but this felt different. There was a finality to the semester ending and us moving on.

"So, do you really want to take me out to dinner?" I asked. He turned toward me and grabbed my waist, pulling me tight into his.

"It would be an honor."

I frowned momentarily while his eyes searched mine.

"What?"

"I was just thinking about what you said. You wanted to officially make you mine, but I feel like being your girlfriend just seems so trivial after everything we've been through," I said.

He laughed—like one of those genuine big belly laughs.

"What's so funny?" I asked.

"Nothing." He shook his head.

"I'm being serious," I pressed. We were getting soaked in the rain, but I made no rush to get to the car. When you lived in Isles, being wet was just part of your whole aesthetic. It wasn't cute.

"Nothing, princesa. I agree with you. I think we are beyond the boyfriend slash girlfriend title."

I narrowed my gaze at him, but let it go, taking him up on our dinner date and leaving the rest shrouded in the cloak of mystery.

He linked his fingers into mine as we ran to the car before jumping in. I took my new place as his passenger princess before he turned on the heat of the car.

"When's our date?" I asked.

"Tomorrow."

"Where are we off to tonight?" I asked because it was Friday and it was usually when we decided the weekend, but this one was extra special because we were done with the semester and both passed, so there was lots to celebrate.

"To our future," he said. I leaned back on the car seat, staring out the window while Rain's hand rested on my thigh, giving it a little squeeze as we drove down Isles. No longer did we have to look behind us or live in fear of leaving the neutral territory. The Den and the Alpha house had made peace with each other.

In that moment, the world opened up as we watched the pine trees thin out, eventually revealing the city beyond the woods. I arrived in Isles as an immature eighteen-year-old, seeking a typical college experience, but what I found here was a mix of the best and worst moments of my life. While painful memories often took center stage in my mind, I needed to remember that this place had also given me the two great loves of my life. I wouldn't trade meeting either of them. I instinctively reached up to touch the tattoo behind my ear, a reminder of the man it represented and the person who gave it to me. I had feared that the world had room for me to fall in love only once, but I was one of the fortunate few who got to experience this earth-shattering, all-consuming love twice.

I was one of the lucky ones who got to be in love with the person who grounded me here on earth. The one who gave me the space to find my own inner strength, the one who encouraged me to be the best version of myself, the one who was so fucking beautiful in every single way. But I was also lucky because I loved someone else up above, too. The one who showed me the darkness in the world. The one who showed me an all-consuming love. The one taking care of our daughter.

I sighed deeply, keeping my eyes shut as Rain's hand gripped my thigh.

"You okay, mi pareja?" he asked. I turned over and drank his beautiful features in. The way his hair tousled, the way his eyes turned hooded whenever he drank me in, the way his arms flexed as he reached out toward me. But I also loved the way he was always checking in with me while giving me the space I needed to feel.

"Yeah." I sighed. "I'm really good," I confessed.

As we descended into Dansport, everything felt just right. The lightness I had finally found in a world once veiled in darkness was a testament to the remarkable resilience of the human spirit. I grasped this marked the beginning of a new chapter, a chance to embrace love and cherish a life brimming with endless possibilities.

*Into the darkness I'll go, and into the light I'll be.*

# RAIN



My wife frantically paced by her phone while she glanced down every second to make sure she wasn't missing a call. She was standing in our library, surrounded by what she called her comfort objects. She'd told me when she was younger she was obsessed with smelling her blankets for comfort, and being by her books gave her the same feeling.

"They are going to call," I told her as she shot me a warning look. A low chuckle came from within as I went to our kitchen and grabbed some of the homemade cider I'd made her with our recent harvest this fall. The countryside was already getting cold, and while it wasn't as freezing as it was at our hunting cabin, it still was gloomy weather.

The perfect writing weather.

As I walked toward the kitchen to admire the rain tapping against the glass, I saw the photo of us on our wedding day. We didn't do anything big, just something small out in the cabin the summer after Ember graduated.

I couldn't help but chuckle as I reminisced about the day that had forever changed the course of my life. It was the day I had persuaded my now wife to join me for what she thought was a regular date, only to surprise her with a heartfelt proposal. I still vividly recalled the amazement on her face as we sat in the restaurant, and I poured my heart out, asking her to be my wife. Her quick and eager agreement filled me with joy, even though I had secretly contemplated marrying her right on the spot. Eventually, we compromised to wait until her graduation the following year.

Our wedding day turned out to be a private affair, attended solely by Pico, Marissa, Walsh, and her dad. My mother declined our invitation. She firmly believed I caused her failed marriage and shattered family. Mr. Ortiz had somehow settled his score with the Cartel, and although I refrained from prying into the details of his actions, my mother remained resentful, blaming me for what she perceived as the ruination of her life.

I took a deep breath. Ember often thought I should be more upset about these circumstances, but she couldn't fathom that I, too, held my mother accountable for her choices, chiefly her decision to marry Mr. Ortiz and then effectively abandon me and Ash to his perilous fate. After enduring years of therapy, I had learned to come to terms with the fact that I couldn't change their behavior. Instead, I had learned to coexist with it, establishing the necessary boundaries.

All of a sudden, the ringer went off and she practically ran back into the living room. She looked shocked while she stared at her phone.

"Go on, pick it up," I encouraged as she clutched the phone in her hand before swiping to answer.

She got up from the vintage couch that she'd thrifted a couple years ago when she dragged me to Dansport's monthly flea market. There were a few photos, including some from our wedding, hanging up behind us. I bought her a house, but she gave me a home.

"Hello?" I could hear the hesitation in her voice but only because we'd been together for the last four years. She was speaking in a hushed tone, which gave me the perfect opportunity to watch her. The way her long black hair hit the center of her back. Her curves were still fucking utter perfection, and I could literally bend her over the couch right now with how hard she constantly made me.

But the most attractive thing about Ember was her brain and emotional strength. The ability of how she takes everything in stride, so I know that even if this phone call doesn't have the best of news, she will take it with ease.

"I did?" she squealed. I huffed a breath out because I took back that thought. And while there was little doubt she would get this, I was definitely the realist in our relationship.

"Thank you so much, Sera. I will talk to you soon," she said before hanging up and throwing the phone on the couch.

"And so?" I asked her.

"I am officially a published author," she screamed as she ran into my arms. I whipped her around as I pressed a million kisses on her forehead.

"Harper Frank Publishing picked you up?"

"Yes," she said, completely out of breath, pride beaming brightly from her smile.

"God, I am so fucking proud of you." I didn't know how many times I'd said that to her in the past, but I knew it wasn't the last time because I was always in awe of Ember Fortin.

"I cannot believe that in just a few short months, everyone in the world will have access to my story—to our story." She laced her fingers in mine as she stepped away from me. "To his story."

A tear formed in her eye, and I gave her a little twist of my lips. "I never doubted they would."

The front door busted open, and I grabbed Ember, pulling her behind me.

"Are you expecting anyone?" She shook her head as I made my way to the front of the house.

"And so?" Santiago's booming voice echoed around the house.

"Jesus Christ, Santi, you scared us," Ember said, moving in front of me and walking toward him.

"I did it." Her smile was contagious, even her eyes couldn't hide the pure joy she was experiencing.

"Yes," he exclaimed, wrapping her in his arms. "I knew it."

"I didn't," she whispered. I used to be envious of how close they were together, but with what the two of them went through together, they shared a deep bond and he loved her. I just couldn't help but be possessive over what's mine.

"I am going to need a signed first edition," he joked with her before telling us he would head to the city to meet with a "friend."

"Really?" Ember questioned.

"She's just a friend, mija." He laughed as he left, and she just shook her head at him.

She pressed the door close and locked the door before turning toward me. I sensed the change in atmosphere as she languidly walked over to where I was standing.

"Rain?" Her eyes darkened with desire as her fingers started to trace circles on my chest.

"Yes, my beautiful wife?"

"I think I need a reward for this," she mused, and I only let out a small laugh.

"Oh, yeah?" The corners of my lips twisted in a devious smirk. "And what is it that you want?"

"You," she said without missing a beat.

"You have me," I murmured.

"No." Her tone was so fucking raspy I swear she could've been one of those sex phone operators and I would've come listening to her talk about her grocery list.

Her fingers touched the bottom of her sweater as she pulled it over her head revealing a black lace bra. God, I loved my wife's curves, and time only made her look more beautiful and enticing. She was everything I could've ever dreamed of.

"What're you doing to me?" I demanded as she let out a little giggle before slipping out of her jeans.

"Come here," I commanded, but she shook her head, a mischievous glint on her cheeks.

"If you want me, you have to find me." She looked beyond me at the door before her plump ass ran outside in the cool fall evening.

"My fucking wife." I laughed before shedding my sweater. A game we'd been playing for years now. I hated chasing after my wife in any other way, but in the bedroom? Game. Fucking. On.

I opened the door and called out for her and laughed when I heard the crunch of the leaves on the ground behind the orchard.

I ran toward her. I was her predator.

"All mine," I growled into the wind as I searched each row of trees to try and find her.

"Come on, mi reina." She was my queen, and I, her king.

I stalked each row, careful when treading on the earthen ground below when I finally saw her sprinting in the open, grassy area between the orchards and our house. The pines provided a gloomy backdrop as her black hair flowed wildly in the wind.

Just as I walked in her direction I heard a splash and chuckled. I took the long way around the house before discarding my pants and my shirt. She was frantically looking out into the woods, when I stalked up behind her, jumping into the pool and covering her mouth.

"Surprise," I murmured into the shell of her ear. It was warm in the pool, but not scalding hot. Well, not until my beautiful wife turned around and I got a full view of her bare tits moving gently with the water, her nipples just above the surface. I rolled them between my forefinger and thumb, watching as they hardened at my touch.

"Fuck," I groaned, and her hooded eyes met mine. My mouth was on hers, pushing my tongue inside her warmth as I flicked it around sucking her dry. Even in the gentle movement of the water, I felt her body against my own. My fingers trailed down her neck to her wet shoulder where I pressed gentle kisses on her clavicle.

"This," I murmured before moving to the next spot.

"Is." Another kiss.

"Mine." I finally concluded before I shoved her legs apart, thrusting my fingers inside of her cunt.

"Oh, fuck." She moaned, an erotic noise that made my cock so hard that it was fucking twitching, begging to touch her sweet little cunt.

I lifted her by her ass out of the hot tub before I continued to fuck her with my mouth. I walked through the open door before depositing her upstairs in our bedroom.

"Spread your legs wide so I can taste your pretty little cunt." I groaned, watching her delicate folds open for me.

"My desperate little wife looking to let Daddy lick you dry?"

"Clean me up," she begged. She was my naughty little minx.

My tongue carefully caressed the outside of her folds as I held onto the back of her thighs for support.

"My favorite meal," I choked out as my tongue continued fucking her damp cunt. Her sweet liquid spilling into my mouth as the hunger within me increased.

"Fuck . . . me" she demanded as she writhed away from me.

"As you wish," I responded before grabbing her ankles and in one swift movement flipping her around so her stomach was against the bed.

"Get on your knees and lift your hips for me." She gasped at my demand as her plump ass slid up high in the air for me.

It was the most perfect view as I spread her cheeks, letting my needy cock press into her tight little cunt.

"You were made for me." I groaned just as I pushed all the way into her. Her hips slid back onto my cock, and I held onto her while she thrust on me.

"That's it, mi reina. You are doing such a good job." I praised as her head rolled back, grabbing onto a handful of hair as I reared her deep onto my cock. Her moan was deep down and guttural as I reached around, giving her nipple a pinch before continuing my assault on her tight little cunt.

"Such a good girl," I repeated. More thrusting.

"My good girl." I complimented as she let out a symphony of moans and groans.

"Come for me, baby," I demanded, and in a second she clenched around me. She would explode all over me soon, so I let out the last few movements, giving her ass one final slap as I detonated inside of her.

She collapsed onto the bed as I slipped my cock out of her before lifting her and walking her to the shower.

"I love you," she murmured as I placed her on the little seat inside the shower as we waited for the water to heat up.

"I love you," I commented back, lifting her chin up so she was eye level with me and gracing her lips with a quick kiss. "Come on."

We spent the next half hour cleaning each other off and basking in the warmth of the water.

"Do you think you'll ever be sick of this?" she asked as I grabbed her a towel to dry off before jumping out and getting one for myself.

I couldn't help but laugh at her words. "Never."

"How come?"

"You are the only thing I've ever wanted. From the moment I tasted your lips, I knew I was totally fucked."

She furrowed her eyebrows. "It's like drinking another milkshake aside from the diner. There is nothing that compares to the chocolate milkshake in Isles. Everything else tastes like shit, right?" She nodded.

"Same thing."

She giggled. "That's weird, Rain."

I shrugged. "It's true."

She leaned over to the basket I'd gotten for the bathroom where I left my T-shirts that she liked to wear to bed and plucked a worn black one from the pile before throwing it on. It was one of those things that had never changed from our time in Isles.

"Turn around." I told her before grabbing the Aquaphor and dabbing it behind the ear.

"It's been months already, I think it's healed." It was. I just liked seeing it. When she came to me suggesting that she would get a matching F on the other side of her ear, my heart literally sank . . . in a good way. I begged her to reconsider it because I didn't want her to feel pressured to, but she insisted. She told me she wanted both of the greatest loves in her life to be known, so she'd gotten an 'F' behind her other ear.

I put a little Aquaphor on it, not listening to her and loving the way it looked branded onto my wife.

"Now it's your turn," she mused, and then I laughed while turning around. I had gotten a similar tattoo that Ash had with a cave and a few bats coming from it, but there was a sun shining onto the cave. "Mi sol."

It was both a representation of everything that we'd gone through, coming into the light from the darkness, a memento to the saying that she used to murmur from her mother and a little memory of their daughter, Sol.

When she finished, I shoved my shirt and some gray sweats on before walking into the bedroom and lifting the covers.

"You are always mine, mi pareja," I whispered as she crawled into bed with her back tucked tightly into the crook of my body.

"Hey, Rain?" she asked in a sleepy tone.

"Mm-hm?" I responded.

"Why do you call me that? Mi pareja. Will you finally tell me?"

I chuckled.

"Because in Spanish, it means my partner. But not just any partner, it's the kind of partner you share a space with—a life with. A partner you're intimate with on all levels. When I met you, calling you my love seemed so trivial because you were so much more to me than that. I always knew you were my partner in this life."

"Wh-what?" Her tears were imminent, but I continued, wanting to explain to her.

"Yeah. I just thought calling you my partner was more intimate than calling you my love or even calling you my life. Being my partner means that you're my equal—the one I lean on when I need support. It means that you're mine."

"Mi pareja," she repeated. I reached over to wipe away the tears already trickling down her cheeks.

"Go to sleep," I whispered into the shell of her ear as she let out a delicate noise of satisfaction.

I gave her a kiss on her lips before tucking her tightly into the crook of my body, where we'd spent the last four years together. We were writing our own story, one that spoke of resilience, courage, and love. I couldn't wait to see what the next chapters would hold, knowing that with Ember by my side, it would be our adventure.

*"I love you because the entire universe*
*conspired to help me find you."*

*–Paulo Coelho, The Alchemist*

# AUTHOR'S NOTE

I know many of you were anticipating this go in a different direction and that Ash was still very much alive. I've seen the reaction videos and heard your responses from the first book, where you were deeply saddened. I hope through this book you understand a little more of what was going through Ash's head and his childhood.

Suicide and grief are life-altering experiences. It's often difficult to comprehend why someone would choose to leave. As I wrote this book, I wanted to convey the profound grief realistically, which is why book one left off on the cliffhanger. I believe it's vital to tackle taboo topics in literature, particularly those related to mental health. Men are often discouraged from opening up about their emotions, which can exacerbate issues like depression and thoughts of suicide. I wanted to highlight that these struggles aren't limited by gender, which inspired me to delve into Ash's story.

Moreover, I wanted to write a book about what the stages of grief look like realistically. Though Ash is no longer with us, I hope by the end of the book, you'll see that life continues after death, even if the road to get to happiness is filled with sorrow, pain, longing and then love. Ember and Rain were able to find each other and form a deep connection even though Ember and Ash were soulmates.

If you're still upset after reading this, that's okay. I had many possible endings in mind, but it was crucial for me to spark a conversation, no matter how big or small, about suicide and depression. I hope you appreciated the complexities of Ember, Ash, and Rain. I think about Ash often—my Ash—and I hope you do too.

See you in the next world,

Vee

Your mental health matters.

If you or a loved one has ever thought about suicide,
please contact the suicide hotline for help.

They are open 24/7.

There is always help and support just a phone call away.

Ask for help before it's too late.

9-8-8

Did you love this story?
Are you not ready to leave Isles just yet?
Coming in Winter 2024/2025 you'll have
the chance to go back to Isles.
Be sure to look out for

**Between Dusk & Dawn**

A dark enemies-to-loves bully romance
featuring Maddy & Walsh Solis.

***Each day a different mask.***

Walsh Solis is a golden boy with a black heart. Behind his straight-A smile, he's in training to become a Mafia commander — and his father's replacement. For Walsh this means duty, obligation, and playing the game.

And girls like Madison don't fit the mold.

Madison Ryan is used to hiding her scars. Good girls don't come from families like hers, no matter how hard they try. But that one secret night with Walsh — the one his girlfriend didn't know about — gave her a taste of hope.

Against his better judgment, Walsh finds himself intrigued by Madison's sad, dark allure. But when his girlfriend gets caught in the deadly crossfire, Walsh and Madison get caught up in a game of who can ruin each other's lives more.

And this time, Walsh has no way to hide his obsession with her...for better or worse.

# ACKNOWLEDGMENTS

I'm not sure where to begin. When I wrote this duet, I was in a very sad place in my life. I had just moved to a new city and felt very lost. These characters provided the companionship I needed most.

Then I published "Into the Darkness," and readers began to see the love and soul this book holds. This book wouldn't exist without you. I read every single message, shared all of your videos, and love talking about this with you all. I truly wouldn't be here without you.

I want to thank my editor, Dee, for helping me polish this book and bring it to life. Thank you for being a cheerleader on my team—never letting you go!

Celena, you championed this book from the start. Thank you for proofreading it, for the calls when I panicked about my writing, and for always being there for me.

I also want to thank Nicole for her second set of eyes on this book. You are so loved.

Thank you to The Author Agency for being the best team to get this book out, and to my PA, Nichole, for your endless support.

To my alpha and beta reading team: Daphne, Alexandria, RC, Julia, Lisa, Sammi, Ariana, and Madison, thank you from the bottom of my heart for helping shape this book. An extra special thanks to Ariana for helping with PR boxes and being my teammate at signings.

Thank you to Luna Literary for the amazing graphics and to The Sparrow Collective for keeping my Instagram looking fantastic.

Thank you to Sandra for the BEAUTIFUL formatting and Haya for the most perfect covers I could ask for.

Thank you to my sweet friend Christina for always cheering me on and keeping me sane.

To the most amazing narrator team I could ask for, Paige and Oscar thank you for bringing these characters to life.

To everyone who has touched this book, thank you so much.

To all the bookstagrammers and booktokers who posted about "Into the Darkness" and everyone who sent me their theories—I love each and every one of you.

Lastly, thank you to my amazing husband for everything you do. Thank you for supporting my wild dreams and letting me read you scenes I was excited about.

Thank you all. I'm going to go cry now for the millionth time.

# ABOUT THE AUTHOR

Vee Taylor is a passionate writer based in the suburbs outside of Chicago. With a lovingly supportive husband, two dogs, and two children, she finds inspiration from her mental health background and uses it to fuel her writing. Her passion for reading and writing began ten years ago, and she hasn't looked back since.

As an avid book lover, Vee is obsessed with all things bookish. She loves exploring new worlds, discovering new characters, and delving into different genres. Her favorite genres include dark romance, romantasy, and good ole smut. When she's not writing, she can often be found with her nose buried in a book or scrolling aimlessly on social media.

Aside from writing, Vee is also a talented photographer. She loves spending time with her friends and family, and enjoys trying new things. With a zest for life and an unwavering passion for writing, Vee Taylor is so excited that you are here on this journey with her.

www.veetaylorauthor.com

**Follow Me On My Adventures**

Thank you so much for reading and supporting this adventure of mine. Your support is beyond words on the page. I would love it if you kept up with the next adventure by following my socials below.

Follow me on Goodreads, Facebook, Instagram, Threads or Tiktok

@veetaylorauthor

Join my Vee's Vixens on Facebook to join a chat group about this book

www.ingramcontent.com/pod-product-compliance
Lightning Source LLC
Chambersburg PA
CBHW071301140726
47996CB00005B/1583